W9-AEA-623

JOYCE CAROL OATES

Other Books by Joyce Carol Oates

NOVELS

Childwold
The Assassins
Do With Me What You Will
Wonderland
Them
Expensive People
A Garden of Earthly Delights
With Shuddering Fall

SHORT STORIES

Night-Side
Crossing the Border
The Goddess and Other Women
Marriages and Infidelities
The Wheel of Love
Upon the Sweeping Flood
By the North Gate
The Hungry Ghosts
The Seduction
The Poisoned Kiss, Fernandes/Oates

CRITICISM

New Heaven, New Earth:
   The Visionary Experience in Literature
The Edge of Impossibility:
   Tragic Forms in Literature

PLAYS

Miracle Play

POEMS

Anonymous Sins
Love and Its Derangements
Angel Fire
The Fabulous Beasts

ANTHOLOGY

Scenes from American Life:
   Contemporary Short Fiction (EDITOR)

son of the morning

joyce carol oates

son of

the morning

A NOVEL

LIBRARY
BRYAN COLLEGE
DAYTON, TN. 37321

VANGUARD PRESS, INC. NEW YORK

61774

Copyright © 1978 by Joyce Carol Oates

Published simultaneously in Canada by
Gage Publishing Co., Agincourt, Ontario.

All rights reserved. No part of this publication may be
reproduced or transmitted in any form or by any means,
electronic or mechanical, including photocopy, recording,
or any information storage or retrieval system, or otherwise,
without the written permission of the publisher, except by
a reviewer who may wish to quote brief passages
in connection with a review for a newspaper, magazine, radio,
or television.

Library of Congress Catalogue Card Number: 78-56428
ISBN: 0-8149-0793-8
Manufactured in the United States of America.

Designer: Ernst Reichl

For One Whose absence
is palpable as any presence—

I will open my mouth in parables;
I will utter things which have
been kept secret from the
foundation of the world.
—Matthew, 13:35

BOOK ONE

the incarnation

i

Whisper unto my soul, *I am thy salvation.*

You have promised that there shall be time no longer. Yet there is nothing but time in the desolation of my soul. A vast Sahara of time surrounds me, and though the frightful minutes pleat when I manage to slip into unconsciousness, the release is so brief, so teasing, that to wake once more to my life is a horror. Am I a brother to anyone in this agony, I ask myself; is it Your design that I awaken to such a brotherhood . . . ? But I don't want mankind, nor do I want the happiness of the individual without mankind: I want only You.

There shall be time no longer, yet we are deep in time, and of it; and it courses through us like the secret bright unfathomable blood through our bodies, bearing us along despite our childlike ignorance of its power.

Is this a revelation, I ask myself. Or an aspect of my punishment.

Save me, O God, by Thy name, and judge me by Thy strength and not by my weakness. If I have come to life again it is in obedience to the simple laws governing the sun, the moon, and the earth; it is not of my doing. My strength is like that of the mist-green reeds that do nothing but bend, with alacrity and cunning, as the violent winds pass over. Or do I think of the delicate young buds of peaches, or the hair-nests of the smallest of the sparrows. I think of the improbable precision of the eye: the perfection of the iris, the pupil, the mirroring brain. I think of my mother's broken body and of my father's swarthy beauty and of my own soul, which drains away in time, minute after minute, even as I compose my desperate prayer to You.

■ ■ ■

It happened that Ashton Vickery one weatherless day thirty-seven years ago climbed the remains of an old windmill on his uncle's property, a .22 rifle under one arm, a shotgun under the other. He was twenty-three years old at the time: long-boned, supple, his pale blue gaze coolly Nordic, set for distances.

"Come along, come along, little bastards, come along, I got all morning, *I'm* not in no hurry."

Atop the partly rotted tower he stood for a while, shading his eyes. Where were they? In which direction? He unlocked the safety catch on the rifle, he unlocked the safety catch on the shotgun. Both guns were his; he had owned them for years. Very finely were they oiled. It was a pleasure for him to caress them, to draw his cheek lightly along the stock of the rifle, to raise the heavy barrels of the shotgun and take aim.

Through the scope he sighted the butchered chickens in the irrigation ditch. His finger hesitated, he felt a queer jolt of pleasure, wishing suddenly to pull the trigger: to tug it back toward him. The well-developed muscles in his shoulders and arms tensed. His mouth drew into its customary grimace — the corners downturned, the upper lip shortened, haughty and imperious. Ashton was a good-looking young man and very much aware of it. He had the Vickerys' prominent cheekbones, their thick unruly eyebrows and hard, square chin; by the age of sixteen he had been taller than his father. His eyes resembled his mother's and were as thickly lashed. Softly he crooned to himself, drawing his gaze along the uneven horizon, in no hurry. "Come along, come along and show yourselves. Come *along* now."

He laid the shotgun carefully at his feet and cradled the rifle in his arms. It was light, lithe, a marvel to hold; a beautiful instrument. Quickly it leaped to his shoulder; quickly it arranged itself to fire. His left arm extended, his right arm crooked: just so! He leaned his face against it, closing one eye. Like this. Yes. Pivoting at the waist, Ashton Vickery could, by moving the barrel as slowly as possible, contain all of the landscape; all of the visible world. He sighted it along the barrel and all was well.

"Where are you hiding? It won't do no good. I can wait. I ain't half so hungry as you — I can wait."

To the north, Mt. Ayr dissolved upward in a haze of cloud; the powerful scope could bring it no closer. Closer in, farmland belonging to Prestons and Bells and Vickerys lay perfectly still, greening wheat and oats and barley, and a field of straight young corn, and a sparse woods of beech and oak. The air was fresh, a little chill. Ashton would have liked it cooler: would have liked to see his breath turn to steam. He hated being overwarm. It pleased him that the sky was overcast and that clouds moved above in sluggish layers, clotted, the color and consistency of skim milk. No sun. Only a peculiar glowering light that was like moonlight, like mist. A blank neutrality in which only a few insects sang, and very few birds. Like sleep, it was; like the dreamless sleep of the depths of the night. Perhaps he was sleeping? — dreaming? The foliage magnified in the rifle's scope and the glimmering surface of the river some distance away and the pallid, dissolving Chautauqua Mountains and the oppressive sky itself (which looked, for a moment, like a soiled concrete floor!) were mesmerizing. Ashton found himself smiling a foolish mindless smile, drawn through the scope and into the vast silence, thinking that this had happened before: many times: and would happen many times again.

But this is false: Ashton Vickery did not really think.

He was not accustomed to thinking, for what was the need?

The rifle was an extension of his arms and shoulders and eyes and soul, as everything he touched was an extension of himself. He did not think, he tasted. He tasted and chewed and swallowed. He was quite content with himself. (Since it had been decided that he would enter into a partnership with his Uncle Ewell, buying a one-third interest in his uncle's general store in Marsena, since it was settled once and for all that he not only could not emulate his father — who had an M.D. degree from the state university — but *would not*, there was peace in the Vickery household. But then, Ashton had always been at peace with himself.) It did not surprise him that women found him attractive, for he found himself attractive when he paused to contemplate himself. Tall, rangy, arrogant, cavalier, he moved about Marsena and the surrounding countryside with an unflagging confidence in his own worth. Had he not, after all, the power to kill? — as he chose? — to kill with grace, with cunning, with mercy or without? The secret of his manhood (which he could not have articulated) lay in his ability to destroy, his willingness to kill, the zeal with which he snatched up his guns. He had first fired a rifle at the age of five, and at the age of six he had killed for the first time. The creature had been a full-grown hare. Ashton was never to forget the amazing kick of the rifle, the cracking sound, the *certainty* — he was never to forget the astonishing life — the livingness — of the rifle as the trigger was pulled and the bullet shot to its mark. The death leap of the hare had been extraordinary; it had torn from the child a gasp of startled recognition. The *livingness* of the rifle and the bullet and the death spasm and his own bright quickening blood: never would he forget.

Patient and tender with the morning, so fond of himself he stroked his own stubbly jaw, and considered: "Ashton can wait. Ashton has plenty of time." Half-mindedly he reached in his shirt pocket for a package of chewing tobacco and bit off a thumb-sized amount and began to chew it placidly, the tip of his nose moving with the pleasurable rhythm. He hoped the morning sun would not burn off the haze; his only prayer was that the still, blank neutrality of the present moment might be extended until he had accomplished what he'd set out to do.

"Come along, you little motherfuckers," he said softly.

It would have been well for them had they been able to run free about the countryside with their jaws stretched wide, like deepwater fish, gobbling up all the life they encountered. They were hungry. It was hunger, that enormous heartbeat. The throb, the palpitation, the lust was for food dampened and spiced by blood. In one barnyard they had cornered a dozen or more chickens and rushed upon them yipping with amazed delight, tearing at their throats — they ripped off the silly squawking heads even where there was no need, no time to linger and eat. A terrified Bantam rooster, all burnished-orange and red feathers, flew drunkenly to the top of a tool shed where none of them could leap; his screams penetrated the morning haze for miles. What a noise! What a commotion! Feathers, blood, flapping wings, scrawny scaly reptilian feet whose claws were as nothing against *theirs*. By the time the human inhabitants were shouting, by the time the first of the gunshots sounded, they were far away and safe, their snouts blood-darkened.

Then again they were hungry, panting with hunger. Where did the hours go? — they trotted in one direction and then wheeled about, panicked by a certain odor; their leader was a ragged German shepherd whose tail had been chopped off close to his rump many years ago, and it was his wisdom to run half blind, his nose close to the ground.

The pack was most commonly sighted along the Alder River, though it was once seen by Carlson Bell as far away as Rockland, north of the city, that is — eight, nine, ten, possibly eleven wild dogs trotting across the paved highway, their fur wild and filthy and matted with burrs, their ears torn, scrawny tails carried low. Carlson braked his pickup truck and skidded to a noisy stop on the gravelly shoulder of the road and reached for his rifle — which was always in the truck with him, for safety's sake — and began shooting before he'd had time, even, to shut off the ignition. He leaped from the truck and ran after them and it was incredible, he claimed afterward, how *fast* they got away; and how sinister it was that they didn't bark or yelp or even appear to take special notice of him: just ran like crazy along a dried-up ditch of cattails and marsh grasses and thistle until by instinct or cunning they came to exactly the right place to jump free of the ditch, behind a screen of dwarf hazels, and then they were in that big swampy woods that goes on for acres on both sides of the old Marsena Road, all mosquitoes and snakes and rot and darkness: and naturally no sane man would follow.

Carlson Bell had fired a few shots after them, not in anger so much as in exclamation. "You see! Here I am!"

But though small posses were formed from time to time, mainly of boys, and though Old Man Arkin prowled out back of his barns all hours of the early morning muttering to himself, his shotgun ready to fire (for the pack had killed not only half his hen coop but had, for the sheer pleasure of it, torn out the throats of all but the strongest of his sheep, and killed his aged half-blind collie — whose piteous yelps Arkin believed he would hear the rest of his life — and in a frenzy of high spirits even dug and threshed in his daughter-in-law's kitchen garden a few yards from the back door), still the wild dogs ran free and struck where they would.

Carlson Bell claimed there were nearly a dozen of them, Ewell Vickery claimed there were even more — and one of them he recognized. It was a mongrel retriever that had once belonged to Harley Revere but must have run off when the family moved to town, a mean vicious stupid creature that had always acted a little wolfish so it was no wonder the Reveres left it behind — but now it had gone wild, now it was a killer. What if everyone drove their dogs off and let them go wild as coyotes! — no one would be safe. Thaddeus Vickery had never sighted the pack but had treated the nine-year-old Belding boy for bites on both forearms and on his right leg (a savage wound — looked like a shark bite, Thaddeus said) after the child had been surprised by the dogs on the Alder River bank — he and his brothers were fishing and when the dogs appeared they ran toward home and, unprovoked, the dogs chased them, setting up a terrific howling and yipping and barking — a horror, a nightmare — but thank God the boys weren't killed — thank God no one had been killed so far. It was a pity, Dr. Vickery said, but absolutely necessary that the boy receive rabies shots; he knew how they hurt but the risk was too great: the dogs might very well be maddened.

The German shepherd, the mongrel retriever, a cockleburr-covered speciesless hound, a rat-sized stunted creature that was probably a coyote. . . . Surprised at their kill, they were sporty and looked like laughter; their stained mouths appeared to be stretched wide in grins, in human grins. They pranced about, howling at the moon like legendary beasts. They scrambled up the sides of ravines and caught pheasants in their jaws, and rabbits, and even flying squirrels; and of course river rats and muskrats, and groundhogs that had wandered too far from their holes. They hunted in the foothills of the mountains where there were no real roads, only overgrown trails; shrewdly they kept their distance from mankind; then suddenly and unreasonably they appeared at four in the morning in someone's barnyard or in the vacant lot behind the white frame Church of the Nazarene where there'd been a fund-raising picnic the day before and where food had been dropped in the grass — or they appeared one Sunday at dusk, out of nowhere, to frighten children playing at a smoldering refuse dump near a trailer village along the river. They were urchins, they were Apaches, they were savage, and savage-sad, their bellies permanently stiffened with mud, their ears laid back against hard mean skulls. Were they dogs, Thaddeus Vickery wondered, or merely stomachs. Hadn't they become nothing but a certain length of guts about which the animal skeleton and flesh moved, frantic with desire . . . ? Howling, whining, whimpering, snarling, deep-bodied growling, panting, yelping, baying, cries very nearly like a flicker's, an uncanny *ostinato* of grieved rhythm, a melody of blunt pain: eyes, brains, and teeth forever in the service of guts.

When they were first sighted a year before, there had been

only three or four of them, and the farmer who came upon them huddled against the side of his barn the morning after a snow-storm — thirty below zero it was, that morning — had not the heart or the wisdom to kill them, but drove them away instead, shouting at them and waving a pitchfork. At that time they hadn't killed very much — there were no tales of their raids — they were garbage scroungers mainly, weakened by hunger, their ribs showing, worm-ridden, brain-damaged, tongues lolling in their steamy mouths. The farmer had taken pity on them and driven them away and it wasn't until the next spring when the pack had grown in size and in meanness that he realized his mistake.

Hunting for deer in the autumn with his friends, Ashton Vick-ery, the doctor's only son, came upon one of their number lying in a pool of dried blood, and a few yards away were the remains of a doe — probably gut-shot by a local hunter and left to stagger away through the woods to die, and so the dogs had come upon it and killed it and devoured most of it, and somehow this partic-ular dog — part shepherd, part hound — had angered the others and they had turned on him and torn out his throat and much of his belly. Seeing that ants were at work on the carcass, Ashton did not linger; but he felt at that time a curious sense of rage, almost a sense of — could it be injustice — of something gone wrong, and very ugly it was, and should be righted. "I'd like to get them dogs," Ashton said to his friends. "Let's go'n get them dogs — what d'you say to that?"

But his friends didn't take him up on it; anyway, they said, how would you know where to hunt them? They're most likely far gone from here.

Then one morning in his uncle's general store in Marsena — a red brick building eighty years old that housed the only barber-shop for twenty-five miles and the Marsena post office — Ash-ton's uncle Ewell Vickery complained bitterly to him about some dogs that had broken into his wife's hen-house the night before and killed seventeen hens, Rhode Island reds that were especially good for laying eggs, and the worst of it was the terrible mess the dogs had made — tossing the chickens around, flinging blood everywhere, scattering feathers to the tops of the trees. No, the *worst* of it was, Ashton's uncle said passionately, that it had taken place so fast. And without much noise except for the hens' squawking.

"Why, that's a real shame," Ashton said, blinking. It was a surprise to him for some reason that the dogs had dared come so close to *him*.

Ewell complained about the fact that the dogs had been running wild now for months and the county hadn't done anything about it, wasn't there a sheriff's posse or a committee or something a while ago, why was everyone so lazy, why didn't anyone show responsibility . . . ? One of the McCord boys claimed to have winged a strange dog with his .22 but the dog was never found; must have run away on three legs. Apart from that, nobody had done anything.

Maybe the dogs were too shrewd to be cornered, Ewell said. Maybe they weren't dogs, but devils, and nobody human could kill them.

Ashton laughed loudly. "What the hell — ?"

"There's got to be some explanation for why nobody's killed them yet or even chased them away," Ewell said.

Ashton shook his head in exasperation. "Shit," he said, "you leave it to me. Take me my guns and set up a blind and wipe 'em all out. Leave it to *me*. . . . Hey," he said, leaning across the counter and extending his hand to his uncle, "you want to place a bet on it? You want to bet on it? One hundred bucks, old man, how's that? One hundred bucks says I can't do it — ? C'mon and shake my hand and it's a bet!"

His uncle waved him away. He seemed rather embarrassed.

"Not one *hundred* bucks," he said, frowning.

"Seventy-five, then! C'mon, you got the cash! C'mon!"

Ewell Vickery stared at the floor and his lips moved as if in a silent prayer and his nephew couldn't help but laugh, it was such a legend around Marsena that Ewell was a miser — getting to be a silly stingy old maid, in fact, with (so it was rumored: Ashton himself helped the rumor along) a fishing tackle box stuffed with bills beneath his and his wife's sagging bed, and a savings account up in Yewville of who knows how much? — thousands, maybe tens of thousands! — yet he stood there, skinny in the chest and arms and legs and paunchy in the stomach, in washed-out overalls and a flannel shirt, the blue Vickery eyes gone all milky and squinting in his face, a man no more than five years older than Ashton's father Thaddeus — which would make him about fifty-two — yet looking shriveled and faded-out and maybe ten years older. It was the miserliness, Ashton thought; he wished he could cure his uncle of it.

"C'mon, old man," Ashton fairly sang, "give me a hand on it! Seventy-five bucks. It ain't like I was asking for a bigger share of your profits, right? Now *that* I don't look to expect."

"It might maybe be dangerous for you —"

"Not *me*. Not me and a bunch of scrawny pups."

"It might maybe —"

"*Might maybe*," Ashton said in his uncle's mournful voice, irritated by the old man's language — for it often annoyed the young man that his family — well, not his family but his relatives — the Vickery and Sayer people spread out through most of the county — were so old-fashioned. Even the word *they* used ("old-timey") upset and amused him. "Look: you going to shake on the bet or back down? Talkin' about them miserable little buggers like they're the Devil himself or something nobody can touch —"

"Watch your mouth, boy: what if there was a customer in here?"

"There ain't any customer in here, not that I can see," Ashton said with an impatient smile, "and what's wrong with calling them buggers if that's what they are? They killed your goddam chickens, didn't they? I don't see no point to talking about them as if they were something so special that nobody could touch — I can't halfway tolerate that kind of a mentality." Ashton felt obscurely threatened and even insulted and it seemed to him that his uncle was partly to blame. But he managed to retain his smile. "If I kill them bastards I ain't gonna haul my ass around the countryside without some remuneration. Fifty bucks?"

"Fifty bucks what?"

"As a bet. Between you and me. You are saying I can't get them and I'm saying I *can*. C'mon, Uncle Ewell, you gonna shake my hand?"

"*You* don't have any fifty bucks that I know of," Ewell said sullenly.

All things must be fulfilled . . . consequently they shook hands, and that evening Ashton whistled cheerfully as he cleaned and oiled his guns, and when his sister Elsa asked him was he going hunting next day, and his mother's big frame filled the doorway of the shed and *she* asked him was he going to take a holiday from the store again and anger his uncle again, Ashton said only that he was taking a day off with his uncle's permission and it was none of their business what he did. "I wouldn't halfway mind, though, if one of you sweethearts packed me a nice lunch," he said.

They both snorted with laughter, but in a few minutes Elsa returned, honey-haired sweet-faced fifteen-year-old Elsa, with the breasts and hips of a full-grown woman ("I pray God she won't grow to be *my* size," Mrs. Vickery said often), leaning in the doorway to tease him. "How far are you going? Who's going with you? Them silly old friends of yours? Just a bunch of over-grown boys, Mamma says; playing around in the woods. You going after a bear maybe? A grizzly? You going after some big game? — maybe out in our woods?"

"Honey," Ashton said, "I'll bring you back the makings for a fur outfit: coat and hat and muff. Dress you up just fine for the winter."

She laughed scornfully but nevertheless made him a delicious lunch of roast beef sandwiches on rye bread, and almond and orange-peel brownies, and a thermos of coffee pale with cream. "This should fuel you up for as far as you're going," she said,

setting it on the kitchen table that night for him to take in the
morning.

"I thank you, sister," Ashton said with mock formality.

"I surely do thank you," he said, eating the last of the brownies
atop the rotted tower.

He drank half the coffee, cold, as he liked it, and saved the rest
for later, and bit off another plug of tobacco, and moved a few
inches so that he was in the shade, and yawned contentedly,
studying the countryside. Did he see its beauty, did he take note
of the birds' morning cries? — a trio of kingfishers by the river,
rattling at one another; a jay singing the gentler of its songs,
liquidy and breathless; a cowbird whistling in a pasture somewhere near. He smelled the wet grass, he filled his lungs with the
scent of wet clover. For a half hour he was neither awake nor
asleep, in a kind of alert doze, his eyelids lowered partway, the
movement of his jaws slowing but never quite coming to a halt.
In his mind's eye he saw the dogs. He saw them drawing nearer.
Still, very still he was, not daring to move even in his dream; but
he could not control the sudden leap of his blood. Ah, he saw
them now, he *saw* them: deranged with hunger and therefore
incautious, flea- and mite- and mosquito-bitten, worm-gnawed,
eyes rolling a sick crazy yellow, tongues aslant, teeth gleaming
inside black-gummed mouths. . . .

He waited.

He waited and it seemed to him that the fresh breeze that lifted
from the river would urge the dogs to him; he sniffed the breeze
and half fancied he could discern their scent upon it. He had no
doubt they would turn up and that he would slaughter them one
by one. It would come to pass sooner or later; if not today, then
surely tomorrow; if not tomorrow, another day; wasn't Ashton
Vickery a peculiar young man (so people said admiringly), brash
and all-in-a-hurry sometimes, possessed of the slow cold methodical cunning of a hunting owl at other times?

He had oiled his guns and laid them atop the pine bureau in
his room and he'd slept a fine, full, deep eight-hours sleep, which

was what he always required; he had slept with the grateful, quivering abandon of a healthy animal, or of a very young child; he had slept as he always slept. A dreamless and absolutely satisfying sleep that refreshed him utterly (as sleep didn't seem to refresh his father: but wasn't it the old man's fault that he worried so much about his patients' illnesses and deaths and debts and quarrels and silly old-maid fears?). Waking at five-thirty, he had jumped from bed and in twenty minutes was at his uncle's farm and parked back of a lane between a cornfield and a cow pasture where the family wouldn't notice his car — for the last thing he wanted was his aunt chasing him up to offer midday dinner, or one of his boy cousins coming to join him, or one of his girl cousins coming to flirt; he had to be alone the way his grandmother had to be alone to pray if he wanted to get the job done.

"Come along, little bastards, little buggers," he whispered.

His father had written a letter to the *Yewville Journal* on the subject of the wild dogs, but the newspaper had not printed it. *That* had infuriated the old man! Ashton hadn't bothered to read the letter since he not only didn't care for his father's exaggerations and the big words he used, he didn't care for reading at all; it seemed to him that if people had anything important to say they would say it out loud and eventually it would get around; what was the need to keep things tiny and secret, writing them down . . . ? He was like his grandparents that way, like his mother's people, who hadn't even gone to school much beyond fifth or sixth grade and always brought the subject up since they were proud of it. Thaddeus Vickery had gone to school for years, years and years and years, and when he got his degree he'd had to borrow money to set himself up in a practice and where had he borrowed money from if not his in-laws, old William Sayer with his immense farm in the valley — ? Now that he had been a doctor for twenty-five years he still hadn't any money, it was Sayer money that kept the house from going to the bank in the thirties, and Sayer money Mrs. Vickery had inherited that allowed the family to be superior to most of the people of Marsena — not that Ashton minded being superior, he rather liked it, but he was inclined to think his superiority had to do mainly with himself, his face and body and personality. Maybe a little with being the doctor's son: that had always impressed his teachers, who'd graded him higher than he deserved. Being the doctor's son, however, was often an embarrassment, since the old man believed he knew the cure to everything if only people would listen, and naturally they were fools for not listening, for not printing his meticulously typed-out letters to the newspaper in town and granting him a public forum for his ideas. Ashton had not read the letter, but he'd had to sit through a meal while his father read the family parts of it in a preacher-like voice, jabbing the air with his forefinger (as he forbade anyone else to do, especially at the dinner table), making some long-drawn-out clever point about the dogs being victims: victims of human beings: victims turned killer in order to survive. They were all abandoned dogs, Dr. Vickery charged, some of them had been pets belonging to Yewville residents who hadn't wanted them any longer but were too kindhearted to have them put to sleep by the Humane Society, so they took them out into the country on a Sunday drive and let them go, and drove away thinking — thinking what? — thinking the dogs would find new homes, thinking farmers would take them in and feed them and give them new pet names and love them? Selfish fools! Selfish criminal insensitive fools! Pet-owners from Yewville and Derby and Rockland and as far away, even, as Port Oriskany, strangers who saw no evil in giving their pets "freedom" out in the country — they were common criminals and should be fined if not jailed and if he, Thaddeus Vickery, were an attorney instead of a medical doctor (yes, Ashton thought, exchanging a glance with his mother, the old man *must* allude to that: what pride!) he would certainly encourage farmers to sue for damages against the dogs' owners, could the dogs' owners be tracked down; didn't these people know it wasn't just farm animals that were slaughtered by the wild dogs, but people had been bitten, a nine-year-old child had been severely bitten and had had to undergo the agony of a series of rabies shots — didn't people know how their responsibilities branched

out to include not just their own families but all families? —
everyone? — everywhere? Old Thaddeus's voice had rung clear
and strong and outraged. Mrs. Vickery murmured assent, Elsa
avoided Ashton's eye so that she wouldn't be drawn into giggling
and sent from the table, and she too murmured assent; Ashton
alone said nothing, his head bent over his plate, eating beef and
mashed potatoes and string beans and cauliflower and glazed
carrots and cornbread and butter as fast as he could, and not
lingering for dessert either — though his mother and Elsa had
made blueberry pie, one of his favorites. How could these "humane" pet-lovers abandon their pets to the vicissitudes of the
wilderness, Dr. Vickery demanded, had they no imaginations?
— no intelligence? Their beloved pets became scavengers, butch-
ers, outlaws, maddened and diseased and terrorized, not even
animals any longer but simply coils of intestines about which
matted fur grew. It was only a matter of time until they killed
someone. A child, perhaps. Why, within Dr. Vickery's memory
there was a hideous case out around Mt. Ayr, a dog had gone
mad and attacked his master and killed him and had acquired a
taste for blood and before he was tracked down and shot he had
attacked a half-dozen people and partly eaten a young child
and —

"Thaddeus, *please*," Mrs. Vickery said suddenly.

Dr. Vickery looked up from the letter, blinking. His face was
ruddy, the pupils of his eyes appeared to be dilated.

"No more," Mrs. Vickery said with finality.

Elsa giggled, Ashton guffawed and slipped away from the table.

"Ashton," his mother called, "don't you want any —"

"Nope: no thanks!" Ashton said.

The dogs were trapped and he killed them one by one, agitated
at first and then more methodical and then, near the end, very
agitated again — shaking with excitement. Such noise! Such
struggle! And the *livingness* of it — the dogs scrambling against
the high walls of the ditch and falling back, yowling, wounded,
crazy with terror — the kick of the rifle, and then, as he drew

closer, the masterful discharge of the shotgun, which tore a partly grown hound in two and ripped off most of the skull of a shaggy coyote-looking creature with a bad leg — and on and on it went, Ashton carried with it, buoyed along by the noise, the desperation, the clawing, the howling and wailing and barking. "Oh you little buggers, take your medicine now, filthy little flea-bitten motherfuckers, c'mon, c'mon, you there! — where you think *you're* going," and since there was no danger now he slid down into the ditch and followed a mongrel German shepherd — a pregnant bitch, in fact — that was crawling through the underbrush, crawling on two front legs, dragging herself frantically — the lower part of the spine blasted away, gushing blood; he ran after the bitch and, standing practically over her, fired the shotgun one last time.

"Filthy little bastards," Ashton cried. "*Now* how's it feel? Now you know!"

Had any escaped? It was possible. He counted eight bodies. But had there been more than eight; had there been more than eight in the ditch? He counted them again, counting aloud. Seven, eight, nine. Ah: nine. Had miscounted the first time. But there were bodies atop bodies, and parts of bodies. . . . He counted again, wiping his sleeve across his forehead. Six, seven. Eight. And was that a dog there or merely part of. . . . Yes: nine. The bitch would have had pups and so he had really killed a dozen of the buggers. See how they liked it now, how did their medicine taste *now*. "Motherfuckers," Ashton said scornfully.

It was quiet. It was very quiet.

No birds, even: all flown away.

Ashton walked carefully among the bodies, for it was necessary that they be dead; no hunter allowed a dying creature to drag itself away into the bush, there to suffer until it died; no hunter worthy of the name. "That didn't hurt much, did it," Ashton crooned. He poked at the head of a Labrador retriever with a bit of Doberman pinscher blood in him, sprawled dead against a rock. Vicious-looking thing, all those teeth. Stained. Broken.

Could have torn a leg off if he'd had the opportunity. One of the dead hounds resembled a dog Ashton had seen somewhere recently — hound with a brown-spotted left ear, a white right ear — might have been from the same litter: whose dog? One of his friends' father's, maybe. Ashton counted the dogs again. Five, six, seven, eight, nine. Or was it ten. Up ahead there, in a tangle of dried-out willow bushes, was something — something that lay very still. Ashton scrambled up the ditch and went to peer down, shading his eyes. It was midday now and the sun was quite strong. A tangle of fur, a bloody grizzly snout, eyes rolled back into its head: ah! Did that make ten now, or did it make eleven?

Ashton laid the guns carefully on the ground and took out his hunting knife, the blade of which was razor-sharp, and went to cut off the dog's ear. That was one. Flies were already alighting on the broken body, buzzing and humming about the sticky blood. Ashton worked fast. He went to each of the dogs in turn and cut off an ear, whistling, not at all revolted, though of course the flies annoyed him. One fly bit him on the back of the hand and he cursed loudly, the sting was so painful.

"*You* want swatting, you sonuvabitch!"

One by one he attended to them, taking his time. He was still excited but he forced himself to work methodically. That heartbeat, that swelling sensation — the queer expansive awareness of — of his own body, his own life — his selfness — *him* — straddling the dogs, working over them, joshing with them as he might in other circumstances; as if, now they were dead, they had become kin to him, prized possessions. They were no prizes, however. Even the coyote had been a wretched specimen. No sheen to the coats, no flesh or muscle to disguise the protruding ribs. The pregnant shepherd was very nearly obliterated — a mass of blood and guts and fur — but Ashton could see that both her ears were eaten pink and scabby by mites on the inside. He wondered casually what the mites would do now, next. Could they remain on the body for a while or must they leap off immediately and find another host? Once on a camping trip he'd been attacked by

sand fleas — he believed that's what they were, horrible little
things so small he couldn't see them, they'd just started rising up
his legs and he'd slapped at them absent-mindedly while he and
his friends were putting up the tent — and after a while of slapping it occurred to him that something was wrong, something
was very wrong, and he began yelping frantically and jumping
about, and at that moment his friends too realized the fleas were
upon them, and crawling up their legs, and —

"Hold still now, Tiger; this ain't gonna hurt," he said, and so
he rose from the last of the dogs, part of its ear in his hand.

Raw appetite and fear, Dr. Vickery had charged, where once
they'd been pets beloved of man. Was there no justice, was there
no —

"Hush," Ashton murmured, thinking of his father. The old
man would not like it when he heard the news, but everyone else
in Marsena would be excited; maybe Ashton's picture would be
in the paper again, as it had a few times before (once when
Ashton was the first hunter of the season to bag a deer, another
time when he'd been hardly more than a boy, fourteen, and had
pulled another boy from the river back of the schoolhouse where
they were swimming, like fools, in freezing-cold water one autumn day).

One by one he put the ears in the paper bag that had contained
his lunch, and then he gathered up his guns and stood at the edge
of the ditch for a while contemplating what he had accomplished. Strange, he thought, that everything was so quiet. Alive
and yelping one minute, dead and stiffening and forever silent
the next. It was the same breeze blowing from the river, the same
breeze blowing up from the field of sweet clover; very distant now
was a hoarse rattling call, a bird's cry of caution. He realized the
tobacco he was chewing had gone tasteless, so he spat it out.

"That's the last time you're gonna trespass on Vickery land and
mess around with our livestock," Ashton said.

He was feeling good. He was feeling very good. Maybe just a
little tired — a little sad. Drained from all the excitement. But

no: mostly he felt good. As if he'd just wakened from one of his deep dreamless nights. His muscles tingled, his brain was jumpy and alert, his eyes felt almost sun-seared from having had so much to attend to; the sensation in his groin had become now almost an ache.

Flies were settling on the dogs.

"Taught you a thing or two, huh?" he said, backing away.

He drove the mile and a half back into the village and parked in the shade of the old carriage house and entered his house by the back door, noisy as always to let his mother know he was home. "Jesus God, Mamma," he called out, "you got some lemonade or something fixed? — my mouth tastes like a buzzard's crotch."

He let fall the bloodstained paper bag onto the table and laughed to think how the old woman would peer into it and scream, but when Mrs. Vickery came into the kitchen she frightened him by the look she gave him and said: "What's that on your forehead? What you been up to?"

"What's what?" Ashton said.

"Paint? Blood? Did something fly into you, did you scrape yourself going through the brush?"

From Uncle Ewell he collected only thirty-five dollars, the most the old man would hand over. (He claimed the pack was much larger than Ashton said it was, at least fifteen dogs, maybe twenty; Ashton must have let most of them escape.) Ashton's photograph was indeed published in the *Yewville Journal*, in a prominent position on the third page of the Saturday edition; posed with the dogs' ears arranged before him on the ground, Ashton Vickery squinted at the camera and managed a somewhat strained smile (for cameras made him nervous: he hated to just stay still and have someone do something to *him*). Ashton and his mother bought a dozen copies of the paper to hand out to all the relatives who might have missed it, and a few friends and neighbors, and in general everyone was well pleased. Dr. Vickery said very little; he spent a while examining the ears, the ragged blood-stiffened ears, but he said very little.

"The old man's jealous 'cause *I* got in the paper and *he* didn't," Ashton laughed, slapping at his thighs.

His mother told him to hush, not to make Dr. Vickery flare up; but probably it was true.

But probably it wasn't: Thaddeus Vickery was never a mean-spirited man.

ii

You are from above and I from beneath; I am of this world and sunk deeply into it: You are not of this world.

Bereft of You for the past three years, I am in dread of dying in my sins . . . I am in dread of the draining-away of my spirit. Once after You swooped upon me so suddenly, like a great hawk, and I only a child at the time, I arose baffled and stunned, and it seemed to me that the soul was a kind of thread: how easily it might be snapped if it were Your will, and thereby loosed from the body! — from the surrounding world!

Now I languish in exile and my spirit is turgid and brackish as swamp water, ebbing daily, draining away. There is an odor of rot and of stagnation: of despair.

Why seek the living God among the dead refuse of the past?

The ditch heaped with bodies, the iridescent winking of the flies, the sky raising itself as the sun burned through the morning haze. Higher and higher the perfection of the sky. Flat, it would see to me now; flat as wallpaper.

Distance is an illusion of the optical nerve.

The past is an illusion of the human brain.

There were moon-bright nights he slept through with that abandon I described. A certain pale, trembling intensity to his sleep: his breath occasionally rattling, his fair face contorted, his eyeballs rolling in his head. He is not dead at this moment — Ashton Vickery, I mean — but the young man he was is dead; someone is dead. It has been promised there shall be time no longer. And so the past is an illusion, a cheat. And yet it cannot be reclaimed.

I am thy salvation. . . .

Of Nathanael it was said by Christ that he should see heaven open, and the angels of God ascending and descending upon the Son of man. Of the child Nathanael it was said that God had claimed him from birth and filled him at certain moments with His power. In his grandmother's strong arms he slept: *Sweet mouse, sweet little mouse, dear one, dear baby, sleep.* His mother's knees weakened when she carried him and her breath grew rapid and shallow and she cried aloud that he should be taken from her and clasped safely in another's arms, for there was grave danger she would hurt him — she would drop him on the floor, or bring him too near the stove; she would squeeze him so hard in her embrace that his life would be smothered.

She was evil, some said. The evil that befell her contaminated her.

You know, however, that this was false, and those who said it spoke falsely, in ignorance and in malice.

You have seen deeply into her heart — You know that no evil resides there.

Do You dwell with her even now? — or have You abandoned her also?

It is said that the poor in spirit are blessed, for theirs is the kingdom of heaven, and they that mourn are blessed, for they shall be comforted; it is said that the meek are blessed, for they shall inherit the earth. The mighty that are exalted unto heaven shall be brought down to hell. . . . But it is also said that to him who has shall be given, and he shall have abundance; but from him who has little shall be taken away even that which he has.

■ ■ ■

One darkly bright October evening Elsa Vickery was crossing
a field on her way home from a Wednesday-night service at the
Emmanuel Baptist Church of Marsena when a man, a man she
had never seen before in her life, stepped onto the path before
her.

She halfway smiled, she was that simple; that friendly.

"Hello?" she said. "What do you — ?"

She had never seen him before in her life, or anyone who
resembled him. He wore a neck-scarf, he was about the size of
her brother Ashton, maybe twenty-eight or thirty years old, he
had tight curly hair that might have been black, his forehead was
strong and bold, his eyes were dark, shadowy, humorless; though
he was grinning at her from the start.

"Who are you?" Elsa asked, her voice rising in amazement.
"Do I know you? What —"

He approached her, grinning. His lips were stretched flat
across his teeth. He spoke in a harsh melodic voice and she
realized he was from the mountains, he *was* a stranger, he was
no one she knew. But what was he saying? She strained to make
sense of it. The words were low and caressing, cajoling. Almost
inaudible. In the moonlight she could see him plainly: the hair
retreating on the temples, the strong bony forehead, the long
aquiline nose, the teasing grin. "Where are you going?" he murmured, "where are you going in such a hurry, huh? — slow
down. No hurry. Lots of time. No hurry." He reached out to
touch her and she shrank away, but she was not yet frightened:
nothing like this had ever happened to her. The voice was murmuring and caressing and cruel. "Where are you going so fast?
Nowhere."

She turned and ran a few steps and there appeared on the path
before her another man, somewhat younger. He stepped out

from the brush and blocked her way, holding his arms wide as if for an embrace.

"Who are you?" Elsa cried. "Who do you want —"

The moon exposed them: they were like figures in a photograph, starkly black and very pale, unnaturally pale. Their hair and the recesses of their eyes and their wide-stretched mouths were deeply shadowed — their faces and hands appeared to be white, a queer glowering bloodless white, like bone.

The young man skipped toward her, boyish, his arms extended.

Elsa half-turned, and saw the man with the scarf close behind her, and ran from the path, stumbling, plunging through the underbrush in the direction of the river. Something was startled up, something flittered noiselessly into the air — bats? — could they be bats? The high grass caught at her legs, tiny thorns tore at her flesh, she heard the man laughing behind her, and it crossed her mind that this might be a game — must be a game. Perhaps she did know them? They did know her? It must be a game. One of them clapped his hands as if driving her before him as if she were a cow or a hog, as if he knew her and she him, as if it *was* a game. But she ran, she ran. It did not matter that the bats fluttered and dipped on all sides, that the underbrush scratched at her legs and hands and even at her face. Were these men brothers or cousins of boys she knew, were the boys hiding somewhere also, could it maybe be the Ackerson brothers, or Ralph Prestone who had been teasing her earlier this evening, could it maybe have something to do with Sarah Grace and Gina — ? Not long ago Duane Ackerson had frightened her at school, saying there was a tear in the back of her dress, and Elsa had screamed a little, though she had half-known he was teasing and she shouldn't be so breathless and fluttery and silly — who are you imitating *now*, her mother would say — and tonight after church services Duane had been glancing her way from time to time though she had ignored him — Or was it her brother Ashton — some friends of his she hadn't seen before — Once he had put a dead mouse in her coat pocket and howled with laughter at her shock, and —

"What's the hurry, hey girl? Where're you going in such a hurry?"

Someone caught her by the upper arm. His fingers squeezed her soft flesh so, she cried out in alarm. It was happening too fast. She could not comprehend the game. She was panting, her hair had fallen into her eyes, her mouth stretched into a kind of smile. "Leave me alone," she said. But was that Elsa Vickery's voice? It came out so broken and feeble, she could barely hear it herself.

Another of them ran up. He made a low throaty chuckling noise.

"Who's this? Who's this?"

"We found us a little surprise."

"Is she one of —" and here Elsa couldn't make out the word, the name: it might have been Wayne or Wade or Ray or something like a jocular snarl, distorted by the long twangy nasal accent. " — one of Wayne's girls come looking for him? Hunting him up? Can't get enough of him, eh, and has to come hunting him up?"

Three or four of them surrounded her now. And still another came running with long strides up from the river, where there was a small campfire. Elsa smelled gutted fish, burned flesh, tobacco, beer, whiskey.

"You ain't told us your name, girl," the man with the scarf knotted about his neck said, scolding. He closed his fist in her hair and gave her a little shake, as one might shake a dog. "Ain't you going to be friendly? Ain't you going to give us a little smile, even?"

Elsa looked from one to the other to the other, still trying to smile, trembling, speechless. Her mouth was so dry, how *could* she speak? Her tongue had gone numb and cold. Were they men she knew or who knew her, were they friends of Ashton's, were they teasing not-meaning-to-hurt, were they acting up because they were drunk and couldn't judge how frightened she was

. . . ? She tried to speak but could not; her throat just closed up tight. Her front teeth hurt where the night air touched them.

In the stark moonlight the men resembled one another except for age. And weight. The one with the scarf knotted about his neck appeared to be the oldest — or was he maybe just the pushiest, the most domineering? They were brothers, she saw that. Or cousins. All had tight curly hair, broad faces, loutish grins. Lopsided grins. They had been drinking, that was it: fooling around: not knowing when their play began to hurt. Fishing on the riverbank and drinking and now teasing poor Elsa, who knew she should laugh and push at them and show them she wasn't afraid, and — Her head was jerked back.

"Why're you so unfriendly? Why're you so standoffish? Hey, girl, howcome you're trying so hard to get away?"

Even now she thought she should smile; must smile. For if it was a game, a joke, if they told about it afterward, why, she would be laughed at — everyone in Marsena would laugh at her. Silly Elsa Vickery! Isn't she silly, getting so worked up over a joke! It hadn't been so very many years ago she and Gina Talbot were chased home from school by the big boys afternoon following afternoon, and it had been only play, the boys hooting after them and tossing horse chestnuts and snowballs and overripe pears in season, and hadn't the other girls been rather jealous because it was obvious the boys *liked* them — which was what the schoolteacher tried to explain to Dr. Vickery, who didn't understand and who was angry, having seen his daughter running shrieking down the middle of the Marsena Road in full view of anyone who happened to look out —

One of the men held her by the hair, and another squeezed her arm again where it already hurt, and still another, a boy, bent forward to touch her breast — how could he dare do such a thing, in front of everyone! She tried to throw herself backward. She tried to break free. *Dear God*, she cried in silence, *dear God please don't let, dear God please* — She stumbled against someone's legs and nearly fell. But they wouldn't let her fall. Beery whiskeyish breaths were hot against her face. Why were they laughing? Why did they want to hurt her? She couldn't believe it was happening and her mind stood off a little from it, astonished, feeling nothing. But then she came back to herself and nothing had changed. The boy had pushed against her, speaking in a light sly taunting teasing drunken voice, saying words she had never heard before but understood, somehow, understood at once: she stared at him in amazement and saw he was hardly more than her own age, and there was a smudge — or was it a birthmark — three or four marks on his cheek — and then her knees buckled.

Dear God —

Oh please —

An arm jammed itself beneath her chin, hard. Pressed itself against her throat, hard. She choked and gagged and tried to scream. There was a taste of grit, salt — one of them put his hand over her mouth.

At last behind that hand, she began to scream.

That afternoon it had been warm enough for Elsa and Sarah Grace Renfrew to sit on the side veranda of the Vickery house, in the sun, making crepe-paper flowers — mainly daffodils and jonquils and daisies — the water lilies were tricky, and the roses demanded a certain precision Elsa didn't seem to have: so she thought it wisest to make only the simplest flowers, since she was wasting paper and her wilted, mashed attempts were disappointing and made her feel irritable and perhaps a little resentful of her friend Sarah Grace. So the girls worked for several hours, sitting at a small oakwood table Dr. Vickery had brought out for them. They carefully fluted the edges of petals, they carefully arranged tiny stamens inside calyxes, and with their very fingertips labored to make the tips of the stamens look real or close to real. The petals and the interior organs were secured by twists of wire, thread-thin, then covered with dark green crepe paper, and the flower itself was then secured to a stem of covered wire, very malleable but not very real-looking. However, it *worked* — it held the flower up, and kept the leaves in place, and looked fairly nice.

She kept glancing at the six or eight daffodils she had already made, rather pleased with them, though the first two were bruised and perhaps the petals were overstretched in places and showed finger smudges — but then, so did Sarah Grace's: they were no better, really. Elsa thought the flowers looked nice. They were for the church bazaar a week from Saturday and she hoped everyone would like them and that they would be bought, not left behind; but probably *someone* would buy them — one of her aunts or even her mother — just to make her feel good. She hoped that wouldn't happen, it would be so awkward. Everyone would know. Sarah Grace's flowers would probably be sold and what if hers, Elsa Vickery's, were *not* — everyone would know and pity her —

"Look what you're doing," Sarah Grace said sharply.

"What — ?"

She had almost knocked the saucer of glue off the table with her elbow.

"I *saw* it," Elsa said, her face going hot.

"You didn't either see it. You were going to —"

"You needn't be so *smart*," Elsa muttered.

"How am I *smart*? Just for saying that?" Sarah Grace whined. But she kept working at the jonquil she was making, her fingers quick and skillful. She was Elsa's age exactly, almost to the day — fifteen years old last May — but taller and thinner and more quick-minded and with a tendency (so everyone said, especially Sarah Grace's mother) to get ahead of herself. "Did you want me to sit here and say nothing while the saucer is skidding off the table — ?"

"All *right*," Elsa said.

Sarah Grace's fingers were so slender, so swift; they looked as it they *knew* ahead of time what they should do — how was it possible? Elsa had to think carefully about each step. First you did one thing and then the next and then the next, and then you fitted the sections together, one step, then another and another, and when she was doing the first she couldn't possibly think of the next, let alone the *next*, while Sarah Grace showed her how you could skip one of the steps by twisting some wire around the stem to begin with and then fitting the petals in and — but it was too complicated, Elsa's head swam, she had to shut her eyes and tell Sarah Grace to please stop: *she* intended to follow the instructions in the book Mrs. Sisley gave them, and that was that. "There's only one way of doing things, Reverend Sisley says — the right way," she told Sarah Grace, who only shrugged her skinny shoulders. So she labored and bit at her lip and sighed with befuddlement and exasperation — if a flower was so difficult to make in nature, if God had such trouble with it, why there wouldn't be many flowers at all — or there would be just the very simplest ones — and sometimes she threw her work down with a small cry of impatience and hurt and began over again, all over again. It seemed to Elsa that her hands were heavy birds, ungainly and sullen, not at ease on the table-top amid the crepe paper and wire and flour-and-water paste.

Sarah Grace was singing under her breath, and Elsa began to sing under hers. She sometimes wondered — did Sarah Grace do such things deliberately to annoy, or was it just her nature? It often happened that the girls got on each other's nerves, though Elsa knew it was rarely *her* fault. She was easygoing, softhearted, *too* softhearted. Where Sarah Grace was all wristbones and elbows and long skinny legs, Elsa was prematurely adult with flesh and a certain overwarm embarrassment. It might be said that Elsa Vickery was the prettier of the two — though Elsa would have protested shrilly and gone bright red, her eyes fairly watering with dismay; but neither girl was nearly so attractive as Gina Talbot, whom they both admired and detested. Sarah Grace was tall and pale and freckled and her two front teeth were unfortunately prominent. Elsa was rather short, with a large spreading frame like her mother's, and her mother's soft, fine, beautiful skin — high-colored for the most part, especially when she was excited or self-conscious, and unfortunately so delicate, so lovely, that the smallest bump or pimple or rash or insect bite could disfigure it: so that she spent long miserable minutes staring at her reflection in the bathroom mirror, wondering if life was worth it, if she could manage to endure, if she could just *live through* the drawn-out space of time it took one of her skin eruptions to flare up, come to a dull, sullen, white-tipped maturity, and then subside and gradually fade. . . . Sarah Grace's skin was blemished, but with her freckles who could tell? It wasn't fair. Elsa eyed her enviously and thought it wasn't fair. At the same time she knew it was wrong, it was sinful, to think such thoughts about her best friend — or about anyone; she knew that very well. Hadn't Jesus made it quite clear. . . . Not once but several times Jesus had been very outspoken on the subject of envy and jealousy and spite and coveting and lusting after in one's heart . . . and Reverend Sisley had preached near the end of summer about the seven abominations — was it from the Book of Psalms or Proverbs — all about discord and mischief, the sowing of evil, the danger of pride, lying tongues, the heart that devises wicked imaginings . . . feet swift in running to mischief, or was it to being a false witness. . . . She had listened closely, rather fearfully (for it sometimes seemed that Reverend Sisley was preaching to *her* — that he knew very well how sinful she was, how she forgot about Jesus for long periods of time during the day, how she was mean and spiteful and silly and petty and jealous and clumsy as a calf, and her skin was always — *always* — broken out in some prominent heartbreaking place), and while she could not always follow Reverend Sisley's or the Bible's argument word for word, she nevertheless knew very well in her heart what was being said. Certain phrases escaped her altogether, certain warnings were baffling and alarming, but she felt vaguely that she understood: she *sensed* the awful, inevitable truth: it had in some way to do with *her*, even when she was most confused. *(For by means of a whorish woman a man is brought to a piece of bread,* Reverend Sisley had read in his high, rapid, breathless voice, glancing up and out at the congregation over his glasses, and blinking as if he'd just run before them with terrifying news, news for *them* out of all the world's inhabitants; *and the adulteress will hunt for the precious life . . . !)*

So she knew it was wrong to harbor mean thoughts against

Sarah Grace, who had been her closest friend since first grade, but *why* did Sarah Grace sing under her breath some bumpy monotonous unrecognizable tune over and over and over, like a mechanical doll, pretending she didn't know how exasperated Elsa was, and only glancing across the table at Elsa when Elsa did something wrong — like dropping a lump of paste onto the unused olive-green crepe paper just now. "Oh *Elsa*," she said, smiling an insufferable superior smile that was meant to be impatient and forgiving and affectionate all at once, as if Elsa were a baby who had soiled her diapers too soon. . . . Elsa blushed and cleaned up the mess with a tissue and said nothing. She had vowed she wouldn't get drawn into a quarrel with Sarah Grace since the last quarrel back in August had been so upsetting, both girls had wept for days, and their mothers had had to get together (though ordinarily Mrs. Vickery and Mrs. Renfrew had nothing to say to each other), and it had been terrible, lonely and terrible, and people had laughed at them, and Gina had carried stories back and forth, and. . . . The first night, Elsa had been too upset to eat, even; she'd sat at the dining-room table with tears glistening on her soft babyish cheeks; asked to explain the circumstances of the quarrel, she could only shake her head mutely, as if her heart were broken. Ashton paid no attention at all, Elsa's mother comforted her in a vague not-very-serious way, but Dr. Vickery was the cruelest. "Have you girls quarreled *again?*" he asked. And then, raising his bushy tangled eyebrows so that his forehead furrowed, and pursing his lips as if he were blowing on a horn or a mouth organ, he sang in a maudlin mocking voice right there at the dinner table —

> I won't holler down your rain barrel
> I won't climb your apple tree
> I don't want to play in *your* yard
> If you won't be good to me — !

— until Mrs. Vickery quieted him, saying he shouldn't tease Elsa because she was really very upset. Elsa herself didn't know whether to be angry at her father, or embarrassed, or whether to give in and laugh with the others, so she just sat there feeling lumpish and cowlike and hot and miserable. But next morning she and Sarah Grace were friends again and couldn't even remember very clearly what they had quarreled about. Suddenly Elsa saw that Sarah Grace had been making two flowers to her one. How was it possible? Sarah Grace's thin skillful fingers, Elsa's pudgy clumsy fingers. But two flowers to her one! Daffodils and jonquils and a small bunch of Shasta daisies, really very lifelike, *very* pretty, Reverend Sisley would admire them, and Mrs. Sisley too, and everyone would want to buy them, and. . . . Of course it was possible for Elsa to work longer and harder on the project. She could stay up every night till midnight in her room, and her parents wouldn't know, and she could make a vow to Jesus to turn in more flowers than any of the other girls, and to make some water lilies too, though the water lilies were awfully tricky and even Sarah Grace had failed with them, and. . . . But maybe it was wrong, it was small-minded and sinful, to pray to Jesus behind Sarah Grace's back? Though it was entirely possible that Sarah Grace had prayed to Jesus on this very same issue and felt no guilt at all. Maybe she had prayed for extra skill, which was why she worked so quickly and made Elsa appear so slowed-down. . . . Thinking such thoughts distracted Elsa, who could only deal with one thing at a time, and before she knew it the paste-saucer fell to the floor; how had her elbow brushed against it when it was nowhere near it — ! The saucer fell to the floor and cracked in three pieces and Sarah Grace said, "See, what did I tell you?" and giggled her thin, mean giggle. Elsa stooped to pick up the pieces. Her face went hot and must have been beet red. Well, the saucer was a *Vickery* saucer, wasn't it, an inexpensive five-and-dime saucer, it was none of Sarah Grace's business, was it? Seeing that the girls were always at the Vickerys' house (so Mrs. Vickery said) and Sarah Grace thought nothing of accepting hospitality from them and helping herself to anything that was offered — date-nut fudge, molasses cookies, cold ham; seeing that Sarah Grace was really a guest of Elsa's this afternoon, sitting in the warm lovely sunshine

on the Vickerys' side porch — she had no right to be critical and
catty, did she? "It was an accident," Elsa said. Sarah Grace bent
over the jonquil she was fashioning, trying not to giggle but at the
same time not trying to keep Elsa from *seeing*, she bit her lips
and pretended to be very absorbed in the tiny fluted calyx and
said nothing. "It was just an accident," Elsa repeated, trying to
force the pieces together again. It was *almost* possible, the pieces
were so big. And the flour-and-water made a nice paste to
hold the pieces together, didn't it? Elsa believed she could
repair the saucer so that no one would ever know it had been
broken.

She hadn't been a clumsy child all along, evidently. So the
family indicated. A plump slow-moving baby, an adorable little
girl, always pink-cheeked and healthy, and her hair — honey-
hued, naturally curly, a little too fine, perhaps, to hold any complicated curls, but very pretty — very pretty. And then around
the age of eleven she'd gotten ungainly almost overnight: grew to
her present height of five feet one, put on weight around her hips
and thighs and breasts, became unaccountably heavy-footed and
clumsy. And tearful. Helping Mrs. Vickery with the dishes, she
sometimes stared in amazement as a plate slipped out of her
hands and crashed to the floor or, worse yet, as a cup came apart
in her fingers — the cup itself in one hand, the handle in the
other. Just the other day, Sunday, after the morning service, she
had somehow walked into the glass door of the sunporch and
cracked three panes, *somehow* that had happened though she
knew the door was there as well as anyone in the family. . . .
"Daydreaming," Mrs. Vickery said irritably. But it wasn't true:
Elsa never daydreamed. (Fortunately Mrs. Vickery was never
very critical of her daughter, being big-boned and not exactly
graceful herself, and she didn't take housekeeping nearly as seriously as most women, which was a blessing. Elsa had once overheard her mother on the phone talking to Aunt Hannah, Ewell's
wife, saying, "Well, the poor girl's at that age, you know, it would
only make it worse for anyone to *pick* on her — I figure she'll
grow out of it in a few years!")

Grow out of — ?

"Damn," Elsa whispered. She had been twisting the little tube of paper that was to be a daffodil stamen so hard that it came apart in her fingers.

"I heard that," Sarah Grace said softly without looking up from her work.

Elsa threw the stamen down and let the rest of the flower fall.

"I said *damn* and I'll say it all I want and I don't care who hears me," Elsa cried.

"I *heard* that," Sarah Grace said.

"I'll say it all I want! I don't *care* who hears me! I don't *care!*"

Sarah Grace looked up at her, astonished, as Elsa began to cry.

She lay where they had dragged her on the riverbank. At first she thought Sarah Grace was still with her. She was crying, and Sarah Grace was staring at her, not knowing what to say. After services she had helped Mrs. Sisley and Mrs. Fifield with the apple cider and the little paper cups and though she hadn't done a thing wrong she had felt very self-conscious. Her breasts were too big, she stood round-shouldered to disguise them, and it occurred to her after she'd been walking around for five minutes that maybe her skirt was stuck to the back of her legs and, worse yet, to her buttocks, but it was too late to pull it away, everyone would see.

She was crying before she woke, a faint frail babyish sound, a wailing deep inside her body. In her sleep she was crying and when she woke her eyes stung with tears and her face was already wet and she could not determine where she was — thrown onto her back in a chilly field, thrown onto the damp trampled grass so that she could stare into the sky, into the strong pale circle of the moon. It was exactly like a light somehow shaded over with pearl.

At services that evening Reverend Sisley had talked to them about Jesus of Nazareth as their closest friend, a friend who was always near them, always close by, listening and sharing and giving strength. Elsa tried to whisper *Jesus* but her lips were swollen and parched. It hurt to move them. She must have hurt her mouth somehow, and the pit of her belly, and deep between her legs, and the smallest finger of her left hand throbbed with pain. *Jesus. Dear God.* Who do you tell your secrets to, Reverend Sisley had asked, peering at them, who is your closest, dearest friend? Who gives you everything you have — food clothing shelter loved ones protection from all harm? The shepherd will provide for his sheep: never doubt: never doubt.

"Jesus . . . ," Elsa whispered.

At the social hour two of the boys had drifted near, unwilling to sit down but evidently wanting to talk; the four or five girls Elsa sat with giggled and kept interrupting one another. There was talk of a new gelding Mr. Ackerson had bought, and Ralph Preston told them about his cousin Enoch who had run away to Canada to join the Air Force, saying there was a war to get to and Marsena couldn't hold him; and there was talk of Miss Fenner who had been their seventh-grade teacher who had quit and moved away last year who was evidently married *and* a mother — which was rather fast, wasn't it, one of the girls murmured and the other giggled furiously, Elsa among them. (Though she had liked Miss Fenner well enough — very well, in fact. Had adored her for an entire year.) And there was talk of. . . . And. . . .

There was talk of . . .

Elsa heard the voices, heard her friends' giggling, but could not get to them. Where were they hiding? She tried to raise her head but the effort made her dizzy. . . . The night sky looked very cold. The moon, and the scattered stars, and Elsa Vickery. "Jesus," she said aloud. Her voice was a disappointment: so babyish!

She had helped clean up in the church hall and then she and Sarah Grace and Rosemary Preston and her younger sister walked home together. It was just nine o'clock. It was quite cold. The Preston girls lived closest, just off the Marsena Road, and at old Mrs. Druillard's house Elsa and Sarah Grace said good night and went in different directions, and Elsa decided to cross the Druillard lot to save steps though she was somewhat afraid of the dark, weedy, jumbled field — thinking there might be snakes, maybe, or rats. In fact she *did* scare up a rabbit. When she saw his white tail she said aloud: "I won't hurt you, don't be so silly!" But the rabbit bounded away, disappeared.

She rose on one elbow slowly and painfully. The others were gone — Sarah Grace and the Preston girls. She could no longer hear their voices. Why did her finger ache so? She stared at it; it hung loose from her hand at an odd angle.

"Mamma? Daddy?"

Her mouth tasted of dirt and salt. Her lips were puffy and very dry. She saw Reverend Sisley holding the Bible shut tight in one hand, his eyes half-closed with emotion, tears streaming down his cheeks. When he wept Elsa squirmed with shame; she *wished* he would not get so upset. It was worse in the evenings than on Sunday morning; worst of all was Wednesday night. No one knew why. Christ's sufferings swept over him, and the sinfulness of mankind saddened him, and no matter how hard he worked there were members of his church who back-slid and would not support him. . . . From time to time he questioned Elsa about her father, but never very intensely; nor did he say much to Mrs. Vickery when she came to church on Sunday morning. Dr. Vickery did not accept Jesus Christ as his Saviour: he didn't think of Jesus Christ at all. So he said. It was shocking, it was disheartening, but there you were — nobody could hope to change Dr. Vickery's mind. *Dear Jesus,* Elsa prayed every night when she went to bed, *please help my father, please guide him to You, please enter his heart so he will be saved.* . . .

Above, the river bats were flying in broken, spasmodic circles. They were like scraps of paper, like bits of rubber. Elsa stared at them, hoping they would keep their distance. What if one got into her hair — !

Mrs. Vickery claimed that a bat had tried to get into her hair once when she was a girl, long ago. A nasty flapping fluttering thing that brushed against her face — can you imagine?

Elsa began to shiver convulsively.

She was alone: the others had run away.

She was alone, so no one could hear if she sobbed, if she made a fool of herself.

She got unsteadily to her feet and something ran down her legs, the insides of her legs. Her head swam. She touched herself — her underpants were gone. Her skirt was ripped. Something wet and warm ran down the insides of her legs, unloosed, free. She stood in one place for a while, not daring to move. It was blood, she knew it was blood. *That* blood.

The moon was somewhere else in the sky; it must have shifted. Cold rose from the earth in waves. Elsa looked down at herself but could see very little. She touched herself gingerly. Why was she trembling so? It was like a shivering fit — she sometimes had shivering fits in the winter and everyone felt sorry for her. Her belly was wet, her thighs and her legs. One of her shoes was off. The smallest finger of her left hand hung at a crazy angle. "Mamma," she whimpered. "Daddy . . . ?"

She held her right hand up and saw that it was wet with something dark. It was sticky. The fingers darkly stained: blood. It was *that* kind of blood. She heard herself whimpering; she was so ashamed, everyone would know, everyone would see. The back of her skirt would be stained.

The campfire had gone out. Or they had doused it with water.

It was painful to walk. Moving her legs was dangerous: it made her bleed more. Her mouth still tasted of salt and grit and sweat. Someone's hand. The palm of someone's hand pressed tight against her mouth.

Dear God, she prayed, *dear Jesus please hear me: please enter my father's heart and bring him to You.*

She found herself walking back toward Mrs. Druillard's house. That way she could take the Marsena Road to the road she lived on and avoid the riverbank and the worst of the darkness and be home in five minutes and no one would know.

The back of her head hurt where it had struck against the ground. There was a torn, raw, throbbing sensation between her legs and in the pit of her belly. Her breasts ached. She staggered, her head swam, she almost fell, she knew she was being silly and everyone would laugh. Where were her underpants — ! And the back of her skirt would be stained.

She had whipped her head from side to side but the hand remained hard against her mouth, pressing against her teeth. Her mouth had bled, was bleeding still. Why had they laughed and jeered, why had they crowded about her, staring, grinning? A voice rose, teasing and cruel; it might have been addressed to a child or a dog.

"Where are you going? — Nowhere."

She had fainted, she had fallen from a considerable height, which was why her body ached. Why she was bleeding. Her knees had gone limp; perhaps that angered them.

She had not wanted to anger them.

Out on the Marsena Road she could see better: she could see the dark rivulets of blood on her legs and the dark stain on her hand. One shoe on, one shoe off. She hobbled along. If any one saw — ! If one of the Bells was looking out their front window — !

Her loins ached. Deep inside her something was torn. And her little finger: she saw that it must be sprained or broken, yanked out of its socket. By now she was nearly home so it didn't matter if she began to cry louder. She heard a baby's wail, and then a low guttural gasping sob.

They had run away: had left her there on the trampled grass and run away.

One of them crouched above her. She could not see his eyes, she could see only shadows. He wore a neck-scarf; he was no one she knew. Nor did he know her. The others ran away hooting to one another and the man with the scarf crouched above her and muttered "Here" and tossed her own sweater onto her — it fell partly on her chest, partly on the grass, but she could not move to adjust it.

They had shoved her legs apart.

They had yanked at her, snatched at her, crowding and jostling one another. Between her legs it had hurt very, very badly: did they know?

She had screamed for them to stop but no one heard.

Now she screamed again. "Mamma! Mamma! Daddy!"

But what could she tell them or anyone, how could she explain? — her underpants gone, her clothing ripped, her belly and legs smeared with her own sour-smelling blood?

iii

And so it came to pass that the only daughter of Thaddeus and Opal Vickery was grievously despoiled, and — wonder of wonders — conceived a child even in her misfortune, and carried it nearly to term: giving birth early one rainy June morning, after eight months of sorrow and some seventeen hours of arduous labor, to an undersized and sickly baby boy later christened *Nathanael William* (*William* in honor of the infant's grandmother's father, deceased some ten years; *Nathanael* meaning *gift of God*); the mother being only sixteen years and one month of age at the time of her parturition.

A dead nature, I have read, aims at nothing; seeks no end. A living nature, however, strives to manifest itself and even to transcend itself and even perhaps — I am shaky on such matters, having had so poor a formal education — to interpret itself. That this violent conception, pregnancy, and birth were aspects of a single coherence, against all odds insisting upon its being, who would dare doubt? — for the mark of Your will was everywhere evidential.

Contemplating the miracle after some three decades, and more, I find myself subject, still, to most upsetting emotions. I do not know, I cannot know, whether the birth of the child Nathanael William was a justification, sanctioned by Your hand, of the violence suffered by the unfortunate girl, in all certainty a virgin at the time of her rapists' cruelty; I do not know whether the gift of this remarkable child was a sign of Yours that all would be

well, and more than well, for the suffering Vickery family —
whose lives were irreparably altered, both in a public and in a
private sense. This would indicate to my way of thinking that
Your gift of Nathanael was a compensation for the earlier outrage, much as Your gifts to Job were signs of Your renewed pleasure in him, his having withstood the torments of Your test upon
him. And yet it may be that the extraordinary gift of Nathanael
William was intended from the very start — even unto the first
days of the Creation.
Before Nathanael was, You are.

■ ■ ■

Awaiting the birth of his grandchild, Thaddeus Vickery did not
concern himself with such riddles, nor did he rejoice in the imminent miracle. He had had time to contemplate his daughter's
and his family's misfortune for many sad months, through a
gloomy autumn and a protracted, most stormy winter and a chill,
rainy spring that advanced and retreated teasingly, and froze the
buds on the favored peach tree he had planted just outside his
office window some twenty years before in memory of the loss of
his second-born child, a boy, who died of a kind of bronchitis
when only three weeks old; he had had time to contemplate many
things, to plunge through many divers emotions, and to come
near to drowning in them, for he was a passionate, readily in-
flamed man, unused to the heaviness of heart imposed upon him
by his daughter's fate (to him incredible: "It can't be possible,"
Dr. Vickery said time and time again, to others and to himself in
the privacy of his office, where he sat by the hour awaiting patients or, very late at night, awaiting a visitation of some kind that
would *explain* the bizarre workings of what was, to him, a soulless
yet not malevolent, and fundamentally *knowable,* universe;
"pregnancy under such circumstances, conception itself — It
can't be possible, it can't *be*").
He and Opal had lain sleepless in the lumpy old four-poster
bed for innumerable nights, neither speaking because they had

already said all there was to say. The disaster could not have happened — not to their sweet, innocent Elsa — not to *them*. That the child should have been mauled and tormented and raped was hideous enough; that she should have been somehow impregnated was insupportable. "No, it can't be possible. Simply can't be possible," Dr. Vickery muttered. For weeks he lost faith in his own powers of reasoning, in his own sanity, and, what was more grievous, in the powers of reasoning and the sanity of his profession, and of science more generally: for if the universe was merely a jumble of unlikely events, why should one devote one's spirit to interpreting it? When he sighed loudly and ran his fingers through his graying bushy hair and said for the hundredth time, "It can't be possible!" his wife said sharply, "It doesn't matter if it's possible or not: the fact is, it *is*."

The rape and its circumstances were hideous enough, and the subsequent pregnancy, but even more outrageous, in a sense, was the fact that the rapists were never apprehended. Thaddeus was convinced they belonged to one of those dirt-poor, sprawling, inbred, diseased mountain families who lived north of Marsena, whose unfortunate children he sometimes saw (he volunteered his services to the public schools in the district, and from time to time a mother would even bring a child to his office, emaciated, glassy-eyed, already near death — for the mountain people feared and despised doctors and were reconciled to the routine deaths of children), and that the sheriff and his men were simply too cowardly to investigate — though naturally they protested that they had done everything humanly possible and had not yet given up. Ashton was not only convinced that someone from the mountains had committed the crime, but that it was, in a way, directed at *him*, the men had known *him*, Ashton Vickery, and wished to hurt and insult *him* in the cruelest way possible, knowing that the rape of his only sister, whom he loved very much, would drive him mad. And not only that: he believed the sheriff and his men knew the rapists and refused to arrest them, not simply out of cowardice (though the sons of bitches were certainly cowards) but because they sided with the rapists against

Ashton and his family. "They think it serves us right!" Ashton said, drunken and aggrieved. "Because we're Vickerys and Sayers — because we're better than them — because Pa's a doctor and Uncle Ewell's got the store — because of *me* — They all say it, they're saying it behind our backs, the bastards, the filthy lying dirt-eating bastards! — saying it serves us right. They don't give a damn about poor Elsa, they're maybe saying it serves *her* right too. Behind our backs they're saying these things while to our faces they're always so sorry — the sons of bitches! If I only knew which ones of them to get."

His parents tried to calm him, tried to reason with him. Neither Thaddeus nor Opal believed the sheriff knew who had committed the crime and was deliberately refraining from arresting them; neither of them wished to believe (Thaddeus the more vehement on the subject) that their friends and neighbors in Marsena, his *patients*, secretly rejoiced in the Vickerys' tragedy and went about saying to one another that it served them right. "No, that's really unacceptable," Thaddeus said angrily. "I *don't* believe that."

"What the hell do you know about this town, or about people?" Ashton said.

"I know the people of Marsena. I've known them for a far longer time than —"

"You don't know anything," Ashton said rudely. "Only what you think you should know."

"Everyone in Marsena is fond of Elsa — you know that. There isn't a girl sweeter, better-liked — There isn't —"

"*Wasn't.*"

"Everyone has stopped by to ask if there's anything they can do, and —"

"Stopped by to pick up some gossip," Ashton said. "Look, Pa: don't tell *me*."

"Don't tell *me*," Thaddeus shouted.

And so they began to argue as they often argued, at the dinner table, while Opal pressed her hands against her ears or rose suddenly and walked away, and they were left alone (since Elsa refused to come downstairs for any meals and spent nearly all that winter in her room, staring out the window, or working indifferently on a quilt, or reading her Bible, or sleeping for long unnatural stretches of time — sometimes as much as fifteen hours a day), shouting at each other, their faces distorted by hatred.

Sometimes Thaddeus and Opal quarreled, sometimes they sat in dignified silence, two aging, distraught, somewhat oversized people whose flesh had begun to melt from their frames unevenly, leaving Opal haggard-faced, her eyes ringed by shadow, and Thaddeus even more nervous than usual, his well-worn, familiar clothes now too big for him, so that he resembled one of those vagrants who sometimes passed through Marsena and appeared at the Vickerys' side door begging for food or money. Much of the time there was simply nothing to say, which was why Thaddeus spent so many hours in his office or was unusually willing to make house calls, even to people who lived miles away; and he had gotten into the habit of remaining in his office late at night, sipping bourbon, playing a form of solitaire he had invented as a medical student desperate for a mindless activity that would calm his thoughts; sometimes reading Marcus Aurelius's *Meditations* or Lucretius's *On the Nature of Things*, books he had admired very much as an undergraduate thirty years ago at the state university. Sometimes he even played softly on his old ocarina, an instrument from his boyhood, made of terra cotta, producing a gentle, sad, feathery, hollow, melancholy sound not quite music. He blew on it very softly, and not very well. And only when he was fairly drunk.

Of course the issue was, from November until late winter, whether Thaddeus should arrange for his daughter to have an abortion. He believed it was necessary, it was incontestably necessary; though the girl's life did not appear to be endangered by the pregnancy (for Elsa, despite herself, was in fairly good physical condition: it was chillingly evident that her *body* did not at all mind being pregnant) it was possible that her mental health was affected. More: she should not have to bear the child of her rapist. It was insupportable, Thaddeus believed. An outrage.

Opal listened and appeared to agree and yet remained silent, her head inclined toward his as if she'd become hard of hearing these past few months, her steady stunned gray gaze never quite meeting his. She was a rather homely woman — agreeably homely most of the time, with a too-long nose, fat cheeks, frizzy mouse-brown hair. Her complexion was lovely, the skin fresh and smooth as a girl's, but she had gotten in the habit of frowning unconsciously and now there were sharp creases between her eyes and on her forehead that looked unnatural, even disfiguring. The period of her womanhood was over, Thaddeus found himself thinking, without knowing what he meant; the period of her femaleness. Over.

Thaddeus had fallen in love with Opal when he was in his early twenties and she eighteen. Hefty, good-humored, with a loud, frank, artless laugh, she had amazed Thaddeus with her warmth and the good sense of her conversation — had truly amazed him, since at their first meeting he had thought her almost comically unattractive. She *was* rather graceless, riding a reddish-brown roan mare across her father's pasture, bareback, or playing a noisy four-hand rondo with one of her girl cousins, or trying to teach Thaddeus a simple box-step dance; but it quickly ceased to matter. In a few weeks he no longer *saw* her. The surprising thing about Opal Sayer was that he could talk with her as he could talk with few women. He could talk about nearly anything: his studies, his difficulties with his teachers, his setbacks, his hopes, even his erratic feelings about *her*. Within a year of their meeting he was very much in love. He believed he and Opal Sayer would never come to the end of all they had to tell each other, and he could not anticipate a time when her opinion would not be the first he would seek on any matter. In a sense, nothing was quite real to him until he discussed it with Opal — even his own feelings were inchoate and baffling until she gave them a name. "Oh, you're just tired," she might say, putting her hand sympathetically on his shoulder, as another man would, or, "Oh, you're *angry* — and you have every right to be angry." And then again, "Thaddeus, you're imagining it all: you're being very childish."

So they had fallen in love and were married in the Baptist church in Marsena, and when Thaddeus's residency at a Port Oriskany hospital was finished they moved to Marsena, where, with the help of Opal's father (it was a measure of Thaddeus's love for her that he allowed Mr. Sayer to give them a substantial wedding gift — several thousand dollars), they were able to buy one of the handsomest houses in the village, built in the early 1850s. It was three stories high, with a spacious veranda and an impressive portico; it was covered in shingleboard, painted white, with dark green shutters and trim; it had a stained-glass window above the front door and a very attractive bay window looking out onto the long, sloping front yard and the unpaved central street of Marsena. There was a brick walk that led to the street, and a gravel driveway lined with magnificent blue spruce; there was a carriage house; and a small barn; and some twenty acres of land, most of it wooded, some planted in alfalfa and clover. The house had been owned by a man named Crofton, who had owned most of the shares of the Marsena paper mill where Thaddeus's father had worked for many years — so Thaddeus had thought it fitting that *he* should buy the Crofton house and populate it with his own children. At the same time he felt rather apprehensive about the move, even before the financial difficulties of the thirties, when a house that size was a considerable burden to maintain. "I'm afraid," he sometimes told his young wife. "I'm afraid we'll just move in and we'll lose it." Opal waved away his doubts. "You're being superstitious," she snorted.

She had an elegant sign made for him, black letters on brass, which swung from a little iron pole set in the front yard. *Thaddeus Vickery, M.D. General Medicine*.

"Nobody will ever make us leave here," she said.

Inside, the rooms were rather dark, though spacious and comfortable. Most of the floors were hardwood, there were oak timbers in the ceilings, the kitchen was enormous, with a slate floor and a fieldstone fireplace and an antique harvest table that had been in the Sayer family for over a hundred and fifty years. There was a dry sink planted with philodendron, the only house plant Opal had any luck with. There was a large fieldstone fireplace in the parlor, and yet another in the dark, cozy room that was to be Thaddeus's office, opening off the foyer but with its own side entrance. (Rare in this part of the world were the floor-to-ceiling bookshelves in the room, which had been Crofton's study.)

As time passed it happened that, without the Vickerys really noticing — for they were both busy, distracted, not very self-conscious people — the house took on a somewhat shabby, run-down look. White shingleboard is very hard to keep up; weeds grow through even the most attractive of gravel driveways, and poke up around the edges of bricks laid for sidewalks; moss takes root and begins to spread on roofs, tiny maples and oaks start to grow in uncleaned gutters. Several of the blue spruce unaccountably sickened and died and were not replaced — Thaddeus never got around to it; the large "silver" mailbox from Sears turned to rust, as did the iron pole from which Thaddeus's handsome sign swung. Opal had no luck with the roses the Croftons had left, and put in marigolds and nasturtiums and geraniums every year, and tried her hand at gladioli, which grew to surprising heights but bloomed feebly. She went through phases when housework appealed to her, and phases when it did not, and since her husband rarely commented on the condition of the house — rarely noticed it, in fact — there were long stretches of time when the windows needed washing and the hardwood floors needed polishing and the molding was filthy and there were smudged fingerprints everywhere. Once Ashton was born, it became almost impossible to keep things clean: Ashton was a restless, careless, rather destructive child.

The first pregnancy and birth was remarkably free of incident, but the second was a difficult one and the infant, a boy (baptized

William Matthew), lived only a few weeks. The loss of the baby brought Thaddeus and Opal closer together but had the effect, also, of breaking their childlike insouciance and their delight in each other: with that death, as Opal put it rather grimly, the honeymoon ended and the business of real life began. At this time Opal was still in her early twenties, big-boned and girlish in a rough way, with a fine healthy complexion and attractive blue eyes, quite pale and finely lashed. Thaddeus, not yet thirty, had begun to discover gray and silver and even bone-white hairs on his head, which sometimes amused him and at other times frightened him. Both realized they were no longer individuals pleased to live together in a large, impressive house, like children given undeserved gifts; they were married — married people; a wife and a husband. The death of the infant had linked them in a way their wedding had not (for the Baptist ceremony meant nothing to them, the "holiness" of matrimony was absurd), and even the birth of their first son had not. They were irreparably joined, married for life; married for eternity (in which, of course, they did not believe: in which Thaddeus vehemently and scornfully disbelieved). "It looks as if we're in this together," Thaddeus had said with faint astonishment at the grave of William Matthew. "It looks as if it's all very serious. . . . Did you know this before? I didn't." Opal had squeezed his arm in silence, to indicate she hadn't known but she knew now.

Yes, Thaddeus found himself thinking from time to time, it was all very serious: life was serious. You woke up and found yourself in it, and then suffered a series of later awakenings that made you realize you could not get out of it; it was no longer *your* life but life itself, a kind of communal, impersonal life in which you participated. But that was unfair! A kind of trick. Just as loving Opal had led to the trickery of that second birth· and that unforgettable death. (Which Thaddeus still could not *understand*, twenty years later: that is, he could not understand why all his efforts to save the child had failed: and of course he had not wanted an autopsy, neither he nor Opal could have borne the thought of an autopsy performed on that tiny body, which had already suffered so much. . . . Only a few weeks before Elsa's misfortune, some twenty-one years after William's death, he had happened to walk through an abandoned cemetery in Childwold, a tiny settlement some miles to the west of Marsena, and came across an aged, weathered gravestone that had nearly broken his heart with its crude naïveté:

BYE BYE MAMMA FROM BABY WILLY

May 5, 1871 — August 11, 1871.

The grief of his own son's early death had swept upon him and he found himself weeping for several minutes, bitterly and helplessly.)

After the second pregnancy, for some reason it became difficult for Opal to conceive a child. They tried — they tried relentlessly, desperately, with a kind of sardonic good humor. The house was so large, they loved each other so completely, surely they were meant to have many children? — at least four or five? Opal went through a spell, fortunately short-lived, of praying for a baby; she went not merely to morning services on Sunday, as everyone did (even, for a while, Dr. Vickery himself, when he believed his position in Marsena not yet solid enough to withstand charges of "atheism"), but to the Sunday-evening service, and the prayer meetings on Wednesday and Friday evenings. After some years she did manage to become pregnant — and then lost the baby, after a bout of influenza; then again, at the age of thirty-one, she became pregnant with the child Elsa, their last-born. And it struck her often as ironic that she, who had had to work so industriously at the business of becoming pregnant, should have a daughter, poor wretched Elsa, who should manage to conceive so very readily at the age of fifteen. . . .

"The odds against it are astronomical," Thaddeus declared.

Opal nodded and said nothing, and as he went on to argue that an abortion was not only justified under the circumstances but the only correct, moral thing to do, the only *sane* thing to do, she sat very still across from him (they were sharing a nightcap at the old table in the kitchen one midnight in November) and appeared to be listening respectfully enough; but when he was fin-

ished she said softly, "Yes — except the baby will be half Vickery.
What of that?"

Nevertheless Thaddeus tried to talk his colleagues at the Derby
General Hospital into approving an operation "to terminate pregnancy" for his daughter; he was convinced the abortion must take
place and that no intelligent person, certainly no professional
colleague of his, would wish to oppose it. But the Chief of Surgery
refused to consider the case. He refused even to submit it to a
committee. "It's illegal in the state and too many people know
about your daughter," he told Thaddeus. "I'm sorry: but what can
I do? The operation *is* illegal."

"I don't understand," Thaddeus said blankly. "What do you —
what do you mean?"

"Abortion is illegal. You know that as well as I do."

"But the girl was raped —"

"It doesn't make any difference. Abortion is illegal, we'd be
vulnerable to arrest, the fetus is a living creature and —"

"It isn't living," Thaddeus said. "It isn't human."

"It's living and it's human. You're tired: you'd better go home."

"Of course, of course it's living, I meant only that — that — It
isn't human — It isn't a human embryo," Thaddeus said excitedly. "Not if we stop it in time. Don't you see? It has no eyes yet,
it's mouthless, sexless, it's hardly more than a worm, a slug, and
if we stop it in time —"

"You'd better go home. You don't look well."

He drove to Port Oriskany, where he argued with the Chief of
Surgery at the hospital there, a man who had interned with him
and whom he had always liked. From there he went to talk with
another former classmate, in private practice in Rosewood, an
affluent suburb west of the city . . . and from there to a clinic in
Port Oriskany where one of the physicians on the staff was, according to rumor, available for abortions if one could afford
them. But he had no luck, he had no luck at all.

"The problem is that everyone knows about her by now," he
told his wife angrily. "The entire county! They sympathize with

me, they're sorry as hell about Elsa, but they won't do anything: they're terrified of being arrested."

Opal nodded slowly. "You don't blame them, do you?"

"Yes, I blame them! For Christ's sake," Thaddeus said. "They might consider *me* . . . they might consider the hell I've been going through. Even if I could locate someone in another part of the state, or in another state, people here know about her and they would wonder . . . they would talk. . . . Could I be arrested after the fact? Could Elsa? But there wouldn't be any proof. Would there? Oh Christ," he said, running both hands through his hair, half-sobbing, "if only she'd miscarry. . . . *You* lost that baby, after all; it happens all the time; there was the Wreszin girl just the other week, lost it in the fifth month. . . . The poor girl, how she bled! Like a pig she bled. Oh God. If Elsa . . . If only. . . If only everyone didn't know about it we could act in secret, we could all go away for a week or two, and . . . Even if I couldn't locate someone to do it I could do it myself, maybe . . . if I could bring myself to. . . ."

Opal stared at him. "That's ridiculous," she said sharply.

"If we got desperate enough . . ."

"There's no *we*, it's only *you*," she said. *"You're* desperate. I never heard of anything so barbaric — you, her own father!"

"But if no one else is willing —"

"Her own father! You're crazy even to think of it!"

"But Opal —"

"Stop it. Shut up. Don't say another word," she cried. "Elsa can live with it and I can live with it. Don't say another word."

"Live with — ?"

"You and Ashton are the ones — *you're* the ones. Elsa can live with it. Don't you say another word about doing it yourself! *Doing it yourself,*" she said mockingly. "As if I'd let you touch her."

Thaddeus stared at his wife. This fat, sallow woman with the frizzy hair and the bleary, slightly mad eyes — what had she to do with him, how did she dare oppose him? She was wearing what might have been a housedress or a dressing gown or a smock

of some kind, shapeless and faded with many washings, and over
this she wore one of his oldest, shabbiest coat sweaters; her cotton stockings were baggy at the knees; her shoes were unlaced.
She gave off an odor of fury and desperation, an animal's odor.
He felt for an instant the dizzying conviction that he did not
know her at all, that she was a creature who had come to life only
in the past few weeks.

"She isn't going to have that baby," Thaddeus said quietly.
"She's only a child. She knows nothing of life, she isn't very
bright — a sweet, warm, lovely girl — a mere child —"

"Both my sisters were married when they were seventeen,"
Opal said.

"— an innocent child with her life all before her. Suppose she
has the baby and puts it out for adoption — what about the rest
of her life? She'll never forget it. She'll never be the same again.
It would be a terrible, tragic mistake to let her have it. I *know*,
I've seen this sort of thing happen many times — and in most
cases the girl at least loves the father of the child, at least *knows*
the father —"

Opal was shaking her head from side to side. Her face was
closed and ugly. "It's too late," she said. "It's out of our hands."

"It isn't too late, for Christ's sake! It can't be much more than
the third week. There are many possibilities . . . but we must
agree, Opal, we must agree that it's . . . it's. . . . That we don't
want the poor girl to have that bastard child. . . ."

"It's too late," Opal said hollowly.

And so they argued, and fell silent; and Thaddeus drove out
again, seeking aid; but he had no luck. All things must be fulfilled
according to Your law and so he had no luck, though he wept
and stormed and threatened and cajoled and offered to pay large
sums of money, until even those colleagues of his who sympa-
thized with him and pitied him and wished to help him lost
patience and refused to see him, saying the situation was a tragic
one but could not be helped: such was the law of the nation, such
was the law of the Lord.

If he had succeeded . . . ?

But the thought is impossible. *Nathanael Vickery never born!* Impossible.

He was not to deliver the baby either, because both his wife and his daughter forbade it. (Just as Elsa had forbidden him even to examine her that terrible night — staggering into the kitchen with blood glistening on her legs, her finger sprained, her heartbeat accelerated and erratic. No, don't touch me! No. Not *you*. — Hysterical, unreasonable. She had allowed Opal to take care of her, while he shouted instructions through the closed bedroom door. And afterward at the hospital, in the emergency ward of Derby General, she had not wanted him in the room with the doctor on duty. She had not *wanted* her father anywhere near.) A midwife from a nearby farm, a coarse, ignorant woman in her late fifties, was Elsa's and her mother's choice, and so Thaddeus sat out the interminable labor in his office, playing solitaire and sipping bourbon and leafing idly through old medical journals and newspapers (war was imminent but unreal as a fairy tale: what did Hitler and Belgium and Luxembourg and the Netherlands have to do with *him?*) and the slim, stained volumes of philosophy he had studied long ago, in another lifetime, when he had been moved by the melancholy glamour of Stoicism while having no awareness whatsoever of its truth.

Elsa's labor began shortly after noon and continued for the rest of the day and well into the night; it was to last some seventeen hours altogether. Thaddeus sipped bourbon, sitting unshaven at his cluttered desk, reading Epicurus, waiting. At the back of his mind arguments continued: she *must* have an abortion, she *must* be rid of the child. The disaster *must* be averted. But it was too late. It was June now, the very last day of June. The baby would be born at 5:30 A.M., undersized, not breathing, the umbilical cord twisted about its neck, a dead thing — evidently dead — until the midwife gave it a panicked shake and it came to life and began to gasp and choke and squawl. Downstairs its grandfather sat hunched in his pajamas and wrinkled bathrobe, reading by an inadequate lamp of the grim measured truths of the "hedonist"

Epicurus, who declared that there is nothing nobler than to apply oneself to philosophy, and there is no greater goal for mankind than the attainment of ataraxia — tranquillity, equanimity, the repose of one's soul. Dare one hope for joy? — for the feverish activity of joy? No. Better the vanquishment of all desire and all strife. The cessation of instinct itself.

Upstairs the girl suffered her brainless sweaty agony, downstairs her father wiped at his eyes, muttering to himself. They had not allowed him to. . . . They had not allowed him. . . . He might have changed the inevitable course of events; he *might* have triumphed. Yet somehow it had not happened. The third week became the fourth, and then the fifth. . . . And then it was the third month. . . . And then the fourth, and the fifth, and. . . . Deeply into winter; emerging from winter and into spring; a cruel tantalizing blizzardy spring; then heavy cold rains. Now it was the very end of June and summer had not yet begun. Unfair, it was unfair. They had not allowed him to scrape her womb clean. They had not allowed him near her, though she was his daughter and lived in his house, under his authority.

In Lucretius he read with great interest that there is no hell (except earth itself), and there are no gods, no intrusion from another sphere into the lives of men. What is heaven? What is hell? Chimeras. Wisps of fancy. There is no spiritual world, only a materialist world in which soul and mind are evolved with the body, grow with the body, ail with the body, and finally die with the body's death. There is nothing permanent: the universe consists of atoms: the law of laws is that of evolution and dissolution everywhere. Wiping at his eyes, Thaddeus Vickery discovered in these ancient, placid words a kind of beauty, a grave and noble simplicity he had not hoped to encounter in his lifetime. The infant Nathanael Vickery was born from between his mother's bloody chafed thighs, as she pushed and pushed to free him from her, groaning aloud, wailing, and Thaddeus Vickery underscored with a shaky pencil a verse paraphrase of Lucretius he could recognize, even in his exhausted state, as mawkish, yet beautiful nevertheless, a wisdom he would never surrender:

Globed from the atoms, falling slow or swift
I see the suns, I see the systems lift
    Their forms; and even the systems and their suns
Shall go back slowly to the eternal drift.

iv

In the beginning there was not the Word, nor words; only the bliss of Your presence. He knew it as light: liquid light. So radiant that it was black; blinding; a blackness ten times black; but light nonetheless, Your radiance.

The infant Nathanael saw through his closed eyelids such realms of light! — and breathed with his tiny lungs the rich warm liquid radiance. It was dearer than blood to him, more precious by far than any physical substance. (Once born, in fact, he could not maintain himself easily in the coarseness of air; nor could he manage to take nourishment at his mother's full, generous breast, though his lips made sucking motions and his distraught mother tried to force him to suck.) He never forgot that radiance, that bliss, and forever afterward in the depths of his soul he sang praises to You. Even in his darkest times he sang praises to You.

He sings praises still.

Like David in the wilderness of Judah: *O God, thou art my God; early will I seek thee: my soul thirsteth for thee, my flesh longeth for thee in a dry and thirsty land, where no water is; To see thy power and thy glory, so as I have seen thee. . . . Thus will I bless thee while I live: I will lift up my hands in thy name.*

In this new landscape how could he make his way? Yours was a realm of such intense light that there was no need to see; his eyes moved in a continual ecstasy, blinded, blind. He saw nothing, neither did he hear. Yet he *knew.* He knew all there was to be known. Your Kingdom: an infinity of Being. Souls unborn, yet-to-be-born, souls transparent and light-riddled as his own. Souls shifting and flowing through one another, light as the seed of dandelions . . . graceful as tiny rainbow-hued fish . . . fragile as butterflies. . . . He was a witness to their agility as they passed through one another and wound about one another, causing small ripples of pleasure, small vibrations of pleasure, almost too intense to be borne. He was a witness to Your love, Your perfection, which was his own. Faceless, eyeless, he had no need to *see*, nor did You contemplate him — nor did You judge him, so long as he was Your own creature. The lifebeat, the jolting of the womb, the terrible constrictions of the womb's wall, the struggle of his spirit as it was fashioned into flesh: the lightning flash of pain as the eyelids were pierced forever: the filling of the lungs, which seemed too small to contain all that they must contain: screams and yells and kicks and squawls and now a ruthless impatience to be born: so You breathed mightily into him and he gasped and choked and quickened with life, and fell headlong into an ecstasy of pain.

In this new landscape he floundered, he groped; he was slippery as a fish and could not take hold. Enormous walls of blood-warmed flesh and milk-taut sacs and his mother's strained, stretched, dead-white belly, skin paler than his own — how could he make his way, how could he take hold? You pulsed along his feathery, downy temples, and stared out sightlessly from his pale eyes, and slipped hot and near-scalding out of his body; You leaned close to him in a balloon-like mass of flesh, You held him to Your jarring heartbeat, his beet-red heated flesh squirming against Yours! And so it came about. And so it was. His lips and his toothless desperate gums closed about Your nipples, but without taking hold, and there was weeping, and sorrow, and discord, but in the end You flowed into him, the pure river of the water of Your spirit flowed into him, and he quickened yet again, and sprang into life.

And his sacred name was whispered to him, that he should know himself as distinct from You, from even Your heartbeat in the marrow of his bone: *Nathanael William Vickery*. So it was then and ever shall be. His sacred name was whispered to him, that he should never forget Your gift of life, Your honeysweet nourishment; that he should never forget, in addition, how he was plunged among the others, many of them strangers who knew You not and scorned You, how he was flesh of their flesh and blood of their blood but in spirit Your creature, with the mark of Your blessing upon him: *Nathanael William Vickery*.

But he was to remember, too, and most vividly and irrefutably, the actual details of his birth. The hurtful air: a sudden chill envelope sticking greedily to his wet hide. The painful pricking of light against his eyes. (Not Your light, which is both glimmering and dark and wonderfully gentle, but the light of the outer jumbled world.) The taste of blood in his mouth. The hammering ringing pulsating noise of his own anguished cry. ("Listen to him!" someone exclaimed. And the circle of glaring faces drew tighter.) Ah, and the astonishment of his first bath! — for though, afterward, years afterward, he was always to be ignored if he claimed, however hesitantly, that he did remember the hour of his birth, he *did* remember, with remarkable exactness, the lapping warmth of the water, the surprising cold and hardness of the porcelain basin, the pressure of hands — strangers' hands — the soft caressing greedy feel of a sponge — for the sponge, larger than a grapefruit, with its queer porous texture, was as real to him, and as living, as the strangers themselves who treated him, from the first, with such startled love, such half-fearful concern, whispering in his presence as if he were incapable of hearing: "Ah, look at him! *Look*. So small. But so alive. . . . He *has* come to us, hasn't he? He is ours."

■ ■ ■

It happened that, one January morning, Nathanael's young mother was preparing a meal for him in the kitchen of her parents' house, and a great uneasiness came upon her, for the house was poorly insulated and its walls could barely withstand the wind out of the northeast (sweeping down from the mountains so relentlessly, day after day), and even the kitchen, always the warmest room in the house, seemed drafty and uncomfortable. "It's cold. Why is it so cold? I hate it here. Why is it so cold?" she said aloud. The baby Nathanael stared up at her; she held him loosely; the giant balloon of her face, the intense glistening eyes, the downturned mouth swayed above him. "Are you cold? Are you hungry? Yes? No? Why don't you speak? Why don't you cry? You don't cry *enough*, says ugly old Aunt Hannah. . . . But I think you do cry enough, I think you cry more than enough. I don't want you noisier. Or hungrier. *I* am your Mamma and *I* know. Are you waking up more? Are you smelling your food? Mashed apricots, mashed peas. Are you hungry? Are you trying to smile — or trying to cry? Yes? No? Why do you stare at me like that? Do you know at last who I am?"

The baby's face strained as if something wished to speak through it. His tiny, perfectly formed lips worked soundlessly. And those eyes! — Elsa stared and stared at them. They were beautiful, they were like her own but *not quite:* like her own but not quite. Pale, pale blue and a bit of hazel, and some hazel-green, and in certain lights flecked with very dark brown. "Looks just like you," the relatives said, "looks just *like* you," smiling their falsehoods, their silly lies, staring at Elsa whom they pitied and hated and would never forgive. "Looks like all of you," said Mrs. Stickney the other day, meaning Thaddeus and Opal as well as Elsa. Her scrawny homely horse-faced daughter Judith nodded her agreement, but when the girls were alone in Elsa's room and Elsa wished to show her the lovely white cashmere baby's shawl one of her aunts had knitted for her, Judith hardly glanced at it; giggled nervously when Elsa asked her about school; clearly wanted to escape. "I don't like you and I never did," Elsa whispered. "Go on out of my room! Get."

Had she said those words aloud? Or kept them to herself, biting her lips until they bled?

Now there was talk of Ashton: getting in a fight all the way up to Yewville, arrested with three other men in a tavern, dragged to the county jail where he spent the night. "Blacked out," he claimed. "Didn't remember a thing." They fined him fifty dollars and let him go, and the talk was of him bringing shame too onto the family — *bringing shame too*, Elsa overheard one of the relatives say to Mrs. Vickery. Words not meant for her to hear. But she heard. She heard everything. Hiding in her room at the top of the house, secret as an animal in its winter lair, she had grown cunning that past winter — the winter of her great distended puffed-up belly — the winter of her disgrace. Something took root and grew in her, inside her; but it was not hers. It was not *hers*. Think of that! It lay coiled up inside her, a bit of stubborn flesh that grew a head, an enormous head, and eyes, and a mouth, and fingers with webs between them, and a jawbone, and a nose, and even a tail! — so the picture book said. (Dr. Vickery had given her several books to read but Elsa found herself unable to concentrate on the printed words. Her eye just jumped all over, from line to line; it was worse than trying to read in school when she was called on by the teacher — and usually made a fool of herself, faltering and giggling. It was worse by far! It was so hard! But she forced herself at least to study the pictures, her lips moving to shape the words in the captions, for she *knew* it was important, all this was important, her father wished her to have knowledge in her mind as well as the creature growing in her belly.) And then, and then gradually the eyes were formed in the bulging head, so it would not be a sightless beast like a creature of the deep, and the tail dissolved, and the webs between the fingers and toes dissolved, and the lifebeat was strong, very strong. . . . "It's too late," Mrs. Vickery had said back in November of that year, sighing heavily, walking heavily about the house. "It's too late: we'll have to live with it," she had said, pausing at about the tenth step going upstairs, always the same step, so that the boards creaked under her weight.

In the night Elsa heard her parents shouting at each other. Or did they shout at Ashton? Or was it the men by the river, she

wondered drowsily, had they returned, had the one with the
knotted scarf returned, come to claim her . . . ? Always in the
morning her room looked the same: the lilies-of-the-valley wallpaper that was discolored, especially near the window (the window frame was warped and rain got in, and Dr. Vickery kept
saying he'd call Lyle McCord to do a little carpentering work one
of these days, but he forgot and Elsa had not the energy to re-
mind him: maybe she'd get pneumonia and die, and *then* how
sorry they would be — wouldn't they?), the bouquet of dried
weed flowers in a chipped blue vase (goldenrod and devil's-paint-
brush mainly, with some corn tassels thrown in, and three cattails that were once quite handsome but now a little dusty), the
Raggedy Ann doll Mrs. Vickery had made for her how many
years ago? — why, it must have been fourteen years at least! —
sitting propped up in the child-sized rocker by the radiator where
it was too hot to sit most of the time when the furnace was
working, and anyway the rocker was too little now for Elsa — if
she sat herself down in it she might be stuck for good. And the
peach-colored organdy curtains she and Opal had made, and the
pinewood hope chest at the foot of the bed, filled mainly with
moth-eaten old blankets and comforters and sweaters Elsa had
outgrown, and the china fowl atop the bureau (rooster, hen, and
three baby chicks almost life-sized), and the picture of Christ
framed in something very ornate that looked like gold, but Elsa
supposed was not gold: Christ with bright-glistening brown eyes,
reddened lips and cheeks, droplets of rich, sullen blood making
their way down his bluish forehead from his cruel crown of
thorns that looked to Elsa just like the briars growing out behind
the old carriage house where she had played as a child, unwisely,
and scratched her arms and legs more than once. All these things
were familiar enough, daylight returned them to her; or her to
them. Blinking in amazement, she would stumble from bed to
look all around the room — all around it — from wall to wall to
wall to the window (where she sometimes stood in her nightgown, shivering, empty-headed, waiting for her mind to fill, staring at the semicollapsed roof of the carriage house and the bro-

ken weather vane, and the pigeons that flew in and out of the hay-door, and, past the mist-shrouded field where Carlson Bell's horses stood asleep, the foothills and the mountains and the distant, almost invisible peak of Mt. Ayr, which was lost to her sight for days at a time in the winter). And gradually a sound in the room claimed her sleepy attention: a sputtering half-whimpering gasping sound; and she would turn, startled, frightened, and see the baby bassinet that had not been there a minute before.

Always in the morning her room, her life, looked and smelled and sounded the same, and felt the same (as her nails scratched absently at a bump on her thigh, or her fingertips drew themselves lightly against the baby's fair downy silky blond-brown hair), and whatever had taken place during the night — whatever shouts and screams and jostlings and jeering laughter and cries of *Jesus*, *Jesus* — simply fell away and were forgotten. Elsa stood barefooted and flatfooted in the daylight world and there, changing a wet diaper for a fresh dry one, sprinkling a vaguely lilac-scented powder onto the kicking infant, she yawned noisily (as she *must* not do downstairs, for Mrs. Vickery said it was rude, and wasn't it bad enough that Dr. Vickery sometimes forgot himself and yawned even louder? — and it was no excuse to say you were tired).

Sometimes Mrs. Vickery scolded; sometimes she sat herself down on the horsehair sofa and, sighing, feeling lazy, would get Elsa to sit close beside her, the baby on both their laps, and talk for long minutes at a time about nothing much: just talk. What kind of jam did Nathanael like best, how tall did Elsa think he would grow, would his eyes change color, or his hair, how did Elsa feel these days, how was her schoolwork going (Elsa was supposed to be working on her own this year, Sarah Grace Renfrew was supposed to be bringing her assignments over, and there was talk of some "tutoring" by one of the teachers: but Elsa never brought up the subject), should they drive to the city one of these days and buy some clothes, maybe a nice winter coat for Elsa, for Sundays — when was she going to start going to church again? Soon? Sometimes Mrs. Vickery talked like this, lazy and loving,

and sometimes she was snappish, and in a bad temper, and Elsa
whispered, "Oh I hate you: you!" and ran upstairs. And sometimes . . .

Sometimes they talked about her in secret. As they had from
the start. They whispered about her, and shouted, and lapsed
into silence. And then she would hear their footsteps taking them
away from each other. Dr. Vickery to his office, where he closed
the door hard, Mrs. Vickery on the stairs, where she paused
midway. She knew. From the start. Her father had taken a sam-
ple of her urine to a laboratory in the city but she knew she was
pregnant, as surely as if she'd been pregnant many times before
and was now only remembering. The nipples of her breasts were
queer and sensitive, and in the morning she was lightheaded,
confused from so many crammed noisy dreams, and she *remembered* a baby's wail — had it somehow been in the room with her?
Some days she was ravenously hungry and hardly cared what she
ate, scavengering in the refrigerator half an hour after dinner,
braving Mrs. Vickery's sharp tongue, but, even worse, her unpredictable tearful pity; other days she vomited up everything, even
skim milk, even weak tea, even honeycomb honey smeared on
whole wheat bread, her favorite breakfast. So there was no need
for her father to run off to the Yewville hospital with the little
glass jar and make a fool of himself; *she* knew.

Then they whispered and quarreled about what she already
knew, and by the time they told her — *after* they had told her
brother, in fact — which both angered her and made her laugh
— she had no feeling about it to offer them, no surprise or tears
or terror. Which baffled them. Alarmed them. Dr. Vickery especially, who kept pushing his glasses up his nose and scratching at
his chin-whiskers as if they were alive with itching, Dr. Vickery
especially wondered at her, speaking slow and calm and a little
loud, as you would do with a child or a deaf person or someone
senile. Did she understand? Did she grasp the meaning of his
words? Did she *comprehend?*

"Well, yes," Elsa said sullenly.

Later the three of them — Mrs. Vickery and Dr. Vickery and Ashton, that is — quarreled downstairs while Elsa was trying to sleep, and she half-heard their words, and ran out of her room and down the stairs and surprised them in Dr. Vickery's study and she shouted at them and called them names, horrible ugly names, and scratched her father's face and knocked his glasses off, and when Ashton tried to catch her she punched him hard in the gut, right in the gut — ! But no: she turned over and fixed the pillow so that maybe she wouldn't hear. Downstairs they raised their voices one final time. Then were silent. Then paraded into the kitchen and Mrs. Vickery opened the squeaky cupboard door and got out, probably, the can of cocoa, and the three of them had hot chocolate sitting around the table and Elsa's mouth watered and she slipped into sleep and there her mother raised a cup of delicious hot chocolate to her lips and she drank it hungrily, lustily, and *almost* tasted it. . . . But maybe she had imagined it all and they hadn't quarreled and it hadn't been about her. If she came into a room they always stopped talking, and smiled at her, and asked her some question or other, and she fell into the habit of shrugging her shoulders and offering no reply at all, for what was the use? She knew she would have a baby, was having a baby, and it did no good to carry on like the rest of them. Her mother broke into tears, and even her father did (once at the dinner table: so embarrassing!), but she had no tears left and it was unfair for them to blame her, for what was the use? ("I don't think the child understands," Dr. Vickery murmured once, in her hearing, and Mrs. Vickery silenced him with a simple, "*Thaddeus.*")

One November afternoon when it was twilight by five-thirty she pushed by her mother in the kitchen and opened the cupboard door and reached for the can of cocoa, and when Mrs. Vickery said, "Elsa, what are you doing? Do you want to spoil your appetite? We're going to eat in under an hour —" she shrugged her shoulders and said brutally, "Well, *you* people had some last night," in a voice meant to be scornful but that came out hurt and childlike; and she realized too late that it hadn't been the night before and maybe she had only dreamed it anyway. . . . Mrs. Vickery had stared at her, too puzzled to speak.

In her womb the thing quivered with — with elation, with rage? With simple lustful hunger?

All the shadows of the big old drafty house deepened. Widened. Only a cunning sleepwalker could make her way through them without tripping.

"Elsa," they said, "Elsa — ?"

But no: she carried herself haughtily enough.

Her father spoke to her tenderly, with love and dread. Behind his voice she heard another but she did not let on. *I will greatly multiply thy sorrow and thy conception; in sorrow thou shalt bring forth children. . . .*

"The child understands the facts of her condition, but she doesn't *comprehend*," Dr. Vickery said. And in her presence, too, as if she were deaf.

Though he was not yet fifty years old his face was lined and leaden-hued, and the soiled cuffs of his long winter underwear showed at his wrists. When he fussed with his pipe, which was continually going out, his fingers trembled; Elsa had to pity him. She watched as if hypnotized while he picked out the old muck and shook fresh tobacco in and tried to light it, sucking noisily. It seemed to take him longer all the time to get his pipe functioning.

"Why do you talk about me so much?" Elsa asked quietly.

"Because, dear, we're afraid you don't really *comprehend* the circumstances of your life now. Of our lives now."

"Do you?"

"What?"

"I said — *do you?*"

Both Dr. Vickery and Mrs. Vickery stared at her. "What do you mean, Elsa? I don't quite — don't quite follow you," Dr. Vickery said.

"Do you comprehend the circumstances of our lives?"

"Elsa — ?"

"Do *you?*"

She glared at them, triumphant. She wanted to burst into contemptuous laughter and banish them all upstairs and out of her
sight.

In her womb the thing throbbed with life, with the beating
pulse of life. She liked to think at such times that it was hers. But
she was not deluded, having guessed at Your enmity with the
world of man.

But the nuisance of merely living! — as long as she remained
with her parents she was theirs, and if they wept they desired that
she weep also; but they did not want her to weep by herself, in
secret.

Of course someone did weep, often. Curled beneath the bedclothes; brushing the tangles out of her hair; trying to shake herself out of her numb, bruising sleep. Sometimes in the early
morning there was the simple excitement of Elsa, an Elsa-as-
always, who broke away from her and dressed quickly and eagerly
for school, paying no heed to *her* tears, and this Elsa rushed
about like the cat foolishly frantic for his supper and took hardly
any time to eat and hurried outside to catch up with Sarah Grace
and Gina and the others, and they called her Slowpoke, as they
used to, and asked her if she'd done her homework, and later on
they sat together in the crowded lunchroom, and passed notes to
one another during study hall second-to-last period of the day.
. . . But most of the time there was just the person pretending to
be Elsa, who lay in bed stubborn and cold and fixed and hard,
who didn't give a damn about Sarah Grace or Gina or anyone
else.

Out of her hearing they talked about an abortion. She knew,
somehow she knew. Maybe she had actually heard the words.
Maybe she had heard them in her sleep. But she knew it would
not happen because the baby's wail had already sounded in the
room with her, in her very bed. It would not happen. Her breasts
grew plump and white and pink-nippled, and the skin of her belly
was shiny white and quite pretty (so she thought, sadly) and so it
would not happen, God would not allow it. She was meant to
have the baby, which was *his* baby, the man with the knotted

scarf, *his*, and no one else's, what was the use of crying or carrying on?

And if, afterward, he came for her — came to claim the baby?
No.

She would stare coldly at him and turn aside as if not recognizing him. She would say: "I don't know you. I've never set eyes on
you." He might plead with her, and say how sorry he was, how
sorry, *sorry*, in a voice like her brother's whine when he'd broken
something in the kitchen, coming in so staggering-drunk, but she
would hardly listen, and she would not look at him at all. "I don't
know you. I've never set eyes on you," she would say coldly.

Why was the baby's food so slow in heating up? — ah, she saw
that she'd forgotten to turn on the burner. Damn it, she thought.

"Damn it and damn you," she said aloud.

It was chilly in the kitchen, as always, which was why she wore
her wool bathrobe and her thick imitation-fur bedroom slippers
and knee-high wool socks. Her hair needed washing; needed
trimming because it grew in unevenly and the ends were split.
She was pale with the long winter, and plain and flabby and
sullen, but any time she wished she could fix herself up, any time
at all: she could be just as pretty as before. As pretty as Gina
Talbot, maybe. She could shampoo her hair and pinch her
cheeks to make them red and maybe dab on a little lipstick, if it
wasn't too noticeable. But what was the use, why should she
bother? Even before she began to show, they hadn't allowed her
to return to school. "She might distract the other students," the
principal explained to Dr. and Mrs. Vickery. "She might alarm
the other girls, the younger girls especially." They had not
wanted her anywhere near. Not even to look at. She could study
at home, they told her, an "arrangement" could be made very
easily, her friends could bring assignments and her work back
and forth, and one of the teachers could be persuaded to tutor
her, and she could take exams just like the others at the end of
the year, and be spared the presence of the other students. The
bigger boys, especially: it might be better for her to avoid them.
"In that way everything will work out for the best, for your daugh-

ter and for the other students, and for her teachers too," the principal said.

Well, that was about Elsa — not about *her*.

She had no wish to fix herself up just to please them, and to pretend to be Elsa again, now she knew how they despised her.

"I know what I know," she said, stirring the baby's food with his own little spoon.

Suppose they looked at her — who did they see? Not her. Not even Elsa. ("That old sad silly cow," she laughed.) They saw someone else and spoke to that person in their heads, their skin tightening, around the eyes especially. There were, naturally, false smiles — even Ashton (who now could barely stand to be in the same room with her) managed to smile. Showed his teeth, anyway. But she didn't mind — why on earth should she mind? It was what they had always done to each other anyway.

The baby Nathanael, beginning now to fret, waving his fat little hands excitedly — did he see her? *Her?*

He had wanted to breast-feed shortly after his birth and she, or someone in her place, had wanted him to do so: but it had not worked. She tried and tried, and the infant tried, and Mrs. Vickery helped also, but it did not work. Straining on all sides: but it was a failure. Reverend Sisley baptized him *Nathanael William Vickery* and Elsa, who had not chosen the name, or anyway could not remember, had not objected, for what was the use? They propped her up in bed, they gave her the creature to hold. It was just like any other baby she'd seen in her lifetime — no smaller than her cousin Marilyn's, which had been born even earlier than hers, a seven-months' baby. Small enough but not *too* small. A nice little tidy weight. Bawling and gasping and wetting even before, it seemed, he would have anything to wet.

Still, he was sizable, when you thought of how he'd been up in her belly, *inside* her. It didn't seem possible, did it? Crammed up inside her, poor Elsa, poor silly sad homely cow. Bearing down on him, bearing down, down, they had shouted for her to *Push! push!* and she'd all but given up, it was so hard, so pointless, when she saw that God would take him anyway: God would reach

down and snatch him up and claim him for His own. Still she
had pushed at whatever it was there between her thighs, stuck up
inside her, hard and cruel as a rock, fighting her all the way,
since it did not wish to be born. The face above her possessed a
raw, immediate beauty. Its complexion was swarthy, its eyes
shadowed, its forehead strong and bold. She screamed at it and
would have scratched at it, but her own eyes rolled back in her
head and were lost. No! she screamed. No, *no*. But who could
listen in all that uproar? There was the stink of perspiration, and
of bowels; the stink of blood. She half thought in her delirium
that the pillow beneath her head, her best goose-feather pillow,
was soaked with blood and would have to be burned.

The face had not smiled. Its lips had parted in a recognition of
her pain — her terror.

"I don't know you," she screamed. "Go away: I don't *know*
you."

Such a long time in the womb, such a long time pushing his
way out! You couldn't help screaming at him, could you? Five or
six or seven of them, the police were told. The sheriff first, and
then the police. Listening. Embarrassed at Dr. Vickery's grief.
Apologetic, and eager to get away. (Elsa was to know that look of
wanting-to-get-away very well as the months passed.) Seven men,
or maybe eight? Who could tell? Her testimony was confused and
contradictory. She could not remember. Then she remembered
— remembered something. A face, a snatch of a name, a voice.
Twelve days in the hospital, unconscious much of the time, running a fever. Doped-up. In that state she could remember something, but it was like a movie she'd seen and could not quite
recall. Maybe it was best to pretend? to lie? She was so sleepy,
her voice fairly drawled. Saliva ran down her chin. Such a baby!
She started crying for no reason at all and couldn't stop until
someone gave her an injection, and even then she didn't stop,
just fell back into sleep into a raving dream where the tears continued worse than ever.

She woke, she yawned, she staggered from bed. What day?
What month? — The algebra book on her desk, face down, the

spine broken. What day? Was Sarah Grace coming this afternoon? But she had made excuses two times in a row, busy with
chorus rehearsals after school, or having to do an errand for her
mother. And the last time she'd come to the Vickery house she
had acted stiff and rather frightened, absolutely *not* looking Elsa
directly in the eye. A nervous gangling giggling girl whom Elsa
didn't like anyway — had never liked. "All right, then, go home,
go away, goddam you," Elsa had whispered.

That long, long winter. Waiting. Waiting for the heartbeat, for
the first kick. Working lazily on a rag quilt, all sorts of crazy
colors and stripes and flowered prints, her swollen fingers moving
clumsily, something to do, something not to think about — was
this scarlet-orange of an old silk dress the color his scarf had
been, but naturally she couldn't have seen? — since it was so
dark? Jabbing herself with the needle more than once. Dropping
the thimble so that it rolled beneath the bed and disturbed the
vapory beginnings of dust balls. Oh Elsa, clumsy Elsa, what's the
use? Not one but several bassinets were offered. So she and Mrs.
Vickery had their pick. Rather choosy with the baby clothes and
blankets that were brought over by relatives, hand-me-downs still
in good condition. Elsa and her mother listened politely as Dr.
Vickery gave the names of various adoption agencies in other
parts of the state — some church-affiliated, some not. There was
a friend of Ashton whose sister who lived over in Shaheen was
desperate for a baby, but she and her husband had no luck, no
luck after eight years of marriage, and the adoption agencies were
so slow, and maybe — maybe they could adopt Elsa's baby? If it
was a normal baby. If it was born without any trouble.

"If that's the Abbott boy's sister," Mrs. Vickery mumbled without bothering to look around, "I'm not so sure. I'd have to think
about *that*."

There were long periods of time when mother and daughter
worked side by side in the kitchen, making noodle dough, rolling
pie crust, preparing an ordinary evening's dinner, and no thought
of *it* intruded; not at all. The radio played country music beamed
out from Port Oriskany and the snow blew stinging against the

windows and the oven heated the room and there was no need, even, to complain about Sarah Grace or the other girls, or some-one-or-other who had said something-or-other that had found its way to Mrs. Vickery's ear. True enough, Elsa was slower than ever before, and sometimes left things half finished (once left the dust mop lying in the foyer right in front of Dr. Vickery's door, so that he nearly stumbled over it), and Mrs. Vickery did have a sharp tongue; but they got along as well as ever. It was important to keep busy. Only when the day came to an end, and Dr. Vickery and Ashton were expected in, did the mood change and Elsa want to run upstairs and hide beneath her bedclothes and cry and cry like a baby. For, if Dr. Vickery had been out on house calls or at the hospital and they heard his car in the driveway, they glanced at each other guiltily and Elsa saw that her mother remembered — remembered everything. And betrayed her in an instant.

Then the baby managed to get himself born, and gained weight as the weeks passed, and sometimes it was difficult for Elsa to remember whose he was and what he meant. Even what his name was (which he seemed to know — the *Nathan* part of it, at least). Mrs. Vickery and Aunt Hannah and Samantha Hurley, Elsa's cousin, and Mrs. Stickney from down the road fussed and chirped over the baby, and sat in the parlor drinking tea and eating fruitcake, chattering while Elsa sat in silence staring at the scuffed toe of her shoe, and about her head flew all sorts of news — the older Preston girl was as good as engaged to Duane McCord, who was now making a great deal of money at one of the steel mills in Port Oriskany; someone's cousin had run away to Canada to join the Air Force and was now training in England; there was to be a stepping-up of the draft before spring; one of the Ackerson boys had turned sixteen and quit school like all his brothers. Elsa blinked, and saw the sweater falling onto her; the cuff nearly poked her in the eye. Had he said anything as he tossed it onto her? Or had he said all he'd wished to say? Strange if they met someday. At a volunteer firemen's picnic, maybe. At

Wolf's Head Lake some summer. "Why are you looking at me? I don't know you," Elsa mouthed. She would be carrying the baby in her arms. Curly-haired, it would be; cute as a button; dressed in blue. "I've never seen you before in my life," she whispered. His eyes pleading, his mouth downturned. But no: no.

Then again, they might have met somewhere else. Years ago. She might have been with other people; with Dr. Vickery, for instance. Remember when he'd been called out to one of the big valley farms, where a young German field hand had been hurt, and Elsa had accompanied him, and Dr. Vickery had set the poor man's broken leg — ? Sunburned, with streaked blond hair, speaking only a few coarse words of English, trying not to cry: a quite handsome young man in his late twenties. *He* might have been so injured, his face stretched in agony, and Elsa and her father might have met him in the rich golden sunshine of harvest. And then —

Was Nathan a good baby, was he sweet as he seemed? — so the ladies asked. And Mrs. Vickery said he was indeed. Hardly any trouble at all. So different from *her* son Ashton at that age. A perfect baby, really, and so quick to catch on, you could almost see him thinking — you could almost make out his anxious garbled words. The ladies talked about other babies, all of them trouble in some way — colicky, diarrheic, "rambunctious." Boy babies were the worst, they all agreed. Elsa and Mrs. Vickery were so fortunate. Mrs. Stickney spoke vehemently, describing in detail the uproar caused by her son during the first year of his life, and told Elsa she was very, very lucky little Nathan wasn't like *that*. "Oh well," Elsa said, pulling her thoughts together. "Well . . . if he was that bad, you know, why probably we'd give him away to someone-or-other. What do you call it? Adoption, adoption something. Oh yes: agency. I mean," she said, faltering as the women stared, "I mean if he was that bad, that *terrible* bad, and nobody could get a night's sleep."

Sometimes Reverend Sisley and his wife came to visit, and she had to be very careful what she said. It was better to say nothing.

So she said nothing. Afterward Mrs. Vickery might scold ("How can you just sit there mute? — have you gone simple?"), but it was better to say nothing, or as little as possible, so she wouldn't make a mistake. Reverend Sisley led them in prayer, read from his Bible, blessed them and accepted their blessing, and smiled at Elsa through his glasses. Sometimes his eyes were damp with tears. Elsa was, he believed, bearing up remarkably well under her burden, she was meeting her challenge head-on; Jesus must be very pleased with her. It was possible, Reverend Sisley said, that Elsa was closer to Jesus than any of them, closer even than he himself, because of her suffering and her courage and the cross she had to bear. Mrs. Vickery and Mrs. Sisley sometimes wiped at their eyes, but Elsa never did. What was the use . . . ? The first time she had met with Reverend Sisley, not long after the rape, he had acted strange with her, he'd fumbled through his Bible and avoided her eye and read passages to her she couldn't follow, or didn't care to follow, something about Eve and the First Sin and woman's suffering and the serpent in the Garden and the apple and angels with swords and God's righteousness, and she had stopped listening, and found it hard to make herself listen ever again. . . . *I will greatly multiply thy sorrow and thy conception; in sorrow thou shalt bring forth children; and thy desire shall be to thy husband, and he shall rule over thee.* Yes: she found it hard to make herself listen.

"Stop thrashing about. What's your hurry? You've got all morning," Elsa said. All morning. There's not a single blessed thing to do but eat, is there?"

But he was crying. He was certainly making a fuss.

"You've got to wait for this to *cool*," Elsa said. (She had allowed the baby food to overheat; it had been boiling furiously when she snatched the pan off the stove.) "Do you want to burn your silly little mouth?"

On a pile of newspapers beside the stove the cat lay half asleep, looking up drowsily at the baby's noise. It was an old tom, battered and lazy, gray-striped, with a face like an owl's, an expression that seemed at times almost intelligent, almost critical. Sometimes Elsa dreamed about the cat instead of the baby, the old gray tom instead of Nathanael William. Did it matter? One or the other? You had to feed them both. Except the cat was cleaner, washed his own coat and took care of his own messes outside, and didn't raise a squawk. If worse came to worst, Elsa thought, blowing on the spoonful of mashed vegetable, the cat could run off and become a hunter and eat birds and mice and rats and even squirrels, and get by, but Nathanael William would just starve to death on his own; he was so puny and helpless. Such a fretful squirming stubborn little thing! What if he crawled away somewhere, what if it was summer and Elsa took him into the woods and he got lost, or she locked him, in play, in the old smokehouse on the Arkin farm where no one went any longer, and came back home and her parents said, "Where's Nathan?" and she looked around, surprised, and said, "Why, I don't know: don't *you* have him?" and it wouldn't be her fault if he sickened and died if she mislaid him and couldn't remember where. . . .

She tasted the baby food and it seemed to be cool enough now, and Nathan was fussing so, and fretting, she'd better start to feed him: so she did; but it must have been too hot because he set up a terrible yammering noise. And this was the good baby those bitches all congratulated her on, *this!* "Oh hush," she said, bouncing him a little on her knee, "just hush. Why are you so noisy? What do you want? What's the point of all your carrying-on?" Gradually he calmed down. His fat fingers plucked at the air, his tiny lips worked. Was he trying to talk to her? Trying to accuse her? She didn't know if he was ugly or beautiful or just like everybody else's baby. She didn't know why he had been born — *why* so much commotion had been raised. She held the spoon a few inches from his wet, anxious mouth and it crossed her mind that his face had no shape at all but was just a kind of squashed-together mass of skin with the beady little eyes poked into it, and the little nose, and the mouth: it was terrifying, that face. It had put itself together out of parts of *her*, her blood and flesh and even her bones, and still it wanted more of her, always more. "Just what is your problem?" she asked. He fretted and blinked and squinted and struggled in her lap, making clumsy swipes at the spoon that came nowhere near the spoon but annoyed her all the same. "What do you want? Why are you so greedy? What's the hurry? Where are you going?" She brought the spoon to his mouth and nudged his mouth open, and he managed to take part of the food, sputtering slightly. His arms flailed. He was quite strong. "Where are you going?" she asked. "Nowhere. Isn't it nowhere? Eh?" She brought the spoon toward his mouth again, but this time, at the very last moment, pressed it against his little pug nose so the mushy food stuck to it; which made him fret all the more. He looked so silly! The next time, she brought the spoon up against his forehead and smeared a bit of the disgusting stuff on him there, and couldn't help but giggle, he was so flush-faced and sputtering like an old man, and kicking so hard. A hot wave of sheer sensation coursed through her. Her voice rose shrilly and began to quaver. "So you're hungry again? Always hungry! Greedy! Where do you think you're going, kicking those legs a mile a minute like that? — You're going nowhere, little noise-box." Trembling, she held the tiny spoon an inch or so from his face, near his eye. He wailed, he threw himself about with an amazing spirit. If he jerked forward in his greed, he might jab himself in the eye — and whose fault would that be? Tossing himself around like that! Such a silly arrogant little noise-box, such a maddening little pig! A voice had rung out not long ago, filling the church with its certainty, its chanting truncheon-hard certainty, and Elsa had half-listened, and half-comprehended, and now the words ran through her in a furious jumble and she wanted to laugh at their craziness: *And if thine eye offend thee, pluck it out, and cast it from thee: it is better for thee to enter into life with one eye, rather than having two eyes to be cast into hell. . . .* Words, words! Such a jumble! They meant nothing, or everything; she had no time to listen; the baby was squalling louder than ever in his hunger and baffled humiliation, and she made a tiny lunge at him with the spoon, and —

She heard her mother's heavy, fast footsteps but it was too late. Mrs. Vickery was already in the kitchen, only a few yards away, and had already seen — had already begun shouting at her.

V

O Lord, You alone are the pulse beat, the arterial blood that flows in secrecy in the darkest, bluest recesses of the soul. How shall I praise You? Even as You have turned aside from me in loathing, how shall I praise You? You knew all my longings from the first; the very light that shone in my eyes was mine no longer. For it is said that as the newborn child is contained in the soul of the world, so is the world itself contained in the soul of the newborn. There is not one without the other. There is not one without the necessity of the other.

My vision, O Lord, is greatly reduced, but I am far from blind, and there are days — mornings, especially — when my right eye is fairly strong, and I experience a painful sense of hope. It does not last, it does not last for more than a few minutes, but I am grateful for all such gifts and pray only that You will see fit to return to me.

What was once measured in hours, and then in days — so very bitterly! — is now measured in years: Your absence. Why did you forsake me, O Lord? At the very height of my power? — the living demonstration of my love for You? And why do You continue to keep Yourself from me, despite my ceaseless prayer? Is Your loathing for me a measurement of my sin? But how specifically did I sin? And do I sin now? Is this very prayer of mine an affront to You, which I make in utter ignorance? How can I know? Who will tell me? Who is a witness? Who can comprehend?

Who is listening?

I endure the world, as You endured it; I dwell in the world but am not of it. So the seasons pass. So the moon and sun spin about my head. I am aging, I am very mortal. The breath of Your love in me has become grievously faint. But I do not despair. I will never despair.

I tremble with the desire to be a witness to Your truth, as I was once; to plunge into the corrupt and ignorant world bearing Your message. Lord, there is none like You! None! Let all the nations hear, let all of mankind praise! But they do not listen — no more now than in the time of David. *They have never listened*. They have most gleefully exchanged the glory of the imperishable God for representations of perishable man, of bird and beast and reptile; they willingly exchange Your truth for lies, worshiping the creature in preference to the Creator. I would raise my voice against them now, as I did in the years that have passed, but I am too weak — I am much changed, as You well know. Why do You keep Yourself from me? Is it my fate to be at home neither in the world of man nor in the realm of God?

■ ■ ■

The child Nathanael dwelled with God, and there was no time when he was not with God. So it was: before his birth and afterward. He knew not the terrible loneliness that I and many others, fallen from Your regard, have known.

The child Nathanael knew the blissful light of Your presence both before his tumultuous birth, and afterward. For many years afterward. He was *Your* child and in his soul there was contained the very soul of Your creation — past and future. He had no direct knowledge of You, nor did he have a word for You. His grandmother soon began to speak to him of God, and of the Son of God, and when they were alone together she would read to him from the Bible, and he listened as if enchanted, for though he had no word for You he sensed that these words were Your words and this history Your history — but he had no direct knowledge, he could not *know*. He knew only what remained with him of Your Kingdom of Light, of utter ecstasy preceding the bitter turmoil of birth.

When he was very small his grandmother hugged him and rocked him to sleep in her strong arms. Again and again. "Don't cry, don't fret, sweet one, sweet little mouse, my dear one. . . . Why should you cry? She can't hurt *you*."

She swayed, holding him tight against her; her eyes glittered strangely with tears; she smelled of soap and milk and bread dough. How he loved her! His tiny fingers plucked at her mouth, her ears, her hair. She sang: "Bye, baby bunting, Daddy's gone a-hunting," and he drifted off to sleep.

He wept and kicked frantically. She was gone.

And then she appeared — stooped over the bed to pick him up, grunting.

"What a fuss! Oh Lord what a noise!" she laughed.

She carried him about with her, grateful for his warm, compact weight. He was hers, was he not? Hers. Her first-born, Ashton, had come too soon in her life — she'd been hardly more than a girl herself when he was born, and she hadn't been ready for motherhood. She had not understood it. Her marriage, her emotional and sexual love for her husband, had distracted her from the baby; he had not quite existed for her. She had loved him, of course. But he had come too soon in her life.

Now her marriage was in the background. Her love for Thaddeus had become a companionable love. She honored him and respected him and believed she could not live without him — would not care to live without him. He was her husband, after all, and they were one flesh, one spirit. They had grown together, in a sense, and could not truly *see* each other as separate individuals; so it was not possible for her to feel a womanly desire for him. Not any longer. Her desire was no longer of the flesh, it was of the spirit — a tremendous hunger of the spirit that only the child Nathanael could satisfy.

She fed him, spoonful by spoonful. Her face grew ruddy again with happiness. In a throaty, husky, delighted voice she sang:

O Galilee, sweet Galilee
Where Jesus loved so much to be
O Galilee, sweet Galilee
Come sing thy songs again to me!

The child's face held such love for her, how could she bear to
gaze upon it? His eyes! His small, sweet, perfect lips! She felt, in
a way, that she was not worthy of his adoration. After all — she
was not his mother. And he would know it, even if he didn't
know it yet.

"Your mother *does* love you, Nathan," she said. "Except she
isn't well. She'll be well soon and then . . . and then she'll come
back to you, wait and see. Do you understand? No? Yes? What a
lovely big smile!"

When she crooned a lullaby or one of the simple gospel tunes,
the infant stared at her with an almost quivering intensity, an
almost painful absorption, as if he were drawing the words from
her: *he*, and not she herself. The way he stared — ! It frightened
her, almost, that he should be so different from other children.

"He knows," she told Thaddeus one night when they stood by
his bed, watching him as he slept.

"Knows — ? Knows what?" Thaddeus asked.

"Everything."

"What do you mean?"

"Everything. He knows everything," Opal said in a soft, trembling voice.

"About Elsa, you mean?"

"Elsa, yes," Opal said impatiently. "And everything else."

Her husband stared at her, frowning. At such times he said
little, as if sensing how she was set in opposition to him, how
stubbornly she would oppose him if he provoked her.

"He isn't like other children," she insisted. "He's deeper — far
deeper than Ashton or Elsa was. You don't remember them, but
I do! This child is much older than they were at his age."

"Older? In what sense?"

"In his soul."

"Ah yes: his soul," Thaddeus said uncertainly.

"He *knows*."

She waited for him to contradict her, but he did not; he was turned slightly away from her, staring at the sleeping child.

"He knows all there is to know," she whispered fiercely.

Her husband did not understand and she despaired of making him understand. He was too much taken up in worldly activities; his soul was broken into fragments, claimed by a hundred people, and more; there was no certainty in him. Lying awake beside him as he slept his exhausted, uneasy sleep, Opal prayed for him, moving her lips silently. She had not prayed for many years; she had joined the congregation at services in those routine, familiar prayers, and often she had sung along with the others, hymns in praise of God and of the Son of God, but she had not truly *prayed* for many years — her soul had not been moved. Since the birth of her grandson, however, she had begun praying once more and there were days when a kind of constant prayer coursed through her, *O God help, O God please, O God have mercy:* from dawn to midnight the words pulsed in her with a fervor she could not recognize as having come from herself.

Because the child had come into the world so accursed, so loathed, she knew she would love it more than she loved her own children. Perhaps, in a way, it *was* hers — her own William, miraculously reborn.

"You seem to know me, don't you?" she asked him. "There's something so wise about you, so precocious! You know all of us, don't you? Eh?"

Opal stared and stared at him. It was impossible for her to get enough of him. Such a quiet, intense baby — blinking at times as if astonished. His tiny forehead furrowed with a sort of intelligent bewilderment, his eyes narrowed, his hands flew like trapped birds. The several words he possessed appeared to possess him: "This," he would say, stammering, shaking his head, trying to point with both hands, *"This.* This this this." And again: "Yes. Yes. *Yes.*" If he tried to nod, the nodding got out of control; his poor little head bobbed and baby spit dribbled down his chin.

Each acquisition of a new word — *no, granma, baby, hot, cold, here, good, bad, cat, granpa, rain, sun, night, hungry* — involved frantic effort, squirming and coughing and sputtering. It was exhausting for Opal merely to watch — if only she could help him! His eyes were large and dark, all iris at such times. It was as if he were giving birth to himself, frantic, unable to stop. "Yes? What is it? What are you trying to say?" she asked in a keen, piercing voice. "Poor dear baby, poor sweet mouse. . . . You know what you want to say, don't you? Eh? But where are the words, where are the words!"

Sometimes when she stared at him she slipped into a warm, consoling trance.

Did not the baby Nathanael assure her by his presence, his mere existence, that all was well? — that all would come about according to Your design, and was therefore not to be dreaded? The birth of Ashton, her own son, had delighted her but had not, for some reason, amazed her; perhaps she had been too young to grasp the wonder of the birth of a child. And Elsa, poor Elsa, had been born after William's death, and after a miscarriage and years of futile effort . . . so that Opal had come to consider herself a luckless woman, probably sterile. But Nathanael was altogether different. He blossomed day by day as she watched, he was not her child in the flesh but hers nevertheless, *hers*, a miracle of beauty and vitality that spoke to her of something beyond herself that she could not have defined. If she tried to explain her certainty to Thaddeus, she faltered and stammered and was conscious of his judging her — the man was always judging everyone! But the infant did not judge, though he possessed great knowledge, an inexplicable wisdom. All that had happened was meant to happen, from the beginning of time. She should not fear: should never fear. How could she, Opal Vickery, set herself against God's infinite wisdom? — wasn't that a sin? It came to her as she gazed upon the baby Nathanael that a single moment's doubt, the mere flicker of an eyelash, was a terrible affront against the Lord and might very well cast the sinner into hell forever.

Reverend Sisley had said from the pulpit that the world was plunged into an era of great turmoil and that many, many must die. It was God's will. Had not God promised that Satan would be loosed from his prison and all the nations of the world drawn into battle — ? A sinful mankind must expect punishment both in this life and in the next.

And yet all would be well. One must have faith.

She must have faith.

The baby Nathanael allowed her to know such things, though she could not have explained how. She hugged him against her breasts, weeping. Her joy was so intense she could hardly bear it. "Oh my dear one, my precious one! How close you came not to have been born! And now the very world is transformed by you — Nothing is the same —"

His small compact weight felt *right* to her. Her body seemed to remember it from a distant past. He belonged nowhere but in her arms, here, at this very moment: for this too was eternity.

Between her and the baby there coursed a sense of recognition, a hot, heady connection of love. His eyes appeared to change hue, like precious stones, deeper, darker, depthless, mesmerizing. He tried to talk, babbling and chattering happily. A fatherless and motherless child: hers: God's. What miracle of Biblical times could compare with this? What work of God's was greater?

"Listen to you! Just listen! You've got so much to tell us, don't you?" she cried.

She carried him outside and held him up, fairly shivering with emotion. The love he stirred in her was enormous — almost frightening — a rich, raw, throbbing hunger like nothing she had ever felt before. Sexual hunger had radiated from her loins and had transformed her in the past; but this sensation radiated from her heart and her lungs and her throat, and seemed to make its way through her entire body, wishing to flow into the outside world, wishing to *love* all of God's creation. She swayed as if in a strong wind, holding the baby aloft.

It was a clear, weatherless morning. There were strands of cloud, the soft querying sounds of mourning doves, an odor of damp from the earth. The baby kicked and struggled and tried to speak, but the sounds he made were indecipherable.

". . . so much to tell us, eh? Don't you? Nathanael William Vickery!"

"What is that you have, Nathan?"

The child held it out to Thaddeus — a feather of some kind, about four inches long.

"Ah, isn't that beautiful!" Thaddeus said. He squinted through his bifocals, drawing the feather across his palm. It *was* beautiful: a jay's feather, blue with black stripes, a white tip, a grayish-white quill. "It isn't for me, is it? Is it for me?"

"Yes," the child said, nodding solemnly.

"That's very kind of you," Thaddeus said, smiling. He wished he could make his grandson smile in return; the child stared at him with his large, troubled eyes as if they had never seen each other before. "A gift, is it? Well — I can use it for a bookmark. It will make a very practical bookmark, won't it?"

The child nodded.

"Where did you find it? — out in the yard?"

The child said something in his soft, quick voice that Thaddeus could not quite understand.

"Speak up, boy. I *don't* think I'm hard of hearing yet. You found it — ?"

"Jesus," said the child shyly. ". . . Jesus gave it to me."

Thaddeus stared at him, still smiling. A joke? A game? *"Jesus* gave it to you? This feather . . . ? What do you mean by that?"

The child's eyes were dark, flecked with hazel and green. There was something prematurely grave about his face — as if the skin were stretched too tight across the slender bones. He was three years old now and had been talking for almost two years, always in the same light, rapid, breathless way, rarely smiling in Thaddeus's presence though he seemed comfortable enough with Opal. Now his lips moved again but his words were nearly inaudible. Thaddeus had to fight the impulse to grab him and give him a good shake. A feather! Jesus! *Jesus!* Was that what his grandmother was filling his head with these days?

"Jesus gave you this feather, did He? Handed it to you?"

The child began to nod, then hesitated. His lips twitched. He was about to smile, perhaps; or cry; he sometimes smiled when Thaddeus scolded him gently, and sometimes cried.

"Out in the back yard, I suppose?" Thaddeus said lightly.

The child nodded. A smile evanescent as a firefly played about his lips. His complexion was smooth and waxy and mauve-pale, his manner cautious and restrained. Thin-armed, thin-legged, with dark curls and large, intense eyes, he was so absorbed in the conversation that his entire body appeared to be trembling. Thaddeus could almost feel the tension in the child's slender body. He loved him, and pitied him. And felt a pang of exasperation. "Well then," he said, sighing, "why don't you show it to your Grandma. *She'll* appreciate it."

But Nathanael would not take the feather back. "No," he said, frowning. "It was for you."

"For me? Really?"

"Yes. He meant it for you."

Thaddeus stared at the feather uneasily. What was the point of this, what was the child's meaning? For there must be meaning to the exchange. It was a game of some kind, a bit of harmless trickery. Perhaps Opal had something to do with it; she often read stories to the boy, many of them adaptations of Biblical tales, and she took him to Sunday school, and then to regular Sunday services. Now that Ashton was gone, and Elsa. . . . Now that her own children were gone Opal had turned all her attention to Nathanael.

Thaddeus turned the feather slowly between his fingers, studying it. The astonishing precision of it: of the meanest, most ordinary feather: was this what his grandson saw, was this the reason he believed Christ had given him the feather? Strange. Unnerving. Thaddeus felt acutely uncomfortable in the child's presence. He loved the boy, yes, certainly he loved him, and yet . . . and yet he was always rather relieved when Nathanael ran off to be with his grandmother.

To Opal he said that night: "Do you think you should encourage him? With this Christ business?"

Opal was turned partly from him, brushing her short, frizzy hair.

"I mean — his fantasies about Jesus, his stories," Thaddeus said. It surprised him that his manner was jocular, almost jeering. He would have liked to speak to his wife seriously, yet his voice kept rising almost to a shout; and he saw that his hands were trembling. "After all, Opal! *Jesus this, Jesus that!* I mean — Really — You don't want the child to grow up with a — an imperfect grasp of — Are you listening, Opal?"

She faced him, her gaze dragging after. Cowlike, placid and stubborn, she stood in her flannel nightgown with her arms at her sides. Her jaw had thickened; her color was ruddy. *She has secrets*, Thaddeus thought involuntarily.

"He seems to believe that Christ is always around him," Thaddeus said, trying to keep his tone light. "No doubt they encourage that kind of thing at Sunday school — ? I know what Reverend Sisley is like. I don't *object* to it, Opal, in adults, but in children who can't differentiate between the world of fantasy and the world of reality, don't you think it's — well, dangerous? Don't you think so, Opal?" he said, almost pleading.

"I know you don't believe," Opal said quietly. She hesitated, cleared her throat, began again: a harsh, ugly blush spread across her throat and her right cheek. "I know it's hard for you to believe. But Christ *is* with us. He *is*, Thaddeus. Whether you acknowledge Him or not — whether you see Him or not. He's with us. I know. — It makes you angry to hear me say such things, but I must say them. I —"

"Opal, please —"

She shook her head wordlessly.

They had had similar exchanges in the past. Since Ashton had enlisted in the Army, since Elsa had gone to board with a cousin of Opal's who lived in Derby, the issue of Opal's religious beliefs

— her religiosity, as Thaddeus called it — had arisen from time to time, always at weak, awkward moments like this. Thaddeus's instinct was to turn from her brusquely and crawl into bed and, in a few minutes, feign sleep. It was not simply that the Christ business annoyed him; it alarmed him as well. He was not at his strongest, having been active since six-thirty that morning: rounds at the hospital in Yewville, a visit to a dying woman, office hours here at the house. And part of the evening spent trying to fix the sump pump in the cellar. . . . But he forced a smile, a sympathetic smile, and took his wife gently by the shoulders, and pressed his lips against her warm forehead. What to say? Oh my God, he thought wildly, what to say? — after thirty years of marriage, to realize you don't know whom you've married —

"We're both tired, aren't we," he whispered.

"Yes," Opal said.

"So we won't quarrel. Not tonight."

"Not tonight."

In bed, in the dark, he couldn't resist: "Except he's only a child, Opal. Entrusted to us."

She said nothing. She was certainly not asleep, however.

"He has no one but us," Thaddeus said.

The bed quivered with her massive, exasperated sigh.

"*No one* but us," Thaddeus said angrily.

She did not contradict him. She would allow him these petty, inconsequential victories.

She knew what she knew: *Christ is with us whether you acknowledge Him or not.* So she allowed her husband to say what he would say and to turn from her and sleep his restless sleep. In the very next room the child Nathanael slept in a bed that had once belonged to Elsa — with railings and a decal of a lamb on the headboard — and she knew he was with God even as he slept a child's deep, intense, dreamless sleep, and that nothing his grandfather said or did could interfere.

Elsa came back to visit once or twice a month, riding with one of the McCords who lived in Derby; she and Mrs. Vickery were rather uncomfortable with each other. "Well, you haven't said a word about my hair," Elsa cried nervously, fluffing her springy artificial-looking waves, and Mrs. Vickery tried to smile, saying, "You always *did* look sweet: you know that," and then they fell silent. They were grateful for the boy's presence, or for Dr. Vickery (who would take the afternoon off, if no patients were scheduled), or even for Mrs. Stickney or the Sisleys or old Mrs. Arkin, who sometimes dropped by when Elsa was back for the weekend. Not that they knew her, or would have recognized her — she was twenty pounds lighter at least — far too skinny, in Mrs. Vickery's opinion — and the lipstick and makeup and high heels and bouncy hair and self-conscious, nervous giggling were a shame; but try to tell a young girl anything, try to make her listen for five minutes instead of rattling on about her job (she was clerking at Woolworth's and was next in line for a waitressing job at a bar and grill, where, she said, she'd make almost twice as much as she was making now) and how she had fixed her room up ("Why don't you and Pa come to visit, just once?" she begged, squeezing her hands together between her bare knees in a way she must have learned from another girl, or from a Hollywood movie) and how she had so many wonderful friends there in the city, Holly McCord who was going with a sailor, someone else who was engaged to a boy who worked in Port Oriskany during the week at the big steel mill, and someone else — a cousin of someone's — Mrs. Vickery remembered, maybe, that girl who'd spent the summer with Rosemary Preston a few years ago — ? Well, *her*. And she was married, and her husband was in Belgium around where Ashton was supposed to be; wasn't that a coincidence? And —

So it was chatter, chatter. Her hands flying about, her fingernails painted bright red.

In Nathanael's presence she was more fluttery than ever, though she rarely addressed the child himself. (Mrs. Vickery noted how the boy stared at his mother, his small lips pursed together: judging her, was he? Wanting no part of her.) She inquired after Marsena people, and certain patients of Dr. Vickery's ("Oh, is poor Mr. Donner still *alive?*" she once asked, wide-eyed), and Vickerys and Sayers generally, and of course Ashton (who so rarely wrote, and when he did, had nothing to say: complaints about the food, mainly, and his wet feet, and an ingrown toenail, and of Negro soldiers he'd encountered in England whose behavior was such, he said, that it had to be seen to be believed — wait till those niggers got shipped back home!), and how the house was holding up, and the outbuildings, and Dr. Vickery's old Ford, and not until she'd run through a list of silly items did she think to inquire about her own son: who was not her son any longer.

"Well — isn't he looking *fine!*" she would exclaim.

"He should," Mrs. Vickery said. "He eats everything set before him, and doesn't fuss, and is his grandma's good, good boy. Aren't you?"

The child nodded shyly.

"He's my *good* boy," Mrs. Vickery said.

But Elsa was not her good girl, not any longer; no daughter of hers, really; it was a relief when she left on Sunday evening and the house was quiet again. Hairpins in the bathroom, a smell of cosmetics and cheap cologne, Nathanael somewhat edgier and jumpier than usual — that was all. "She isn't Elsa any longer," Mrs. Vickery told Thaddeus rather bitterly. "I don't even know her."

"That's nonsense," Thaddeus said.

But she knew what she knew. Though she didn't say anything to the boy, didn't bring up the subject of his mother at all. Why, when it wasn't necessary? When the boy rarely brought up the subject himself?

Rarely asked about Elsa, and never — wasn't it odd, wasn't it a relief — never about his father.

"That's a blessing at least," everyone told Mrs. Vickery.

vi

Of the many signs and wonders attending Nathanael Vickery's life, there were seven revelations of extraordinary magnitude: seven times when God seized him in the flesh: seven small crucifixions, from which he recovered with increasing difficulty. The last and most terrifying was made to him at the age of thirty-four, when he addressed a multitude of over one hundred thousand people in the fairgrounds at Patagonia Springs; the first, and gentlest, was made to him at the age of five.

■ ■ ■

At that time there lived in the foothills of the Chautauqua Mountains, some eighteen miles north of Marsena, a young Pentecostal preacher named Micah — Brother Micah Tannebaum. He had married at the age of seventeen, and his wife, who was a year younger than he, died giving birth to a stillborn infant; not long afterward Micah was called to God and commanded to spread the Gospel according to God's instructions. Which he did, declaring himself self-ordained: Brother Micah Tannebaum of the Mt. Lambeth Tabernacle of Jesus Christ Risen.

Working alone one summer he refashioned an old one-room schoolhouse, converting it into a church with a pine pulpit and rows of chairs in place of pews. He painted most of the outside of the wood-frame building, and fixed the crumbling chimney, and mowed the overgrown weeds; he even laid linoleum tile on three-quarters of the floor. A tall, broad-shouldered, slow-speaking young man whom everyone pitied at first, and then came to admire, he drove tirelessly about the countryside, even up into the mountains, recruiting Christians for the Mt. Lambeth Tabernacle. He never argued, never raised his voice. It was simply that the Holy Spirit had descended upon him one midday and bade him repent of his personal sins and accept Jesus Christ as his Saviour and then to spread the Gospel to all quarters of the earth — to those who would listen, and to those who would not. His manner was simple and direct. In front of a group he often became rather emotional — "breathed upon" by the Holy Spirit, he called it — but in ordinary discourse he was unemphatic, good-humored, rather charming. He rejected absolutely the fire-and-brimstone preachers who tried to terrify good honest Christians, just as he rejected the "big city" preachers who had drifted too far from the Bible and pulled things out of newspapers and the radio to talk about — even Methodists and Baptists, some of them, who were becoming corrupted by the times. Christ's teachings, he said, were clear enough. God's will was clear enough. For the most part men were confused and ignorant rather than evil — the men he'd encountered in his lifetime, anyway; they only needed awakening and instruction, and their salvation would be guaranteed. If the Devil was loosed from the bowels of the earth, going about his destructive work, causing crop failures, armies of cornborers, ice storms in early September, tornadoes, deformed births, the war in Europe and in the Pacific, all this rationing and scarcity and inflated prices — if the Devil was moving freely among mankind, why, the thing to do was meet him head-on: acknowledge his presence but show no fear. Resist temptation, but more than that — actively confront the Devil and drive him away.

Within a few years Brother Micah's congregation consisted of between fifty and sixty full-time members. And of course there were often visitors at his church, since it was known that he performed miracles.

One Friday evening in midsummer, not many days after the fifth birthday of her grandson, Opal Vickery took the boy with her to a prayer meeting at Mt. Lambeth. She bathed the child and dressed him with care in the navy blue suit she had made for him, a replica of his grandfather's only decent suit, though without the vest; she bathed herself and powdered her large, clumsy, vulnerable body and put on several dresses before she decided upon the right one — a flowered cotton print, predominately white, with long sleeves and a full, swirling skirt. Despite the heat she pulled on cotton stockings, tugging and stretching until the seams were straight. Her skin grew ruddier, her breath scant.

"If you come across any of those three-inch screws," Dr. Vickery said as they were leaving, "you remember to get me some, will you? Because I —"

"Yes, of course. Yes," Opal said, fairly dragging Nathanael out the door. The Bells' car was parked in their driveway; they must hurry; it was already past six o'clock. And she did not want the child to blurt out innocently that they wouldn't be going shopping in town at all — they were going to a prayer meeting up in the hills. (Dr. Vickery must not know: he would have been scornful, and possibly rather angry. He had been disapproving of the Baptists for some years now, having stopped attending church entirely; but his attitude toward the Pentecostals was brutally comtemptuous. Nor did Opal want people in Marsena to know where the Bells were taking her, for what if word got back to Reverend Sisley?)

So it was with a sense of daring, of illicit adventure, that she settled into the back seat of the Bells' car, trembling with her own boldness.

The dense layered sky above the mountains cracked and appeared to shift with sudden flashes of heat lightning: soundless and lovely.

"Look!" the child whispered, pointing.

"That's summer lightning," Opal said. "That's no danger."

"Is that where we're going? Up there?" he asked.

She peered at him with a mother's keen, critical eye, and saw that he wasn't afraid; not at all. His skin glowed and his fine dark eyes were brighter than usual, as if he felt, as she did, the excitement, the daring, the possible recklessness. . . . And Mrs. Bell, half-turned to them, was recounting in her flat, nasal, bland voice certain events that had occurred in Brother Micah's ministry thus far that *she* did not necessarily believe, nor did she disbelieve. Her husband Carlson, behind the wheel, kept nodding emphatically. He interrupted her at one point to say: "It's in the Book. Ain't it? For anybody to read that's got a brain. Our Lord Jesus Christ appears to His disciples, after His death, and He says . . . He promises. . . . Something about devils, casting out, and laying hands on the sick . . . laying hands on the sick: healing: ain't that so? I don't have the words set down but they go like that. Ain't it so?"

"Nathanael knows the passage, don't you?" Opal said.

The child, who had memorized many verses of the Gospels, lowered his gaze and did not reply. Opal touched his stiff little shoulder. She saw that his hands were clenched together — was he shy of the Bells? — most likely, though they were next-door neighbors — but *why* must he be shy? It was within the boy's power, Opal believed, to conquer his own childish fears. She loved his gentleness, his gracefulness, his sweet, preoccupied moods — so wonderfully different from the little hellion her own son had been, and from the rowdy unthinking *ordinary* children of her neighbors and relatives; at the same time she was passionately proud of him when he managed to recite, as he did upon occasion, passages from the Bible. (He had memorized Chapters 1, 6, 8, 12, most of 14, and most of 18 and 19, of the Gospel of St. John, and had brought pride to the Marsena Baptists by winning for their Sunday school first place in a county-wide competition only a few weeks earlier; and he knew many other passages besides, particularly those that had struck Opal as the most moving and the most significant.)

"Don't you know it, honey?" she whispered.

Carlson Bell was driving along the narrow, unpaved road with a caution Opal thought exaggerated. She was impatient to get to Mt. Lambeth, a small settlement on the north fork of the Eden River that she hadn't seen more than a half-dozen times in the past thirty years, since it was out of the way and there was no reason, ordinarily, for her to go there. Dr. Vickery journeyed up there occasionally, on medical business — routine physical examinations and ear-nose-throat and dental check-ups at the single public school — and nearly all he ever had to say about that part of the country was that the war had hit it even harder than Marsena: a pitiful number of young men killed or wounded or lost, and a considerable number moved away, probably permanently, to work at those high-paying jobs in the defense plants in Port Oriskany and other cities on the lake. "The countryside is emptying out," he grieved often, blaming the Government that was shifting everything about from under their feet and had no heart for the poor farmers who could barely make a living unless they owned enormous farms and could afford to install fancy machinery; blaming the federal and state and local politicians; blaming history itself. Opal only half attended to her husband's gloomy prophecies now, having lost interest — or was it faith — in his reading of the universe; how had she ever, as a young girl, believed in him so uncritically, so proudly? (And during the long war years she had refused to talk with him about the "progress" of the war, had refused to listen to the radio broadcasts he was so addicted to, and had turned her gaze aside from the newspapers and magazines that dwelled so gluttonously upon destruction, as if God had not provided for His own children all along: as if these half-dozen years of evil were very important in the light of eternity. She cared for her son Ashton, of course. She prayed for him daily, sometimes hourly. And yet even he came to seem curiously unreal. . . . It was as though by running off and enlisting before the Government called him, without a word to his parents and certainly without a care for *their* feelings, he had somehow abdicated his blood connection with them.)

Yes, they were a disappointment — her husband, her son, and her daughter.

But as Mr. Bell drove slowly along a road that was hardly more than a bumpy cow lane, raising enormous clouds of dust behind them, she heard herself echoing Thaddeus: "This part of the country is emptying out, isn't it? Such a pity. . . ."

Rocky hills, small scrappy farms, houses little more than shanties with tar-paper roofs and bales of hay dragged up against their foundations for warmth; barbed-wire fences badly in need of repair, scrawny gray sheep, the texture of poverty, of futility; a pity. Strange, that it should be surrounded by such physical beauty — such blatant, indifferent physical beauty. Most of the Chautauqua Mountains were pine-covered, but the two highest peaks, Mt. Ayr and Mt. Lambeth, rose delicately snow-capped, distant and glorious in the slanting rays of the late-afternoon sun. "Praise God for *that*," Opal thought.

Mrs. Bell was speaking of a rumored case of healing Brother Micah had evidently performed. He had laid his hands on someone's head — and terrible migraine pains had disappeared.

"And a ringing in the ears as well," Carlson Bell said.

"Well," Opal said slowly.

"And more than that, Opal. Much more," Mrs. Bell said fervently.

Opal stared at her neighbor's creased, smiling face, and at Carlson Bell's thin profile. She knew Carlson had not been well this past year. He had aged, hadn't he? — looked eighty years old, though he couldn't be much more than sixty-five — tried to keep up his robust, slightly cranky manner, but there was no disguising the sallowness of his skin and the fact that he had lost a considerable amount of weight. Leah Ackerson said she'd heard it was a tumor under his arm, draining away all his strength, but Violet Preston said it was "blood trouble," and naturally Opal could not question Amanda Bell about it; though the women had lived next door to each other for decades, there were certain matters they never discussed. (Anything to do with money, or trouble with family members or relatives: anything that was a blow to pride.) Nor could Opal question her own husband about Carlson because he never spoke of his patients' troubles. He *never* violated their privacy, as he chose to put it. It was like pulling teeth to get out of him the mere fact that someone-or-other had come by the office, though Opal could see the car plainly enough in the driveway. . . .

"More than that?" she said faintly.

They were almost at Mt. Lambeth now. Carlson slowed to five

miles an hour, driving over a one-lane bridge with a rattling wooden floor and no railings. Below was the narrow, lazily meandering north fork of the river, rather shallow at this point and, in the near distance, glittering like a snake's scales.

Beside Opal the boy squirmed and she realized she had been squeezing his tiny moist hand unconsciously. They glanced at each other — Nathan timorous, Opal apologetic — but the boy must have misinterpreted her look because he said in a guilty undertone that he remembered the verses now — he *did* remember them.

"Jesus rose on the first day of the week," he said softly, eagerly, "and after that he appeared in another form, and . . . and *Afterward he appeared unto the eleven as they sat at meat, and upbraided them with their unbelief and hardness of heart, because they believed not them which had seen him after he was risen. And he said unto them, Go ye into all the world, and preach the gospel to every creature. He that believeth and is baptized shall be saved; but he that believeth not shall be damned. And these signs shall follow them that believe; In my name shall they cast out devils; they shall speak with new tongues; They shall take up serpents; and if they drink any deadly thing, it shall not hurt them; they shall lay hands on the sick, and they shall recover. . . .*"

Mr. Bell said, "Amen!" to this, at the very moment that Mrs. Bell, expelling her breath as if something had both frightened her and caused her to laugh aloud incredulously, said, "*Serpents* — !"

"How old is the little one?" an elderly woman asked Opal, peering at Nathan. Her face was a mass of wrinkles, her eyes were like tiny bits of glass, most of her teeth were missing, yet she was smiling happily. Pulled down tight over her forehead was an olive-green knitted cap; she wore men's shoes with the toes cut out.

"He's five. Just five the other day."

"Five!"

The woman gaped at Nathan, smiling even more widely.

Other women drew close, frankly studying Opal's dress and her shoes and the black patent handbag she was carrying.

"This is your first visit with us, isn't it? Oh, you'll learn from Brother Micah! You'll *learn!*"

Evidently Brother Micah had not yet arrived. The congregation was waiting for him outside, talking boisterously, shaking hands with one another and even embracing — Opal had never seen people so openly demonstrative, and even *men* — men embracing one another: what a sight! Cars and pickup trucks were parked in the cinder driveway and along the road, practically in the ditch. There must have been forty or fifty people, all of them cheerful, rather overloud, as if they'd been drinking — but they had not been drinking, since drinking was forbidden. It was odd that all the men should be gathered in one group and the women and children in another. Carlson Bell had gone at once to join the men, without a word of explanation, and Amanda had led Opal and Nathan unhesitatingly to the women. Opal noticed there were a number of very young children, even toddlers, even infants in their mothers' arms.

So much smiling! So much good-natured chatter! All these people knew one another well. And seemed extraordinarily fond of one another. It was possible, Opal thought, that they were all related — these were mountain people, after all, and who had they to marry except one another? For some reason their exuberance made her uneasy. She held Nathan's hand tight, hoping he wasn't frightened; hoping she had not made a mistake, bringing him here. These were such impoverished, gaunt-faced, drab people. . . . Their accents all but hurt her ears, and the clothes they wore . . . ! A pity. A shame. But the boy wouldn't know, wouldn't judge. Nor would he tell his grandfather. Opal hadn't even the need, she knew, to caution the child against telling Thaddeus; he sensed what she wished him to do or say, and what not to do or say; there was never any disharmony between them.

Exactly at seven o'clock Brother Micah drove up in a car with a rusted fender and a rear window mended with cardboard, and everyone surged forward, calling out greetings. These were the *friendliest* people, Opal thought, almost with disdain. Even the children darted forward crying hello and their mothers made no effort to restrain them.

Brother Micah was a tall, strapping young man with a sun-burned face and strangely long blond hair and fine green eyes, set rather close together. Opal stared at him. She had hardly an eye for the woman and the two men and the boy of about fourteen who climbed out of his car, Brother Micah so drew her attention. He *was* tall — at least six feet three or four. And those green eyes! And that surprising hair, which reached to his shoulders! Opal felt herself smiling, grinning, with a kind of confused alarm. Brother Micah Tannebaum. A self-ordained preacher. A healer. A worker of miracles. Here in this impoverished Mt. Lambeth, in this old whitewashed church with the clumsy steeple and the homemade sign Brother Micah had probably done himself — *Mt. Lambeth Tabernacle of Jesus Christ Risen* — proud black letters shakily outlined in gold.

"Bless you, brother! Bless you, sister!"

So the greetings went. Everyone was joyful, eager, perhaps a little tense. Brother Micah's eyes glittered and he did not hesitate to embrace everyone who came near, and to shake hands with those who held themselves off shyly, like Opal and Nathan. "Bless you, son!" he cried. "I know you've traveled a long distance to come here tonight!"

There was a family resemblance among Brother Micah and the people who had ridden with him. The woman's hair was straw-colored; the elder of the men — who carried a wooden box, lidded — had Brother Micah's strong, square jaw; the other, carrying a guitar and a harmonica, could have been a younger, slighter twin of his; and the fourteen-year-old, clutching a ukulele, had Brother Micah's close-set green eyes and his broad, sloping shoulders. They all appeared to be radiantly happy. Who are these people, Opal Vickery thought suddenly, and why am I here? She blamed her husband, she blamed Ashton; and, most of all, Elsa.

Brother Micah opened the church door, which was unlocked, and his congregation began to crowd in after him.

"Is something wrong, Nathan?" Opal asked, seeing that the boy looked frightened.

He murmured something she could not hear.

"Yes? What is it?" she said, stooping.

"I'm afraid," the child whimpered.

"Nathan, afraid? Why are you afraid?"

He shivered.

She bent over him, brushing his warm forehead with her lips. "Silly little mouse, what's there to be afraid of? Your grandma's with you, isn't she? What's there to be afraid of?"

Yet her own voice was rather shaky.

"God —" the boy whispered.

"Yes? What?"

"God is in there —"

"What?"

"God is in there: I'm afraid," he said with a twitch of his head.

Opal stared at him, shocked. "Well — Yes — I mean — I mean, shouldn't He be? I mean — It's a church, there will be a prayer meeting —"

"God is in there," Nathan said, staring past her at the doorway. His lips had gone white.

"Yes," Opal said nervously, helplessly, "but — But — God loves you, doesn't He — loves all of us — I mean —"

The boy was staring at the doorway, unhearing.

"Nathan, aren't you silly!" Opal cried, and pulled him along.

For what else could she do, having come so far?

The service was informal, noisy, even a little rowdy. Brother Micah spoke briefly, in a loud and euphoric voice, and led the first of the songs — "What a Friend I Have In Jesus" — while the guitarist played his instrument and the fourteen-year-old strummed feverishly at his, and then Brother Micah addressed them all again, in a slightly more subdued voice, and read from the Bible, and Opal tried to make herself relax — these were good country people, after all, good Christians like herself, why should she be so nervous, so apprehensive? Yet it seemed that everyone was apprehensive. At least keyed-up. Tense. Their singing voices were loud and brash, almost defiant. Nasal, flat, twanging — almost an underlying note of hysteria. Or was she imagining it? She sang with the others, softly, and was pleased to see that Nathan tried to sing as well, or was at least mouthing the words.

She was both amused and relieved when they sang a song Nathan's Sunday-school class had learned:

> The wise man built his house upon the rock
> the wise man built his house upon the rock
> the wise man built his house upon the rock
> and the house on the rock stood firm —
>
> The foolish man built his house upon the sand
> the foolish man built his house upon the sand
> the foolish man built his house upon the sand
> and the house came tumbling down!

Perhaps it was the heat lightning that illuminated the darkening sky from time to time, as if punctuating the congregation's fervor, or perhaps it was the crowdedness in the church — the odor of bodies, the damp heat. But the atmosphere grew more and more charged; the voices shriller. Opal's gaze was drawn from Brother Micah's glowing face to the wooden box that had been placed on a chair at the front of the room. She had the idea that everyone was looking at it; staring at it. The singing grew louder, people on all sides were clapping, a few were so moved by the percussive rhythms that they could not remain in one place but had to dance about in short hopping exhilarated steps, bringing the palms of their hands squarely and flatly together.

Brother Micah called out to them in a thunderous voice, both hands raised. His face appeared to be luminous, as if lit from within. "Brothers and Sisters in Christ! Brothers and Sisters and Children beloved of Christ! How happy Jesus Christ is tonight, seeing you all here! Hearing you! Not a one of you that's a stranger to Him! Not a one! Not the oldest or the very, very youngest! Or the babe in the womb! Not a one of us that's not His brother, or His sister, or His own beloved child! How very, very happy —" Opal shrank from his loud, brash voice, not knowing what to think, how to respond. He was so *noisy*. And all around her men and women were calling out, half-singing, still clapping their hands, radiant and perspiring with joy. Someone was playing the harmonica softly. Brother Micah held his Bible high above his head and, eyes shut tight, began to recite in a heavily rhythmic, chanting voice. A number of people joined him, crying out snatches of words Opal half-recognized, words she *did* recognize, but voices overlapped, crossed, warred with one another. The harmonica's notes were eerie and shrill like the voices, sliding from one pitch to another, never quite predictable, and then the guitar joined in, and the ukulele, and more clapping, and even foot-stamping; and above the din Brother Micah's strong, triumphant voice raged: *The Spirit of the Lord is upon me. . . . The Spirit of the Lord is upon me. . . . The Spirit of the Lord is upon me, because he hath anointed me to preach the gospel . . . he hath sent me to heal the brokenhearted, to preach deliverance to the captives, and recovering of sight to the blind, to set at liberty them that are bruised. . . . This day is the scripture fulfilled in your ears. This day is the scripture fulfilled in your ears! O my Brothers and Sisters in Christ, O my dear ones, my beloved ones, my children —*

He snapped his long hair out of his eyes in a whiplike motion.

A short, stocky red-faced man at Opal's left began suddenly to scream. "Christ is in this place! Christ is in this place!" and others joined in, their voices rising, wailing. Opal's eyes jerked in their sockets. She could not control the panic that rose in her, swiftly up from the pit of her belly, into her constricted throat, into her dry mouth. Her heart beat violently. About her men and women were shouting, shrieking, weeping. Opal had attended revival meetings in the past, she had even helped Reverend Sisley arrange for visiting preachers to come to the Marsena Baptist

Church, where they sometimes pitched their canvas tents in a nearby field, and she had been moved, many times, she had been genuinely moved to come forward for Christ, and to weep painful, astonishing tears, yet something was different tonight: something was different: she could not comprehend what it was.

"Christ is in this place!"

A young mother standing just in front of Opal took up the cry, her head thrown back, her mouth stretched open; her entire body began to tremble, the head and torso most violently, almost convulsively. Someone took her baby out of her arms — she surrendered him without opening her eyes, without missing a beat of her harsh, agonized, ecstatic cry. *Christ is in this place! Christ is in this place!* Others began shaking spasmodically. The singing was no longer singing but a wordless, pounding, thunderous chant. An elderly woman cried out in tongues: a high, staccato, rapid gibberish: this too Opal had witnessed before, but she had never been so close to it, she had never really *heard* it until now. Her heart lunged, her throat closed up tight. So much noise! Such an intensity of bodies, faces, voices! And their clapping! Their stamping! The floorboards trembled, the very walls and ceiling of the building trembled — what if something happened, Opal thought wildly, what if the church was shaken from its foundations and the roof suddenly buckled? What if everyone pitched forward at once, drawn to Brother Micah by his trumpet-like voice, his radiant face? She and Nathan would be trampled, would be lost — She and her child —

It was madness, Opal thought, for her to have come here: to have risked so much.

It was madness for her to remain, gripping the boy's hand so hard, so desperately hard: but she dared not release him.

It was madness —

And then the man with the guitar, hollow-cheeked, his face glistening with sweat, threw the guitar aside and went to the box and thumped on it with his fist. And another came forward, another man, his body twitching, his face contorted into a mask of incredulous surprise and delight — and he too pounded on the box with both fists. A collective groan arose; there was one single, gigantic heartbeat that meant to fly out of its shackles, out of its imprisonment; Opal screamed aloud, a choked, stifled cry like a gull's, a cry of sheer terror. What if — ? What if — ? It could not be, it must not be; and yet — What if the heartbeat burst from its imprisonment in the human body, locked in there behind the embracing ribs? What if — ? "Oh Jesus, Jesus," she whispered, "please don't let it happen, please, please don't come to us, not now, not *us*, please, *please!*"

People were pushing forward, crowding blindly forward. But not all: not everyone. (Even in her panic Opal saw that there were others like herself who held back; she saw with sickening gratitude that neither of the Bells was eager to come forward, though Carlson's expression was of remarkable *interest* — as though he were an incidental witness, a passerby gawking into a flaming house; and Amanda was swaying groggily from side to side, her lips slack, her eyes unfocused.) Above the cacophonous din Brother Micah was shouting. Warning: only those to whom the Holy Ghost spoke directly, only those into whom the Holy Ghost had now descended, should come forward.

"The others of us here tonight must obey the Scripture and not tempt Christ! Do you hear — not tempt Christ!"

He held his arms wide, appealing to them all.

The lid of the box was unfastened and the guitarist gave it a heave — tossed it to one side. And then, barehanded, his shirt sleeve rolled up to his elbow, he reached into the box and gave a cry and yanked out a snake. Opal stared, speechless. A snake, was it a snake? — a snake? It appeared to be a copperhead.

On all sides people were moaning, near to weeping with excitement; with a kind of baffled, torturous pleasure.

"Only if the Holy Ghost has descended! Only if the Spirit is upon you!" Brother Micah cried. "Come forward, come forward! My Brothers and Sisters in Christ! In the Holy Spirit! But if God does not call you forward tonight remain where you are — do you hear — remain where you are! Do not tempt Christ! Do not tempt Christ by tempting the Devil, do you hear? It shall come to pass as God has promised," he said, his voice lifting and falling in a queer, forlorn wail, "as God has promised, my Brothers and Sisters, that God will pour out His spirit upon all flesh: and our sons and daughters shall prophesy, and our young men shall see visions, and our old men dream dreams — do you hear, do you hear? It shall come to pass! And God will show wonders in heaven above, and signs in the earth beneath — it shall come to pass! Here! Tonight! Now! Among us now!"

Not knowing what she did, Opal reached out, grasping at someone's arm; she came near to fainting. At the front of the crowded, hot room a man was holding a snake high above his head and its tail twitched convulsively, flicking against his hair. She stared, she saw, yet she could not absorb the sight. A *snake*. *Snakes. Poisonous snakes*. The box contained snakes and she had known it all along, a part of her had known all along: snakes: serpents. *They shall take up serpents*. A part of her had known all along.

Now Brother Micah was clutching a thick, fat snake — was it a water moccasin? — urging it to coil about his neck. Stupefied, rather sluggish, its head turned from side to side and its eyes were dull. Opal wondered, a *water moccasin?* Slumped heavily about Brother Micah's neck? Its dark scales glimmering against the man's white shirt, its entire length dazed? — a *water moccasin?* She stared, she saw, yet she could not quite believe. The scene before her was impossible.

"They wouldn't have water moccasins here, not water moccasins and copperheads, not deadly snakes: no. Not here. No," she whispered. "Not poisonous snakes. . . ."

The interior of the little church shook with cries and shouts and moans and pleas and harsh, hard, childlike challenges. *Let the Devil do his best*, went the cry. *Let the Devil try us!*

The elderly woman in the knitted cap reached into the box and drew out a twisting, whipping, golden-hued snake. She held it firmly in both hands and raised it toward her face, her eyes now shut, her frail little body quivering violently.

Opal stared. Was the woman going to kiss the snake? Kiss the snake? A copperhead, it was: no mistake: a copperhead. Was she going to — Someone reared up in front of Opal and she could not see. A terrible wave of dizziness rose in her, her eyesight blotched, yet she remained on her feet — rooted to that spot as if unable to move. "But they wouldn't have poisonous snakes," she said. "Not *poisonous*. . . ."

Now Brother Micah was crooning, swaying dreamily from side to side. He held the enormous snake in place around his shoulders, one hand grasping its tail, the other its ugly flat head. It was as if he were gripping an old, familiar enemy, an affectionate rival. His expression was beatific.

"Come, Devil," he said, "do your best! Do your best! Strike — and your venom will be overcome by Christ's love! Strike — and you will be overcome! Those who believe shall be saved, and those who believe not shall be damned. The Lord God of Hosts is with us tonight. The Lord God of Hosts has descended into His witnesses and they shall overcome the Devil and his poison and all his works. . . ."

There were cries of "Amen!" And again, "Amen, Amen!"

A song was begun, spontaneously; garbled at first and then with fierce, militant clarity —

> He's got the whole world
>   in his hand
> He's got the whole world
>   in his hand
> He's got the whole world
>   in his hand
> He's got the whole world in his hand!

Brother Micah gave the snake to another man, who accepted it gratefully, though he staggered under its weight. The woman in the knitted cap was crooning to her snake as if it were a baby; and another woman, middle-aged, her plump face streaming with tears, was trying to embrace her, trying to embrace her and the snake both. Mother and daughter, they appeared to be. The young boy who had been playing the ukulele had let it fall and was now caressing a squirming olive-brown snake held by another person, a woman with a flushed, ecstatic face. Opal stared as the boy stroked the snake with both hands, more and more desperately, and, as if not knowing what he did, he began to tug at the creature, trying to get it out of the woman's grip.

> He's got the little children
>   in his hand
> He's got the little children
>   in his hand
> He's got the little children —

Opal gagged; a pool of something black and foul had gathered at the back of her mouth.

Brother Micah stooped to pick up a child, and it looked as if the child was holding a snake — yes, one of the copperheads. The thing gave a crazy lunge and struck against the child's face, its tail flicking agitatedly. The child, gripped tight in the crook of Brother Micah's right arm, had a queer, pinched, waxen face, and his eyes were nearly all whites, as if they had rolled partway back in his head.

Nathanael — ?

When Opal saw that the child was hers she could not even scream, she could not even move — something descended upon her, crude and flatly black as the underside of a shovel, striking against her head.

She fainted dead away.

vii

And so it happened that the Spirit of the Lord descended into the child Nathanael Vickery when he was, to all outward appearances, no more than five years of age; and from that time onward, for nearly three decades, the Holy Spirit did reside within him, flesh of his flesh, close as a splinter beneath a fingernail. Nathanael's eye glared dark with the molten heat of the Lord, plunged deep in time as a bird diving starkly and cleanly into the sea, leaving the surface affrighted but rippleless, undisturbed.

If he did not speak of his early visions it was because, lacking a sense of their strangeness, not knowing they did not appear to everyone else, he was simply ignorant: simply a child.

In a waking trance he saw Jesus, and heard Jesus's gentle words, and even took Jesus's hand when it was offered to him. As everyone did. After all — they sang of Jesus, did they not? They smiled happily, their eyes glistened with joy, they knew all the words of all the stanzas, did they not? *He walks with me and He talks with me, and He tells me I am his own. . . .* Reverend Sisley spoke easily and companionably of Jesus; it seemed to Nathan that the man was only telling them what Jesus had told *him*, and that was why they must listen, must honor his ministry. (Years later, talking with the theology student Japheth Sproul, Nathan had to admit it still seemed preposterous to him — that the altogether goodhearted, zealous Baptist minister had not, in fact, directly spoken to Jesus at all; had never even *seen* Jesus!)

Something moved above the cradle — a hand, a face? — and though Nathan could hear raised voices in the darkness he was not frightened, for the person who stared at him, leaning over his motionless, crafty little body, surely meant him no harm. *Nathan? Nathanael?* The voices rose and fell. Distant, they were — caught up with the wild, buoyant cries of the wind at the top of the house. There was a man said to be his grandfather, and a woman said to be his grandmother. And another woman said to be his mother. He had pressed himself against her body, trying to burrow into her soft, warm, intoxicating flesh, but he had failed: and so he lay alone in the dark — alone, waiting, staring at the stranger who approached him.

No need for fear. No need to cringe beneath the covers, his knees drawn up against his chest. Jesus saw, Jesus knew. *Nathanael?* He whispered.

The voices quarreled as they must, and someone wept; and the noise was mixed in with the sound of the wind, picking at the shingles of the roof.

"*They* cannot touch you, not even to bless you," Jesus said.

Nathan listened eagerly.

". . . certainly not to hurt you," Jesus said.

(Which turned out to be true.)

"The inhabitants of this world cannot touch you, neither to bless nor to hurt," Jesus whispered. "Will you remember? For you are of the same substance as I — you are not like other men."

Nathan stared. He knew he must reply, but he did not know what words to use. And so he said nothing — but as his dry lips twitched, Jesus heard and understood just the same; Nathan's unvoiced words slipped into His heart as a thread is slipped into the eye of a needle — in an instant, with extraordinary grace. And so it came to pass that Jesus knew in His heart what Nathan wished to say, and He drew closer to the bed, saying, "Will you remember? Always remember? The fruitless sorrow of the world of other people, and *my* blessing — ?" and the fingertips that touched Nathan's overheated skin were cool, marvelously cool. He was to remember them, that particular startling pressure, all his life.

"I thank you, Jesus," he whispered.

So he knew himself blessed by Christ from that hour forward.

Yet in a dream he could not resist fighting his way to a mirror, to *see*; to *know*. The mirror would tell him whether the mark of Christ's fingers was on his forehead and whether the secret baptism would be proclaimed to the world.

But there was nothing — no sign.

Merely a child's face. The chin rather weak, the nose long and pale and sensitive, the eyes dark, the lips trembling. A dream-face trapped in a dream-mirror, across which dream-fingers groped frantically. No sign? No sign?

"No? No? But why?" he cried aloud.

For days afterward he tried to tell his grandparents about what had happened during the night. He chattered, he interrupted himself, words flew from him in garbled breathy patches; he flung his hands about. His grandfather pretended to be listening closely. Then he peered at him over the top of his glasses and gave him a rough hug, saying, "What a lively little cuss, eh?" and made him a present of a twist of stale licorice out of the box he kept in his desk drawer, to hand out to children who behaved well when he examined them; and so Nathan knew that his grandfather did not understand. His grandmother appeared to be more interested. She questioned him closely about Jesus — what He was wearing, what His hair was like, what words, exactly, did He use — and gazed with love at Nathan as he spoke, brushing his hair from his forehead. "Jesus *did* come to you, and Jesus *did* bless you," she said, stooping to embrace him, "and do you know why? Because you're made in His image. Because He loves little children best, little children like yourself — because He is always with you."

Words choked and frightened him. Sometimes he stammered — there was so much to be said, and adults did not take time to listen, not to really listen. If he ran into the kitchen to tell Grandmother Vickery that Mrs. Stickney was coming up the front walk, or that one of the heavy quilts she was airing had fallen to the ground, she reacted at once; she believed. If he ran up to her to speak of Jesus she smiled and listened patiently, and when he paused, breathless, overwrought, she dampened a cloth at the sink to press against his forehead and asked if he would like something cool to drink — fruit juice or tomato juice? And wasn't he exciting himself too much? He had a weak chest, he often began coughing helplessly and couldn't stop for several minutes.

There were times when he despaired of explaining anything to them, and so he tried to draw instead — feverish spirals and eyes that stared and stared and stared, as Christ's did: looking directly into your soul. The eyes gave way to suns, the suns to balls of blazing flame. It exhausted him to do these drawings, hunched over strips of shelving paper his grandmother had given him; his heart beat quickly as his hand moved, knowing that he must fail — it was impossible to draw what he had seen. Christ's gentleness, Christ's sorrowful, patient smile; the bruises and scratches

on His forehead; His somber, loving voice as well — impossible
to express all that he had witnessed! So he crouched above the
messy drawings, trembling with frustration.

Then he tried to write, imitating his grandfather's handwriting
and other handwritings he had seen. He filled up pages he dared
not show anyone, fearing they would laugh; certainly the other
children in the neighborhood, and his cousin Davy Sayer, would
ridicule him — already ridiculed him for the stories he told. And
then again he could not resist showing what he had written to his
grandmother, and sometimes to his grandfather as well — for it
seemed to him that they *must* understand, that his meaning was
clear enough. Hadn't the frantic lines and squiggles that ran
across the pages been driven by a passion that went beyond Nathan, that came directly from God? —

But his grandparents saw only

and sometimes humored him by saying that in another year he
would learn to write. But clearly they did not understand.

In the Mt. Lambeth Tabernacle of Jesus Christ Risen it was
Jesus Himself who appeared to Nathan and beckoned him to
come forward.

And so he obeyed. As he was always to obey.

The singing and the chanting and the raucous, discordant
music faded; the floorboards ceased to tremble beneath his feet;
his panic lessened. *Nathanael*, came the whisper. *Nathanael: you
know Me: come forward*.

He had known beforehand that something would happen to
him that evening. He had known. Ascending into the foothills,
clutching his grandmother's damp hand, he had known; and he
had been frightened. The Holy Spirit would pour Himself into
Nathan's flesh and that flesh would be illuminated; and what if it
were burned away, charred hideously? — what if everyone who

gazed upon him screamed in horror? Yet it must be: it must come to pass. He would not dare resist. Thus far nearly every visitation of Christ had taken place in secrecy, sometimes in his bed, sometimes in the carriage house or in the unused chicken coop; or back in the woods, or the irrigation ditch, where he could talk aloud freely and not be overheard by his grandparents or other children. Every visitation had been gentle and dreamlike and assuasive; the person of Christ had not been overwhelming, not very *physical*; His message to Nathan had always been a private one. But Nathan had known as Mr. Bell drove them deeper and deeper into the foothills that the evening's revelation would be like no other he had ever experienced, and that he would never be the same again.

The midsummer heat: the noiseless bodiless flashes of lightning: Grandmother Vickery's and the Bells' increasing nervousness. It was clear that something was going to happen. He felt his heart race and he had to fight the instinct to move about, to shift his weight from foot to foot, to mutter aloud. No, he didn't want to be here tonight; not in the poorly whitewashed little church with the clumsy steeple; not in the presence of Brother Micah, whom God had surely touched. A moment's exchange of glances — Brother Micah's queer green eyes flashing into his — and he had known, had *known*. There would be a revelation, the very landscape would come crashing through the windows, the clotted, layered sky would be pierced; nothing would ever be the same again. *Jesus*, he begged, *don't come for me here: not here: not tonight.*

Brother Micah led them in prayer. Nathan pressed his hands against his face, shutting his eyes tight. Words scuttled about, brushed near him, fell away. He had no need of words. Then the little congregation began to sing, keeping time with the music by clapping hands and stamping feet. The building shuddered and rocked. Nathan's mouth went dry. When he drew his hands away from his eyes he saw that the interior of the church was bathed in light, and for an instant he thought it was lightning, or the setting sun, or a prodigiously bright moon. Brother Micah's face glowed with perspiration, the guitarist's narrow, intense face glowed, the boy with the ukulele played as if the Holy Spirit Himself were guiding his fingers — and still Nathan prayed that the miracle would not happen. Not in front of so many people — so many witnesses.

He heard his name called. The voice was a familiar one. *Nathan. Nathanael.* The light grew stronger, searing his eyes. He would have liked to hide his face but there was no hiding from the Holy Spirit.

The floor shook beneath his feet. He was being drawn forward, like a sleepwalker he was being drawn forward; the interior of the church blazed. Dimly figures danced about him, their faces indistinct. The brilliance of the Holy Spirit was such that ordinary human beings were hardly more than blurs, shadows, phantasms. Suddenly he remembered having seen such creatures before — in a void of sheer, quivering light, a radiance ten times brighter than the sun, where bodiless souls flowed into one another, blending with tiny stings of pleasure, fainting together like water plunging into water. Before he and God were separated: were two. Before the turbulence of birth.

And so he was no longer terrified. It was a coming-home, then; a return. The Holy Spirit drew him deeply into the center of the void, setting his feet hard upon the rock of faith, of God's love. How could he wish to resist, how could he have been frightened? *For you are of the same substance as I,* Christ had whispered. *You are not like other men.*

At the very center of the palpitating light there was not the human figure of Christ but the spirit, the form of Christ: Christ's voice: toward which Nathan hurried. *Nathan, Nathanael. My own child.* No one else mattered. No one else existed. Brother Micah had disappeared, Grandmother Vickery had disappeared, no one was in this place but Nathan, nearly blinded by the intensity of God's light. He was aware of dim, shadowy things, of illusory creatures; mere phantoms of the Devil's imagination. He was aware of the fact that through God's intervention he, Nathanael Vickery, had absolute power over these creatures, and that they could do him no harm.

Suddenly he was being lifted bodily into the air. It was Christ Himself, now in His physical manifestation, who bore him aloft, caught snug in the crook of His muscular arm. The Devil's creature whipped and coiled about them futilely, lashing against Nathan's face. But it had no power! No power! The Devil himself had no power! Christ cried in a ringing, terrible voice, holding Nathan high above the multitude so that all could see: *Verily I say unto you, Except ye be converted, and become as little children, ye shall not enter into the kingdom of heaven. . . .*

It was midnight before he came out of his trance, and even then he could not speak coherently. His small taut body was bathed in perspiration; his hair had become a damp, tangled mass of curls; the pupils of his eyes were dilated. Dr. Vickery examined him, whispering to himself in his panic. "What? What? What has happened to the child?" Mrs. Vickery, frightened into speechlessness, brought wet cloths and a rubber bag filled with ice water to control the fever. "Oh my dear God, what has happened to the child?" Dr. Vickery whimpered. He seized his grandson's pale, peaked face in both hands and stared into the boy's glassy eyes; he could not keep himself from crying openly.

They put him into their big double bed and kept watch at his bedside. All that night Nathanael thrashed about, babbling, spittle edging out of the corners of his mouth, his eyes rolling. Dr. Vickery was concerned lest he swallow his tongue, or gnaw at the inside of his mouth, or dislocate his neck by whipping his head about so violently. "What has happened? What has happened?" The boy had been in perfect health — he had had no more than a cold that past winter, which he'd thrown off within a few days. And he had not been bitten by the copperhead. (The miracle was that no one had been bitten — no one at all. The snake-handling part of the services lasted between twenty and twenty-five minutes, and involved some six poisonous snakes and at least a dozen people; yet no one had been bitten, and the evening ended upon a jubilant, triumphant note.)

But the child Nathanael continued to throw himself about, his legs kicking, his teeth grinding furiously; he clawed at the sheets they tried to draw up to his chin. Dr. Vickery, who knew about the Pentecostal ceremony but not about the snakes — for his wife had not had the courage to tell him — stared at the child's pale, contorted face and could not think what to do. It was as if all his medical training and his years of experience had left him — had never been.

What has happened to our strange, beautiful child, he wondered, is this the start of a neurological disorder? — a kind of epilepsy? Is it some sort of fever? Did he see something no one else saw?

And how should he be treated?

viii

His linen was never quite clean, and his little potbelly strained against his trousers. And his beard, graying more quickly than the hair on his head and being less bushy, less curly, sometimes took on a mangy, feeble appearance: so that, glancing at himself by accident in the unflattering mirror of a patient's bathroom, or seeing his image rearing up defiantly in a glass, he sucked in his breath in alarm and did not know, when expelling it, whether to sigh mightily or to laugh.

"Not quite the handsome old dog I used to be, eh? But no matter, no matter! Having women chase you — what's the use? — only a lot of silly goddam fuss — needless complications — little melodramas — *I* never gave a damn, to tell the truth — was always a one-woman man, for better or worse, in sickness in health etcetera. You don't believe me? It's true, it's true!"

He muttered to himself, to Nathan and Mrs. Vickery and

friends who stopped by, raising his eyebrows to show he was jesting — he *was* jesting. They should not take him seriously. He loved to complain about his own ailments —*"Physician, heal thyself!"* — is that what you're thinking, Nathan?" — and about his patients' naïve faith in him; he loved to complain about those patients who were fanatically loyal, running to him with the most trivial of symptoms, and those patients who were indifferent to their own health — "As if they live in a body not their own, which they operate like a car or a tractor: which isn't *theirs*. Such ignorance! Such *asses!*" There were those who paid their bills at once, in cash; and those (a growing number, unfortunately) who put off paying for months at a time, expecting Dr. Vickery to bill them as if he were running a big-city kind of business; there were those (also a growing number) who did not pay at all. It was logical for them to pay in installments for cars and refrigerators and overpriced clothes, but for health? — for their *own* health? Then there were those who not only wouldn't pay, but couldn't; and it was important that he respect their pride, their desperate vanity, by appearing to believe they refused to pay out of stubbornness or even meanness, rather than that they were unable to pay at all. So he must press them for payments: but not too emphatically. And he must be sharp enough to distinguish between these people; an error on his part might lead to humiliation all around.

"You let everyone take advantage of you," his brother Ewell complained. "Then they imagine they can take advantage of *me*."

But Dr. Vickery was inclined to make excuses for them; he had the idea, after all, that he knew them better than anyone else did, since he tended to their bodies. Perhaps he was mistaken — his vanity often led him into sentimentality — but he defended them nevertheless. "They didn't ask to come into the world," he shrugged, "especially not *this* world. Especially not as themselves."

The recent war had come upon his generation too swiftly: far too much had happened. One day they had been assured there would be no war, there would never again be a war, and the next day there were confronted with enormous scare headlines and a peacetime draft and amazing prices, and finally the speeding-up of events that led to Pearl Harbor and the war in Europe — and everything shifted about, tossed into the air and allowed to fall where it would. Dr. Vickery had read about the Nazi concentration camps, he had studied certain photographs, and he had not quite — he had not quite been able to comprehend. (His wife, and many other Marsena citizens, did not read about such things at all: considered them none of their business.) Too much had happened since the late thirties. He could not hope to absorb it all; so he argued himself into believing he knew as much as he needed to know for his time and place. "I'm just a small-town G.P., after all," he said often. There were younger men pressing forward — let them struggle as he'd struggled. Someday they would replace him; very good. He was willing to be replaced when the time came, but it would not be for many years. He planned to retire at seventy or seventy-five, or eighty. There was no hurry. When the time came he would be replaced by younger men, and he would not resist; but that time was far off.

And of course doctors were badly needed in the country, especially in the more impoverished areas. Most of the young doctors wanted to live in the cities.

In the meantime the furniture in his office and waiting room was becoming shabby; the walls needed to be stripped and repapered; the carpets were worn flat and colorless with age. Even his old hourglass, a gift from his father-in-law many years ago, no longer performed as it was meant to: grains of sand had stuck together in coarse clumps so that the opening between the two glass spheres was blocked. "Time" could not be recorded at all; it had simply come to a stop. And he desperately needed new equipment for his office. He leafed through professional journals and bulletins, studying the advertisements, baffled and dissatisfied. It was the effect of the war, perhaps, the effect of recent history: too much for anyone his age to absorb. The truths he believed in were those of the body, the body's anatomy and its immutable laws; he had pledged himself to these truths at the age of twenty-five, and nothing else — certainly not glossy photographs of office equipment — seemed very significant.

"Why am I here?" he asked himself. "Why here on earth? What purpose does my life have?"

To give aid. To do no harm. To console, to attend, to stand beside.

To help create the conditions for health.

To acquire as much knowledge as is humanly possible.

"There is no *Thaddeus Vickery* otherwise," he said.

He had lost his childhood faith in God one humid afternoon in the early twenties, in the cadaver room at the state medical school, and he had never regretted that loss — in fact he had hardly noted it. A doubtful allegiance to the "soul" had been purged by the stink of disinfectant and in its place Dr. Vickery had pledged a far more substantial, far more noble allegiance — an allegiance to the human body and its human, humbling laws, to the great law of Necessity itself. He believed not in Truth but in truths, in a universe of truths, and he believed these truths were available to human beings; they were not muddled or mysterious or forbidden, nor were they the possessions of gods — of wrathful murderous deities. What was God, in fact, except the not-yet-known, the not-yet-articulated? One acquired truths through the willful effort of one's own human labor, not through the caprice of supernatural beings. And these truths were permanent, or as permanent as mankind required.

All this he had explained to Mrs. Vickery many times. And she had understood him in the beginning. He felt she understood him even now but, for some inexplicable reason, she pretended not to understand — pretended not to be his wife, his Opal, his quick, bright, bold, audacious bride. She *knew* he spoke the truth and that his entire life had been dedicated to this truth, but she pretended to scorn it, and very nearly to scorn him; he would, in fact, have preferred her outright scorn to the sort of malicious, insufferable pity she showed for him — discussing him at great length with Reverend Sisley, praying for his eternal soul, whispering about him to their grandson. Certain sorrowful events of their shared life — the death of their second son, and Elsa's rape and illegitimate pregnancy and her elopement, so-called, with another woman's husband (a sailor who now worked in a factory in Youngstown), and Ashton's estrangement since his discharge from the Army — were laboriously reinterpreted in the light of Thaddeus's refusal to be redeemed, his refusal to accept Jesus Christ as his personal Saviour — the very vocabulary infuriated him! It was ludicrous, it was intolerable, yet it was so — and he lived with it, he even managed to live fairly happily with it. (Because, perhaps, he never quite believed his wife was serious. How *could* she be? Opal Sayer had too much good sense!) What had happened was not allowed to slip into the past but must be reexamined, reinterpreted, submitted to judgment. If Elsa went bad, if Ashton had drifted from them and they didn't know if he was married or not, or even living with a woman or not, surely such misfortune must be their fault? — his fault? Surely it must be in response to certain acts, certain sins? *His* sins?

"I happen not to believe in sin," Dr. Vickery said contemptuously.

"Yes," Mrs. Vickery said. "Which is why you are so unhappy."

"I am not unhappy."

"So wretchedly unhappy."

"*I am not unhappy.*"

So they picked at each other, not quite quarreling. And the boy, hearing them, seemed embarrassed. By the age of eight he had developed a peculiar, almost alarming precocity, not so much of the intellect — though he was intelligent enough — as of intuition: an ability to sense the feelings of others, to register the emotions of others. "The boy can read minds," one of the relatives said, breathless with exaggeration, and over at the Baptist church where he often taught Sunday school and occasionally gave a Bible reading and a brief sermon at the regular services, it was thought he was a "born preacher" and that God had "singled him out" — but Thaddeus knew such statements were absurd. The boy was precocious, unusually sensitive, rather *too* sensitive for his own good. Quiet, subdued, obedient, sweet, soft-voiced — a beautiful child, certainly, with lovely eyes and a pale, serious forehead and a slightly receding chin that emphasized his delicacy: a model child, any grandparent's dream of a child. He was *there* to be marveled over, to be adored, and if he ever thought of his true parents — his mother and his father — he never said a word.

"What would you like, then, for Christmas?" Thaddeus asked.

The boy smoothed down a dog-eared corner of a page of the old medical encyclopedia.

"You must want *something*," Thaddeus said lightly.

A tiny pulse throbbed in the boy's forehead, near his left temple. Thaddeus found himself staring at it, thinking, *The child is alive: look*. (For he sometimes dreamed of his grandson in a childsized coffin, and himself doubled over in grief.)

"A bicycle for next spring? A pony? An air rifle . . . ? But you don't care for your cousin Davy's air rifle, do you? So I don't suppose you would want one of your own."

"No," Nathan said.

"No — ?"

"No thank you."

The boy spoke so softly, Thaddeus sometimes thought he must be going deaf. And when he asked the boy to repeat himself, his own voice sounded brusque and irritated; and it often seemed that he was scolding the child. Which he was *not*. But the boy blushed guiltily and became even more tongue-tied than before.

"Your grandmother tells me you've been making excellent progress with your organ lessons," Thaddeus said, "and one of these days I plan on dropping in . . . sitting in the back of the church, maybe, and just listening. You wouldn't mind? . . . But we couldn't get you an organ, now could we? I mean the real thing. They're not like pianos, are they? — that you can haul around? Pipes and valves and pedals, a colossal instrument, not for a private home. So we couldn't very well buy you *that* for Christmas."

"I don't want any organ," Nathan said. "I mean . . . Thank you, but there's the one at church — that's the only one I need."

"Yes," Thaddeus said patiently.

"I don't know if I'll keep taking lessons. I don't know if it's the right thing. It's not clear . . . I don't know. . . ."

His voice trailed off oddly, as if he were no longer addressing Thaddeus.

"Well," Thaddeus said, sighing, "whatever: whatever. You think about it, will you?"

Nathan stared at a point several inches beyond his grandfather's right shoulder, frowning; obviously thinking quite hard. But he came to no conclusion: his expression did not relax.

Thaddeus was seated at his old, battered, enormous desk on a Sunday afternoon, a snowy Sunday in late November. It pleased him that his grandson had come into his study — had been sitting for the past forty-five minutes in the leather easy chair that faced the desk, leafing through a medical book of the 1920s. The child's eyes were green-brown, ringed with hazel, and his fair, near-translucent skin had never looked more delicate. Though it was said of Nathanael that his voice changed considerably when he read aloud from the Bible or taught Sunday school, Thaddeus had never heard this "voice" and could not quite believe in it. He saw only a child eight years of age, small-bodied, remarkably composed but obviously rather shy.

What was there for them to talk about — grandfather and grandson? For they must talk, they *must* talk. Thaddeus loved the boy desperately and felt at times he would lose him — that something would happen and the boy would sicken and die suddenly and the enchanted period of Thaddeus's grandfatherhood would be terminated — and he himself would die shortly afterward. It was nonsense, of course, for they were both in good health. It was nonsense. Yet he was obsessed with the thought, and wanted the boy with him as much as possible. But what was there for them to talk about? If he started to explain certain functions of the body, if he started to describe certain medical procedures, he soon heard his voice become pompous and impersonal, slipping into the rhythms of a long-dead professor at his medical school whom he had always disliked; even more disturbing was the fact that Thaddeus often got things mixed up, confused Latin words, sputtered and swore at himself and changed the subject. . . . So he offered the child a twist of licorice, or he began to fuss with his pipe, which always took at least five minutes to prepare. Loving was one thing, talking another. Loving was a state of the soul; talking a mere activity. *Loving. Talking.* To express the one, he felt the need to plunge into the other. And why did the boy never seem to help? Perhaps — though Thaddeus did not wish to think so — his wife had poisoned the child against him.

This afternoon he had brought up the subject of the impending holiday season. Which meant, for him, food and drink and presents — not presents for him, especially (though his patients could not be talked out of bringing him things: they were so superstitious), but presents for Nathan, who was after all only a child. But the boy had no interest in Christmas gifts, in the excitement of secret buying; he did not seem to understand it. ("Why, your own mother used to love Christmas! Used to be a silly little *baby* over Christmas!" Thaddeus wanted to shout in exasperation.) It meant for him the day of Christ's birth. But that day was not to be singled out, evidently, from the entire matrix of events that constituted Christ's life . . . and Thaddeus steered away from *that* subject.

"I'm not going to argue theology with an eight-year-old," he thought.

He was a grandfather and he had a grandson, a remarkable child, and what was he to do with the child? As Nathan grew up, he reasoned, he would lose interest in his grandmother's universe and gravitate toward *his*; there was no point in forcing the issue, no point in arguing. The "religious business" was a sham and a pretense and the child was caught up in it, helplessly, but he would have enough sense to snap out of it without Thaddeus's direct intervention, wouldn't he? That was obvious. In the meantime, however, how was Thaddeus to guide him? He made the books and magazines in his study available to the boy, and encouraged him to ask questions, and . . . And even read to him from Marcus Aurelius and Lucretius. . . .

Several years ago he had bought Nathan a small wagon, on impulse one day in Derby, for no special occasion — no birthday, no holiday — and when he'd presented it to the boy Nathan had thanked him sincerely enough, and then had clearly not known what to do with it. At the same time, Nathan had not wanted to hurt his grandfather's feelings. And so he had made an effort to play with the wagon, pulling it back and forth in the driveway, in full view of Thaddeus's study. . . . Watching him, Thaddeus had felt a thrill of something close to dismay. For the child was behaving the way he believed a child should behave, yet somehow it was not convincing; it was forced, obscene. A lie. It was obvious Nathan wanted so much not to hurt his grandfather, how could Thaddeus help but love him? — pity and love him? "Look what you've done to him," Thaddeus had said to Opal bitterly. "You and the Sisleys and the rest of them — ! Bleeding him dry, aren't you, so there's nothing left for *me?*" Opal had seemed, surprisingly, to understand his bitterness. But she said only that it had nothing to do with her or the Sisleys — it was God Himself, Christ Himself, claiming their own child.

"Shit," Thaddeus muttered, not caring if she heard.

But what was *play?* How did you explain to a child what *play* was? Other children in the neighborhood played, sometimes in Nathan's presence, and sometimes Nathan made an attempt to play with them; but it was unconvincing.

"Go outside," Thaddeus often said. "Take Elsa's old sled, go over to the Ackersons' hill — coming home just now, I saw a bunch of kids there. Go and join them, eh? The fresh air will do you good." If he was going to a friend's or a relative's house where there were small children, he offered to take Nathan along: it would be good for him, wouldn't it? Opal would send cookies or brownies or fudge along with him. Opal too seemed to want him to do these things, to be a normal child; at least some of the time. At other times she interrupted Thaddeus rudely, saying the other boys were coarse and ignorant and brutish and Nathan was well rid of them. "You don't understand your own grandson at all," she said.

But he tried. And failed. He tried often, and failed; and tried again, speaking jocularly, hoping to make the boy laugh. (How *did* you make a child laugh, Thaddeus wondered, when your life depends upon it?) His jokes called forth that solemn, contemplative stare, a half-twist of the lips that might have been pitying.

"Even your grandmother will be disappointed," Thaddeus said, "if you say you don't want anything this year. She's a woman, after all — she likes to fuss, she likes surprises. So if —"

The child had spoken. He stopped short, fingering the edge of the encyclopedia.

"Yes? What? I didn't quite hear," Thaddeus said, leaning forward.

". . . many things already," Nathan said softly.

Thaddeus cupped his hand to his ear. "Eh?"

"We have too many things already," Nathan repeated, blushing.

"Too many things already . . . !" Thaddeus laughed. "Us? *Us?* Why, Nathan, we're practically *paupers*; if this upcoming year is anywhere near as bad as last year . . ."

Nathan was shaking his head slowly.

"That isn't true, Grandfather," he said.

"Not true . . . ?"

Blustery, buffoonish, Thaddeus let his pipe fall and exclaimed softly. "God*dam*." Out of the corner of his eye he believed he could see, still, the tiny blue vein in the child's forehead. Which was proof, wasn't it . . .? Proof that the child's heart was beating . . . ?

"Why are you shaking your head, my boy?" he asked, taking care not to shown his annoyance. *He* was the doctor, after all, and in this part of the country he was never challenged. Though he might play the fool when he wished, he was never seriously challenged; and *never* in his study. "You know nothing about my financial affairs, about the mortgage payments I owe on the house, the property taxes. . . . Do you? You know nothing."

Nathan stared at a point in the air somewhere between his grandfather and himself, frowning. It occurred to Thaddeus suddenly that the boy had come to him this afternoon with a deliberate plan in mind; he wasn't a youngster lonely for his grandfather's company. (It was possible that Mrs. Vickery had something to do with it. She had been awfully quiet since coming back from church that noon, had hardly spoken throughout dinner.)

Thaddeus waited, stiffly, uneasily, knowing the boy was going to speak. He could feel the child's anxiety: the very air tensed. How strange it was, how uncanny! To keep his gaze from straying onto Nathan he cleaned the old stale tobacco out of his pipe and tamped down new, grateful for the stark strong fragrance, its pungency, its *reality*.

Speaking softly and not very coherently at first, Nathan began by saying again that they owned too many things. The house, the land, the car, money in the bank. . . . (At this point Thaddeus guffawed: *money in the bank!*) There were people who had nothing, Nathan said; people who hadn't even places to sleep. Yet they were all related, they were all brothers and sisters, all God's children. And. . . .

"All *related* . . . ?" Thaddeus said strangely. He lit his pipe and sucked noisily at it. Nathan took no notice of the interruption but continued, speaking distractedly of the "poor" who are always with us, the meek in spirit, the brokenhearted, the captives. . . .

There was a catch in his voice, a clicking in his throat. He sucked for air, seemed to swallow air, and sat for a moment utterly still.

"Nathan?" Thaddeus said softly. "Are you all right?"

"Jesus told us that if we want to be perfect," Nathan said more firmly, "we should go and sell what we have, and give to the poor; and we will have treasure in heaven. Jesus *said* that. He said it plainly, you can't mistake it, how can anyone mistake it? I've heard Jesus's voice. I've heard Him say those words and I've heard Him say them to me, to *us*. It was Vickerys He had in mind!"

Thaddeus continued sucking at the pipe. His thoughts raced, he felt rather dizzy and dispirited. He wanted to laugh, to wave away the child's hysteria, but at the same time the air felt too heavy to part. "You seem a little peaked," he said uncertainly. "Every Sunday exhausts you, getting over there at nine o'clock and staying as long as you do, and now on top of everything playing that goddam organ. . . ."

"I've heard Jesus's voice," Nathan said. "Over and over again the same words. *If thou wilt be perfect, go and sell that thou hast, and give to the poor, and thou shalt have treasure in heaven: and come and follow me —*"

The boy's voice rose shrilly at the end, almost plaintively. Thaddeus could hardly bear to look at him — there was something about the child that jarred, that hurt; it was as if Thaddeus's very soul were being hurt.

"Nathan," Thaddeus said sharply.

"Grandfather," the boy said at once, blinking.

Thaddeus felt a wave of sheer dislike pass through him. Again he wanted to laugh, but he dared not even smile; it was best to keep his face rigid, neutral.

"If we want to be perfect, Jesus told us what we must do," the boy said more softly. "He never meant for people to have so much that they couldn't even think what presents to give one another for *His* birthday — He never meant that at all. There's nothing He said that —"

"*If we want to be perfect*," Thaddeus said. His voice was higher-pitched than he had wished. He did not want to hear himself mocking the boy, for it was so easy to mock him; yet he seemed to be mocking him nevertheless. "But why should we want to be perfect? You, me, anyone? Eh? Why perfect? Why *perfect*? The way we are's good enough, isn't it?"

"— nothing He said has to do with such things," Nathan went

on calmly. "I asked Him about this house here, and all the things we own, and He said it was more than we needed: far more: and that it would be joyful for us to give away most of what we own, or all of it: that we couldn't really understand Him until we were poor."

Thaddeus stared at the boy and could not believe what he heard.

"*What* are you saying . . . ?"

"Grandma said, when I asked her, that you had bought the house out of vanity. So that people would look up to you, and envy you. And because you wanted to fill the house with children. So the house is big, there are many rooms that aren't used," the boy said, his voice rising slightly again, almost melodic, frail and reedy and yet persistent, maddening. "There is too much in our lives. All these books — these magazines and newspapers — all these things to confuse us. There is too much, we should give most of it away, or all: and then we shall have treasure in heaven."

The child was utterly serious. Piteously serious.

"Your grandmother has been telling you lies," Thaddeus said angrily. "Her and that ignorant old Baptist preacher, that fool Sisley — putting this sick nonsense in your head! How *dare* they try to infect you —"

"It's Christ Who counsels me," Nathan said.

"Christ! Who is Christ!" Thaddeus cried.

"He says you will never know Him, so long as you mock and ridicule. He says —"

Thaddeus laughed loudly, waving the child away. No, it was impossible: it was really impossible. The child was insane. His only grandson was insane. Comely, almost beautiful, with those striking eyes and that sensitive face — so obviously an intelligent boy, spiritually akin to Thaddeus himself — and yet insane. There was no getting round it now. The old woman was insane and she had infected the child. He blamed her. Suddenly he detested her. And Reverend Sisley, and Mrs. Sisley, and the others — the others! They were all insane and he alone knew the truth.

The child was leaning forward now, his thin shoulders raised as if in apprehension of Thaddeus. It was evident that he was greatly moved; Thaddeus had the idea that he was trembling inwardly. The madness of a child! The Christ-madness of a child! It was unthinkable, obscene. Had Thaddeus not been so dispirited, he would have tried to calm him, to change the subject, maybe to lead him out of the study and into another part of the house, or outdoors. . . . But his expression remained harsh and rigid; his lips were fixed in a queer smile he could not alter.

Nathan drew his shoulders up even higher. In a rather cold, reedy voice he said: *"Kiss the Son, lest he be angry, and ye perish . . . when his wrath is kindled but a little."*

This was too much, this was intolerable: this Thaddeus truly could not bear.

He began shouting. "What? What? Kiss the — *what?*" He threw his pipe down and got violently to his feet, knocking his chair backward against the wall. "Look, my boy: let Christ kiss my ass, do you hear? *Kiss my ass!* Christ and the Father and the Holy Ghost or whatever — let the bunch of them kiss my *ass*, do you hear? Eh?"

Nathan blinked at him, uncomprehending.

"I've had more than enough of this crap from you and your grandmother and everybody else," Thaddeus said. Though he was angry, he fairly barked with laughter — his grandson's shocked expression was hilarious. He imagined Opal and the Sisleys and most of the village of Marsena crouched outside the door, listening, astonished and frightened. Very well, then, let them listen! Let the world listen! "They can kiss my ass, you got that? The bunch of them! Your precious simpering Christ, and God the Father, and whatever the Holy Ghost is supposed to be. All I approve of is the Creation, do you hear? And even that wasn't done right — even that was bungled. Only a drunk or a madman would have perpetrated such a —"

It was then that Nathan, his face dead white, made a peculiar clicking sound in his throat and gasped for breath. His body shivered convulsively. His eyes seemed to go dead, to go opaque.

"Nathan?" Thaddeus cried.

The boy appeared to be getting to his feet, lunging forward. But he had no strength; his legs buckled. He fell heavily onto the floor, the side of his head grazing one of the legs of Thaddeus's desk.

And in that manner You manifested Your displeasure to him: in that manner You poured Your spirit into his meager flesh.

ix

Heaven and earth were joined together in a massive embrace, their parts coiled together, convoluted. It was a darkness many times the dark of an ordinary night. Yet Nathan could see: he could not have prevented himself from seeing.

Heaven and earth in an embrace of many arms and legs . . . roots and giant tendrils and enormous vines and the branches of trees and of rivers, boulders like human muscle, rock and salt and ice and precious stones. Immense walls of granite. A terrible cold. On the far side of the walls a movement, a tear in the night's substance—and the Lamb of God appeared, climbing out of the darkness, out of the cavern that tunneled so deeply into the earth, blazing and triumphant. In His company were a host of angels, resplendent in light, quick-darting as birds. As the darkness at Christ's feet increased, becoming a sort of element like water, and then like dirt or mud, the light about His radiant face grew more powerful, so that Nathan could hardly bear to look. *Thou Jesus, son of David! Lamb of God, which taketh away the sins of the world!* But this was not the gentle Christ Who had appeared at Nathan's bedside years ago; this was a Christ blazing with light, holding a sword aloft, His hair and beard darkly gleaming, His eyes glaring. As He rose from the darkness — which sucked noisily at his feet — He drew with him a multitude of souls, the souls of the blessed who would enter heaven with Him on that day. Thousands upon thousands of the saved, rising from the cavern as the old earth passed away — and they too blazed with light, their faces radiant, suffused with joy.

Bodiless, no more than a painfully quivering pair of eyes, a fissure in the darkness, Nathan Vickery stared at Christ and Christ acknowledged him from His pinnacle in the heavens: lowered His immense sword so that, for an instant, its tip was pointed toward him. *I am a child of the wrathful God*, Christ cried in a terrible voice. *I am not to be mocked.*

And so Nathan cried out for forgiveness for his grandfather; and his cries rose to the outermost reaches of heaven and penetrated into the very depths of the earth, where light had become thickened into rock; but Christ did not reply. Aloft, ringed with flame, His face gigantic now as if pulsing with anger, He merely gazed down upon the child Nathan with a stern, contemptuous, jeering look. *Jesus, thou son of David, have mercy*, Nathan prayed.

Have mercy.

■ ■ ■

After Nathan recovered from his vision he attempted to tell his grandfather of the danger to his life, but the old man would not listen: would not tolerate the child's warning voice. "If you repent," Nathan said, panting, "if you beg His forgiveness —" But the old man refused to listen. He stormed out of the room, he slammed doors, he hid from the Word of God, and thereby brought about his doom.

"He will die if he doesn't repent," Nathan told his grandmother, who swallowed as he told her of his vision — of Christ and the angels and the blazing, dazzling flames — Christ and His terrible sword — Christ and the multitude of the saved, who were being lifted out of the darkness and borne aloft into the

Kingdom of God. She swallowed, and blinked, and hugged him
against her, but said nothing. Christ and His sword and His angels and His saved, Christ and His terrible words of warning
directed toward Nathan — and the tip of the sword pointed
earthward, toward *him*, as if he were the focal point, the axis. As
if all that must be fulfilled would be fulfilled through *him*, and
none other.

"He will die if he doesn't repent, if he doesn't beg God to
forgive him," Nathan sobbed, burying himself in his grandmother's embrace.

They prayed for Thaddeus Vickery, that his heart would be
softened and his willfulness melted away; and his soul exposed to
Christ at last; and his doom averted. They prayed that You, in
Your infinite love, would touch him — would raise him to You,
unrepentant though he was. As the days and nights passed they
prayed fervently, hidden away from him. He understood what
they were doing — correctly interpreting his wife's strained, anxious look and his grandson's pale, wasted little face — and this
infuriated him all the more, for he was a man of intense feeling,
quick-tempered and stubborn and fatally proud.

"You're mad," he said to them. "You're sick. Get out of my
sight!"

The child Nathan was all nerves now: weasel-like, jumpy, furtive, not very attractive. His face was pinched, yet curiously illuminated; his eyes were bloodshot still (since his convulsive fit and
the hour-long coma that followed, the whites of his eyes were
threaded with blood), and yet intense, almost glaring. Thaddeus
had seen such children up in the hills, in the mountain set-
tlements: undernourished, feral, often stunted, often brain-
damaged. Not very attractive. In fact quite ugly. Repulsive. Wiry
and quick as animals, with the sly, frightful grace of animals. Yet
cruel: cruel as demons. "I pity you," Thaddeus shouted. "Get out
of my sight!"

He had brought the child back from the dead. In a state of
terror he had felt for the heartbeat, but there was none — he had
felt for a pulse in the wrist, in the neck, but there was none. The

boy had stopped breathing, his eyes were unfocused, a terrible clammy coldness seemed to rise from him, a coldness of death. One moment he had been normal enough, or nearly; he had been upset by Thaddeus's remarks, and a little pale, but not distraught; the next moment he was having a fit of some kind, choking and gasping for air, and he had pitched forward onto the floor, writhing, helpless. His heartbeat? Was there no heartbeat? No breath? His lips had gone bluish-white. His body gave off a close, rank, panicked odor.

"Nathan, Nathan . . . !" Thaddeus cried.

But he had brought the child back from the dead. Crouched over him, awkward and grunting, a droplet of perspiration falling from his own face onto Nathan's like a solitary tear, he had forced the child's breathing into motion again: had forced a ragged, rattling breath into the boy's lungs again: and so the child lived. Thaddeus had the ability to labor over his patients' bodies with a gentle, rather blind, methodical thoroughness that was not affected by his personal nature, not even by his grief or alarm. He was "gifted" as a doctor, so it was said; but he dismissed the very idea as absurd. At crucial times his hands acted of their own accord, springing into life with a quick, sure alacrity, and he had a certain talent for diagnosing — but he would not have wanted to claim such abilities as his *own*. It was enough for him that a patient survived, that his body rose again to health; gratitude made him uneasy.

And so, too, with his grandson, he had the idea that his hands, his instinctive, unhesitating mechanical movements, were responsible for bringing the lungs back to life. Of course the child had not been dead — his breathing had stopped and his heartbeat had stopped, or at least gave the appearance of having done so, but he hadn't really been *dead*: he had simply drifted off a little from the shore of life, of living, and Dr. Vickery with his deft practiced hands had reached out to grab him and haul him back to land. That was all.

Nathan had awakened, babbling incoherently, and then sank back into a kind of stupor, semiconscious, delirious. But alive,

alive. Thaddeus carried him to the horsehair sofa and covered him with a blanket. Was it a form of epilepsy? Might it even be asthma? Or what had once been called hysterics? He would make an appointment to take the child to a clinic in Port Oriskany for a complete series of tests. He knew (though not well) the staff neurologist; he would telephone the man first thing in the morning and describe in detail his grandson's symptoms and. . . .

"We'll make you well and this terrible thing won't happen to you again," he said, stooping to kiss Nathan's cold forehead. "Poor child. Poor baby. Poor love. . . ."

Yet it happened, despite the efforts of Nathan and Mrs. Vickery to arouse Dr. Vickery's awareness and love of You, that a tragic estrangement took place in the household, and as the days passed, darkening always earlier as the winter solstice approached, Thaddeus turned more and more from them, a querulous bitter stubborn man. He was not old — he was by no means old — yet he fell into the habit of muttering to himself, continuing arguments with his wife when he was hidden away from her, late at night, in his study or prowling about the darkened downstairs of the house.

"Repent! Repent!" he whispered, clapping the fist of one hand into the palm of the other. "Repent: so the Devil whispers."

He hid from his wife and his grandson in his work. He had never worked harder. A ten-hour day was not unusual with him but now he kept office hours well past dusk, and rose early to make house calls, and stopped by the home of a new, young doctor who had recently begun a practice on the Yewville Road and who was said — so the gossip went, cruelly and characteristically — to be bitterly jealous of Dr. Vickery, who had every patient in the area in his pocket: and the meeting with the doctor went very well indeed, and Thaddeus was satisfied that they parted friends. (He intended to refer certain of his patients to the younger doctor; not generosity but simple pragmatic wisdom — he had far too many patients already.)

Yes, there was oblivion of a kind in his work, in the exhaustion it brought. What did it matter that his wife and his grandson were mad, and mad with spite against him, what did it matter that they cut themselves off from him and no longer loved him, but only stared at him with their insufferable pitying concerned eyes — ? He had always forgotten his personal problems when he was in the presence of people who needed him; there were times, scattered throughout his decades of work, when he had even forgotten, or put aside, rather severe pain and discomfort (the start of an attack of appendicitis at the age of twenty-nine, the agony of an impacted wisdom tooth in his mid-thirties) simply because he was too busy with his patients. And so, now, during those terrible December days that followed the second of Your revelations to Nathan Vickery, Thaddeus obliterated himself in his work, in the symptoms and illnesses and misfortunes and fantasies and despairs of *other people*.

I'm afraid, they wept, that I have cancer. A lump, a pimple-sized bit of flesh, stubborn and gristle-like, might it be cancer, might it be my death? Plantar's warts — what pain! And no dignity to it. I'm afraid, they cried, that my heart is going bad: I can't seem to catch my breath in this cold weather. The youngest of the McCord girls came in, accompanied by her blowsy hard-faced sarcastic mother (whom Thaddeus remembered as one of the young wives he had *almost* adored, many years ago) who acted as a kind of nurse, brusque and methodical and merciless, as Dr. Vickery did a vaginal examination of the daughter: fifteen years old, sullen and terrified and quick to scream before the instrument was even well in, a wan, pretty, doomed child, at least three months pregnant by Dr. Vickery's estimation, and infected with gonorrhea. ("Did she think it would just go away?" Dr. Vickery asked Mrs. McCord, and Mrs. McCord said, "She didn't think about it at all.") A twelve-year-old boy brought in with a cracked rib: pain, but an easy break: easily tended. Dr. Vickery, they said, my blood pressure — is it my blood pressure? — my skin feels tight to bursting and there's a ringing in my ears sometimes and my eyesight goes dark. I'm afraid: can you help me? Sore throat; deafness; lingering colds; flu; lice; fever; difficulty with breathing; arthritis; bleeding from the rectum; a terrible itch in both eyes; backache; stiff joints; insomnia. But I don't want to go to a hospital, they said, their faces stiffening; my mother never went into a hospital, never once, had nine children at home and lived to be ninety-four and died at home, never *once* went into any hospital. Dr. Vickery, they said, it's nothing much, is it? How soon can I get back to work? Erratic heartbeat; rickets; faintness and dizziness; a problematic pregnancy; a one-year-old who threw up most of his food; Mrs. Stickney with her bladder problem; Carlson Bell with his roundabout way of pleading with Thaddeus to lie to him.

At times he was not only exhausted but depressed, when it seemed to him, despite his natural optimism, that health and well-being were a narrow lane winding through a jungle of enormous, lustful, crazy vegetation . . . that one could toil to the end of his strength and his spirit's endurance and keep the pathway cleared for only a brief spell, a few days at the most: for no human effort could halt the avalanche of sheer rapacious nature. And he would recall the situation in his own household, and his very being seemed to shrink, to cringe, for where was his solace now, if no one loved him? — if no one cared for him? His daughter Elsa lived three hundred miles away with a man he had never met, and his son, a war veteran, a grown man now of thirty-two, had become even more of a stranger to him; Ashton had left this part of the country entirely and had sent home no address. And Opal and Nathan had turned against him. Where was his solace, his strength? He needed a sort of blind, naïve courage in order to keep the pathway cleared, an almost arrogant optimism: otherwise he would weaken and fail. . . .

He took his meals alone in his study and slept on the old horsehair sofa, not wanting to be with his wife; dreading her look of supplication and disapproval. And her pity. Sometimes he heard her talking to the child in another part of the house and he wondered if they were talking about *him*. He kept to himself, proudly, with a kind of rancorous satisfaction. If he ate only haphazardly, stuffing himself with cold cuts and pieces of bread and cheese, refusing Opal's hot dinners, if he sometimes went without breakfast, taking only black coffee, smoking a few cigarettes, what did it matter? — what did it matter to his family? One morning he had an attack of dizziness and a prickling sensation passed over him, a feeling of pins and needles in his left arm, but he simply waited for it to fade; he wasn't going to waste his energies in self-pity.

Alone at night, unable to sleep, he padded about his study in his bedroom slippers, playing softly on the old ocarina (whose gentle, soft, hollow tones blended with the wind and seemed to lift him out of his isolation, throwing his loneliness out into the winter night where it had not the power to cripple him), pausing now and then to sip at a glass of bourbon. Afterward he turned on his reading lamp and sat hunched at his desk, studying the slim battered volume of Marcus Aurelius's *Meditations*, turning page after page, absorbed, enraptured, exclaiming to himself: for he had never encountered any wisdom as profound and as reasonable as that of Marcus Aurelius, there was no other voice that cut so keenly into him, that awakened in him so passionate a certainty. From the very first, as a young man, he had always read the *Meditations* as the expression of a strong, self-determined, entirely enviable and even rather optimistic personality, not unlike himself.

He wished he might haul Opal and the child in here, to instruct them. Reason and the art of reasoning: there is no higher law. *All is but thinking so.* One must be like a rock against which the waves of the sea break unceasingly, never surrendering to emotion — neither despair nor joy, terror or ecstasy. Superstition is abhorrent: the martyrdom of the Christians repulsive. One lives within one's mind, one's disciplined reason. Knowing that all things vanish swiftly, one accepts the universe as it is — a universe of change, flowing about us, flooding against us, bearing us away. Only the present moment is real. *Time is but a point, reality a flux, perception indistinct, the composition of the body subject to easy corruption, the soul a spinning top, fortune hard to make out, fame confused. Physical things are but a flow-*

*ing stream, things of the soul dreams and vanity; life is but a
struggle and the visit to a strange land, posthumous fame but a
forgetting. . . .*

Night after night Thaddeus studied the *Meditations*, and leafed
through medical journals and magazines, and fussed with his
pipe, and drank too much, and wondered how long his wife and
grandson could hold out against him. He tried to contemplate his
own position in terms of Marcus Aurelius's wisdom. *You shame
yourself, my soul . . . while you allow your happiness to depend
upon the souls of others.*

"Yes," he said, "that's so: that's so."

It pleased him that the Emperor had been contemptuous of
Christianity and that persecutions of Christians had taken place
during his reign. Their ignorance, their superstition, their very
passion would be distasteful to a man of reason, as it was distasteful to Thaddeus. More than that, it was despicable. Intolerable.
A plunge into the abyss — a wallowing in the most brutish and
unhuman of instincts. *Repent,* they commanded, *repent or
die. . . .*

He marked his place in the *Meditations* with a scruffy blue-jay
feather he used as a bookmark, and turned to the Bible.

It was after midnight when he began reading, and he read
throughout the night. Hunched over his desk, his head lowered,
his eyes straining against the poor light, he read and could not
believe what he was reading. It had been many, many years since
he had even opened the Bible, and during church services he had
been in the habit of luxuriously daydreaming, so he came to the
Bible almost unprepared. It was as if he had never heard of the
Gospels, and of Christ's teachings; as if he were an alien confronted with a new language that he must understand or be destroyed.

He began with St. Matthew. At the back of his mind were
various Sunday-school tales, and the simple, rather touching
hymns everyone loved to sing, and the image of the Child Jesus,
meek and mild, answering hatred with love. But it was not so.
The Gospel according to St. Matthew presented a self-righteous,

intolerant, wildly egotistical, and even megalomaniacal personality — Jesus of Nazareth who confuses and bribes common people with miracles, who brags that He has not come to bring peace on earth but a sword, who threatens His enemies (those who merely choose not to believe in *Him* as the Son of God) with hellfire, a furnace where there shall be wailing and gnashing of teeth for all eternity. Why had Thaddeus believed that Jesus was fundamentally a loving person? It was not so; not so.

"The man was psychopathic," Thaddeus whispered.

The sudden knowledge sickened him and he felt, for an instant, weak with fear. Yet he read on. St. Mark, St. Luke, and St. John revealed the same person: Jesus of Nazareth who was vindictive, crafty, sly, opportunistic, and hypocritical. But, most of all, bullying. Cruel and sadistic and bullying. Hateful. The words of undeniable wisdom — that mankind should be loving and forgiving and considerate of one another — were not original with this man, but commonplaces; possibly Hellenic, possibly Oriental? What was original in Jesus was His insistence upon His own divinity: *Strait is the gate, and narrow is the way.* And again: *He that is not with me is against me.* Terrifying the multitudes with His threats of hellfire and endless agony, preaching an idiotic, blatantly untrue dogma that intention and act are equal, and involve equal responsibility, Jesus of Nazareth taught that one should forgive one's enemies while fully intending not to forgive *His:* for *His* enemies were to suffer horribly. Childish and unjust, whimsical, rather savage; a truly impulsive personality that did not hesitate to curse a fig tree because it had no fruit for him when He happened to be hungry, thereby causing the fig tree to wither and His disciples to marvel at His powers; the petty hero of a host of absurd miracle tales that make the point (the intention of Matthew, Mark, Luke, and John notwithstanding) that only an exhibitionist can compel the "love" of the masses. Thaddeus read and reread certain passages, hardly able to comprehend the nature of what was being revealed to him. Like most atheists, he had assumed, patronizingly, that the Christians who surrounded him on all sides were goodhearted, idealistic, deluded people who tried gamely to live up to the high moral principles of Jesus Christ, their Saviour, but naturally failed since they were not perfect. No doubt Dr. Vickery himself had said upon occasion, with the weary irony of centuries, that the churches had "perverted" Christ's teachings, and that — most embarrassing cliché of all — if Jesus were to reappear on earth again, He would once again be crucified. Now, rereading the passages that dealt with the crucifixion, Thaddeus's sympathies were entirely with Pilate, who struck him as the only reasonable man in the narrative. Jesus had clearly wished to be crucified, He had forced others to participate in his martyrdom; like a spiteful, selfish child He had to have His way — for only *His* way had any value. "A maniac," Thaddeus said softly. "A criminal. A simple-minded zealot who certainly intended to purge Israel if He had had enough power. . . . Is this the man everyone adores, is *this* the man who has shaped the Western world?" One must love Him — or suffer in hell. There was no other way. God could not be reached save through this self-proclaimed Messiah, who harbored within Himself a chilling contempt for humanity; who so despised life that He railed against it, slandering the flesh and all natural desires, urging His followers to martyrdom. It was repulsive. It was fascinating. That Thaddeus Vickery at the age of fifty-six should at last *see* . . . should at last penetrate the mystery of the loving Saviour. *For I am come to set a man at variance against his father, and the daughter against her mother, and the daughter in law against her mother in law. And a man's foes shall be they of his own household.*

"Murderer," Thaddeus said.

It was not long afterward that Thaddeus Vickery, entering the kitchen of his house by way of the back door, stomping snow off his boots, saw his wife and grandson at the big wooden table working together — rolling and cutting dough for noodles, it seemed. The room shimmered with heat and the odors of food. So fragrant, so dense! Dr. Vickery had been out most of the day and was unusually tired, and when he stepped into the warm kitchen it was as though he were stepping into an element thicker than air, somehow clotted, viscous. He found it difficult to breathe. The very flesh of his face, his jowls and cheeks, sagged heavily; when he uttered a greeting his words came out muffled and inarticulate. Such fatigue! He had not felt so tired in recent memory. And his left foot was all pins and needles from the cold.

Opal turned to him, her broad face flushed, the crease between her eyebrows deeper than he recalled. An old woman, he thought sadly. Nathan, bent over the table, slicing with painstaking care the rubbery, flour-sprinkled dough, looked up at his grandfather with a quizzical, searching gaze, his expression startled. Was he about to smile? To call out a greeting? A warning? The long curved bread knife in his hands caught the glare from an overhead light, through the smudges of flour and dough, and a wire of some sort — it must have been a near-invisible, scalding-hot wire — darted from the tip of that knife to Thaddeus's left eyeball. It *was* a wire: Thaddeus screamed as he felt it pierce his eyeball.

In an instant it ran back to his brain, plunging everything into darkness. The entire left side of his body caved in. He heard the start of the scream, not its finish; he felt only the caving-in, the collapse, the violent falling-away of his body and not the impact of the floor itself. And he saw nothing. After the wire pierced his eye he saw nothing — not the child's face, not the child's look of terror, of guilt: nothing.

X

Thaddeus Aaron Vickery, born 1891 in the village of Marsena, died on the evening of December 21, 1947, at 10:15 P.M., in that same village. He died of a massive stroke that fell upon him without warning; and in Your mercy You saw fit to allow him death without the intervention of consciousness. He was mourned by all who knew him — by hundreds of people who attended his wake and his funeral, and who appeared to be, in some cases, quite stricken with grief at the loss of Dr. Vickery, as if they had imagined that he was exempt from the laws of Nature and of God, and might have lived forever. He was especially mourned by those closest to him, his wife Opal Sayer Vickery and his grandson Nathanael William Vickery.

As it is said in the Book of Isaiah: *All flesh is grass, and all the goodliness thereof is as the flower of the field: The grass withereth, the flower fadeth: because the spirit of the Lord bloweth upon it! surely the people is grass. The grass withereth, the flower fadeth: but the word of our God shall stand for ever.*

BOOK TWO

the witness

i

Before Your creation was, You are.

And we who are Your children wait patiently for You to return — to breathe life into us, to save us from the terrible waters that threaten to overcome our souls. Save us, O Lord, is our prayer in these dark times. Save us! We sink in deep mire, where there is no standing: we are come into deep waters, where the floods overflow us.

Save me, O Lord, for am I not obedient unto You? Am I not patient? Am I not one of Your children?

It did me no good to be impatient.

There is no loneliness, O Lord, like that of a man whom You have once loved — and then abandoned. But this You know full well: for it is not possible that You do *not* know. For You come before all Your creation and in it we are swallowed whole: in You we are swallowed whole.

You are the Alpha and the Omega. You are the soul, and at once the whisperer unto the soul: *I am thy salvation*. You are He who writes these words and He who reads them, You are both myself and my terrible longing for You, spread out now throughout my body, packed tight against the envelope of my skin.

Like the wretched desire of Nathanael for the young woman Leonie: filled to bursting.

A nightmare! A raging pain behind the eye! A loathsome thing even to contemplate so many years later! . . . Yet he triumphed over it and was one with You and was beloved of You, a blessing denied most of Your children, however obedient and loving they are.

Do You hear? Do You listen?

It was Your promise that there shall be time no longer and I attend still upon that promise. We are in the last days, perhaps in the last hours. For it is said *All the wicked ones You will annihilate*. And again it is said by Jesus, regarding the last days, that this generation that is now will not pass away until all these things occur — until the world order is overthrown and the Kingdom of God is made manifest. Yet I remain deep in time, O Lord, sunk deep in its mire so that my very breathing is threatened. I dare not sleep except in a sitting position, for fear of the terrible nightmares that overflow me when I lie down naked and defenseless. There is such torture in the hours, O Lord, in the minutes that pass unheeding since that day nearly four years ago when You saw fit, in Your infinite wisdom and justice, to abandon me. Yet I am not impatient. I have not the energy for impatience any longer, nor would I tempt my Lord and my God a second time with my childish cry that He show His face at last. . . .

Several months ago I began this prayer, composing it as a petition to You, a ceaseless plea. And it is evident that You approve of my labor, for though there are difficult, painful hours there are, from time to time, unpredictably, moments of grace: of sheer grace: when I write quickly and fearlessly and know myself closest to You. I hope, O God, that You will judge me by Thine own strength and not by my weakness.

My prayer is not one of anger or impatience, nor is it one of lawless curiosity and speculation. I am forever obedient to You: forever meek and humble in Your sight. My prayer is an utterance of faith, of infinite faith. I would not have begun it except my longing for You struck so mercilessly deep one night, I could not see how it might be possible for me to endure that night, or the next, and the next: for the nights are long, O Lord, in Your fallen world. (I do not mean that I found it difficult to sleep; restful sleep has eluded me now for years. I mean that I found it difficult to endure the night, and even to conceive of the possibility of enduring it.)

Consider the silence of the night sky: the clouds of night that break the sky into rudderless clumps, moon-glaring, frantic with wind. What solace? What comfort? It is only October, yet the air is stark and cheerless, as if we were plunged already into winter. The breath of the night is the breath of Your absence, O Lord. And the leaves in the poplars outside my window — ! A frenzied whispering, a ceaseless plea. *Why do You forsake me?*

There is no loneliness so bitter as that of a man whom God has once loved fiercely and has then abandoned. No human love can satisfy him, nor can any human pleasures drug his senses. In the immensity of God's disregard he languishes like a child who cannot eat, slowly and piteously starving to death.

What torments me even further is the fact that the composition of this prayer is such a painful, such a relentless undertaking, for I who compose it must also live by means of it, sucking and gasping for breath. Could anyone witness my struggle, he would be moved with pity for me, and perhaps with revulsion as well: for in our world those who suffer are not long tolerated, and spiritual suffering is not honored at all. And could anyone glance through the effort that has already occupied me for months, wrung from me drop by drop by drop, he would be astonished to find it so brief. A lifetime, and so brief! So quickly read! The labor of these sleepless nights could be scanned in a few hours, and dismissed as merely unsightly, as unpretty, and thrown aside — for such is the nature of the fallen world, and pity is rarely offered those who suffer each alone.

Why do You forsake me? — a question no one wishes to hear.

■ ■ ■

How strange a form his being took, the girl thought. He was so sweet-voiced when he wished to be, and then again so strident, so powerful — his voice ringing clear and bell-like as her own father's voice when he was preaching at his very best. It did not seem necessary for him to read from the Gospels; evidently he knew great blocks of passages by heart; and he did not shout them out mindlessly, as other preachers sometimes did, and as the one or two child preachers she had heard had done (like queer wind-up toys, those strange children, no feeling to them, no subtlety), but he spoke the words as if they were his own, as if the Holy Spirit did indeed speak through him, consoling rather than frightening, brightly and hypnotically conversational rather than ranting. . . . How strange that that eleven-year-old boy was given out to be Nathanael Vickery, Reverend Sisley's boy from Marsena: for it was clear to her that she knew him and had heard him preach many times before, that he had been this way before, and that her father could not fail to recognize him as well.

"Is *that* the Vickery boy, the one they talk about?" Leonie asked.

She stood at the rear of the church, her arms folded tight beneath her breasts. It was a warm June evening, a Friday, and every pew in the church was filled. It was not *her* church; she had only stopped by on a whim, having nothing to do since her father was out of town for the rest of the week — preaching a revival out in White Springs for the Evangelical Christian Missionaries' Alliance. She was Esther Leonie Beloff, the daughter of the Reverend Marian Miles Beloff, renowned in this part of the world; and his fame made her self-conscious, and rather pleased, for it seemed to her obvious that she and her father were set apart from other people, from her father's congregation and his many admirers, for instance — that God had chosen a special destiny for them both.

"For *him* too," she said, staring at the Vickery boy. He was now leading the congregation in prayer: not droning as most preachers did, but speaking, almost singing. His voice was melodic, yet strong enough to carry to the very rear of the room: to her. Was he a freak, Leonie wondered, was he truly marked by God as her own father had been marked (for Marian Miles Beloff had begun his preaching ministry at the age of thirteen), were the things people said about him true . . . ? "Yes, just listen to him!" she said, stifling her laughter. "Eighty-five pounds and his little-boy face gleaming with sweat and his voice like it just pierced through a cloud — oh dear heart, isn't he something! I'll take him back home with me."

A Disciples of God church on the outskirts of Rockland: asbestos siding, interior smelling of newness, cheap varnish and cheap paint and something earnest, eager. Disciples of God wasn't *her* church, wasn't her father's. His church was fairly new too but it was made of brick, set atop a hill in North Yewville, the lawn unevenly green but a lawn nevertheless: whereas the earth outside this little crackerbox was all barren and lumpy. She wasn't from Rockland, was only visiting a cousin of her mother's while her father was away; she didn't know the regular minister and didn't care to know him; it was only Nathanael Vickery who interested her. Such a frail child, small for his age, and big-eyed — she could see that even at this distance. And it was true about him being so gifted. She would have to tell her father it was true: that boy-preacher everyone was talking up, from Marsena, *was* the real thing. Once you heard him, there was no mistaking what he was.

Now they were singing "Rock of Ages" and Leonie joined in, feeling elated, zestful, knowing that people near her would begin to hear her voice — she had been trained as a gospel singer from earliest girlhood: her voice was powerful and muscular and confident — and would be dying to turn around to see who that soprano was.

> Let the water and the blood,
> That from Thy wounded side did flow. . . .

Leonie sang loudly and lustfully, her eyebrows arched high. She was sixteen years old, with a rich, olive, rather oily skin, and black hair that curled and frizzed out about her plump face. She had a woman's body, mature and full, almost stout, with surprisingly thin ankles and small stubby-fingered hands and delicate wrists. Beneath her solid chin was the hint, the merest hint, of a second chin; hardly more than a crease of soft, rich-complexioned flesh. She had wide, full, lovely lips, and a rather snubbed nose, and pale green eyes that appeared to be slightly slanted in her face, like cats' eyes — and catlike too was her sly, smirkish grin and the general sinuousness of her manner. She loved to use her voice, which was genuinely striking, and so she sang so forcefully that the young boy preacher could hear her — wasn't he peering and squinting in her direction, a frail little boy in a suit too large for him, his damp hair plastered to his forehead as if he'd been laboring out in the sun? *Let me hide myself in Thee:* Leonie sang almost shrilly, sending the words over the heads of the men and women who stood before her. She knew all the words, knew them without understanding them, sang without faltering in a kind of hectic daze as her father and his assistants had taught her, and it seemed to her that the boy preacher *did* hear.

> Rock of Ages, cleft for me,
> Let me hide myself in Thee. . . .

The service was coming to an end. She judged it to be moderately successful, for an ordinary weekend service: no laying-on of hands and casting out of devils and healing; only a few people speaking in tongues; only a few people rushing forward in hysterics to the altar rail to throw themselves at Christ's feet. *Let me hide myself in Thee.* . . . The boy preacher had handled the excitement very well: he hadn't appeared to be alarmed by it, as far as Leonie could judge. (Maybe he was just too innocent yet and hadn't had any real difficulties, any *real* hysterics thus far in his ministry — ?) No doubt in Leonie's mind that the boy was genuine, that he had the call. And he was such a sweetheart with his curly dark hair and his big eyes and his shimmering trembling melodic voice that rang out everywhere! She wouldn't half mind taking him back to North Yewville with her as a surprise for her daddy and as a baby brother for herself. She wanted more family, she *needed* more family . . . a sister most of all, but a brother would have been fine: such a pity that her mother had died so young! The Vickery boy hadn't any family either, except for his grandmother. (Was that big ruddy-faced woman in the front pew Mrs. Vickery? — tears streaming down her cheeks and shoulders heaving as she sang?) The rumor was that his mother had died at childbirth and she hadn't been married and that God Himself had intervened to be the infant's father: maybe it was true, maybe it wasn't, but just the thought of it made Leonie shiver.

"*He's* the one," she thought. "What will be, will be."

Though Leonie had been in Rockland only a day or two, she had been hearing about the Vickery boy all that time, from one person or another, mainly women friends of her mother's cousin, or neighbors who were always dropping by. (On account of her presence, she judged: after all, she *was* the Reverend Marian Miles Beloff's only daughter.) It was said of the Vickery boy that he fasted for days at a time in order to purify his body, and that he had queer eating habits, more complicated than those of Catholics or Jews. ("Or Moslems?" Leonie had said brightly, as if she knew all about the eating habits of Moslems.) He was so close to God, it was said, that if someone spoke to him too abruptly, unannounced, he didn't hear at all; he was with God and deaf to man at such times, and it took him a while to "come back." He could remain for hours on his knees, praying. ("But he sounds like a *monk* or something!" Leonie squealed, thinking of her father who rarely, these days, got onto his knees: and if he did, someone had to stand close by to haul him up again.) He knew most of the Bible by heart, of course. He could play the organ just wonderfully — and it used to be a sight to see him, so small, sitting on the very edge of the bench so he could reach the pedals; he'd begun playing when he was very, very young. ("My daddy started playing the accordion and mouth organ when he was six," Leonie said. "Is he maybe like that? The music just comes out of nowhere, out of the air? — that's what my daddy used to say.") There were times when he kept to himself, in a darkened room, fasting and praying and begging God for a sign, and when he emerged from his isolation there would be something strange and altered about him — his eyes frosted-looking, or his teeth edged with blood, or bruises on his arms and legs and neck, or the indentations of nails on his palms. Much of the time he was a quiet, dutiful, sweet-faced boy whom Reverend Sisley could trust with anything, but there had been two or three occasions when he had given such impassioned sermons and led his people in such impassioned prayers that there had been spontaneous healings — written up in the newspaper, they were, and witnessed by dozens of people who *swore* to the truth of what they saw: an elderly woman cured of a blockage in her throat that had prevented her breathing right for twenty years; a twelve-year-old girl cured of "nerves"; the brother of one of the church's deacons cured — for seventy-eight hours — of some terrible pathetic trembling that had come over him a few years before, causing his arms and legs to quiver, and even his eyelids. And there were other cures, other occasions; other rumors. ("But the boy doesn't have a healing ministry, does he? I never heard *that*," Leonie cried. Her own father hadn't been called by God to a healing ministry — a healing ministry being, as he said repeatedly, a very serious thing.) People disagreed about him, because there were those — men, especially — who just didn't take to the spectacle of a boy preacher, and who probably would have scorned Christ Himself when He first began speaking to the multitudes. But everyone who heard the Vickery boy preach did agree he was no ordinary boy — not by a long shot. "You drop by the church and peek in and see what you think," Leonie was told, and though she held off assenting, she did fully intend to go. ("But I hope he isn't deformed somehow," she said. "The last child preacher I heard, at the 'Vangelical Conference a few years ago, was a little girl with a block shoe or something — built up so her one leg was even with the other, you know? And she was a wizened little ugly thing just loud-mouthed, coached by her mommy and daddy, that was all, and not speaking for the Lord at all: not a bit! They put her up there for the collection, thinking they would rake the money in, but they failed utterly as my daddy and the other men said — *failed utterly*. But I expect this Nathan Vickery isn't on the order of *that*.")

So it turned out he wasn't, he wasn't a fraud or a fake or demented or silly; Leonie judged his presence as good as that of just about any preacher she'd heard, except for the big-name ones like her own father, or the Reverend Bill Branham, who was even more famous, or Sister Hannah Price out of Dallas, Texas, who had preached an unforgettable sermon in Cleveland about eighteen months ago — the sick and the lame and the blind and the deaf had truly been aided that night, as Leonie Beloff could testify, having seen with her own eyes the miracles that transpired, and having been so excited by Sister Hannah that she came near to fainting a half-dozen times and *did* faint on the way home, despite the fact that her father tried to joke her out of it. The Vickery boy wasn't quite on that level, because he was, well, too commonsensical and even-speaking, and Leonie had the idea that he was rather intelligent for a child his age, or for a person of any age; and being intelligent just didn't set right up on a stage or at a podium. But he was genuine. Christ dwelled within him and there was no mistaking that.

"Yes. *Him*," Leonie thought.

The hymn ended with a long-drawn-out *Thee*.

Now Leonie bethought herself that she should skip around the crowd somehow and introduce herself to tonight's visiting preacher, and to his grandmother (that horse-faced woman *must* be his grandmother, though they didn't look anywhere near alike: the way she was up there hugging him, as if he was a baby!), and to the Disciples of God regular minister himself, but the evening was awfully warm, and her mind was drifting off onto . . . drifting off onto those boys she had been ignoring by the pharmacist's that afternoon, those loud-mouthed smart-alecks who had been teasing her on account of her wild frizzy hair and asking her who she was, was she maybe a new girl in town? — and would she like a Coke or a soda? — or a ride out along the river? — and frankly she had had enough of piety for one evening. ("I'm just not that serious-solemn boohooing making-a-big-fuss-over-Christ kind of Christian: not me," Reverend Marian Miles Beloff said repeatedly, and Leonie was exactly the same.) And there were so many other people milling around, wanting to shake the boy's hand, and the regular minister — white-haired, with glasses and a squint and a funny little rosebud mouth — looked so dull, and the place *was* awfully warm. . . .

So Leonie ducked out of the church without introducing herself to anyone at all and by the time she saw her father again, Tuesday of the following week, she had half-forgotten about Nathanael Vickery, and anyway they had more important things to talk about: such as the fact that Reverend Beloff was going to be financed for a gospel program on a radio station in Port Oriskany, and that meant they would have to move (again: they had moved some five or six times in Leonie's memory), and there was the possibility too of a revival circuit later that summer, or anyway part of a circuit, if a certain deal pending with the famous Bill Branham didn't fall through. (It seemed that Reverend Branham gave so much of himself, he was often incapacitated; and there was need for competent backup preachers, provided they weren't *too* competent.)

"Oh, I heard the most darling little-boy preacher out in Rockland, at a Disciples of God," Leonie thought to say finally, but Reverend Beloff only grunted a reply, possibly he hadn't even heard, and Leonie — who had caused something of a minor scandal in the neighborhood, having been seen talking and laughing with utter strangers on Main Street and having been glimpsed, on Sunday evening, riding in someone's jalopy out on the highway — thought it best to steer their conversation away from the subject of Rockland in general. Which was fine with Reverend Beloff, who, as he expressed it, always lived with one foot in the future.

So Leonie did not meet Nathanael Vickery at that time, nor did Reverend Beloff take the slightest interest in him. But when he came into their lives several years later Leonie was to remember him at once, with a hot, quick flash of certainty, a sense of intimacy, as if they had known each other very well, like sister and brother; as if they had always known each other. So *that* is the form His being takes, Leonie was to think. *That*.

ii

Dr. Vickery's sudden death had so upset his wife, and the memory of him — his face beet-red and contorted and one eye practically popping out of its socket, and those terrible convulsions! — stayed with her for so long, night and day, that it was several months before she could deal with the estate: all the legal problems, the taxes for the district and for the county and for the state and for the federal government; and curious inexplicable claims made against her by people in the area who said Thaddeus owed them money for repairs or services — not exactly barefaced lies, but cruel exaggerations or distortions of the truth. (The Derby mechanic who checked over Thaddeus's car and made routine adjustments tried to claim that Thaddeus owed him three hundred dollars — and Opal might have paid if her grandson hadn't suggested she go through the papers in Dr. Vickery's drawers once again, hunting for canceled checks.) It was a bitter, bitter thing, this death: and in a way Opal would never forgive her husband for it.

"His last look was one of anger," she said often. "Fury. His face was so wrinkled and red, he was *glaring* at the boy and me . . . !"

A massive stroke: coming from nowhere, totally unexpected (though Dr. Vickery *did* have high blood pressure), and lethal. He was never to regain consciousness but died within a few hours; and at the very end, thank God, his face acquired a look of genuine peace.

She did not know if she had loved him; how could she have *loved* so stubborn a man, who had set himself in such blind, ignorant opposition to the Lord? She went for days without weeping, troubled by the fuss relatives and neighbors insisted upon making; and what a nuisance, the man's small army of patients! — all of them brokenhearted, a few quite terrified at the thought of losing him, as if *he* were the sole physician in all of the Valley. "You'll get along without him," Opal said sternly, displeased with so much noisy sorrow. "He was only a man, after all — only mortal."

In secret, of course, she and Nathan prayed for his soul. Nathan led the prayer, his small pale face practically hidden by his hands, and the two of them remained on their knees for long dreamlike delirious minutes on the bare floorboards of the attic. The prayers went on and on and Nathan's voice rose and sank and rose again, choked with tears, and Opal could only murmur assent, beginning to sob, racked with the pain of her loss, and the pain of that last ugly sight of Thaddeus — falling to the kitchen floor in his old worn-out overcoat, his once-handsome face like a gargoyle's, hideous with death. Or was it God, was it the revelation God made to this unbelieving, scornful servant Thaddeus? — not death at all that had astounded and angered Thaddeus, but God? — *God?*

"Why did he die like that?" Opal asked, angry herself. She was not quite coherent; she was rather exasperated with her husband. "Like *that?* — so fast, and without any preparation?"

"All things must be fulfilled," Nathan said slowly.

She inclined her head toward him. She did not fully understand, but she assented.

"All things must. . . . Yes," she said.

And so Opal Vickery managed to deal with the legal and financial problems her husband left her (for he died intestate, like many another physician), and some eight months after his funeral she was in a position to sell most of the property: a great deal of the money went for taxes, but a fair amount was given to the Marsena Baptist Church and to the Evangelical Missionaries' Alliance. A year after his death she signed over the house to a homeless family the Sisleys had heard of, an arthritic cabinet-

maker and his wife and seven children who had been living on
welfare up in Yewville, crammed into a bungalow; most of the
furniture went with the house — the sofas and tables and chairs
and Thaddeus's old desk and even his old useless hourglass —
since Mrs. Vickery wanted nothing to do with it. She was talked
into taking along some of the finer antique pieces, and several
ceramic doorknobs, when she and Nathan moved into the Sisleys' house — which was a fairly large house right in town, a
stone's throw from the church. The Sisleys had often complained
of loneliness there, since they had no children. It had occurred
to them from time to time that the Lord meant for them to share
their home, but the opportunity had never so obviously arisen in
the past.

"Now we're all together," Reverend Sisley said, deeply moved.
"And it feels right, doesn't it? — that's how you can tell the Lord
is smiling upon us. It *feels* right. A new family is born out of the
sorrow of loss, a new union is made in the eyes of the Lord, and
all is well. It just *feels* right, doesn't it?"

He gave Nathan lessons, and spoke of sending him to Bible
School in a few years (the minimum age was supposed to be
sixteen but perhaps an exception could be made in Nathan's case:
Nathan *was* so obviously an exception) if there was enough
money; he gave over the Sunday-school classes to the boy, since
Mrs. Haas, who had been in charge of them for years, was so
badly ailing; and allowed him to lead prayers and read the Gospel
and take over entire services now and then, since the boy's presence in front of the congregation was so mature and so assured
— and wasn't it a surprise, when the boy often seemed so shy, so
tongue-tied in person? almost, in a way, *backward?* But he surely
came to life when he was preaching the Lord's wisdom and there
was no doubt that Reverend Sisley's congregation approved, for
not only did more people show up for services when it was known
Nathan Vickery would be presiding, but the collection was always
more generous — always. "It's partly because he's a child," Reverend Sisley told his wife, careful to let her know his feelings were

not hurt, his dignity *not* bruised, "but mainly, I think, because the Lord is behind him and supporting him all the way. The Lord is *really* enthusiastic about Nathan."

The Reverend Thomas Sisley was in his mid-sixties at this time, slow of speech, partly deaf, an amiable smiling man who nodded a great deal, perhaps because he couldn't always be certain of what people were saying. His best days were behind him, he readily admitted; he *had* been a passionate witness of the Gospel at one time, back in the early years of the century and well up into the twenties. He *had* moved many hundreds — or was it thousands — of people to come forward for Christ; and the Lord had been generally well-pleased with him. So he believed, so he was given to believe.

"Now it's only fitting that a new generation springs to life," he said. And to the boy himself he said: "All you have to do, Nathan, is trust in the Lord. Nothing more. The Lord asks you only to do what you can — and He's with you all the way."

"Yes," said Nathan softly. "I know."

"And the Bible is the only tool — and I would say mainly the Gospels, if reading is a chore and your eyes bother you, you know: the Gospels are enough to get you through. There's other parts that are said to be beautiful, like poetry, and a lot of history in them — and things for scholars and theologians to quibble over, you know — but how important is all that? After all — *The time is fulfilled, and the kingdom of God is at hand: repent ye, and believe the gospel.* The Lord doesn't really require anything more."

The child listened closely, and appeared to agree.

"He never sends us anything beyond our strength," Reverend Sisley said.

His wife was said to be several years his senior: white-haired like her husband, but less amiable than he, at times rather waspish, even tearful and petulant (on account of her legs, the pain in her legs: which was much worse in wet weather). She had wanted Opal and Nathan to live with them from the first, but shortly after they moved in she began to pick at the boy (who was always creeping around the house, she said, padding around like a cat, so that her heart practically failed her when he came up behind her and spoke; and his eating habits were so odd — why give up meat, was he a Catholic, and why no milk or eggs, and never anything sweet like cake or pie or cookies or even apple cider?). And she was moody with Opal, who certainly tried her best to be deferential and self-effacing and sisterly. She burst into tears with little provocation, and kept to her room for days at a time, faint of breath, imagining she would die soon and be out of everyone's way. It hurt her very much that Mrs. Vickery could organize the women's meetings without any trouble, and take care of most of Reverend Sisley's mail and financial arrangements, and that she could handle the housekeeping and most of the cooking and even find time to go out and visit the sick, as Mrs. Sisley had once done. It hurt her that people were whispering all sorts of things — that she, the minister's wife, now had two full-time servants so she could laze in bed all she wished, and that Reverend Sisley had somehow gotten hold of the late Dr. Vickery's money (a fortune, it was rumored in Marsena: certainly he must have put away thousands of dollars over the years), and was using Nathan Vickery more and more often, being on the edge of senility himself. So she kept to her room, and when she reappeared the three of them pretended to be delighted to see her — as if this wasn't her own home, where she belonged by rights.

"Still," she thought, "we are all brothers and sisters in Christ. *That* goes without saying."

■ ■ ■

A slow soundless explosion of light, of sheer dazzling blinding light that obliterated the walls and the ceiling and the floor of the room, and swept Nathanael Vickery away from earth altogether: so You saw fit to manifest Yourself on the eve of the boy's twelfth birthday.

He was unable to rejoice in Your magnificence because in his astonishment he had neither breath nor strength. O Lord! Lord God of Hosts! His vision failed and his soul seemed to cringe, to shrink. What was happening? Where would he plunge? In the soul-battering effusion of light there was neither height nor depth, there was nothing to seize, nothing to flatten himself against. You appeared: and the earth fell away.

He had been fasting for some time. For days. Secretly, for days. He hid himself from the others so they would not interfere — not that they dared interfere with his love for You. He hid himself in preparation for a sermon he was to give in a day or two, under Reverend Sisley's direction. Hour after hour he studied the Bible, reading even those passages he had memorized years ago, sternly reading and rereading. *I am the door. I am the door.* His sermon was to be on that subject. And so he studied the Gospel of St. John; and the Book of Revelation; and then he opened the Bible at random, praying for Your guidance, his fingers trembling as if he sensed himself on the brink of an extraordinary experience.

And so it came about that You manifested Yourself to him for the third time in his life.

(Of course You dwelt with him at all times, and Jesus was his inseparable companion, advising him, encouraging him, giving him strength to withstand the ignorant taunts of his classmates at the country schoolhouse, and even their physical blows — but the visions You sent him were something else entirely. There was one aspect of God, Nathan believed, that resided in him and was identical with his soul, being of the same substance; but there was another aspect of God, unknown, unknowable, that came upon him from without, swooping down upon him without warning. God in this form was a rare trembling brightness that pierced the eye and snatched away the breath. It did no good to cry for aid, or for mercy, for this God was oblivious of human pain.)

Christ appeared. His hand was thrust out. For an instant Nathan was too terrified to respond.

"Nathan," came the command. *"Nathan."*

The hand was enormous, hard and muscular; the fingers were like claws.

Blindly he reached out — blindly he took hold of the stranger's hand.

Ice stretched to every horizon. What was this place? Creatures were trapped in ice, in solid ice. Creatures with human forms, human features. Who were they? Why were their screams silent? These were sinners who had turned aside from God, Nathan was given to know; these were the souls of the damned. He stared, a spell upon him. He could not have spoken had he wished to. What was this place? Christ's fingers squeezed his tightly together. The sinners were trapped in ice to their breasts, to their chins, even up to their mouths; it was a coldness ten times colder than any Nathan had known previously. Ah, such cold! Such hurt in every breath! He would have fled, but Christ held him fast. "I am the door," Christ said softly. "By me if any man enter in, he shall be saved: but if he shall not enter in he shall be damned. *He shall be damned.*"

The sinners' contorted faces were too ugly to contemplate. Nathan shrank away. He hated it that their eyes snatched piteously at his. Did they recognize him? Who were they? Mute, encased in rock, trapped, doomed, damned: he felt a terrible revulsion for them. For it was possible that his soul would slip toward them, weakened by pity, and not even Christ's flame-like presence would be sufficient to free him.

And if he saw his Grandfather Vickery among them — !

"Take me away. Please take me away," he begged.

Exulting, Christ led him forward. What was solid earth, solid ice, shattered to a million fragments; Nathan had to shield his eyes.

A forest, a jungle: steamy hot. At first it appeared to be deserted. The heat was so powerful that Nathan could not gauge it — he felt it as a solid wall slamming against him. What were those creatures? Stooped, misshapen, eyeless . . . ? Christ squeezed his hand so tightly that Nathan winced. It was crucial that he be awake, that he be alert, and not succumb to this terrible heat.

Vapors rose, like fingers, into the opaque sky. Water easing into steam. Mist. Elsewhere there were pools of seething liquid, flaming like lava, and in these pools (he had to blink droplets of perspiration out of his eyes in order to see clearly) were human forms. . . . Some waved their scrawny arms, some lay mute and inert as if dead. They swayed from side to side, whimpering like dogs. "I am the door," Christ whispered. "I am the door not all would pass through."

Nathan's soul was transfixed with wonder. He did fear Your son, but feared even more any expression of his own weakness. What shame there was in it, and in him! What shame that he should cringe before the bright-dark glowering face of Your son!

"This is the place of those who sinned with their flesh, and turned away from me," Christ said.

Nathan stared. At first he saw nothing — no one. And then he saw a vast crowd, creatures not quite distinct from one another and from the misshapen earth that held them, nearly swallowed up in mists that stung saltlike with heat. These had once been human beings, Nathan was given to know. But they were human beings no longer. They were stunted, deformed creatures, missing parts of bodies. Many were eyeless; in some cases scar tissue had grown unevenly over the empty sockets. Women's breasts dripped blood. Nathan wanted to shut his eyes, but could not. He was given to know that he must look: he must learn.

Ah, such blood! It was unclean, glistening on bellies, on the insides of thighs; droplets were forced out of nipples, causing great pain. Nathan felt the screams of the women though he could not hear them. No! No! Stop! He stared in horror as an enormous black snake, larger than a water moccasin, overtook one of the women and fastened its teeth onto her breast. What a silent convulsive shrieking! What a nightmare!

Yet Christ would not allow him to fall back.

It was given him to know that all was well: for these were sinners, each and every one of them was a sinner who had rejected Jesus of Nazareth as his Saviour.

"For I alone am the door," Christ said.

His whisper was loving, ticklish to the ear. Feathery-light. If Nathan burst into laughter, if he began to scream — ! But he did not scream. He bent forward to press his burning cheek against Christ's hand, which was cold and stern. "You alone are the door," he said.

In the distance, on all sides, the earth was moonlike, a jagged horizon of craters without vegetation. No life could endure here; yet there were people on all sides, fighting one another even as they gasped for breath. Arms and legs coiled snake-like; heads fought bodies. There were jaws without faces, double rows of teeth that tore and tore and devoured. What a clawing, pummeling, moaning, panting, writhing, shrieking! The air rocked with delirium. Something darted up Nathan's nose, tickling him outrageously, daring him to laugh aloud or shout or sneeze.

"You alone are the —"

Human figures struggled in the mud nearby, with grotesque shapes that must have been wild beasts of some kind — boars or hogs. They thrashed about hopelessly, grunting and sighing. Nathan felt their rage; it communicated itself through the vibrations of the earth, which rose into his body, up into his bowels and heart, sickening him. Not far distant a creature dragged itself off from the others and began to vomit. Black clayey-cold blood, sticky clots of blood — what a horror! Nathan could not help staring. He too began to gag. What if he vomited up his own tissue, his own blood? He tasted something vile, darkly sour, at the very back of his mouth. What if —

Christ urged him on, now gripping him by the upper arm.

"There is no help for those whom God has abandoned," Christ said. "You would do well, Nathan, to consider your own soul. Don't waste your pity on them. You must keep to the path, Nathan, and never look too closely at what surrounds you. And never doubt! You must keep to the path, Nathan! The path! The path!"

Something lifted — white and insubstantial as a muslin curtain — and Nathan woke feebly, and then woke again: to find himself outside.

It was night. Had he been sleep? Had he stumbled from his bed, groggy, half-conscious? He was outside, in a field. Behind a darkened house. But where was Reverend Sisley's house, where was Nathan's bed? And the Bible he had been reading . . . ? "The path," Nathan whispered hoarsely. Christ gripped him still by the upper arm, a presence so close it could not be seen. The grass was wet, Nathan's bare feet were wet, he began to shiver lightly with the cold. But was it cold? Where did the cold come from? Wildly he woke himself, forcing his consciousness back. If he could keep his eyes open he might not sink into sleep. "The path. Where is the path," he begged.

Christ allowed him to see the overgrown elderberry bushes along the fence . . . the rear of the old, partly collapsed carriage house . . . the Bells' outbuildings not far away. Ah, he was home: safely home: and Grandfather Vickery was in his close-smelling cluttered wonderfully messy office, reading at his desk. And Grandmother Vickery was in the kitchen. In the kitchen? Awaiting him. He was only a child, a very small child. He knew nothing. He had no sermon to preach, there were no frightened faces ringing him around, reaching out to him for help — Pray for me, pray for me — there was no one at all who wept for salvation, no one.

Yet Christ gripped him tight and would not let him go.

"All that you have seen, Nathan, will be as nothing compared to the sorrow that will be yours," Christ whispered, "for you are guilty of the sin of pride. Have you not known? Have you not guessed? For these many months, even for years, you have offended the Lord with your loathsome pride, until your very being is an abomination to Him. For it is said that wickedness shows itself in pride and must be humbled. Have you not known? A wicked person walks as you do, Nathan, with a froward mouth

. . . he speaks with his feet, he teaches with his fingers, he knows not the vileness he himself carries. Frowardness is in his heart, he deviseth mischief continually, he soweth discord. Have you not known, Nathan? All these days? All these hours?"

Nathan's teeth began to chatter with the cold. He would have lost all strength and sunk to his knees had not Christ held him up.

"Have you not known? . . . You must only give praise to the Lord, Nathan, all the days of your life, for there is no other wisdom, Nathan. And you must learn humility — you must be humbled this very night. Otherwise calamity will come upon you without warning: suddenly you will be broken without remedy. For there are six things the Lord does hate above all else; yea, seven are an abomination unto him. A proud look. . . ."

Nathan strained to hear Christ's words. There was a shrill ringing in his ears and his senses reeled and he could look neither up nor down. He was fixed as if in a block of ice.

Pride.

Pride?

"The sin of pride," Christ said gently.

Now the strong hands urged him forward. The white veil was ripped away again, and again Nathan was awake, blinking wildly. What place was this, where was he going? Who propelled him onward? The sharp grasses must have hurt his feet but he could feel no pain, no sensation at all. His hair was stirred limply in the breeze. Was it summer, still, or was it suddenly winter? So cold! "You are guilty of the sin of pride," Christ whispered, His voice nearly inaudible now. ". . . thinking to set yourself apart from your brothers and sisters . . . imagining yourself superior . . . fasting, and prayer, and overzealousness in going about my Father's business. . . . How have you dared set yourself apart from all of humanity, doing such things in the name of the Father, Who knows you not? They who exalt themselves shall be humbled: so it is written, and so it will come to pass. They who exalt themselves will be humbled. And they who humble themselves will be exalted."

He stumbled forward. His hands pulled the barbed-wire strands apart. This way? Here? Someone was sobbing aloud in terror.

On all sides of him the creatures fluttered and clucked and flapped their wings in panic. "Pride," Christ said, close against his ear. "Pride. Pride. Have you never understood?"

He had not eaten for so long, now his throat and the back of his mouth were flooded with an acrid, ugly liquid tasting of metal. Like rust, it was. Like black blood. He began to gag, forced himself to swallow it down, and gagged again, his eyes rolling.

Had anyone seen him come in here? Had anyone been watching?

Christ gripped him now by the back of his neck. There was no escape. "Your purity is an abomination," Christ whispered. Ah, what a stench! The odor of chickens: their excrement like dried, clotted paste, and their feathers, and the damp, stale straw in which they nested. There was no escape. He woke continually to the darkened coop, to the squawk and flutter of the chickens, to the taste of vomit in his mouth. He was awake now: this was no dream: the skin that reeked of perspiration was his own, glowing a feeble phosphorescence in the dim light. He stood in his bare feet in a stranger's chicken coop with one of the creatures flailing crazily about him, caught by its neck and one pumping wing. There was no escape. He was Nathan Vickery, Christ held him close, there could be no escape save through the door. *Whoso eateth my flesh, and drinketh my blood, hath eternal life; and I will raise him up at the last day. For my flesh is meat indeed, and my blood is drink indeed.* It could not be, Nathan thought, that Christ wished to humiliate him in this way: it could not be that Christ wished to destroy him. Yet it was so. It was happening, he was fully awake now, quivering with horror: it was so. He choked, he gagged. Pride, pride! Nothing but pride! What was the veil that separated him from all of creation except pride? And that pride must be humbled.

"You must be defiled," Christ said, "before you can be raised up again. You must be defiled before you can be perfect, even as I am perfect. Do you understand, my child?"

Nathan held the struggling creature before him. He wished to cry out from the depths of his soul *No, I will not! No.*

The darting beak, the tiny mad eyes, the limp scabby comb, the frantic wings: horrible. And the clawing feet. Horrible! Yet he forced its head into his mouth. As Christ gripped him tight, he forced the creature's head into his mouth, deep into his mouth. It was horrible, horrible. He would vomit up his very soul. His vision seemed dislodged, seared around the edges like a scrap of paper settling upon a fire in the instant before it is consumed. If only it were a dream — ! But it was not a dream: he was fully conscious of what he must do.

"My child . . . ," Christ whispered.

iii

In the years that followed, You saw fit in Your infinite wisdom to raise your servant Nathanael Vickery once again, and to endow him not only with life and breath (for after the sacrifice of his pride that June evening the boy remained speechless and only partly conscious for several weeks) but with rare powers of preaching and healing and prophesy. It soon became evident to all who heard him that his ministry would be a great one; that You had blessed him with such powers as would allow him to go into all the world, and preach the Gospel to every living creature, as Christ did exhort his first disciples.

Unnaturally silent as Nathan was in his private life, he came into his own whenever he preached or addressed his brothers and sisters in Christ, however small the group. Then he was enlivened, fiery, fierce: his meager voice gathered strength and became rich, brilliantly and throbbingly rich, with an almost painful intensity, so that many of those who heard him preach were moved to ecstasy and to tears by the mere sound of his voice: the *sounds* of God's voice as they are uttered by one who has sacrificed himself to God in absolute humility. *Lord, Lord* — the boy would cry, and it seemed to all who witnessed that a power seized him, literally seized and possessed him, and transported him beyond himself. It was said this power could even be seen if one looked closely enough, or if one were endowed with sensitive eyes: it manifested itself in a luminous glow on the boy's face and hands. (This unmistakable sign of the Lord's blessing first appeared when Nathan was fourteen years old, preaching one evening in a small store-front church in Muirkirk, deep in winter, deep in the notorious ten-month lockout of the Muirkirk Textile Company, which was never to be satisfactorily resolved: for the company closed its doors and attempted to declare bankruptcy, and under cover of darkness one night certain of its workers — men and women both, it was said — broke into the old building and smashed the machines and set fires, so that the building was entirely gutted. At the time of Nathan's visit to the Muirkirk Church of Jesus Christ Risen the factory had been locked against its workers for nearly seven months, and though most of the rather sparse group who came to hear him that freezing night were millworkers and their wives, and the elderly fathers and mothers of these people who assuredly felt great bitterness in their hearts for the owners and were hardened against Christly love and charity and the forgiveness of sins, nevertheless the boy's impassioned voice and the mesmerizing motions of his small, slender hands startled them into wakefulness, into fear and love of the Lord; and when it became evident to certain of the congregation that the Holy Spirit had descended into him, that their prayer meeting had been blessed by God Himself, there was great excitement — individuals burst into song, into ecstatic prayers, their own faces shining with love of the Lord and with joy in their certainty of His love for them; and it was said that the wood-frame building trembled with the intensity of Nathan Vickery's voice; and gale-like winds started and stopped and started again; and one by one, as if plucked out of their seats by the Lord Himself, men and women came forward to declare themselves for Christ, to fall to their knees at the boy preacher's feet, weeping, crying aloud in such voices as were never heard before in Muirkirk or in all of the Eden Valley.)

It came to pass that You endowed Nathan Vickery with the ability to alleviate suffering, and even to cure certain illnesses; though his powers of healing were not consistent, and though the boy himself nervously rejected all such claims, it was soon evident that at certain times and in certain circumstances the power that dwelt about his face and hands, pulsing and ebbing and leaping and darting, did have the effect of erasing pain as if it had never been. The first time he laid hands on a suffering person — a woman in her sixties, a farm wife from the hills of Shaheen who was said to have been in pain for many months, generalized throughout her body and undiagnosable, so the doctors claimed — it was remarked upon by all who witnessed the event that an almost flame-like light glowed about his hands, licking onto the woman's bowed head, licking and streaming down her shoulders, and vanishing at once: in an instant, in a half-second. The entire congregation was rocked with amazement, and when the woman rose to her feet, baffled, blinking as if she had been asleep, and declared herself in a slow, dazed voice free of pain — of course there was uncontrollable excitement, and others came forward, some declaring themselves already cured of their afflictions before the boy could even touch them! Great thanks were offered unto God: there were hours of singing and chanting and clapping, punctuated by shouts of the faithful who spoke without knowing they spoke, as the Holy Spirit breathed His power into them. For it was as if the mere presence of the boy Nathan Vickery excited the awareness of God, and drew Him near. There were individuals whom such powers frightened, and these shied away from him, and even uttered doubts behind his and his grandmother's backs: among them, unfortunately, was the wife of the elderly Reverend Sisley, now bedridden, querulous and spoiled. And there were others, as naturally there would be, and must; for is it not written that the world cannot hate the ordinary man, but *must* hate the extraordinary . . . ? *Because I testify of it, that the works thereof are evil.*

So Your Son spake, and so it is.

But the vast majority of those who heard Nathan Vickery, and who witnessed his powers, testified with great enthusiasm that he was indeed blessed by the Holy Spirit, and that he had gifts that went beyond those of the famous preachers of the day. (For it was an era of miraculous events, a time of signs and wonders: there were revival meetings and itinerant preachers and vast crowds that gathered in sports arenas, awaiting salvation; there were healing ministers like the Reverend Aaron Miles, and Sister Hannah Price, and Bill Branham, and Brother Joe Wallace, whose fame spread across the continent; and even locally there was the Reverend Marian Miles Beloff, whose special ministry celebrated the Power of Constant Baptism, and whose congregation numbered in the thousands.) While Nathan himself remained for the most part silent about his gift, those closest to him, his Grandmother Vickery most of all, began to proclaim that he would soon rise out of the obscurity of the Eden Valley and bear witness to all the world of the Gospels and of the fact that the world's nations were entering into the era of Great Tribulation, and that the end was close at hand.

"Seven years of war, of agony and madness," Mrs. Vickery said, while her grandson sat nearby, stiff and uneasy, his face pinched after the ordeal of his preaching (for it was not uncommon in those days, before Nathan could deal with his exceptional gifts more wisely, that he might lose between five and seven pounds in a three-hours' space of time; that his stomach and throat would close up and he might be unable to eat for a day or two afterward, and his grandmother would have to spoon-feed him warm milk and soup), "and then those who survive will be taken up by Christ Himself and His church, and Christ will reign for one thousand years. . . . Nathan knows, don't you, Nathan? It's as he says. It's all in the Bible. But you have to know how to read it, don't you, Nathan?"

And he would murmur an assent, his thin hands clasped, his gaze dark and brooding and abstracted.

"Nathan is one of God's chosen and he knows, he *knows*,"

Mrs. Vickery said passionately. "And in time all the world will know."

He was a polite, dutiful grandson, courteous with all his elders, never minding that Reverend Sisley either nodded, smiling, without hearing what he said, or asked him to repeat himself again and again, chiding him for mumbling; never minding that Mrs. Sisley had him running up and down stairs on errands, or down the road to the store for supplies, as if he were a servant; patient with members of Reverend Sisley's congregation who sought him out in secret, wishing to bare their souls to him, only to *him*, as if he had the power of forgiveness, as if he were Christ Himself. (They pleaded with him to cure their illnesses, to relieve their "heaviness of heart"; they begged him to lay his hands upon them though he insisted he had *not* the power of healing; a woman once journeyed to him from the Moran Creek area, bringing with her a deaf-mute child of nine who appeared to be retarded, or brain-damaged, and could he make the child well? — could he make the child normal?) Toward boys and girls his own age he was abstracted, remote, not shy as much as simply inattentive; unaware of them as young people like himself. Or perhaps he did not consider himself a young person, perhaps he did not consider himself human at all . . .

He had been attending school only sporadically since the seventh grade, and at the age of fourteen he dropped out altogether. What was the purpose of such learning, why should Nathan Vickery, of all people, sit at a cramped desk and memorize historical dates and lists of presidents and kings and wars, and do ridiculous mathematical problems, and diagram sentences . . . ? All his teachers readily agreed he was a remarkable child: there was something uncannily wise about him, something aged and remorseless and unsettling. He had not much information (in history he always scrambled dates, literally transposing numbers as if such details not only did not matter but were altogether absurd; in mathematics his brain simply balked, and he could not see that a term known as an *answer* was related in any inevitable way to another term known as a *problem*), but he possessed an unmistakable knowledge, a knowingness that transcended mere facts. "He's a genius," one of his teachers said uneasily, wanting him gone from the class. "He doesn't need anything we can offer him," the principal of the school said, smiling, uneasy as well (for Mrs. Vickery's manner had become more and more imperial as she aged, growing ever more stately and massive), wanting him gone from the school. "And the other students are so troublesome, it's impossible to control them, what can any of us do? Your Nathan is obviously going to be a man of God; what can *we* offer him that he needs . . . ?"

So he quit school, and it was a relief to him to be freed of the boxlike classrooms and his teachers' expectations and the rough, noisy, unpredictable companionship of his classmates, whose hostility had upset him less than their awed interest. They did not puzzle him, for they were his brothers and sisters in Christ, and if they mocked him, well, it was familiar enough, for hadn't Christ been mocked before him . . . ? Struck by a green pear or a rotten apple or a hunk of mud, brayed at by a six-foot farmer's boy, *Your mamma's a whore, you ain't got any daddy, funny-looking scrawny skinny Vickery*, or approached by one of the more intelligent boys or girls in whom the agitated love of Christ was blossoming, Nathan felt equally clumsy, for the world of the schoolhouse and the schoolyard was not *his* world; not his domain. He was conscious of the authority of his teachers and did not want to interfere with it, did not wish to set his own authority in opposition to theirs, though he realized it was a higher authority and that his wisdom went far beyond theirs. His time would come, his kingdom would be revealed. He was not impatient.

After leaving school, however, he made an effort to continue his education. Unlike certain men of God whom he had met, Nathan felt no pride in ignorance; and it was necessary that he know enough to combat Christ's enemies when he encountered them. He believed the Devil tempted those who knew too little even as he tempted those who knew too much. A genuine call would eventually take him everywhere in the United States, across the continent, and to foreign lands. . . . Must he know foreign languages? Must he be capable of speaking with foreigners in their own languages? Or would God somehow aid him when the time came? He did not know. He worried that he must learn French, German, Russian . . . Chinese . . . Italian, Spanish . . . African dialects. . . . Marsena had no library, and they rarely drove to Yewville; and the library there would not have been very helpful. Must he know the histories of these foreign lands? Must he know *everything* in order to teach the Gospel?

It seemed unfair.

Perhaps that was the wisdom of the truth that *Few are chosen*. . . .

It was a pity, then, that Dr. Vickery's books were lost to him! Nathan could have wept to think of the riches of his grandfather's bookshelves, now gone. The contents of a single shelf might have occupied him for many months. His grandfather had owned not only innumerable books of a scientific and medical nature, and an entire set of the *Encyclopedia Britannica* for the year 1934, but odd, slim volumes of philosophy and verse, some of them in foreign languages. French, was it? Or Latin? Or German? If Dr. Vickery had lived, perhaps he would have been able to teach Nathan these languages. . . . Perhaps they would have been able to converse.

But he had not lived. And Nathan's grandmother had gone about industriously throwing his things away: his few decent clothes to the Salvation Army in Yewville and the rest — the tattered sweaters, the baggy and stained trousers, the frayed shirts, a shapeless hat — to the refuse dump outside Marsena, along with other personal items and all his books and journals. A full afternoon's labor it had been for Mrs. Vickery and Nathan, lighting with caution the gasoline-drenched things and raking them over and up to meet the air so they would burn thoroughly. Heavy hardback books, the old ocarina, a skull (whether human or plaster Mrs. Vickery did not care to determine) found at the bottom of a drawer, gloves with holes in the fingers, old bedroom slippers worn thin. "It's better so," Mrs. Vickery said, flushed with effort. "The clothes are no good to anyone and the other things are worthless, and the books — well, the books haven't any place in Marsena. They're what led him astray in the first place."

Nathan tried to protest, but both Reverend Sisley and his wife agreed that the books and journals should be destroyed. What were they but godless creations, the Devil's work perhaps . . . ? Since there was never any mention of God in those books and journals it might be interpreted that the Devil had cleverly guided their authors, who were blind and deluded men like Dr. Vickery himself; atheists who pretended to knowledge they did not possess. In any case there was no one in Marsena who could read them, and it would have been a sin had they been allowed to fall into children's hands.

Watching the books burn, squinting against the sullen ponderous smoke that rose from them, Nathan wanted to protest again: Couldn't he have just one of the books? Just one? But Mrs. Vickery was rather agitated and he knew what she would say; it was pointless, it would have upset her, it would have been cruel. And after all, Christ had said clearly enough that man cannot, by taking thought, add a single cubit to his stature.

Mrs. Vickery and the Sisleys agreed that Nathan might acquire a globe or a book of maps, however, since it was possible that someday in the near future he would travel great distances in the service of the Lord. "I can't see anything harmful in that," Reverend Sisley said with a smile. So Nathan borrowed a world atlas from one of his former teachers and spent many hours studying it. The world . . . the *earth*. He grew unaccountably excited when he scrutinized the maps, nearly as excited as when he read Scripture aloud to himself; his fingers stroked the smooth pages as if he were blind and compelled to seek a secret wisdom. How strange the book seemed to him, how puzzling, how exquisitely mysterious. . . . He exhausted himself in his effort to grasp the concept of the earth as a mental construct, partitioned into sections, contained within a *book*. At times his head ached with the strain of trying to comprehend. For it was a paradox, wasn't it? — that there was a geographer's idea of the earth set out clearly and neatly in the pages of a book, and a real earth, an irrefutably real earth, that carried the geographer and all the rest of humanity with it, hurtling through space? He tried, he tried very hard for weeks, to "see" the larger earth in terms of its representations in the atlas: nations, continents, hemispheres. And most crucial of all he tried to "see" the earth as God's earth, His original creation, still living, still in the process of being created. The effort made Nathan feel faint and slightly ill. Never did the Bible puzzle him, since he read it, in a sense, from the inside — as if God-in-Nathan were writing the Bible even as he read it; but the world atlas puzzled him. Ah, how was it possible that men matched neat little diagrams in their heads with the vastness of God's creation! How was it possible they could delude themselves into doing so, century after century? He walked alone in the fields, along the river, along the highway. He studied the hilly, jagged terrain that should have been familiar to him, and the look of the sun in the sky, and the *precise* look of the clouds in their ever-changing design. And it seemed to him vanity that men should attempt to cram the wide earth into their books, as if by doing so they might conquer it.

It was given to him to know that, when the time came, the Lord would provide sufficient knowledge for him — sufficient for him to conquer the earth in his own way. When the time came.

Since that evening in June, just before his twelfth birthday, when Christ in His infinite mercy had helped him to defeat the sin of pride in himself, Nathan had acquiesced in his fate. He realized that his destiny had been set for him from the start of the world, from the very beginning of time. It was not simply that he refused to question his destiny, but that there was nothing in him that might question it. Who was he to set himself apart from his fate — ?

It was clear that he dwelt in a body, that he animated a machine-like body that was somehow *his*, his responsibility; it was clear that this body, especially the face, was known to the exterior world as *Nathan Vickery*. Inhabiting this machine, this fleshly shell, he existed only for the glory of God, and when he was not actively preaching the Gospel or studying the Bible or speaking with God or Christ, he did not really exist at all.

"Exist . . . ?" Nathan thought. "Do I exist . . . ? But in what way, and why? And *how?* . . . It seems so unimportant."

He dwelt high in a tower, behind the eyes, the living eyes, of a creature known to the world as *Nathan*. But he was not Nathan: and surely Nathan was not himself. For this creature, this fleshly thing, had come into the world at a certain moment in time, on a certain date — June 30, 1940, his birth certificate declared — while he himself had lived from all time, before time; in eternity. There were fellow Christians who wept that they had drifted from God, or that God ceased to hear them, but Nathan found it difficult to comprehend that any human being at any time was capable of imagining himself *not* with God. "But how is God apart from you?" he would ask these suffering people, these sinners, in his gentle childlike wondering voice. "Don't you feel Him with us now? At this very moment? *Here? Now?*" He was bewildered, he half-thought such people were misrepresenting themselves to him for some unfathomable reason. Reverend Sisley himself came to him in secret and asked him questions about the Bible, problems that had been bothering him for many years. The Creation: the Incarnation: the Resurrection: the Tribulation to come, and the Rapture, and the Last Judgment: the old man believed all these things, and accepted them, but what did they *mean?*

"What do they *mean?*" Nathan asked, astonished.

"I know they are true, I know the Bible sets the truth before us," the old man said slowly, almost drawling, "but . . . but. . . . But what does it all mean, Nathan?"

Nathan stared at Reverend Sisley, his eyes filling with tears of pity. For it was evident that the old man had come to the very end of his ability to comprehend Your existence: he stood like a man before a darkened glass, rubbing desperately at it to clear away a space for his vision, not knowing that what he does is futile. Nathan answered him gently enough, saying, "There is no meaning. There is only God."

"*There is only God . . . ?*" the old man said, grimacing with the effort to understand. "But. . . . But. . . ."

And he fell silent, his lips quivering.

All men cannot receive this saying, save they to whom it is given, Nathan thought. But he did not say these words aloud, since he did not wish to hurt the Reverend Sisley's feelings. And it would have been futile anyway, would it not . . . ? For only those with ears are capable of hearing.

"There is only God," he repeated, "and all meaning arises from God. We dwell in God, and God in us. Those of us who are chosen by God must work the works of Him that sent us while we can, for the night comes when no man can work: why question the meaning of what we do? It's our heartbeat," he said softly, strangely, so that the old man drew back a little, in awe of him, "it's the very motion of our blood. . . . Do you hear it? That whispering, that fluidity?"

The old man stared at him, uncomprehending. He was too baffled even to nod as he usually did.

"To talk of *meaning* — !" Nathan said, his face contracting with revulsion. "To talk of *meaning* in the presence of our Lord!"

iv

What was his life?

A vapor.

So it is written: a vapor that appears for a short while and then is gone forever.

Yet it had the feel, the sensation, of permanence. There were times when it appeared to slip out of his body . . . when he was highly excited or fell into a swoon; and always when Christ approached. Was it his soul, his breath, his unfathomable incalculable *life* . . . ? It had the capacity of detaching itself from his body in an instant and flying free, like a butterfly borne along by a surprising gust of wind, or even like a scrap of paper. From a distance he might then be a witness to his own physical being, left behind in a state of unconsciousness or paralysis. He could hear what was being said and he could see with absolute clarity the anxious expressions on his grandmother's face, and the queer pinched blankness of his own face, but he felt no real alarm, for You were always close beside him. *There is nothing to fear*, You whispered, *so long as you obey me*.

At other times the body made its claim; the body pulled at him slyly. He found himself inhabiting his body like liquid filled to the very brim of a vessel, quivering as the vessel quivered, stirred at times to an odd reckless excitement.

What were the senses? What did they mean? How was the soul attached to them? The sense of sight especially puzzled Nathan, for it seemed to him that above all it was through the eyes that the world sprang into one's soul. "Is it possible that the Devil reigns over the senses?" Nathan wondered. "Wanting only to distract us from You. . . ."

Even when he was preaching the Gospel, standing before a packed church, even then his senses tugged at him, played with him, sought to distract him. Odd pricks and flashes of merriment, perversity, rudeness, anger — surely it was the Devil tormenting him! He existed only for the glory of God and so he knew that the exterior world should not matter. It should not *matter*. He was addressing souls and not people; not bodies, certainly. The bodies sat in pews or in folding chairs, the faces were turned toward him, eyes fixed upon him, but he was not addressing those illusory shapes: he was a soul speaking directly to the soul of another, and of another, one individual at a time. As Christ brought about the salvation of each individual singly so did Nathan, Christ's servant, hope to bring individuals to salvation one by one. There was no *crowdedness* in God's Kingdom.

Yet, as he spoke, certain quirkish, unsettling thoughts buzzed about him. He would have liked to flee from them, to dart away and abide with You until such time as the thoughts died down, but evidently it was not within his power to detach himself from his temporal body; only through Your grace might the miracle occur. And it could never be anticipated. He had to tolerate his doubts even as he despised them. One of the things that puzzled him was the fact of other people — whether they were physically real as his senses seemed to indicate, or whether their fleshly appearances were as illusory as he knew his own to be. There was no doubt but that God existed, for God animated everything. And Christ had gripped him so hard, and so cruelly. . . . Christ existed, Christ was certainly more than a vapor. But Nathan could not be sure whether he himself existed, and whether other people existed. The flesh was ephemeral, after all. It ripened, rottened, passed away. The spirit abided forever. This he knew. What was the self but a pinprick, a point of light, existing somewhere behind the eyes . . . ?

In the beginning was the Word. So there were words. Inevitably: words. The Bible was words, and he, as a supporting preacher, as a young man beloved of God and of his followers, must immerse himself in words. Did it matter what he said? Did they listen carefully to what he said? They heard the music of his voice, they gazed upon the motion of his hands, and were brought to tears by what he represented. It was said that an unearthly glow danced about him at times, when he was most transported out of himself, preaching, and he did not doubt that the phenomenon was witnessed, though he had no true awareness of it himself.

Yet he was hardly perfect; he felt himself marred and soiled and degraded. For even as he stirred his listeners to tears and to ecstatic outbursts — cries of *Amen* and *Yes* and *Thank you, Jesus* that appeared to be ripped from the very flesh of his people — his senses wandered, he was troubled and distracted, his gaze darted everywhere and would not be still. Leading a prayer meeting on the second night of a four-day Celebration of Praise arranged by an interdenominational organization in Kincardine, standing on the makeshift platform beneath a fairly large tent, knowing himself to be in perfect control of his voice and his gesturing hands, he was nevertheless keenly aware of certain individuals in his audience. It was foolish, it was an error, to be so very conscious of one or two or three people, when all that mattered was the communion of souls, the souls of strangers stirred by his words: which were not *his* words but those of God. He was merely a vessel, he was merely a pathway for God's love to be channeled into the world; he knew himself insignificant, transparent. Yet he could not always control his vision. Though he spoke calmly and then with rising excitement, and then calmly again, though the words he said flowed from him with never the slightest hesitation or stammer, it was as if a part of him edged away from that powerful melodic voice, claiming its own freedom.

("How did you learn to speak so well?" other ministers asked him. They were respectful enough but curious, almost doubting his youth; as if he must be older than he appeared. Nathan could not explain, and so they turned to Reverend Sisley, or to his grandmother. *Take no thought how or what ye shall speak: for it shall be given you in that same hour what ye shall speak.* Was it possible these men of God did not understand . . . ? Nathan wondered, and not for the first time, whether other people were as close to God as he himself was, and whether they understood God's wisdom as much as they claimed. The gorgeous rhapsodic language of the Bible sounded through him, the Holy Ghost descended into him and spoke through him, how could they fail to recognize it? And yet they stared and gaped at *him*, at Nathan Vickery! As if he had created himself!)

Yet his gaze wandered. A fragment of his consciousness broke free of his speaking voice and seemed to stand apart from him, judging him. How strange he appeared, this "Nathan Vickery" whom so many local people admired! His eyes were darkly bright and glittering, his skin was pale, hot-looking, fiercely ascetic, his hair, falling to about the level of his jaw, swung ragged about his face. He had come to resemble one of the Sunday-school pictures of Joseph as he met his brethren: the gaze dark and urgent, the brows knitted, the lips rather dark also, grape-colored. A creature, a living presence; yet what had it to do with *him* . . . ?

Most disturbing of all was his consciousness of certain individuals in his audience. It was not their souls he saw, but their
external appearances; something about them drew his gaze to
them compulsively, maddeningly. He *could* not force himself to
remain unmoved . . . ! In Kincardine his eye alighted upon a
red-haired, plump boy in the third row, who sat with his mother
on the aisle. A child of about eleven, wearing horn-rimmed
glasses, baby-faced, yet smirking — his lips curled upward in a
queer hateful grimace. How was it possible, Nathan wondered,
even as he continued speaking, how was it possible that the child
refused to be moved by him but set himself in stubborn opposition to the love Nathan offered? While on every side of him
people were profoundly absorbed in Nathan's words . . . ? And
he had noticed a girl in the front row, far to the left, also rather
plump, who in coming into the meeting had pushed her way
through the crowd, stony-faced, her mouth set in an attitude of
derision. *She* was the most disturbing, so he made every effort to
keep from looking at her. When it was necessary for him to turn
in her direction he tried to prevent his gaze from slipping onto
her, warning himself that the mere sight of her would be painful
and would arouse worrisome doubts. Yet it was hard to blot her
out. She sat stoutly in her folding chair, staring boldly at him,
unsmiling, as if in disgust. And her hair was alarming: black and
wild and frizzy as unraveled rope. . . . Nathan tore his gaze from
her and continued speaking. But he found himself looking at
another face, this one at the very rear of the tent, belonging to a
gaunt-cheeked man of middle age, in farmers' overalls. He too
was unconvinced, he too stared coldly at Nathan, unmoved.
When Nathan led the group in a hymn the man only pretended
to sing, mouthing the words without enthusiasm — A *mighty
fortress is Our God* — while his expression remained unchanged.

They were sinners, Nathan knew. Unrepentant. They resisted
him, and in resisting *him* they resisted Christ.

But he too was a sinner, to allow himself to be so distracted. It
maddened him, and frightened him, that he should be so helpless
— that he should fail to control his thoughts. Even as he

preached Christ's Gospel he was divided against himself, his gaze seeking out — of the nearly two hundred people before him — those several individuals who resisted him, as if he were no more than a petulant child who must always have his way and must always be loved.

What did it matter that at any prayer meeting or Sunday service there would be individuals who held themselves apart from the rest . . . ? When other preachers spoke and Nathan was in the audience, he was well aware of their frequent failures, he could easily sense the boredom and indifference of the audience; and there was no doubt that he himself was a superb speaker, far more successful than most. Yet his gaze kept drifting back . . . drifting back to the smirking red-haired boy and the censorious farmer and the girl with the frizzy black hair. Had Christ faced these people? Had Christ triumphed over them? Or had they mocked Him, had they placed themselves at the very front of the crowd that gawked at His pain-racked body on the cross? Nathan felt a touch of terror, of panic, that he *must* move these individuals. The others were assured: they were his. Some wept openly, some were making their way forward to the mourners' bench, declaring themselves for Jesus. He had them, he knew them, for years now he had been drawing them to him, his impassioned voice dropping to a whisper and then rising again in a curious plaintive wail, almost a cry, that was peculiarly his own. These were the sinners who stumbled forward to be saved, and were saved, but their declaration of faith in God had been preordained from all time and Nathan could not be genuinely surprised by them. It was the others who fascinated and challenged him. He felt that he must reach out and touch them, grip them tight, force them into submission. . . .

In the confusion he lost sight of the farmer and the red-haired boy. People were in the aisles now, pressing forward. Nathan stood with his arms outspread, his face dripping sweat, and suddenly he saw the girl again: the girl with the black hair. But she had risen from her seat and was approaching him, like the others. He stared, unable to look away. Stared. The girl's hard, defiant expression had softened, and her cheeks were damp with tears, and she was certainly making her way forward to declare herself for Jesus: making her way forward as Nathan had willed.

A miracle!

Nathan hurried down from the platform, down to where men and women and young people were kneeling on the hard-packed dirt floor. Some were weaving from side to side, declaring their sinfulness and their love of Christ and their desire to be washed in the Blood of the Lamb. Nathan blessed them, blessed them. He was exhilarated despite his fatigue. A miracle! At the end of the row the girl stood, moon-eyed, rapt, speechless. She was staring at him. He had broken through her sullen demeanor, he had conquered her in the name of Christ! She staggered forward as if drunk. Surely she wasn't drunk . . . ? A young woman of about twenty, not exactly fat, with a darkly glimmering rich skin and greenish catlike eyes and magnificent hair that frazzled out about her shoulders as if charged with electricity. It struck Nathan that she was unusually attractive. "Brother Vickery," she cried, "Brother Vickery —" reaching for him, grasping at his hands. She was his height exactly; she swayed on high heels; there was a tense, frantic tone to her rather throaty voice. She didn't appear to be drunk. She smelled of perfume — lilac? "Brother Vickery," she wept, "you have saved my life here tonight . . . you have looked into my heart . . . you have brought me to Jesus after so many years. . . ."

Though Nathan's lips were numb, he heard himself say, as he had said hundreds of times, "Bless you, Sister!"

"You don't know what you have done! You don't know what a miracle it is, a sinner like myself, a lost girl, a *bad* girl. . . ."

Her eyes were glazed with love of him, her lips were moist and slack, her breasts strained against the pink, satinlike material of her blouse. She gripped both his hands tight and pressed against him, sobbing. He could not step aside. Others were crowding him, pulling at him, calling him by name. "Brother Vickery! Brother Vickery! Oh thank you . . . !"

He stared at the girl's face, at her eyes that seemed all pupil.

He squeezed her fingers in his without knowing what he did. A miracle! His heart hammered and he could not break free. There was no voice in him now: no Jesus: he stood paralyzed as his spirit seemed to rush forward, concentrating in his eyes, throbbing in his eyes.

"Oh, Brother Vickery, *thank you*," the girl wept.

Which was how Nathan Vickery first encountered Esther Leonie Beloff.

V

Never did Nathan succumb to love for Leonie, not love of the sort he felt for his Saviour, and for the Lord. Nor did he love her as he loved his Grandmother Vickery. He felt only a coarse, sickening desire for her and a contempt for both of them: clumsy straining flesh-locked creatures as they were.

His lust for her was perverse. It frightened him. He wondered at times if he were going insane. For it was insanity, wasn't it, for one of God's creatures to desire another so violently that God Himself was obliterated — ?

(Nor did it help for him to bring the subject up, in his characteristically shy manner, with her father. The Reverend Marian Miles Beloff with his cold, shrewd, merry eyes, and his gold fillings, and his pitted cheeks that were nevertheless powerfully attractive, was not a man to listen carefully to others, not even to Nathan, whom he came to be very fond of: he nodded vehemently, interrupted, punctuated his own remarks with bursts of hearty laughter. At times he appeared to know what Nathan meant, but to discount it. At other times, near the end of their relationship, he appeared to know what Nathan meant and to feel a sort of impatient exasperation for the boy, as if he did not mind Nathan's depraved lust at all and wished only not to hear of it.)

In her stockinged feet she stood only about five feet four. She was feisty-chinned, always in high spirits, always acutely conscious of her appearance. She wore off-the-shoulder blouses when she dared, and colorful skirts, and patent-leather belts that pulled her waist in tightly so that her hips swelled; she loved jewelry of all kinds — imitation pearls looped carelessly about her neck, crystal earrings, a rhinestone brooch in the shape of a horseshoe. Her red-velvet jewelry box was stuffed with gifts from admirers, bracelets and chains hopelessly tangled together, ornaments with jewels missing, single earrings. Much of the time she wore, proudly, a jade cross on a genuine gold chain, which her father had given her to celebrate the start of his gospel program on a Port Oriskany radio station.

Of course she was a believer, an ardent Christian. Her own father had performed her baptismal immersion many years ago, dunking her in a cold-running creek, and she had risen sputtering and giggling, washed in the Blood of the Lamb. "It happened once and it's good for all time," she told Nathan lazily. "I don't *need* to think about it." She spent most of her time going to movies, reading comic books, attending to her hair and her clothes and her nails, and housekeeping for her father whom she loved dearly, though the house overlooking Lake Oriskany was fairly large. But she didn't want any maids poking around in their business — especially not any blacks. "People are always trying to worm their way into my father's life," she said, "and I wouldn't doubt but that they'd sell his toenail cuttings and bits of his hair — you know, like whatdoyoucallit, that the Catholics have — relics? Relics. People are so *stupid*." She was the lead singer on his radio program, performing sometimes by herself and sometimes with the Gospel Choir, a group of five young women and six young men who sang hymns in rich, quavering, honeysweet tones. Her voice was surprisingly strong. When she sang she shut her eyes, and her expression took on a stark, spiritual quality, a look of vague alarm. Her skin gleamed with health, her teeth were broad and white, her very flesh seemed to strain proudly against her clothes. Her favorite hymns were "The Old Rugged Cross" and "Rock of Ages," which usually brought tears to her eyes though she had sung them hundreds of times since she had begun her career at the age of four. ("I think of the rock as a pillow," she told Nathan, raising her shoulders in a shiver of delight, "with a kind of crease or hollow in it that you could crawl into to hide and nobody would ever find you.")

She was not illiterate: she could read the newspaper if she took time, and headlines never gave her any trouble. She liked to puzzle over cartoons, she was very much moved by love comics and screen romances, and she was able to pick out the tunes of popular songs on the piano, hit or miss, without any sheet music at all. Nathan disliked the sort of songs he sometimes happened to hear on the radio, he thought the music rude and profane and some of the lyrics unclean, but Leonie had a craving for them and sang them under her breath, mixed in with gospel songs, as if there were no real distinction. "Music is music," she said, raising her plucked, arched eyebrows. "It's all to beautify the world, isn't it? I like to spread a joyful noise." Reverend Beloff disapproved of her painting her fingernails and rinsing her hair in a blue-black dye, since his radio listeners would disapprove if they knew, but Leonie paid him no mind. She offered to give *him* a rinse and to trim his eyebrows, which were getting old-mannish lately, straggly iron-gray hairs going in all directions. It was quite likely that his gospel program would be taken up by a local television network for Sunday mornings at nine and he should naturally look his best.

Both Reverend Beloff and his daughter, Nathan soon discovered, were lazy, vain, utterly charming people, unlike anyone he had known in Marsena. They were both physically attractive though somewhat big-boned, and their faces were unusually large and broad, drawing all attention to them, absorbing all the light in a room. They were short-tempered, peevish, silly, and exas-

perating, and yet they were firm believers: God and Christ and
the Holy Ghost were real to them as living people and, like living
people, they were capable of being deceived. God played hide-
and-seek with mankind during the week but was likely to be
ever-present on Sundays, fiercely intrusive on one's actions and
thoughts. Still, He could be misled and deceived, as certain
clever Old Testament figures knew very well. The important
thing, Reverend Beloff, tried to explain, was simple love for God
and fellow man and faith in the Scriptures and what else matters?
— not a thing! Officially he did not smoke or drink strong bever-
ages of any kind, not even coffee, not even cola (which was
known as "dope" and which certainly did contain caffeine), nor
did he participate in gambling of even a mild type — not even
checkers or gin rummy; he talked repeatedly to his congregation
about poverty, celibacy, humility, and the need to be reborn —
baptized, in fact — every minute of every day. All of which he
certainly believed. Though he frequently drank and often
smoked cigars and had an uncanny gift for choosing winning race
horses (only, he explained, if he didn't use his brains but simply
scanned the list of horses and allowed his pulses to flutter mysteriously at the right name), though he owned a fair amount of real
estate in Port Oriskany and Derby and North Yewville (which
would, he believed, expand like crazy in the next decade), and
had several very casual mistresses in the state, and was so vain he
sometimes wore corsets beneath his powder-blue suits, and
makeup on his smallpox-scarred cheeks, and a wide-brimmed
black hat of the softest imaginable wool, fashioned in London,
still he was not a hypocrite: he *did* believe in the superiority of
his beliefs, even when he was not inclined to practice them. "The
Lord God," he often bellowed over the air, "is a mighty fortress
— a Rock of Gibraltar. There ain't anything much you can do to
injure *Him*. You can turn and walk away and come crawling back
on your hands and knees, and He's just gonna pick you up in the
palm of His mighty hand and give a good chuckle, you know? On
account of He *ain't* susceptible to every little breeze and quiver
originating in the world of man! No He ain't! He's above all

humankind's pettiness and sees into every heart and sees both forward and back, and there ain't anything that would shock Him, not any little piddling sin at all. He's ready to forgive if *you're* ready . . . if you're ready to be baptized anew every moment of every day." And then he would go on to explain his special theology of baptism, which had saved thousands of souls thus far, and which was set forth in easy-to-read detail in a booklet he had written, "The Power of Constant Baptism," available to his listeners for $1.98.

For radio and preaching purposes he possessed a liquid-smooth voice, but in ordinary conversation he spoke raspily, interrupting himself often. In bright sunlight his eyes ached, so he wore glasses with blue-tinted lenses. Nathan had known the man for several months and had been his First Assistant for six weeks before he discovered, quite by accident, that Reverend Beloff's left hand was not a hand at all — he had lost his flesh-and-blood hand as a child of nine, in a threshing machine, and had worn a hook for a while, and had then been fitted out with an artificial flesh-colored hand, complete down to imitation fingernails and dark hairs on the knuckles, by an admirer who owned an artificial limb factory in Des Moines. "Why, boy, you look white as a sheet!" Reverend Beloff laughed. "All on account of this-here *thing*? You'll get used to it, son. Get used to everything in time."

Nathan stammered that it was a wonderful invention. "It looks the same as a real hand," he said nervously.

After that Mr. Beloff sometimes let his artificial hand fall on Nathan's shoulder heavily, as a joke, just to see him start.

"Us Beloffs just can't take things too seriously," he said. "Not that we're the kind of twice-saved Christians who run around yelling hallelujah every minute of the day. But it's in our nature, so to speak, to figure that if Jesus healed the unclean lepers He will take care of us too. Not that we mean to take things too lightly and backslide: that we would never do. But we like a good laugh, eh?"

Nathan forced himself to laugh in their company, though in fact he rarely understood why they found amusing the things they did. (And what *was* humor, anyway? Why did people break into profane peals of laughter, their faces creasing like infants' faces? What was a joke, why were jokes so valued, so sought-after? He did not quite understand and, humorless, ascetic, vaguely shocked, had the idea that Leonie and her father were pretending most of the time.) It had taken him several days to grasp the fact that Esther Leonie Beloff had simply been pretending to be saved that evening in Kincardine, staggering toward him like a drunken woman, practically falling against him in her gratitude and zeal. And how she had laughed, afterward, her eyes shut tight and her pudgy little chin creasing against her throat: the entire performance had been a fraud, a deception, a joke.

"Leonie shouldn't ought to have done it, not with a hard-working boy like yourself," Reverend Beloff said soberly when they were introduced. "I wanted to meet you, son, and was fully intending to drop in myself after services, you know, but she had to slip in first — always trying to outfox her daddy, playing her damn-silly little jokes. I *hope* you aren't offended — ?"

"No," Nathan said slowly, "I'm not offended."

Leonie giggled, brushing his arm with her own, squeezing his cheek.

"You're just a doll," she said. "You're so *perfect*. I wouldn't ever hurt you, Nathan, not in my whole life. You're *not* offended, then?"

"Of course not," Nathan said. He paused, blushing. Both Beloffs eyed him closely. "I've never been offended in my entire life," he said.

vi

And so it happened that the Reverend Marian Miles Beloff, pastor of the Bethany-Nazarene Church of the Risen Christ, and famous throughout the state for his gospel program (which had

at first been broadcast only once a week, Sunday evenings at
seven, but was soon increased to several times a week because of
listener interest), saw in Nathanael Vickery a means by which
the living message of Christ might be brought to the multitudes.
"No, you certainly don't need to go to any Bible college," Reverend Beloff said impatiently. "That would be a ludicrous waste of
your time. You'd know more than your teachers, you'd be overwhelmed with trivia, and what a loss to America, Nathan Vickery
stuck away somewhere for four years — ! I won't hear of it. I
won't. I'm a graduate of the Eastern Bible Institute myself, and I
have a Bachelor of Divinity from Berklee Theological Seminary,
and a half-dozen honorary degrees, and what do they mean?
Nothing! If I've achieved a modicum of success, my boy, it has
nothing to do with formal training. . . . No, it's entirely a matter
of the Lord's interest in us. His gifts, His power. His energy
channeled into *us*. Your benefactor Mr. Sisley means well, I
suppose, but he knows very little of the world, and after talking
with him for five minutes I came away wondering if he'd even
had a call, to be quite frank; and I'm rather suspicious of this fund
he says he's been raising for you over the years. I asked to see the
account, but he got very nervous and tried to change the subject,
and couldn't seem to hear what I said, so I'm inclined to think
there isn't any money for your tuition anyway . . . or if there ever
was, the old man has siphoned most of it off for his own use.
Does that surprise you, Nathan? It shouldn't. And it shouldn't
matter either. You can put your trust in the Lord and in Marian
Miles from this day onward."

"I don't know," Nathan said slowly. "I would have to think
about it. . . ."

"No, you certainly don't need any formal training. Anyone
who's heard you preach can see in your face and hear in your
voice the unmistakable tones of the Risen Christ, and Bible college would only interfere with your natural gifts. You *don't* want
to be a settled-down Baptist minister with a back-country church,
do you? — or even a city church? You're meant for something
more illustrious, for the most select of the evangelist circuits, for

radio and television, for huge auditoriums and arenas — truly you are! Truly. First you'll begin as my assistant — my First Assistant, in fact — and we'll see what sort of mail and love-offerings you get from the faithful, and every third Sunday or so we'll feature you, and you can lead a Wednesday-evening praise meeting at my church once a month and we'll see about *that*: though I would be very much surprised if the congregation didn't warm to you immediately. I have an eye for success, and an ear. . . . And from what my shrewd little girl has said about that revival hour out in Kincardine, I gather you're one in a thousand and there's not a thing to worry about."

"I would have to discuss it with my grandmother," Nathan said. "She's lived in Marsena all her life and. . . ."

"Can Christ come from Marsena?" Reverend Beloff said shrilly, raising his eyebrows. He stared at Nathan for a long dramatic moment. Then he smiled and leaned back in his chair with his hands clasped behind his head, sighing. "We know the answer to that, don't we? My enemies say I'm slowing down, Nathan, but don't believe them. They spread slanderous rumors out of sheer picklish envy. I'm not slowing down at all, but I do admit to being at that time of life when an afternoon nap is helpful, and I'm about ready to accept with gratitude and humility my followers' offer of a vacation in Hawaii over the Christmas holidays . . . and the prospect of working with a bright and talented young assistant like yourself is pleasing indeed. I can't keep up my break-neck pace forever, after all! I'm only a mortal man, regardless of what some people think. I must watch my health; Leonie is always after me to cut down on fats and starches, the poor child worries so about my health, poor little girl! . . . but I can't blame her, I suppose; I'm all she has in the world and if something should happen to me she'd be alone. So we would both rejoice, Nathan, if you and your grandmother would agree to jump aboard with us and cast in your lot with ours. You *do* have a prodigious talent but at the same time you must learn your craft. I can help you immeasurably with the practical side of theology. . . . You didn't happen to see that slanderous story in the Sunday

feature last month, did you? No? A former associate of mine sold some information regarding me and the Church of the Risen Christ and the Doctrine of Constant Baptism; betrayed me, in fact, as an act of revenge, though at one time we had been very close and he'd been apprenticed to me, in a sense. . . . Not that I harbor any ill wishes against him: it's his privilege, as it was Judas's privilege, to betray whom he will. But as long as you didn't see the shameful, spiteful article. . . . And anyway, my attorneys and I fully expect to receive not only financial remuneration for the insult, but a full-page retraction as well. Otherwise I won't be responsible for what the Lord may decide to do to the guilty parties! . . . I like it, Nathan, that you're so young. Seventeen, are you? So young! Christ was a young man, a very young man. It's His youth, His vitality, His impetuousness, that are so appealing. If He had been, well, my age . . . forty-nine, that is . . . it's possible that certain of His actions would seem inappropriate. Certain of His teachings as well. Or shouldn't I say such things? You seem rather troubled, my boy; I hope I'm not disturbing you."

He got to his feet and walked Nathan to the window of the hotel room, sighing, remarking on the view, sliding his arm around Nathan's slender shoulders. For a man of his size he was surprisingly light on his feet; he gave off a pleasant odor of cologne and tobacco. (He was spending several day in the city as a guest of one of the local churches, having been engaged to help with a building-fund campaign now in its final weeks.) Nathan would have liked to draw away but could not. He stood obediently at the window with Reverend Beloff, staring at the sky, at the mountains in the distance, seeing nothing. Perhaps it had been a mistake to come here. What interest had he in a radio ministry? The possibility of a television program? Huge crowds? He had preached to gatherings of two hundred people, and while the experience had been enlivening in a strange, tumultuous way, he always wondered afterward whether the message of the Lord might not be dissipated in all the excitement. So many people, so many souls, and his solitary soul presuming to address them; wasn't it folly? And the drugged feeling afterward, a dazed euphoria he found very unsettling. . . .

"Lovely view, isn't it," Reverend Beloff said companionably. "The river glittering in the sun . . . and the hills . . . and the fruit orchards . . . and the mountains. Are you from the mountains, Nathan? No? Not exactly? There's so much *space* out there, space and distance and time, the visible universe spread out before us; it makes a man almost dizzy, doesn't it, almost frightened at how small he is. Or don't such thoughts occur to you? You're so young, and the Lord is so much with you, I don't suppose such thoughts do occur to you . . . or possibly . . . possibly any thoughts at all. Ah! To be young again! To be young again, and *you.* . . . I see in you, my boy, a wondrous future. I see in you a means by which the pagan American continent may at last be brought to God. Not that the American people are wicked: not at all! I'm not sure I exactly believe in wickedness, since I've experienced so little of it. Anyway, the Devil takes care of that for us, don't he? — siphoning off the evil for his own purposes. No, the American people are not wicked, Nathan, they are merely pagan and childlike and easily confused . . . and doomed to burn away like vapor in the heat of the sun, unless someone comes to their aid. They are hungry for a true prophet, for a *true* evangelistic voice. They are ravenously hungry for the signs and wonders that attend the coming of one of God's chosen witnesses. . . . It isn't possible for you to deny the Lord, my son. I saw in you from the very first instant of our meeting one in whom the Lord dwells, unmistakably — unmistakably! The yearning in your voice is something I alone can hear, I alone of your hundreds of admirers, for at one time I had it myself . . . and then it was taken from me. . . . But praise be to the Lord, Who works in His own mysterious ways! He ravels and unravels our destinies for us and we cannot resist. What do you say, Nathan? What have you been thinking?"

Nathan was thinking that he would have to spend days in solitude, meditating, before he could hope to confront the Reverend Beloff and his offer. Yet he heard his voice raised in immediate response. "Yes," he said softly.

Someone else had spoken — ?

He had not intended to speak and yet it was his own voice.

"Did you say — yes?" Reverend Beloff asked, delighted.

Nathan hesitated. He did not quite know where he was. Staring into the distance, at the unclear, filmy horizon, aware of a stranger's heavy arm on his shoulders, he felt his throat constrict with an emotion close to panic. Yes. No. But the Lord spoke through him and there was no turning back.

"*Yes*," he said in a whisper.

"Bless you, my son," Reverend Beloff said, deeply moved.

Just as he never regretted any action You led him into, so Nathan did not regret his apprenticeship to Marian Miles Beloff, or his relationship with the Beloffs; though over the months and years he came to suspect that it was, in part, Leonie Beloff who had tempted him into leaving Marsena, and Leonie Beloff who had drawn him most powerfully into his new life.

She was four and a half years older than Nathan. Though she went out often with a number of men, some of them nearly as old as Mr. Beloff himself, she was said to be engaged to a man named Elias Carroll, a deacon in the Bethany-Nazarene Church of the Risen Christ and the owner of a small canning factory. He was thirty-eight years old, a widower with a retarded daughter, a tall, stocky man given to long pauses; he was said to be very devoted to Leonie, though he would not press her to marry him until she was ready. "Oh, he's sweet enough, but not anywhere near like you," Leonie complained to Nathan, poking him in the ribs. "Not pretty like *you*."

"You mustn't distract Nathan from his work," Reverend Beloff said. "You should respect his privacy, dear."

"But I do! I certainly do! I respect everything about him," Leonie said, fixing him with her sly green eyes, winking behind her father's back. "Seeing as how I'm practically engaged to Elias, and practically dwindled into a dowdy old married woman like the ones that fuss around you, Pa, don't I have the right to tease a sweet little boy like our Nathan? I certainly don't mean any *harm*."

She coached him with his part on the Reverend Beloff's radio program, explaining that he must speak slowly enough and clearly enough for the most dull-witted listeners to understand, since they would not be able to pick up any meaning from his facial expressions or the movements of his hands; when Reverend Beloff and his troupe took on a Sunday-morning television program as well, Leonie insisted he come downtown with her to pick out appropriate clothes ("You can look modest, hon, but you can't look *poor* — you don't want to dismay and terrify our audience, do you? They just *hate* being poor and they don't want any reminders!"), and she trimmed his hair herself with a scissors and a razor, since he refused to go to a barber ("I'm not going to shorten it one bit, I just love that kind of *hurtful* way you can toss it around when you get excited; but I think maybe it should be evened up — otherwise you might look lopsided, you know"), and scolded him for grimacing and rolling his eyes when it wasn't necessary and he was just searching for words ("On a platform you can do that all you like, but on television you hadn't better: it picks up the least little shrug and twitch and tic"), and applauded him more than anyone when he did well. She pawed anxiously through each morning's mail, brushing aside even those envelopes that contained cash or personal love-offerings like rings or wrist watches or loose jewels, looking for letters specifically concerning him. ("Listen to this one, Nathan — he thinks you are the very Second Coming itself! And this one, *this* one: the woman is obviously mad with love for you!")

Sometimes she ran her fingers lightly through his hair, sometimes she leaned close to him, suddenly, and blew in his ear. Though other people were around, she thought nothing of lifting his hair and kissing the back of his neck, so that he gave a start and cried aloud; and of course she laughed at him then.

Nathan could not help staring at her. He could not help think-

ing about her. She meant nothing by her behavior; she was almost as impulsive and playful with one of her father's organists
as she was with him, yet he could not keep his thoughts from
drifting onto her. Only when he was totally absorbed in studying
the Bible or preparing his talks or meditating was he freed of
Leonie, and in her presence he became increasingly nervous, so
that it seemed to him everyone must know: must be whispering
and laughing about him.

Why must a man be attracted to a woman, Nathan wondered.
Why *must* it be . . . ? It should not have stirred his blood so
violently, that she pinched him or kissed his cheek or squeezed
his hand, running her thumb lightly across his palm; it should
not have mattered in the slightest. Yet he could not help his
feelings and there were times when he could not stop himself
from staring at her, frankly and openly. A kind of knife thrust
seemed to jolt him through the eyes when she appeared: he simply could not control it. Leonie in her pink-and-white cotton
dress that fitted her tightly across the breasts and was cinched in
at the waist . . . Leonie with several loops of grape-sized imitation pearls around her neck . . . Leonie with her ridiculous rattling bracelets, her gardenia perfume, her square-cut diamond
engagement ring, her open-toed shoes with the amazing spike
heels. . . . A glistening, pulsating, heedless life shone through
her; it seemed to leap into him from her, without her awareness.
Almost from the start of their acquaintanceship Nathan began to
dream about her, waking in horror as every nerve-end in his body
fused to a scalding needle point, and broke, and spilled: though
he groaned aloud for deliverance, there was none. And he came
to see that she was unclean, that her playfulness was really the
Devil's work, and that God Himself must have wished for Nathan
to be confronted with her so he might triumph over the temptation of the flesh she represented.

He puzzled over the situation for days at a time. Why must a
man be attracted to a woman, or to any manifestation of the
world at all? For the friendship of the world is enmity with God.
And the exterior, physical aspect of another human being is the

least significant part of that human being. He puzzled over the riddle, he meditated upon it, he knelt and put the question to Christ Himself. God *is*: acts through: fills all of His creatures completely. Wasn't that so? There was a kind of aura around people that Nathan sometimes saw clearly, and this aura rendered the physical aspect of their being inconsequential, for it suggested that only the interior, only the spiritual, was genuine. He did not *care* what others looked like — he did not really *see* them. Nor did he think of himself in visual terms. (After meditating for hours he lost all awareness of himself as a physical creature and could not have said who, or what, he was: his existence was reduced to a pinpoint of consciousness that seemed to be floating in a lightless, colorless void.) Since all are God, and all is God, there should be no attraction of one aspect of God to another, but only the brotherly affection of like for like. Nathan was well aware of the vulgar jokes that circulated about revivalist preachers and their attraction to young converts — young women whom they touched and embraced sinfully while the women were transported by the joy of the Lord; to his astonishment, Reverend Beloff himself sometimes made such jokes. But Nathan truly felt no differently toward those converts who were attractive young women than he did toward men, or toward the elderly, or the crippled, or sick, or dying: his hours with God had allowed him to know that one soul was as another, that God was all in all. Even the commonplace sentiment that we are all brothers and sisters in Christ was finally irrelevant, since the soul possessed no sexual differentiation.

The several incidents of Nathan's "healing" had occurred when his vision was obliterated and he seemed to be somehow within the sufferer's consciousness, in complete union with the other's soul. Like a man standing in a darkened cave with a flashlight in his hand, Nathan was able to penetrate the darkness surrounding the other person, and to discern the cause of sickness. A gluey black substance, vile and clotted, squidlike, sluglike: an element foreign to the other's nature: which he was able to drive out, as if it were something living. (*Was* it in fact a living creature, a devil? Were such things, which seemed to Nathan rather more like thoughts, snarled and ugly and deathly thoughts, what Christ had seen as devils and had driven out of the afflicted?) At such times Nathan was carried far out of himself, in a kind of trance, no longer conscious of his actions; nor did he have any real wish to know what he did, for fear it would lessen his effectiveness in the future. He did not care to stress this side of his ministry, since it didn't seem to him that God had called him to it in any clear way. And Reverend Beloff was uncharacteristically cautious: "I'm fearful of introducing anything so controversial in our campaign for souls, Nathan, at least at this time, on account of the competition, for one thing, and for another the risk of law suits — do you know about that two-million-dollar suit pending against Sister Price out in Kansas for allegedly contributing to the death of a diabetic child? — and right here in the state that snake-handling preacher who was arrested and sentenced to a prison merely because some idiot squeezed a rattlesnake too tight and it bit him and he fell over dead! — as if *that* was the preacher's fault, when it must have been ordained from all time! It's a touchy, highly specialized area of service, Nathan, and you have got to do an exhaustive amount of screening before you let the afflicted onto your program. . . . Christ Himself, now: you only hear of His successful cases, right? And you don't know how long the lepers remained cured and the dead stayed above ground and the devils kept their distance from those they were driven out of."

It seemed to Nathan obvious that the only reality was interior and invisible, and that the senses — particularly the sense of sight — lied, and when he was most himself, most united with God, he knew this to be so. But the rest of the time he was baffled, even a little chagrined: even a little angry.

Leonie Beloff! Noisy, gleaming with perspiration and good health and high spirits, hurrying about in her absurd high heels, her hair flying; kittenish, spoiled, insolent, crude, utterly charming. The Devil peered at Nathan through the young woman's pale green eyes. The Devil smiled and winked at him. Nathan

would have liked to shield his own eyes, to turn away in alarm.
Or he would have liked to seize Leonie by her plump shoulders
and shake her until her teeth rattled. *Stop! What are you doing!
Why are you tormenting me!* She was unpredictable as a small
child, and as outrageous. At a banquet in the basement of the
Bethany-Nazarene Church, a creamed-chicken-on-biscuits supper in honor of a visiting missionary, Leonie tapped her father's
artificial hand with a spoon, playing on the fingers (which gave
off an eerie hollow sound, vaguely musical); another time, only a
few seconds before their television show began, she let loose an
enormous yellow butterfly in the studio, saying it was the Spirit
of Creation; her costly engagement ring was returned to Mr.
Carroll inside a chocolate cupcake she had baked herself. Nathan
noted, and was disturbed by, the fact that she deliberately won
over his Grandmother Vickery — who by all odds should have
detested her — by presenting her with little gifts: ceramic birds
she had made herself in the church's Arts and Crafts class, hand-
kerchiefs with Mrs. Vickery's initials embroidered on them, pots
of African violets, Fanny Farmer chocolates, rhinestone
brooches. "She's a little flighty but goodhearted," Mrs. Vickery
said. "The important thing isn't whether a girl has a loud, raucous
laugh or not, but whether she's generous and considerate of others." (As Nathan's position with the Beloff troupe became more
secure, and his reputation grew, Mrs. Vickery became increasingly gracious; she wore long dresses of dove gray or magenta or
dark brown with full sleeves, dresses that resembled party gowns,
and her iron-gray hair was bleached to a lovely snow-white, and
waved every Friday afternoon at a downtown hairdresser's, and
she spoke calmly of the probability of the coming of Christ within
her grandson's lifetime: since it was clear to anyone with eyes and
ears that the world was in the Final Days and the Apocalypse was
close at hand.)

Leonie said of Mrs. Vickery that she was a sweet old girl, tough
as a buzzard, exactly the kind of mother — or was she his grandmother — that Christ Himself would have preferred. "She'll protect you from the multitudes, hon, the women especially,"

Leonie laughed. "Or don't you maybe *need* to be protected from the women . . . ?"

Nathan blushed and tried to change the subject.

He could not have said if he loved Leonie or hated her; or whether, in his deepest self, he had any feelings for her at all. The Devil was only using her, he knew, and she could not be blamed for Nathan's own failings — he tried to make himself remember that important fact. Even the Devil had no power, no reality, except what Nathan allowed. Sin sprang only from the will, the refusal to cleave to God and turn away from the world: sin was more a matter of weakness than misdirected strength.

Nevertheless he feared sleep, and knelt by the side of his bed for hours, hoping to summon God to him. It had been years — many years — since God had manifested Himself to him. The command to humble himself, the agony and the nausea, and the long bout of illness that followed: terrifying at the time but now, he saw, a sign of God's blessing. He would have welcomed even another frightful visitation if it would strengthen his soul, if it would annihilate Leonie Beloff in his sight. . . .

vii

How long will You keep Yourself apart from me, O Lord? how long will You hide Your face from me? How long shall I take counsel in my soul, having sorrow in my heart daily?

The loneliness.

Empty of mind, empty of heart.

Now it is December and very cold indeed and there is nothing to say about my craving for You that I have not already said a hundred times. Early in the morning, before dawn, I walk outside in the snow in my bare feet, hoping to feel pain; hoping to feel something. Overhead the stars are fading. The sky is coarse and

curdled. Sparrows awake in a tumult, in the straggly hedge outside my window, and their frantic chirping mocks the despair of
my soul.

I am no longer ill, it is said. But neither am I well.

Why do You continue to forsake me, seeing that I am broken
in body and mind and spirit these many long months! The cruelty
of Your disregard, the remorselessness; the indifference. For out
of the south comes the whirlwind, and cold out of the north, and
by Your breath is frost given to the earth.

And that is all.

Long ago there was Nathanael Vickery and he dwelled with
You in the blissfulness of utter peace. On the surface of his being
there was agitation, as the surface of a body of water is pricked
and disturbed and appears to shudder and to disintegrate, yet is
constant and whole. Long ago he dwelled with You while he
established himself firmly in the world of man, achieving a success in that world that ordinary men might bitterly covet, and he
had no care for money, no care for fame, or the high regard of
men and women; for it was given unto him to see heaven open,
and the angels of God ascending and descending upon the Son
of man, and though his body exerted itself in this world his spirit
triumphed elsewhere, being of the same substance as Your nature. Why should he have taken thought for his life, for what he
might eat or drink? — for the comforts of his body? He inhabited
a body but was not of it. *Take therefore no thought for the morrow:
for the morrow shall take thought for the things of itself.* So it is
written, and so Nathan believed.

∎ ∎ ∎

"You and I could marry," Leonie said lightly. "You're how old?
— eighteen? — why, eighteen's old enough for anything! First
time I saw you, you were only a boy, skinnier than you are now
and edgy as a weasel and your voice the strangest, hauntingest

sound I ever heard — it just went through me, went through me in waves, and the thought came to me that I already knew you: that we'd met before and would certainly be meeting again."

"Then you played that trick on me," Nathan said slowly.

"Oh no, honey! You were just a boy that first time, no more than twelve or thirteen. It was a few years before Kincardine, I forget where — Rockland, maybe, or the outskirts of Yewville. Which? I just sat there and tears came into my eyes because you were the sweetest, most *controlled* child-preacher I ever heard in my life — like you weren't a child at all, but mature as you'd ever get in this lifetime. No, hon, that wasn't Kincardine and it wasn't the night we met. I just slipped away that first time . . . I didn't come forward to bother you at *all*. Because I knew we'd already met, and that we'd be meeting again soon."

"Maybe you ought not to have come forward at all, ever," Nathan said. "Maybe you should have slipped away that second time too."

"But why do you say that!" Leonie cried, hurt.

Nathan wrapped the rest of his sandwich in a paper napkin and sat immobile, staring at the littered picnic ground.

"*Why* do you say that," Leonie said, snatching the sandwich from him and throwing it away. "You're just spiteful, you're just mean. And anyway my daddy would have sought you out within the year — he'd been hearing about you and he needed a new assistant and it's always been in his head, you know, to get himself a boy protégé because *he* was so young himself when he started out: and my daddy always gets what he wants."

"He wanted you to marry Mr. Dietz but you aren't marrying him," Nathan said.

"Well, I might just marry him! I don't know. I haven't decided."

Nathan saw that she had drained her cup again — was it the second or third — and wondered if he should take the bottle away from her. She glanced at him, seemed to be reading his thoughts, and sloshed some gin into the cup he had set down by his feet. "Go ahead and drink it! Drink it right down! You're not going to sit there like a goddam Methodist or something watching me get drunk and casting me down to hell in your narrow little mind! Go *on*."

Nathan's fingers were trembling so, he could barely grasp the cup handle. Must not let her see. She was staring at him, waiting for him. Impatient. Tearful. "I really don't want —" he began.

"I said go *on*."

He sipped at the gin. An astonishing sensation — something flame-like darting up into his nose, into the cavities of his skull. His eyes watered. He began to cough and could not stop coughing.

". . . avoiding me like I was some nasty contaminated woman," Leonie was saying in a child's perplexed voice, "when all I wanted . . . all I intended. . . . Christmastime, when I gave you that nice sweater I spent two damn months knitting, and you just gawked at it in the box and wouldn't even soil your fingers by taking it out — !"

Nathan wiped at his mouth, confused. He stared at Leonie but could not make sense of what she had just said. Her face was so flushed, her eyes so bright and angry! — it frightened him just to look at her.

"Just mumbled some kind of embarrassed thanks, and that was all! That was *all!*" Leonie cried.

"I didn't —"

"You didn't! Didn't *what?*"

"I didn't mean —"

"Didn't mean *what?*"

In her exasperation she kicked out one long gleaming-smooth bare leg. She was wearing a black-and-white flowered sundress with a halter top that showed her lovely, olivish-tanned shoulders and her plump chest and even the pale tops of her breasts. Nathan narrowed his eyes against the magnificent glare of her and tried to recall the subject of their conversation. He had not wanted to accept Leonie's invitation of a ride in her father's second-best car out along the shore of Lake Oriskany; he had known from the bright, cool, rather sardonic tone of her voice

that she would soon become emotional, yet he had heard himself
accept with alacrity — for he was unable to refuse Leonie when
she truly wanted something from him. *I need counsel about my
future*, she had said mournfully, *and I have no one to talk with
except you*.

"Didn't mean *what?*" Leonie repeated impatiently.

He was staring at her bare legs, at her slender ankles, at her
small pretty feet. Each toenail had been carefully painted a rich
orange-red. The color of ripened peaches. The taste of sweet
ripened peaches. And her fingernails also. And her lips. Nathan
took another swallow of the gin and managed to stifle a cough.
". . . didn't mean to be rude," he gasped.

"Oh! Oh well," Leonie laughed without smiling.

"At first I didn't know, did I, whose present it was . . . I looked
all through the wrapping paper and the tissue and. . . ."

"Oh yes, you had to search out the name of the mysterious
person: oh yes," Leonie said, "you couldn't possibly have
known. . . ."

"Everybody was looking at me," Nathan said, blinking rapidly,
"and I felt like a fool, and. . . ."

"Naturally you weren't a fool, were you?" Leonie said. "Never
in your life. Not our Nathanael Vickery."

Leonie jumped to her feet and ran over to the car and reappeared a moment later with her purse, an enormous russet-
colored straw bag with an over-the-shoulder strap and a big brass
sunburst catch. She fumbled inside, hunting up her cigarettes.
They were in a 14-carat gold case with her initials on it; a love-
offering from an admirer, perhaps. "Don't you dare scowl at me,
my boy! I'll smoke if I want to. I'll do anything I want to. There's
nobody within miles except some boats out there, and even if
there were. . . . *Why* do you look so disapproving all the time?"

"Do I?" Nathan asked, puzzled.

"Even when you're not frowning you're, you know, judging,"
Leonie said with a fastidious shiver, drawing near so she could
gaze down her nose and across her cheekbones at him, "you're
always *aware*. There's you on one side and the object of your pity

or scorn or charity or whatever on the other side. Sometimes I feel," she laughed, "you're going to reach out and hocus-pocus me and cast out my devils — ! And *then* what? Then I'll be so lonely, what will I do?"

Nathan tried to laugh, realizing she was joking: must be joking.

"Even your laughter is a judgment," Leonie said bitterly. "It sounds like goddam sandpaper scraping against itself."

She lit a cigarette with her gold lighter — which *was* a love-offering; Nathan remembered the day it had come by special-delivery mail to the television station — and dropped the lighter and the package of cigarettes back into her purse and let the purse fall into the grass. Though they were both supposed to have dressed for a picnic, Leonie wore open-backed high heels, white, very new-looking, and a half-dozen thin bracelets that clattered with every move of her arms, and a dress with an unusually tight skirt. Nathan had no true awareness of his clothing — a white shirt, a pair of drab dark trousers, dark brown socks and scuffed black shoes. Today was Sunday and he had, of course, worn a tie earlier, and a coat of some kind that matched the trousers. Tonight, when he led the Evening Praise Service at Reverend Beloff's church, he would put the tie and the coat back on. He rarely thought about what he wore, or how he appeared to others, despite Leonie's frequent criticism, and even on the warmest summer days he wound up in his usual outfit, more out of absent-mindedness than indifference.

At the moment he was uncomfortably warm.

"*Look* at you eying the world and finding it wicked!" Leonie cried.

Nathan tried to smile because he knew she was joking, teasing, and that was one of the things that exasperated her — his failure to catch on to her jokes. "I don't find the world wicked," he said uneasily.

"You don't *find* it at all!"

Nathan narrowed his eyes against the angry accusing glare of her face. Though he had had only a swallow or two of the gin, it seemed to him that the very top of his skull had loosened; there was a sensation of ticklish, frightening hilarity in his throat and the upper part of his chest. If only he needn't gaze upon this young woman . . . if only he needn't *stare* at her. For she entered him, pierced him, through his eyes: at the point where he was weakest. Was sin itself always a matter of the senses, Nathan wondered suddenly, and might mankind be freed of the deathliness of sin if the senses were somehow obliterated . . . ? Was it the wish of the Lord that the spirit be reduced triumphantly to a bodiless shimmering indestructible essence that could not be assaulted and violated by the illusory world?

But Leonie was calling to him.

"Look, Nathan, the poor things — Look —"

At the edge of the clearing, where a sparse pine woods began, two very skinny dogs had appeared. A third poked its head around an overstuffed trash barrel.

"They're scavengering for food," Leonie said. "They look so *hungry*."

She stooped to get the half-eaten sandwich of Nathan's that lay on the ground and brought it along with the rest of the picnic food to where the dogs cringed, eying her fearfully. Nathan too came forward, thinking there might be some danger — Leonie was so bright and blithe and talkative that the dogs might be frightened — but nothing went wrong: Leonie simply tossed the food to the dogs, murmuring, "Why, you poor things! You look so hungry! Wherever did you come from, all burdocks and mud-splashed and bedraggled . . . ?"

All three were mongrels, with long ungainly tails. The largest, which was so shy of Leonie and Nathan that it half-crawled along the ground, its back legs grotesquely flattened, must have had a bit of collie blood in it, judging from the contours of its head. Whimpering, barking in short excited gasps, it ate the turkey scraps Leonie gave it in a single paroxysm and then swung around, cringing, and trotted back into the woods. "Poor things," Leonie cried. "Are you lost? Isn't it a shame! Why don't we take one of them back with us, Nathan, this smallest one here — Are you a boy or a girl? Eh? Why are you so afraid of me? I don't have anything in my hands, I don't have anything to hit you with! Wait, where are you going? Oh wait! Aren't there any more leftovers for them? Wait —"

Nathan had found it difficult to concentrate on the dogs. He stood behind Leonie, watching her. Had he dreamed of her like this the night before? The scene was so familiar: even the way sunlight fell broken and splotched upon her bare shoulders was familiar: surely he had been in this place before! There was such life in her, such rich warm lustrous heedless *life*. . . . He should have turned away, he should have shielded his eyes against her. But he could not. He felt lightheaded, not himself, on the brink of doing something outlandish — breaking into laughter or shouting. He joined Leonie in calling after the dogs. "Here! Come back! *Here!* Nobody's going to hurt you!" When Nathan's voice was raised, or when he sang, it seemed to him that a superior power laid hold of him and the voice wasn't *his* at all: it was both melodic and strong, sinuous and graceful, a stranger's startling and rather marvelous voice. (He had discovered while visiting one of Reverend Beloff's charitable institutions — only a home, really, in a converted mansion in a decaying residential section of Port Oriskany — that, no matter how sickly and apathetic people were, they could nevertheless be awakened by song, by gospel songs especially; it almost seemed as if, with the Lord's sudden power, even the mute could discover a voice within them they had not known was there.)

"Poor things! But I suppose they were mangy and diseased, you know, wormy," Leonie said, hunching her shoulders for a moment in an attitude of pity and disdain.

"God has abandoned them," Nathan said slowly. When Leonie turned to him, fussing with an earring, he said in a somewhat louder voice: "God has not abandoned them."

"Oh, no. No, I suppose not," Leonie said. She pursed her lips in a childlike manner and clasped her hands before her; the red-orange nail polish gleamed handsomely. *"Behold the fowls of the air: for they sow not, neither do they reap, nor gather into barns; yet your heavenly Father feedeth them.* And aren't we a whole lot better, my boy, than *them?*"

Leonie stepped laughing into his arms, pressing herself against him, nuzzling her warm face against his shoulder and neck. Nathan was accustomed to her teasing, but the very touch of her alarmed him: he felt sexual desire as if it were a blow, a violent affliction. Blood seemed to drain rapidly out of his head, rushing into the pit of his belly, into his groin. He managed to step aside from Leonie, holding her by the shoulders, trying to be as playful as she. Was she drunk? Pretending to be drunk? It was extraordinary how beautiful she seemed to him, even with her hair wilder than usual and her small snub nose gleaming with a film of oil. Her eyes — but were they, properly speaking, *hers?* or her Creator's? — that faint sly green, so thickly lashed, like a near-transparent stone or shell: her eyes were the eyes of his dream, shining upon him, making their claim.

"Oh you and your silly *Touch me not!*" Leonie laughed. "I always thought that was the most unnecessary and ungenerous and just plain silly thing Jesus ever did, flinching back from his own poor grief-stricken mother like that — imagine! *Touch me not!* Oh just imagine! I wouldn't have tolerated it if I'd been Mary! I wouldn't! *Touch me not; for I am not yet ascended to my Father.* I wouldn't have tolerated half the nonsense of those times! Imagine, for a woman — life for a woman then — just imagine, Nathan! And you're almost as maddening right now, though I believe in your heart you are *really* sweet and loving. . . ."

Nathan laughed and turned away and went back to the picnic table, walking stiffly and self-consciously, knowing Leonie was staring at him. Could she tell? Could she sense? He picked up the bottle of gin, meaning to take it back to the car; meaning they should head for home since it was getting late; but he found himself pouring two more drinks for them instead. . . . And time seemed to pleat, a long delirious moment seemed to swell, and burst, and he heard his own voice inside his head trying to determine whose hands those were, what was the nature of flesh and bone and blood, was there a precise meaning in the arrangement of dark hairs on the backs of his fingers, the particular size and shape and texture of his fingernails, the slightly raised bluish veins on the backs of his hands . . . ? He half-shut his eyes, feeling the pull of the Lord. The light of the day was not sufficient to withstand the powerful pull of the dark, for what meaning had a stranger's thin, trembling hands, what meaning had the cloud-streaked blue sky and the blue-gray waves of the lake and the pines at the periphery of his vision, compared to the signs and wonders of the Lord?

But Leonie gave no heed, Leonie had no idea: she came up behind him and slid her arms around his waist, loosely, playfully, and pressed her cheek against his damp shoulder.

"I don't want to go back. I suppose we should go back. I just love driving a car, this car specially, but I don't *want* to go back . . . the way they yowl those songs it just goes through me like the beginning of the flu! I swear. Wish I could sing even louder than I do and drown the lot of them out and not have to hear *them* . . . and then Daddy smiling like he does and thanking them, saying the Lord must be well-pleased with so much enthusiasm, well — ! I *know* what Daddy is secretly thinking just like I know what I am secretly thinking. And tonight you're in charge, aren't you, and it's like you don't even hear the dreadful flats and sharps and mispronounced and scrambled words; all the noise just whirls around your head and leaves you untouched: which must be a blessing indeed!"

Nathan took hold of her wrists to disengage himself. Then he could not move. His head slumped on his breast, he felt suddenly a sense of paralysis, danger and yet paralysis, as if all the strength had drained out of his body except the strength that beat so cruelly in his groin. Leonie hugged him tight for an instant before releasing him. "Oh a final drink is a good idea," she said airily. "Maybe I won't hear the faithful yowling and bawling myself tonight. Except I have to drive back home: *you* never got around to learning, did you? Or anyway you don't have a license. Imagine, a boy of eighteen not knowing how to drive a car, isn't that the silliest thing — !"

Leonie sipped at the gin. Nathan saw his hand raising his cup in slow motion. A wax-glazed paper cup with a paper handle. The liquid was colorless and clear and yet so powerful. Rising into his brain, clouding his vision. He sniffed several times. He coughed. His coughing echoed curiously in his head so that he thought he heard noise at a distance — the stray dogs barking in the woods. But when the coughing spasm stopped he heard nothing except the usual summer sounds: the thrumming of insects, the calls of hidden birds.

"*You* and I could marry, instead of me and Harold Dietz," Leonie said, sitting back against the picnic table. "You're younger than me but I don't care. Do you? Younger but anyway smarter: some of the time. And wouldn't Daddy be delighted! Oh, he wants you in the family, he truly does! He's just plain jealous of anybody else taking a look at you, like that what's-his-name, the evangelist out of Cincinnati, nosing around with queries about Nathan Vickery! The thing is, hon, and don't ever let on I told you, the thing is that Daddy could pay you more than he does, and there's no need for you and your grandmother to pay us rent for that bungalow, that's all a tax write-off, I think it's just mean of Daddy to keep charging you after all this time! So if this Brother Asa or whatever his name is, if he makes you some kind of an offer, hon, don't just turn it down but come to Daddy with it and make him increase your salary, or anyway come to me and I'll coach you what to say — are you listening? Daddy knows you are worth a lot more than you're getting, there are donations and pledges and inheritances tossed our way because of *you* — in addition to all the money Daddy has naturally been getting by himself — but the thing is, Nathan, he keeps such business matters secret: only him and his attorney and financial adviser know how much the church has now: not even his poor daughter is allowed to know! So you'll have to be very clever, and when the time comes I can coach you, otherwise — But aren't you listening? *Aren't* you? Well, I suppose Christ wouldn't have cared about such things either, I suppose I'm just shallow-minded and cheap and don't understand you at all, no more than I understand Christ — I mean I love Him, you know, and accept Him as my personal Saviour — but — but I don't *understand* Him, that He should get betrayed like that and trapped and killed when he knew all along about Judas and could have escaped — couldn't he? — and maybe lived to be a nice old man, healing people and explaining to them about the Kingdom — ? I don't understand Him and I don't understand you but that's what's so sweet about you, Nathan, and why I think you're so precious; you could be my baby brother sometimes and at other times, when you're preaching, I think *My God! who is he!* — and just sit there hypnotized. And I could listen to you, anything you had to say, just anything, not even what you're saying so much as, as you yourself: your voice. But why are you blushing? You've heard all this a million times now from everybody!"

Nathan stepped toward her, and hesitated. The very sight of her hurt him: his eyes ached. He was trembling. His throat and jaws had gone rigid. If he should shout at her, if he should burst into laughter? — or into tears? He never cried. He had not cried for a decade. Why was he trembling? He finished the gin so that he could set the cup down. Why was he trembling? His eyes flooded with tears and a single tear ran down his cheek. Leonie saw it and leaned forward and licked it with her tongue. Then she kissed him. Nathan put his arms around her and kissed her, on the lips, lightly.

"Don't you like me? Oh you *do* like me, don't you?" Leonie said. "I'm just so fond of you, I'm crazy about you, aren't you sweet — ! Oh you're just so sweet! There's nobody like you in the world!" She lifted her face to him and clasped him around the neck and Nathan found himself hugging her, his palms flat against her back, rigid against her back. He kissed her; in a daze, in a fog. There was such life, such sensation in his lips, in his tongue, it was as if that part of him had stirred into life, strange to him. And Leonie's lips as well. And her warm, damp, writhing body. "Do you like me? Do you love me?" she whispered.

Nathan gripped her tighter, kissing her. He could not stop. She ran both her hands down his back, quite hard; she slid her fingers inside his belt, inside the waist of his trousers, and clasped him tight.

"I don't think anything would be a sin between you and me," Leonie said. "Because we're like brother and sister. In our hearts. Aren't we? Or maybe I am your Mamma? Oh, I would love to be your Mamma! I would take care of you forever and comfort you and cook for you and hold you tight and if any time the world hurt you, why I would be there — I would always be there. There can't be any harm in it, can there? Any sin? Nathan?"

His soul had shrunk, had drained away. There was nothing but Leonie, her flesh, her damp face, her lips. Her arms around his neck. Her dreamlike soft wailing voice. He kissed her more desperately, and pressed his face against her neck, against her shoulder, seizing her around the waist, stooping awkwardly to kiss her breasts. His soul had shrunk, there was nothing but the urgency of flesh, the cruel hard beating pulse of blood, that filled him so that he could have groaned aloud with the pain of it, and the humiliation. "Do you love me? Do you love me?" Leonie whispered. Nathan pressed himself against her, as if wishing in his anxiety to caress the entire length of her body with his, eel-like, desperate, out of breath, impatient. She clasped his head against her. Her fingers closed in his hair. "Nathan? Nathan? Do you love me?" He slipped to his knees clumsily and hugged her around the hips and pressed his face against her belly, whimpering, gasping for breath.

"Oh Nathan maybe you — Maybe you shouldn't —"

She spoke so sharply, in so startled a voice, that he drew back at once. He stared up at her, blinking in amazement.

Leonie straightened her skirt, trying to smile; she brushed his long hair out of his eyes and off his damp forehead. "I mean — you know — maybe you *shouldn't*. I —"

She stepped away from him and he remained kneeling on the ground, panting like a dog. His face burned. Another tear rolled down his cheek and he wiped it away himself, quickly, with his shoulder.

"I'm sorry," Nathan said hoarsely.

"There's no need to be sorry!" Leonie said. "There's no need! I mean — I mean I'm just —"

"I didn't mean to frighten you," said Nathan.

"You didn't frighten me. I mean, I — I just don't — I don't *know* quite what to —"

Nathan got to his feet shakily. He saw that his knees were dirty but he hadn't the energy to brush them off. And there were lipstick smears on the front of his white shirt. But he hadn't the energy, the spirit, to really take note. He stood with his head bowed, his chin almost against his throat. Inside him, mocking him, great leaden waves of blood beat against the frail envelope of his skin, wishing to burst free.

"I have to get married someday," Leonie said, sniffing. "I mean — I mean — My husband would want — You haven't ever made love with anyone, Nathan, and I haven't either: I mean not really! Do you know what I mean? And so I think — And Daddy would be so — And I could get pregnant, hon, just think of that — what a surprise *that* would be for all of us!"

"Yes," Nathan said.

"What did you say? — I couldn't hear."

"Yes."

"If I got pregnant, you mean? Oh my God yes! What a fuss, what a catastrophe — and what a shame for you, Nathan, with such a career ahead! You're only eighteen years old: you're only a boy."

"Yes," Nathan said softly. "I understand."

He wiped his face with both hands. He was both exhausted and edgy, jumpy. Leonie continued to talk, though she kept her distance from him and he could not make sense of her words on account of the clamoring in his ears. With a fist he rubbed his eyes, hard, first one and then the other, and he saw clearly a creature — a woman — struggling in mud, struggling to rise, as an enormous black snake wound itself around her body. *Sin. Filth. Those whom God has abandoned.* The snake's teeth were fixed on one of the woman's breasts and a trickle of blood ran down across her belly.

"I alone am the door," Nathan whispered.

Leonie poured the rest of the gin in her cup. She had begun to cry.

"I just feel so sad now, I feel so broken-down — I'm so ashamed of us both! But it was my fault most of all."

Nathan's breath was still quick and shallow. He stared at the ground for a long, long moment, not knowing quite where he was.

"Harold is so sweet and patient, he said he'd wait till I made up my mind one hundred percent, but I'm not good enough for *him*, I feel so wretched and awful, and now I've hurt your feelings, and you *know* I cherish you over any living thing on earth except my daddy — why, I wouldn't hurt you for the world, and look what I've done! It was my fault, it was all my fault," she said, sobbing, "and now everything is ruined between us like there was a death or something between us and I'm so miserable I could just *die*. . . . But you wouldn't want me to get pregnant, would you, Nathan, and cause all kinds of grief to everyone? Because Harold really loves me, he *really* does, and wants me to be his wife, and Daddy is anxious for it to turn out well this time; he was surprised about Elias, and maybe a little angry because I didn't tell him I had broken the engagement until days went by, and he said I was just irresponsible and I'd be lucky if any man would marry me at all! So — do you understand, Nathan? I'm so ashamed of myself —"

"It's all right," Nathan said thickly.

"It *isn't* all right," Leonie cried. "Everything is wrong, I hate myself, I wish I was dead — I wish God would strike me dead!"

Nathan's head jerked back. He stared at her: and she drained the cup, her eyes shut and her forehead furrowed as if in pain. But nothing happened. God did not strike her dead. She finished the gin and stood for a moment with her eyes closed and her hair wild about her face, swaying.

"We'd better go back," Nathan said.

"I don't want to go back ever!" Leonie screamed. "Leave me alone!"

Shortly after Nathan had joined Reverend Beloff's staff and came with his Grandmother Vickery to live in a northwestern residential section of Port Oriskany, there was a scandal in that part of the city: one of the wealthier members of the Anglican Church was indicted for his part in a complicated scheme involving the bribery of public officials so that certain areas of the city might be re-zoned for light industry, and at the height of the news media's interest in the man and his associates he killed himself with a double-barreled shotgun in the basement of his enormous home. There was an investigation, more facts were released to the newspapers, and within a week Marian Miles Beloff made his way to the grief-stricken widow, insisting that she see him, insisting that she allow him to speak to her; for he had had a special vision sent by the Lord regarding the death of her husband and the part he must play in the widow's future life. Though she was an Anglican, and a fairly religious woman, she agreed to see Reverend Beloff, and after several hours of intense conversation she emerged a totally changed woman — a convert, a saved soul, a new member of the Bethany-Nazarene Church of the Risen Christ. "In my previous life I saw through a glass darkly," the woman said, "but now I see clearly — now I see clearly. Reverend Beloff has opened my eyes!"

In the years that followed she gave an undisclosed amount of money to the Bethany-Nazarene Church, and nearly one hundred acres of pine woods in the foothills of the Chautauqua Mountains, and miscellaneous items including a large freezer unit for the church's kitchen, and several chairs and sofas in good condition for the Bethany-Nazarene Rest Home, and some priceless Royal Doulton china for the Reverend Beloff's own use, and a 1958 Cadillac, in excellent condition, also for the Reverend Beloff's own use. The Cadillac was a stately black with extravagant chrome trim and Reverend Beloff accepted it gratefully, though in fact it was to be only his second-best car, since he already owned a Rolls-Royce — also a gift from an enthusiastic convert to his church.

So the car became Leonie's, and Leonie loved it and drove it for the most part with care; but she was in no condition to drive it back to Port Oriskany on this Sunday afternoon. While Nathan tried to hold her shoulders to comfort her, she stooped over, gagging, finally vomiting, and afterward she nearly fainted, for she had never been so sick in her life — had never been so wretched in her life.

"I don't care if I die! I hope I do die!" she sobbed.

Nathan found the car keys in her purse and led her to the car, his arm around her waist. She was so sick! The poor girl was so sick! He would drive them back himself.

"But you don't know how to drive," Leonie whimpered.

He put the key in the ignition and turned it on. A sudden strength gripped him: he could drive the car if he wished: he could do anything if he wished.

"Nathan, you don't know *how* to drive, you'll get us both killed," Leonie said. But she half-lay in the seat beside him, the back of her head against the window. Her legs were all in a sprawl, the skirt of her dress was stained with vomit and hiked up above her knees. And her lipstick was smeared messily across her face and even on her throat: Nathan hardly dared look at her.

"Jesus will guide me," Nathan said.

"Nathan, honey, please — please don't get us killed — Maybe you better —

"I said Jesus will guide me," Nathan repeated, pressing on the gas pedal.

"Oh but honey — Wait —I —"

The sound of the powerful motor encouraged him, the quick response when he pressed the pedal excited him. He felt a thrill of certainty; he could not make a mistake.

Leonie mumbled a feeble protest as the car rolled forward.

Nathan gripped the wheel hard. He sat erect, his head slightly inclined in an attitude of watchful reverence. Was it a sign of the Lord's grace that he could take control of this powerful automobile, that he would be able to drive it back home without any real difficulty? — without danger? (For he had no doubt, he really knew beforehand, that there would be no danger.) His pulses throbbed. He could do no wrong. Once on the open highway he pressed on the accelerator until the car was moving at sixty miles an hour and he felt not the slightest tremor, not the slightest pinch of alarm. Leonie moaned and hiccupped and muttered to herself and fell asleep.

"There's no danger," Nathan said. He was feeling quite elated now; he had forgotten the humiliation of his raging, thwarted body and his burning skin. "No danger. How could there be danger? We can't die. I can't die. Not *yet*. Anyway, Jesus will guide me safely back home, seeing as how *He* was responsible for bringing me out here in the first place: one of His tricks and temptations! Isn't that so?" he said. But there was no one to note the ironic edge to his voice.

viii

Though Marian Miles Beloff had been called by the Lord to do His work on earth when he was only a boy, it was not really until his mid-thirties that he hit his stride: at which time he resigned his position with the First Baptist Church of Indian Springs, Minnesota, and founded his own church, based primarily on the Doctrine of Constant Baptism. (Beloff's church incorporated, and went beyond, the fundamental Protestant rules of repentance, salvation, baptism, communion, and charity.)

In a dream the Lord revealed Himself to Beloff, teaching that a man, after his initial baptism (which should be total immersion, and no adulterated, anemic ceremony consisting of the mere sprinkling of a few drops of water), must continue to will his own baptism and to be washed in the Blood of the Lamb every morning of every day, and every moment of every day if possible; so that he lived in an eternal "present tense" with Jesus Christ as his Saviour. All his worldly hopes and ambitions and fears and anxieties he must surrender to Christ, and as much of his personal possessions and income as was practical, so that he lived like a child, pure and innocent and without regard for the world, neither for its pleasures nor pains. To neglect baptism was to court disaster, Beloff warned; but to practice it faithfully was to be guaranteed salvation. "So long as a Christian lives in the eternal 'present tense,' he has no past at all," Beloff explained in his sermons and in his numerous pamphlets, "and therefore he accumulates no sins. He is like the lilies of the field and the birds of the air, totally without sin — he cannot *miss* being taken up by the Lord God into His Kingdom under these conditions!"

It was in the early forties that Beloff took to the road, addressing crowds in rented halls, in high-school auditoriums, in sports arenas, and occasionally in Baptist or Methodist or Congregational churches whose pastors were friendly enough to allow him the use of their buildings in return for a share of the collection; he was not too proud to appear at county fairs and volunteer firemen's picnics, and even at carnivals. Stocky, exuberant, with his smallpox-pitted cheeks and his broad, warm smile and his voice that had, in public, the timbre and the dexterity of an auctioneer's, he was soon able to amass enough capital to make a down-payment on a church of his own and to settle there for ten months of the year. (Until his early fifties Marian Miles Beloff always spent a fair amount of time on the road, bringing his doctrine to the multitudes.)

It was in 1946 that he acquired the church, and by 1950 he had a congregation of nearly two thousand. By 1955 he was forced to move to a new church, since his congregation had doubled. His radio and television work brought him into contact with additional tens of thousands, some of whom were remarkably generous with their donations. (Donations were of two general kinds: cash and material goods. There were the regular weekly offerings and love-offerings and sin-deflectors, a concept unique to the Beloff church; and from time to time large and usually unexpected gifts and inheritances.)

"The American people are not tight-fisted and suspicious," Beloff said often. "They are naturally charitable; they *want* to give. But where are the organizations worthy of their generosity? The pity is, there are so very few."

The Bethany-Nazarene Church of Jesus Christ Risen sponsored the Christian Teen Ranch and a local rest home for elderly, indigent invalids, as well as a young men's and women's Bible class, a missionary society, and a fairly large Sunday school. From the very first there was a special emphasis placed on music: Reverend Beloff hired a professional organist and a professional choir director, and outfitted his choir in robes of wine-dark velvet. Though he had no singing voice himself, he was powerfully moved by song and believed that through music of a particular sort the souls of the unregenerate could be awakened to Jesus.

Christianity is a religion of joy, the Gospel is uniquely ours — why therefore must we live in terror of the future? Marian Miles Beloff stressed joy, thanksgiving, the forgiveness of sins, the spontaneous giving of gifts, the assurance of salvation. As a young man he had tried anger and righteousness but found it extraordinarily hard work — like reeling in a thirty-pound catfish with no help. Pacing about platforms in shabby rented halls or beneath tents, he had called sinners forward to be saved in a passionate, impatient voice, pleading, begging, threatening, bursting into tears of relief as the first of the converts stumbled forward; he had sometimes shouted at the Devil as if he had sighted him in the audience holding back sinners in his grip. At his most excited it seemed he could preach for minutes at a time without drawing breath.

But his competition on the road was even angrier, and possessed what must have been an even greater loathing of alcohol and tobacco and immoral behavior; so Beloff couldn't keep pace.

As he grew older he relaxed, his doctrines softened, he was willing to content himself with a moderate local success and to leave nationwide fame to others. By the time he took on Nathan Vickery he had developed a friendly, winning, even rather puckish personality. It was true that in general his followers were aging, as he himself was aging, but they were wonderfully faithful and their generosity increased year by year.

As he had hoped, Nathan Vickery pulled in a younger audience; but curiously enough, he attracted the middle-aged and the elderly as well. His painful sincerity, his raw shameless childlike emotion, the uncanny Biblical intonations of his speech, which seemed, in him, altogether natural: all were extraordinarily successful. Reverend Beloff could not have predicted the degree of his success.

"You have a shrewd eye for talent," he was told by the owner of the local television station.

"The Lord directs my judgments," Reverend Beloff said, frowning.

During the three decades of Beloff's ministry many hundreds of sinners had come to him, many suffering souls had knelt before him, brought to true repentance. There had been a dairy farmer who wept in Beloff's arms not a minute after his tearful conversion, confessing he had drowned his younger brother when he was eleven and had hardly given it a thought since, until that very evening; there had been a highly articulate woman of middle age, a public school principal, who had gone into hysterics at one of Beloff's prayer meetings, accusing herself of not having loved her mother enough during the mother's lifetime; there had been, and continued to be, men and women violently repentant of their adulterous behavior and desperate to be saved; there were church deacons and members of the Ladies' Aid Society who confessed in terror that they had never *really* experienced God, and wouldn't He know their claims to love Him were fraudulent? There were widowers who half-believed they had killed their wives, and widows who half-believed they had killed their husbands. There were young husbands jealous of their own babies, regretting they had ever been born; there were young wives and mothers who wished to run away, to disappear; there were elderly women who confessed, sobbing, that they had stolen from their dying relatives in anticipation of inheriting, or in anticipation of not inheriting. Beloff's own wife, who had left him in 1937, two years after giving birth to Leonie, confessed to him on the evening of their first meeting that as a child she had gloated over her elder sister's death by scarlet fever — and it was her conviction that Christ would never forgive her, that He would never find it in His heart to forgive such a loathsome sin. (Beloff had fallen in love with the girl's desperation; he had believed, not altogether wrongly, that only he could assuage it.)

But one of the most puzzling sinners in Beloff's long experience was Nathan Vickery himself.

From time to time the boy alluded to sinful and unclean thoughts, and Reverend Beloff naturally told him not to be disturbed: such thoughts were all very normal. "The flesh is a temptation we all encounter," he said frankly. And laid his right hand, his good hand, on Nathan's shoulder to comfort him — for weren't they both men, weren't they both *flesh?* He would have liked to tell Nathan about his own early sexual experiences and particularly about his years of anguish before these experiences, but something in the young man's face discouraged him. (He sensed that Nathan Vickery could not possibly be consoled by having his sins swallowed up in a vast anonymous sea of others' sins: for was *he* not altogether different, one of the Lord's chosen?) Once, after Leonie had been teasing him more mercilessly than usual, Nathan followed Beloff around for an entire afternoon, too shy to say anything other than the fact that he was "troubled" about something, about someone: and taking his burden to Christ didn't seem to help very much. "That's understandable," Beloff said, wishing only to escape the young man's tense, ascetic, somehow alarming presence, "I mean it's understandable that you're troubled. But I'm confident that Christ *is* helping you, whether you know it or not."

"Are you?" Nathan asked.

Beloff stared at him but could not determine if he was being sarcastic or merely naïve.

One Friday morning in early September, when Beloff had hoped to spend several uninterrupted hours going over his financial records preparatory to a meeting with his accountant, which had been set for that afternoon, Nathan knocked at the door of his study and was so agitated that Beloff could not send him away.

"Yes — all right — of course, of course! — you're welcome — welcome at any time, as you know," Beloff said heartily.

Nathan sat stiffly on the edge of a chair facing Beloff, and for several painful moments he said nothing at all. He had never learned, Beloff saw with pity and a certain measure of irritation, to make the small, pointless, kindly social remarks necessary in the world of man. Now eighteen years old, grown to a height just over six feet, he was curiously childlike and adult at the same time: his manner was without guile, uncalculated, but his features had grown stark, even severe, and his eyes appeared in certain lights to be absolutely colorless. They had a quality of remorseless antiquity about them, like stone or glass or ancient coins. His hair fell past his collar, shaggy and uneven — Leonie must be neglecting him now. And unless Beloff was imagining it, there were actually two or three gray-white hairs in an untidy strand that had fallen over his forehead.

Beloff tried to make him relax, tried to joke in his usual bluff manner — inconsequential remarks about staff members, or last week's visiting missionary and his penchant for apple cobbler, or the weather — but Nathan merely sat there, staring at the floor. His features were unsoftened by humor and his chin seemed less fragile than usual, perhaps because his lips were pushed slightly forward, as if he were pouting or trying not to speak too suddenly.

Finally he spoke softly: so softly Beloff had to strain to hear. Something about the Devil, the Devil's presence. But it was a presence inside *him*, he knew, and he could not blame anyone else. ". . . which makes me wonder if . . . if. . . ."

"Yes?"

". . . if I should continue with my work, because I . . . I don't think I am worthy. . . ."

He fell silent again, not meeting Beloff's eye. His features had the strain of those of a high-wire aerialist.

Beloff sighed, and leaned back in his comfortable swivel chair, and clasped his hands carefully behind his head. The living fingers of one hand slid precisely into place and locked with the sensationless fingers of the other hand in a routine, automatic gesture Beloff found comforting.

"Well. *That's* a farfetched thing for you to say, you of all people!" he laughed. "Absolutely farfetched. . . . If it's impure thoughts or whatever, that sort of thing, well, if you think the Devil is singling you out for temptation, why would you want to surrender? Turning aside from the Lord's work would be exactly what the Devil would wish most, wouldn't he? You don't know his psychology as I do! Haven't lived as long! . . . And anyway, Nathan, we don't teach as the Roman Catholics do that the least little thought will plunge you into hell eternally: the least little thought or deed, even. Don't you understand and accept our doctrine?"

Nathan continued as if he had not been listening: "The Devil isn't a person, but a presence. The Devil is a way of seeing. Sometimes he has me entirely — my soul. And when I look out into the world I see the world through *his* eyes, and it's unclean and contaminated and ugly and graceless and . . . and God has abandoned it . . . and God has abandoned me. That is the Devil. He's with me now, sitting here with me now. He's jeering at me. I can almost hear him. Sometimes when I preach I *can* hear him, a voice running alongside my own. It's like an echo. It's my own voice he has taken over and altered to suit his evil intentions."

He shook himself unconsciously, like a dog.

Marian Miles Beloff remained leaning back in his chair, smiling. He felt the need for a smile: he dare not let it fade.

"Yes — Well — I'm not sure I follow you exactly, but — Isn't it *thoughts* you have, or *feelings* — about women, maybe? Isn't that it?"

"That's just the smallest part of it," Nathan said coolly.

"It *is*?"

"Like my littlest finger to my body," Nathan said, raising a hand and extending the smallest finger at an awkward angle. He held it there for several seconds, contemplating it.

He might have been miles away and staring through a telescope, Beloff thought. Regarding his own flesh and blood with a look of utter detachment and unrecognition.

"If it has maybe to do with my daughter," Beloff said, faltering at first and then resuming his hearty tone, wanting Nathan to know he didn't at all *judge* him: for who was he to cast the first stone, when it came to lusting after women? "If it has to do with Leonie . . well. . . . Well then: she'll be married in three weeks, won't she? And Harold is taking her on a nice long honeymoon trip. So maybe the problem will disappear . . . ?"

Nathan flicked his hair out of his eyes and looked shyly at Beloff. "But I still might think of her," he mumbled.

"You won't see her nearly as often, you know. She'll be changed, she'll be very busy running that big house of Harold's, she just won't have *time* for any of us, you know; isn't that a comfort?"

"I still might think of her," Nathan said.

"But you must think of someone, after all," Beloff said benignantly. "It's your age, it's your time of life, you must think of *someone* — a girl, a young woman — after all! Maybe you'll meet someone else —"

Nathan stared at him, shocked. "But I don't *want* this weakness," he said.

"It isn't a weakness necessarily," Beloff said, faltering.

"It certainly *is* a weakness," Nathan said, his lips twisting in contempt. "It isn't *me*. It gets in the way of my God and casts an ugly shadow on Him."

"But God would understand, you know — I mean God *does*

understand: the spirit is willing but the flesh is weak. Isn't that a comfort?"

"I don't care if God *does* understand," Nathan said. "I'm the one that is afflicted, not God. I don't like it. I don't like anyone or anything coming between me and God."

Beloff ran a hand through his hair, perplexed. "But it's written that the flesh is weak. . . ."

"I'm not flesh," Nathan said curtly.

Beloff guffawed in honest surprise. "What? *Not?*"

"I'm spirit. We're all spirit."

"But housed in bodies, aren't we? Mortal bodies? Aren't we?"

"Yes. But the bodies are insignificant."

"They are? . . . Well, I suppose they are, in a sense. But God gave us these bodies. He gave his only-begotten son a body, didn't He?"

"Not really," Nathan muttered.

"*What?*"

"He didn't give Jesus a body: He gave Jesus the image of a body."

"What's that — the image of a body? The what?"

"He gave Himself in the form of Jesus the image of a human body, so that He could appear on earth and be seen by our eyes. That's all."

Beloff stared at the young man's pale, intolerant face. Was this heresy?

"Nathan, my boy, just *what* are you saying? I never heard of such a — a tongue twister —"

"Christ merely used a human body," Nathan said in the slow, rather melancholy, rather eerie voice that was his preaching voice, though he spoke much more softly. "Just as we all use human bodies. It was the flesh He was crucified on: His own. The Romans who crucified him, the Jews who betrayed him, everyone who witnessed His agony was Him. Us. We are not two, we are not multiple; we are one. Christ is here. I am Christ while He abides in me and speaks through me. I am never *not* Christ even

when He is distant to me. . . . Christ abides in you, Reverend
Beloff, and is listening to me, to my words, and understands the
truth of them at this very moment: He was never flesh and blood,
He was spirit from all time, before there was flesh and blood or
creation itself. He was —"

"Wait," Beloff said, sitting forward now, bringing his elbows
firmly down onto his desk. "You are talking, my boy, about our
Saviour: about Jesus Christ Who died for us on the cross, Who
suffered and bled and *died* so that we might be reborn. He descended into hell and on the third day rose again, and afterward
ascended into heaven to sit on the right hand of —"

"God doesn't have a right hand," Nathan murmured. "He
doesn't have any hands."

"He *does*," Beloff exploded. "If the Bible says so, He does! He
can have all the — He can have all the hands He chooses —"

"Christ was crucified on the cross of His own flesh, which
wasn't really His," Nathan said slowly. "The Romans who nailed
him to the cross, the Jews who betrayed him, and we who live
afterward — we are that flesh that crucified him. But we are more
than flesh. We're *proverbs*."

"And how do you know all this?" Beloff said.

"I don't know anything you don't know," Nathan said.

"This business about Christ not having a body — If someone
heard you — Don't you accept Him as your living Saviour, Who
died for your sins? He was born of Mary, wasn't he, and lived in
Nazareth, and John the Baptist baptized him — ? Didn't that all
happen?"

"Yes," Nathan said.

"It did? But —"

"He took on the image of a human body so that what had to be
fulfilled was fulfilled. He could have been an animal, or a flower
— He could have been vapor — He had a form the way water
has a form as liquid and can change into steam or ice or snow.
The form changes, the essence doesn't. He was spirit. Beneath
his appearance of flesh was a terrible, unshakable reality. He was
spirit, like us! He was just like us!"

"Nathan, I think you'd better leave my study. I think you'd better spend some time today on your knees, asking God to help you. The things you've been saying — Why, if any of our followers heard you, how confused they would be, how frightened and angry — You can't *say* such things, Nathan!"

"You certainly know all these things yourself," Nathan said curtly. "But you've forgotten. Or you're pretending to have forgotten."

"Know all *what* things?" Beloff cried.

"That the Spirit of the Lord is not material."

"Are we talking about the Spirit of the Lord — ?"

"The Spirit of the Lord gives us breath, and sustains us, and without it we would not exist in the flesh," Nathan said. "But the Spirit of the Lord isn't bound up in flesh."

Beloff reached nervously and absent-mindedly for something to hold: a paper clip, a fountain pen. He was sitting now with both feet pressed firmly against the floor, like a sprinter about to jump into motion. As Nathan spoke he guarded himself against nodding, as he usually nodded, in his warm willingness to agree with nearly anything that was said. The words Nathan Vickery spoke seemed, one by one, absolutely reasonable and compelling, and the young man's stony certitude was mesmerizing; and it was possible that he *did* know something Beloff did not, for wasn't he in the habit of praying hourly? — constantly? "Jesus inhabited the body as we inhabit the body," Nathan repeated, "but He was *not* contained within that body. *Ye are from beneath;* he said to the Jews, *I am from above: ye are of this world; I am not of this world.* When we take Jesus into our hearts we ascend with Him into the realm of the spirit — when we allow lustful or unclean or egotistical thoughts to enter us, we are weighed down back to earth and lose His blessing. God and Christ are one. God and Christ and I are one. God is outside of time, Christ entered time, I took on my physical form accidentally in time and must transcend it if I want to be saved. . . ."

"*If you want to be saved,*" Beloff repeated blankly. He was fussing with his fountain pen, turning it round and round between his fingers. Nathan's hard-edged voice was intimidating: in fact, it was rather frightening. Though perhaps it wasn't the young man's voice, or even his queer urgent manner, but the possible truth of his words that was frightening. What if Nathan were right? What if it were actually Christ Himself speaking at this very moment, using Nathan's voice? Marian Miles Beloff would be utterly ignorant, utterly bereft. . . . He was unaccustomed to arguing with other people in any logical, systematic way, pitting his beliefs against other beliefs. It had never been *necessary* for him to argue, since he knew the Scriptures as well as anyone. But Nathan's knowledge of the Bible was different from his own, and far different was the young man's raw, ungiving soul, which seemed to be peering through his eyes from a great distance, detached, somewhat contemptuous. It was the very spirit of Jesus of Nazareth Himself, Beloff thought suddenly, involuntarily: imperious and princely.

"You said — *If I want to be saved*. Do you mean you *aren't* saved?" Beloff cried. "In your heart, after all these years of spreading the Gospel, you *aren't* saved?"

Nathan regarded him with the same fixed, remote gaze. After a long moment he said: "No."

"Now, Nathan, that's just — that's just talk: farfetched talk. Even if I can't agree with this strange idea of yours, I *know* you are one of us and always have been. There's no doubt in my mind that —"

"No one is saved," Nathan said flatly. "Not until his life on earth is finished. He's got to walk the razor's edge every day — one misstep and he may be plunged into hell. *That's* obvious."

"It is — ?" Beloff said, letting the pen fall from his fingers. "But I thought — I — Now you wait," he said, confused and stricken, "you just wait, my boy. According to Christian doctrine we believe in the sacrifice of Christ and the forgiveness of sins and the resurrection of the body — the *human* body — on the Day of Judgment. And we believe — Of course there's a hell, Jesus speaks of it quite frankly, a hell of brimstone and suffering where sinners are cast — But — But through His sacrifice, and through

baptism — total immersion — Through His sacrifice we are redeemed of —"

"God is a spirit that abides in each of us," Nathan continued,
"and so we are all one. If I narrow my eyes just a little I can see
through the eyes of my brothers and sisters — I can see through
their eyes *almost* as easily as through my own. In Christ there is
no male or female, there is only Christ. There is only spirit. So
it's the Devil that comes between us, making us strangers to one
another so we can lust after one another. The Devil distorts our
vision while pretending to sharpen it."

"The Devil does *what?*" Beloff asked, his voice rising as if he
were close to tears. "I don't follow a word of that. Not a word!"

"The Devil causes us to lust after one another's bodies," Nathan said softly. "To confuse us. To come between us and God.
To make us think we're not spirit but only flesh — trapped in
something that drags us down."

In his agitation Beloff groped about his desk top, staring at
Nathan, trying to think: how should he reply, what should he
say? He was not accustomed to being contradicted. He was not
accustomed to feeling himself so outmaneuvered, so manipu-
lated. In fact, he did not know whether Nathan *was* contradicting
him now. The young man's concepts were so bizarre, his vocabulary so strange, it was impossible to know what he meant. A
heretic, was he; or a fanatic of the sort Beloff had always feared;
or perhaps he was an atheist — ? A deathly temptation to Reverend Beloff's lifelong faith?

"The Devil wants us to think that Jesus Christ was really a man
and that He really died," Nathan said, "to blind us to the fact that
Christ came before our idea of Him, and we came before our
own idea of ourselves, and Christ *is* us. To blind us to the fact
that Christ only happened to take on the form He did — as if He
couldn't have taken on any form at all! It's the Devil who gives us
sexual feelings, to blind us to the fact that we're all one substance —"

"All one substance? What do you mean?"

"Before Christ *was*, God *is*. Before my fleshly being came into the world, *I* was. Reverend Beloff, you know very well the truth of what I'm saying: you *know* God is a spirit and that our souls are always with God and never *not* with God. Even in hell it's God hiding behind the flames and the big black snakes and the jaws that snap at one another and the howls of the damned, who only believe themselves to be lost — Even in hell it's God, it's Christ, it's a form of *us* behind the visions — as if we were hunters sighting our prey through a scope but the prey was *us* — looking through what we thought was a telescopic lens when it was only a mirror! Reverend Beloff, you *know* that you know. Everyone knows in his deepest soul. Once the Lord Jesus Christ rid me of my false pride by forcing me to tear off the head of a living chicken with my —"

Beloff rose with a shriek. "No more! Stop!" He could bear it no longer: he snatched up an object from his desk and threw it at Nathan. "My God, stop. Do you hear! Do you hear!"

The object struck Nathan's left knee and fell harmlessly to the carpet. It was a jar of Carter's midnight-blue ink; fortunately the top was screwed on tightly and the ink didn't spill.

Standing behind his desk, Beloff looked like a cornered steer. His chest heaved, his eyes were wide and bright and glaring. He tried to speak but could not. His hands shook. It was a terrible moment, but with a crestfallen dignity uncharacteristic of him Nathan merely picked up the jar of ink and set it carefully atop the desk and left the room without saying a word, without even glancing back over his shoulder.

ix

What day it is, what time, what year — I have no recollection. I walk in the cold-glaring winter sun, partly blinded, one of my eyes pitted with darkness. *There shall be time no longer:* so it is promised. But we are not yet delivered. Why standeth thou afar off, O Lord? You have not yet raised us out of the vaporous world; You keep Yourself from Your children these many centuries.

Carelessly dressed, shoes without socks, shoes chafing damply at my heels. I am a figure now of mirth: of shabby terror.

Empty of spirit.

If the sun penetrates the armor of my skull, if my sluggish bone-brittle body is warmed, what does it mean? Is it You stirring at last in me? A blessing? A new voice?

The hands clutching at me, seeking redemption. Faces swollen to the size of clouds, staring, gaping, with ulcerous eyes. A woman's distended belly — great drooping bulbous lardish breasts pressing down upon the earth. In the sanctity of rocks there are sudden shifts and creases: hideous wounds. A scarred oak fairly howling with the memory of an old pain, an old humiliation. The whorls and labyrinths of the ear, the intestines, the genitals. . . . A new blessing, this nightmare? A new voice, this guttural murmuring that rises on all sides of me?

Look at him!
Who is he?
He's drunk — watch out!
Who is he? Where did he come from?
What is he trying to say?

By Your breath is frost given to our earth.

■ ■ ■

On the morning of Good Friday, shortly before the morning service he was to lead, Nathan Vickery found himself in the kitchen of the house he and his grandmother rented; he had pulled open one of the cupboard drawers and with both hands was groping inside.

His Grandmother Vickery came into the kitchen. She was dressed for church: she wore a handsome, somber dress of mauve and gray, with a white lace handkerchief folded several times and tucked into her belt, and a small black hat with a black veil and a bird's silky jet-black wing, poised as if to dart away. She smelled harshly of soap.

What was she saying? — what did she want of him on this morning of all mornings? Sounds flew about Nathan's head but did not coalesce into words. Broken bits of noise, insubstantial and inconsequential. Whatever made them *human* Nathan could not have said.

She was a tall, erect, wide-shouldered woman, rather mannish, her skin still remarkably smooth, even taut across the cheekbones, her eyes intelligent and rueful. She had held him as an infant against her large, soft, formless breasts, she had rocked him and sung to him and brought him to life. Perhaps he would have lapsed into death had it not been for her: perhaps he would have lost interest in life, would have sighed and faltered and become extinguished. *My dear one, my sweet little mouse. My love.* In a sense Nathan remembered quite clearly, as if it had been yesterday and not nearly nineteen years ago. In another sense he was forced to reject the experience altogether: for it had happened to a mere form, a creature of piggish bawling flesh he had now transcended.

Her voice this morning was grave, troubled, querulous, yet oddly pleased. She was complaining of her son Ashton, who had shown up again to borrow money: as if he had any intention of repaying the money he had already borrowed from Nathan, back in November!

He was spending it on a woman, Mrs. Vickery knew. That woman in the house trailer outside town, the one who had kicked her husband out, a slatternly creature, wasn't she? — an alcoholic. Only twenty-eight years old but an alcoholic. He was spending it on her, and on liquor for himself. Her own son! — now over forty years old! — with his handsome, ruined face, his nose disfigured by broken veins, his eyes grown shrewd and malicious. She *knew* he was spending all his money on liquor for himself and that horrible woman. And what of his own wife, and what of his children? Why would he never answer questions about his life?

She prayed for him daily but it seemed to do no good. And of course Nathan prayed for him, for his only uncle. But in vain.

Nathan saw in his hand a paring knife, an inexpensive stainless-steel knife from the dime store.

Unsleeping the night before, and the night before that, with no appetite for food or drink, he had felt something begin to unfold inside him. Had it to do with the passion of Jesus Christ, with His agony on the cross; had it to do with Nathan's own sense of himself as befouled; had it to do merely with the chill of early spring, the procession of sunless weeping days . . . ? Great dark wings struggled to unfold, and he did not resist, did not dare resist. He was given over to it: to God. He would not resist. O *God have mercy on me*, he had cried, but he did not expect mercy and did not really desire it.

He tested the point of the knife with his thumb and found it not very sharp. But it would do.

Mrs. Vickery saw what he held in his hand, and for a moment said nothing.

He was half-blinded, still, by the powerful vision of the night before. His eyes kept a ghostly afterimage before them; colors were neutralized, dimensions were flattened. A woman was speaking to him but the sounds were noises, bits of noise, jabber. He saw as God would have seen, he heard as God would have heard: before man had been created and given life.

Yes? What?

She laid a hand tentatively on his arm: Did he know what time it was? The service would begin in —

Not wishing to be touched, Nathan drew away. He slipped the knife into his pocket and stretched all his fingers out wide, as a child might have done, to show that his hands were empty. He managed a smile. Mrs. Vickery stared at him. She had hugged him close against her massive body, she had kissed him and rocked him to sleep: her own baby. Now he smiled coldly upon her and had no need to say *Woman, what have I to do with thee?* — for she understood very well without his speaking.

Faltering, she reminded him of the time. He must not forget a necktie, she had set out a clean one for him, and —

He thanked her in his meager, trivial, ordinary voice, and turned to leave. *That* voice was not really his; but he must use it in the world while speaking to ordinary people.

The great dark straining wings opened, the light burst forth, he tensed himself against terror, knowing his punishment was just and even merciful. For days, for weeks, he had had a premonition of this visitation from God; he had known it would come soon. Leonie was gone, he rarely thought of her now, he rarely woke to those piercing-sweet, lustful, ugly dreams of her, all that was gone, vanished — yet he had known he must be punished for such thoughts, and protected from them. The Devil would have no difficulty in choosing another woman to send to Nathan: there were women and girls in the congregation, even in the choir, who gazed at him in that bold, yearning, half-unconscious way Leonie had. . . .

It had been years since the darkness had broken open in him, and the paralyzing light had burst forth. Yet when the vision came — when God appeared — it was as if no time had elapsed since the last vision. The Nathan that was now shrank, pleated, disappeared; had never existed. Always that aspect of his being had been secondary, only superficial, an appearance for others' sakes, and not Nathan himself. But the deeper self was not Nathan: was not a frightened young man who had to clench his jaws tight to keep from crying out in terror: was not human at all.

Pale-lipped, dazed, he slipped on his suit coat and hurried the half block to Reverend Beloff's church. He was late — very nearly late. The hours of wakefulness had been a mistake, perhaps; he was suddenly exhausted; and the ordeal lay before him. Humility. Prayer. *I am the door. . . . Let not your heart be troubled: ye believe in God, believe also in me. . . . I am the way, the truth, and the life. . . . If thine eye offend thee. . . .* An hour or more of almost intolerable radiance, so that he lay paralyzed on

the floor, unable even to move his head or shut his eyes. My
God, my God. Why such pain, why such humiliation? He had
sinned, of course, both in deed and in thought, and perhaps he
had sinned through his own self-loathing as well, and for his
almost ungovernable sense of his own superiority. It was pride,
pride as well as lust. Leonie had clasped her plump arms around
his neck and kissed him wetly and hungrily and he had kissed her
in return, with a child's desperation, as if he might suck the very
life out of her and come to an end of his desire for her; and at the
same time he had shouted *Whore! slut! pig! I hate you!* And so
he had sinned against God and against the woman herself, who
was innocent, who had been innocent all along of *his* lust. It was
not she but the Devil who stirred Nathan at the very root of his
being, and it was not she but Nathan himself who was guilty of
succumbing to this temptation, and even welcoming it.

She had drawn his head down to her breasts, had arched her
back so he might press his face blindly against her. Faint, whimpering like a sick animal, he had clasped her tight about the hips
and sunk to his knees before her, to kiss her wildly, frantically,
between the legs. His senses were filled to the brim: there was
great danger that he would burst, and destroy her: or plunge
himself so violently into her that she would be torn. Yet it was
another time, it was Good Friday. He hurried along the flagstone
path. Leonie was gone, Leonie had moved away, the rumor was
that she and Harold were expecting a baby in the autumn, he no
longer thought of her, no longer dreamed of her, did not wish
her dead. What was that music? The marchlike solemnity of
Good Friday, the organ's chords that filled the church so one
could hardly breathe. Nathan hurried but was without fear. Last
night he had been fearful enough, but this morning he was
purged of fear, for what could harm him in the world of man?
— *he*, whom God Himself had touched?

A packed church, which would please Reverend Beloff. People
standing at the rear. Two television cameras and those uncanny
overbright lights — for the service was to be televised locally —
and one of the directors from the station, awaiting him. He ap-

proached, he listened, he appeared to comprehend. A part of him was quite human and ordinary, almost untouched by the interior light. He spoke courteously enough with his numbed lips and did not flinch when someone straightened his tie and suggested he comb his hair back off his face. Yes? Like this? Thank you.

The organ continued, its bass trembling so that the very earth seemed to shake. Deeper the chords plunged, and louder: JESUS OF NAZARETH THE KING OF THE JEWS. The choir sang. Leonie was not among them. Nathan had transferred the paring knife from his trousers pocket to his coat pocket and now he touched it through the cloth, one finger after another, caressing. Just so had he kissed Leonie, through the cloth of her skirt, wishing only to thrust himself into her and destroy them both. But it was not Leonie: it was the Devil. Jeering, smirking, a redheaded child with glasses, a gaunt-cheeked man of indistinct age staring emptily at him, reflecting nothing, absolutely nothing. The choir sang. One by one the verses declared themselves. Nathan came forward as he had always come forward, calmed by the knowledge that his ministry was nearing its end, that he would deceive the faithful no longer.

The agony of Gethsemane. The kiss of Judas, the bewilderment of Pilate, the condemnation and the crucifixion. His voice broke, speaking of it. Spikes through His hands! — through His poor naked feet! Most intolerable of all, the public display of His suffering: for all the world gaped and sneered and felt no pity. Our pain is nothing like His, cannot begin to approach His. *My God*, He cried, *my God, why hast thou forsaken me?* The unendurable shame of His humiliation, the mystery of His physical breaking, His collapse. . . .

Accustomed to strong lights, Nathan gazed out at the congregation, at the rows and rows of people. They were *his*. He had no doubt of it. They were expectant, looking to him for the emotion they should feel. Upturned staring faces, strangers' faces, brothers and sisters in the suffering, broken body of Christ.

Nathan spoke calmly to them, his voice rising now and then in that small tremulous wail that so charmed them and held them fast, though he was rarely conscious of it himself. He had spent some forty-eight hours meditating upon the betrayal of Christ and the crucifixion and now he wished to take them through that ordeal, asking them to imagine the insult of the weight of the cross on His shoulders, and the insult of the hostile, mocking crowd, and the brute fact of Calvary itself; the sickening horror of the scarlet robe, the crown of thorns, the reed to be carried like a scepter in His right hand. *Hail, King of the Jews!* And the crucifixion itself, in the place called Golgotha. Spikes driven through flesh — through blood and tissue and bones. Ah, the cruelty of it! The cruelty of the world! Nathan's voice began to shake with the sorrow of it. How *could* it be borne? That the Son of God should be broken in His innocent flesh and nailed to a cross for the multitudes to jeer at — that they should mock him with the words THIS IS JESUS THE KING OF THE JEWS. But most piteous of all was His despair. For He had called out to His heavenly Father, in His final agony, thinking God had betrayed Him —

Nathan had spoken so passionately, had brought the packed church to such a pitch of emotion, that a number of people were crying and his own eyes were wet with tears. In a trance he continued, speaking now of the crucifixion of all men upon the cross of the flesh, and of mortality, and sin, and time. He was drawing near to the end of the service, and to the end of his ministry. In a sense the ceremony was completed: God had instructed him the night before and he had known it would be done without hesitation and in that instant it was already consummated. He had only to act out God's will, which must be fulfilled in time, though it exists prior to all time. Crucifixion: the humiliation of the flesh: the breaking of one's body upon the cross of mortality, sin, and death. What Christ endured all mankind must endure, for He goes before us in His human form, a model for us, a warning. He too felt the impulse of pride, and did not always

resist it. And so He must be broken as we must be broken. . . .
As for the hypocrites, Nathan said breathlessly, raising both arms
in an angry appeal, how shall they be dealt with?

In the silence that followed he felt a single tear roll down his
cheek.

The upturned faces, the expressions of absolute concentration:
they were his. But he was going to release them. It was he, Nathan Vickery, who was the hypocrite. He had spoken week after
week of the need to be cleansed in the Blood of the Lamb; he had
spoken of sin, and the fact that the wages of sin is death; yet all
along he had been sinful himself. Didn't they believe him? Didn't
they? But it was true — it was true! He was guilty of lust and of
pride. Most grievously, he was guilty of turning away from the
Lord, of being distracted willfully by the temptations of the flesh.
A single moment's distraction, he cried, might be sufficient to
plunge us to hell forever, though God would not be so merciless;
how much more reprehensible must be weeks and months of
sinful contemplation —! Didn't they believe him? In their inno-
cence they remained unconvinced, they could not *fathom* such
hypocrisy. But he would instruct them. He had set aside this day
for a public confession and a public humiliation. He, supposedly
one of the chosen, had falsely presented himself to them. He
appeared to be a man of God but he was in fact a sinner, a
hypocrite, a criminal. . . .

More and more passionately he spoke, now out of breath. At
last they were beginning to believe him. There were whispers,
ripples of surprise and alarm and bewilderment, a look of utter
consternation on the face of one of the cameramen, who had
barely been paying attention to Nathan's preaching until now. At
last, at last! He would have liked to step down among them, he
would have liked to lower and flatten his voice so that it was no
different from their voices. But he must continue. He must complete the ceremony.

On this Good Friday he was going to take leave of them, and
of his ministry. And he was going to demonstrate to them an act
of pure sacrifice. (He had taken out the paring knife and held it

for them to see, like a magician who has no tricks, no guile.) For Christ has taught us that it is better to be maimed than to be cast into hell whole in body. And Christ has shown us how He submitted to His own destruction, not without emotion, but surrendered to the agony of the body, which was to be the agony of all men, not scorned by Him even in His divinity. How then should Nathan Vickery be spared? How had he spared himself for so very long?

If thine eye offend thee. . . .

He told the congregation that what he was going to do was an ugly, brutal, and senseless act; it was willful; it was perverse; and no one must imitate him. He told the congregation, which listened as if intoxicated, making no move to stop him, that so public an act was sinful in itself, and that its grotesque exhibitionism would be — when he recalled it in later life — part of his humiliation. He *knew* what he was going to do was senseless, but he did it in defiance of sense, and in obedience to God's command. For God Himself had ordained this ceremony. Nathan must be punished, he must be broken and humiliated publicly, for he had embarked upon a public career in God's name, and God was very displeased, and must now be placated.

Woe unto the world because of offences! for it must needs be that offences come; but woe to that man by whom the offence cometh! Wherefore if thy hand or thy foot offend thee, cut them off, and cast them from thee: it is better for thee to enter into life halt or maimed, rather than having two hands or two feet to be cast into everlasting fire. And if thine eye offend thee, pluck it out, and cast it from thee: it is better for thee to enter into life with one eye, rather than having two eyes to be cast into hell fire. . . .

A woman screamed, and then another, and another. One of the choir members in her long velvet robe started forward, as if to stop him; but it was too late. A man shouted. It might have been one of the television technicians, or the organist, or a parishioner who sat close enough to see exactly what was happening. But it was too late. Nathan had brought the point of the

knife without hesitation to his left eye, to the center of the eyeball, and without hesitation he had pressed it inward, his left
hand grasping the small handle and his right hand steadying it.

Pain? Blood? His own cry of anguish?
He was never to know.

BOOK THREE

last things

i

Midwinter.

Stasis.

Silence for weeks: my prayer has been broken off.

What do I know of Nathan Vickery?

The difficulty of re-imagining. Re-visioning. What is lost, re-mains lost.

The folly of resurrection.

Will we rise again in our bodies, they begged.

He was struck to the heart by their greed and would have turned aside, but the Christ in them spoke to the Christ in him and he replied as gently as he could. They heard not his words but the music of his words, and went away comforted.

He who is without ears hears best.

And again they said to him, *Are we indeed in the Final Days, and how will we know we are among the Chosen?*

He saw it was the Holy Spirit testing him, in the voices of strangers. And so he gave comfort as it was ordained he do, and they fell to their knees weeping in gratitude, having been delivered from the fires of hell which were promised in both worlds: in the world beyond, and in this world of the twentieth century.

For we have entered upon the Final Days and the Beast has arisen to sweep all before him.

But perhaps even the Beast knows us not?

The air is brittle with cold. It is a strain merely to look — to narrow one's vision against the prismatic slices of light — to make the necessary connection between one thing and another.

Fragments of ice, ice molecules. Invisible. We are warned not to walk too quickly in the cold, not to breathe too deeply, for the lungs will be pierced by tiny ice pellets and great pain will result and in some cases even death.

I have acquired a secondhand radio. It plays softly all night, a gentle harmless droning, a counterpart to my unsteady prayer. Another voice. Voices. They are strangers, but familiar, aggressively familiar. Someday I will be bold enough to reply to them. At the present time I am mute — sounds stick in my throat — for if I have not You to speak to, to whom shall I speak?

I want no man, but God. I want not the trivial happiness of man, but the tumult of God.

I want —

■ ■ ■

To Port Calmar he came in November of 1965, William Japheth Sproul III, twenty-seven years old, slight-bodied, clever, given to fey obsessions, and seeking, as he told himself derisively, Tillich's God beyond the God of theism.

Though he could have afforded a plane ticket, he made the journey from Connecticut by bus — an eerie, dreamlike, jarring eighteen hours during which he believed he did not sleep at all, though his thoughts were troubled by stray flattened visions and snatches of sound he could not recognize. Shy and arrogant, and needing privacy with as much desperation as others need communality, he had followed the bus driver's directions about putting his suitcase up on the rack, but had spread his books across the seat beside him in order to discourage anyone from sitting there.

He arrived at Port Calmar in late afternoon. It was already growing dark: a light, cold rain was falling. He had not thought of bringing an umbrella. He had misplaced his gloves, or had forgotten to stick them in his pocket; distracted by the excitement of this adventure, he had worn the trench coat he'd been wearing all fall, instead of his warmer overcoat. The wind off Lake Oriskany was rather strong and he had no curiosity about the city, so he remained in the Trailways bus terminal, sitting in a secluded corner beside an unattended shoeshine stand, reading V. W. Slosson's *The Millennial City* and taking notes in the loose-leaf notebook he carried everywhere with him. From time to time he glanced up quizzically, as if he had forgotten where he was. With his small frame and his fair, boyish face and his slightly harassed manner he looked like a student preparing for an exam; he looked a decade younger than his age.

At first it appeared that time would pass slowly in this drafty, unattractive, noisy place, then he became engrossed in his reading and glanced up to see that it was six forty-five, and then a quarter after seven; and then he realized he had forgotten about eating. The Seekers Convocation was scheduled to begin at eight o'clock. He had no idea where the Port Calmar Civic Arena was located. He got to his feet, suddenly panicked, and opened his suitcase — which was filled for the most part with books — and threw the Slosson book inside and wondered if he should store the suitcase in a locker or take it with him. It was too late to find a restaurant. "God, You see? — what a fix! It's *always* the same," he said half-cheerfully.

He decided to get rid of the suitcase, and bought a ham-and-cheese sandwich in an automatic vending machine and ate it as he walked along. Rain was falling more steadily now. While William Japheth was painfully shy in the company of people he knew, he was sometimes rather assertive with strangers, so he did

not hesitate to ask directions to the Civic Arena, though people
looked at him oddly: it might have been the sandwich, it might
have been his prim schoolboy eagerness, or his impatience with
people who seemed not to know what he was talking about. (His
accent was substantially different from theirs. *Their* accent was
for the most part nasal and drawling and twangy, faintly ludicrous.)

There were two civic arenas in Port Calmar, one in the old
downtown, one in a northern suburb. William Japheth decided
his man must be booked for the old one so he made his way
there, following darkened streets, crossing one enormous but
nearly empty boulevard, his head bent against the wind from the
lake. The adventure was so absurd, so pointless, what did it matter that he was miserable with the cold and rain? — journeying
eighteen hours in order to hear a revivalist preacher whose name
was unknown, faced with the prospect of turning around and
taking the eleven-thirty bus back home (for he dared not miss
Tuesday morning: he had to present a seminar on the Jewish
apocalypse of Baruch), and enduring another sleepless and hal-
lucinatory eighteen hours. It wasn't altogether clear to him why
he *was* here, though it had pleased him enormously to irritate
certain of his classmates by speaking of the evangelist Nathanael
Vickery, of whom no one had heard. Nor did they seem to recall
the incident that had taken place six years earlier involving Vickery: his melodramatic blinding of one eye on Good Friday, before
a church of horrified onlookers and a television audience. (Still
an undergraduate at Princeton at the time, William Japheth had
been struck by the news-wire photographs of Vickery and the
accompanying stories that, though they were brief and had the
air of being confused and misleading, seemed to him fascinating:
ghoulish and ridiculous and fascinating. To take Christ's para-
bolic remarks literally! — and to *act* upon them, as if one's life
were in some vital way connected to those remarks!)

Quite by accident he had come across an announcement of
Vickery's "return" in one of the smudgily printed tabloid publications — *Gospel News*, or *Good Times*, or the *Christian Broth-*

erhood — the Divinity School subscribed to and that were rarely read, except for amusement. *Nathanael Vickery. The Seekers for Christ.* Who the Seekers were, William Japheth had no idea, though he suspected he knew well enough, across a distance of many hundreds of miles, exactly what they believed and even why they believed it. The name *Nathanael Vickery* had sounded familiar. Had he ever listened to the man, had he seen him on television? Had he met someone who had heard him preach? It was a surprise to discover that Vickery was so young — two years younger than he, in fact — when his name was so vaguely, so teasingly familiar.

Nathanael Vickery?

He had fallen asleep very late one night only to wake abruptly a few minutes afterward, a jabbing pain in one eye. Ah yes: yes. His dream had provided the answer. His body — a coward's body, eager to acknowledge pain before pain became a reality — had provided the answer. Of course he knew about Vickery, he had read about Vickery years ago, he had been shaken and amused and contemptuous of that *If-thine-eye-offend-thee* performance. He had thought Vickery was finished, as indeed Vickery seemed to have thought. Quite obviously the young man had gone mad. But the ways of Pentecostals are not our ways, William Japheth thought wryly, and so the evangelist has returned . . . and so I must make a pilgrimage to Port Calmar to hear him.

The Civic Arena was an aged, soot-blackened, foursquare building only a few blocks from the waterfront district. It appeared to be the only building in sight that was still in use: directly across the street was a partly gutted warehouse, its walls torn violently away to expose stairways leading nowhere and wires that had the look of veins; down the block was a boarded-up building that had once been the Seaview Tavern: Dine & Dance.

A number of people were approaching the arena, however. William Japheth crossed the street to join them, the collar of his coat turned up, his glasses streaming with rain. He felt unaccountably excited, even exhilarated. It must have been the effect of the hurried walk against the wind and his memory of Nathanael Vickery of six years before. And the sight of the marquee, advertising wrestling matches on Fri. & Sat. nites, and *Seekers Convo* Sunday at 8 P.M.

Admission was a "suggested donation of one dollar."

Immediately inside the arena William Japheth saw someone familiar — a middle-aged woman and a girl of about twelve who had boarded the bus a few miles outside Port Calmar.

Half the arena had been roped off. In the center was a raised platform covered with what appeared to be linoleum tile. A few technicians were setting up the microphone and the speaker system, and a stocky, bald man in his fifties, in a blue serge suit with a vest, was giving orders nervously. He looked, Japheth thought, like a fifth-rate minister of some sort: dechurched for drinking, probably: Vickery's manager?

What a dreary place! Someone had pulled a canvas tarpaulin only partway over an unsightly pile of equipment beneath the platform. The ceiling was remote, splotched, above glaring lights; the windows were protected by grills; there was an odor of chill and stagnation, the stale distress of innumerable bodies. A pot-bellied man with a fringe of white hair, clad improbably in a uniform, stood chatting with an elderly couple who were taking their seats in the very first row. Japheth saw that he wore a gun belt and a holster — he was armed!

Fifteen minutes to eight. Ten minutes. The steeply banked rows of seats were not filling up quickly. Japheth cringed as he looked about, fearing he might see someone he knew, someone who knew *him*. But that was unlikely, wasn't it? Music began. Organ. Someone was playing chords heavily, pompously. The notes were overloud and wheezing faintly about the edges. "Rock of Ages" played as a military tune. An organ with foot pedals, played inexpertly but with a certain degree of audacity. Someone excused himself, as he passed Japheth to sit a few seats away. A solitary individual, a man of about thirty-five, in a gabardine suit with a white shirt and no tie, and a profile that struck Japheth as demented. The man began to sing in a low, quavering voice. *Let me hide myself in. . . . Let the water and the. . . .* Two rows

ahead, a group of five or six young girls filed in. Two had
bleached their hair an identical shade of bone white. One wore a
bright red coat with an imitation leopard-skin collar. They were
shopgirls, Japheth reasoned, opening his notebook and fumbling
for a pen, or perhaps factory workers. . . . Wasn't there a textile
mill in Port Calmar? Several mills? Canning factories?

He must take notes tonight.

Or write a letter to Audrey — who did *not* understand why
he'd left her this weekend.

(They were not engaged because they didn't believe in engagements, but they hoped to be married in a year or two; and in the
meantime, since Audrey was teaching French at a girls' private
school in Quincy, Massachusetts, they had only weekends to be
together.)

A number of obese people in the audience, Japheth noted.
One woman barrel-shaped, in fact shapeless, her hair remarkably
pert and shiny — or was it a wig — orange-red wig — obviously
not her own hair: how monstrous she was, and yet how placid,
how *hopeful!* Staring at the door through which the evangelist
would appear; mouthing the words to a too-familiar hymn. Japheth bent over his notebook, writing in a crude shorthand of
his own invention. Though he was the son and grandson of
scholars and certainly intended to be a scholar himself, in fact
could not take seriously any other profession — for what other
profession gave a man such knowledge, and hence such power?
— he liked to play at being a writer at times, a poet, even a
sociologist intent upon taking careful note of the obvious, for fear
that no one else would care to preserve it: and so he scribbled
descriptions and impressions in his notebook, hunched over in
the cramped seat, his fingers working furiously: and he realized,
not for the first time, that the act of writing in so alien and
confusing an atmosphere was a comfort to him. *And there was
given me a reed like unto a rod: and the angel stood, saying, Rise,
and measure the temple of God, and the altar, and them that
worship therein.*

The obese woman with the orange-red wig. The man beside

her, not very clean-shaven, looking like a caricaturist's idea of a poor farmer. Jacket with sheepskin lining, a plaid shirt, no tie, cheap lightweight trousers. . . . Eyes sunken in his face yet curiously alert: Japheth noted uneasily that the man appeared to be looking at *him*. (But how could he know William Japheth Sproul III was an outsider, a mere observer? — that he had come not to participate, not even to be a witness in the strict sense of the word, but merely to observe with a clinical objectivity?)

"It's filling up, isn't it?" a woman exclaimed close beside him.

Japheth looked up, startled.

"Five minutes to eight and it's filling up and looks like a real nice crowd, a real nice friendly crowd," the woman said excitedly.

"Yes," Japheth said, trying to smile.

A woman of about thirty-eight or forty. Alone. In surprisingly good clothes — a cloth coat of some high-quality material, shoes that were not scuffed and run-over but looked new and fashionable, as far as Japheth could judge such things (for his mother and her sisters, being economically well off, had made it a point to dress themselves with care and discretion); small-boned hands, the nails manicured but not painted; the hair neatly arranged, not bleached or stiff with hair spray; the accent clear enough, not nasal and drawling. She might have been a schoolteacher. Probably *was* a schoolteacher.

"Is this the first time you've heard Nathanael Vickery?" Japheth asked shyly.

"Oh no! Heard him in Flambrugh last spring, and before that in a real little church in White Falls where my brother-in-law's the pastor," she said. "I don't belong to the Seekers. I'm still holding off, I guess, tarrying, as they say," she said breathlessly. "I don't *know*. Do you?"

"*Know* — ?"

"Those people close to the front, all those people — and the ones standing in the aisle, you see? — where that boy is holding a placard — they've all made their decision for Christ, they've been baptized, they're Seekers. Brother Nathan intervened for them. The Holy Spirit came into them and they *know* — it's said you either know or you don't, there's no hesitation at all. I haven't eaten since eight o'clock this morning and would have gone longer except I get so dizzy; why, coming down these steps here I felt so lightheaded for a second I was almost frightened," she said, leaning close to Japheth so he could hear her over the organ's noise, and possibly so that she could, with a shrewd sideways glance, see what he was writing — *was* he a reporter, maybe? — with his glasses and trench coat and fastidious squint he looked like someone not-usual. (He managed to shield his notebook with one arm — unobtrusively, he hoped; he had a naïve childish fear of offending strangers.) "But I haven't had time to study the Bible like I should. I *work* all week, five days a week. It isn't like I sit home, you know, and have hours with nothing to do. . . . Have you come to join them tonight, do you think?"

"Join them — ?" Japheth said.

"The Seekers. Nathan's people. Sometimes you have a *feeling* that the Holy Spirit will come into you, and sometimes you are taken completely by surprise. I just don't *know*," she said, giggling nervously, fussing with one of her earrings, "I can't sort out my feelings from what might be — oh, I don't know — going without eating or the music here or the nice people here — And wait till you see Nathan — he's a true man of God, no doubt about it — It's maybe the case that the Holy Spirit *has* led me here this evening because just the other morning I woke up with a sore throat and I thought *Oh no! not again!* — because I had a terrible case of the flu last spring — and there was the Convocation tonight in my own home town and I felt so brokenhearted if I had to miss it — and — And anyway this morning I woke up feeling all well: the sore throat and the cold had gone away: and I went to church and just gave thanks and it's *maybe* the case that the Holy Ghost is preparing me for something tonight, but I just don't *know*."

A man and a woman and three children stumbled past Japheth's legs and took their seats immediately to his right. The man was surprisingly young to be head of a family — he wore a leather jacket badly cracked about the elbows, and his straight black hair, stiffened with grease, was combed harshly back from his face. He glanced at Japheth, and Japheth at him, but their eyes did not meet. Ordinarily Japheth would have felt intimidated by such a creature — there had been one on the Trailways bus, in fact, an unsmiling young man in his late twenties, tattooed on one wrist, cruel and reptilian about the eyes: one of the unemployed, Japheth thought, one of the unemployable. (Though possibly he was a factory worker or a gas station attendant. But even these jobs were now said to be scarce.) The man's wife was hardly more than a girl, twenty-two at the most. She wore shoes with spiked heels and pinched toes, no longer fashionable so far as Japheth knew, and sheer black stockings, and a royal blue dress that looked rather festive; her pretty face was heart-shaped, her lips darkly pink (she was one of the few women in the place who wore makeup), her voice as she scolded and chattered was bright and quick and inflectionless. On her left hand she wore a wedding band and an engagement ring with a ludicrously small diamond in an outsized setting — which her young husband was probably still paying for, Japheth supposed.

Now they were singing "What a Friend We Have in Jesus": a smiling woman in a white wool dress was leading them, standing at the microphone and moving her hands in wide, awkward, enthusiastic motions. The glaring ceiling lights dimmed abruptly. Japheth thought *I can't escape now* and felt a flicker of panic, for perhaps it had been a mistake, he would go away exhausted and disgusted and confirmed in his contempt for people, and Audrey would quarrel with him ("If you don't *believe* in Christianity why on earth are you a seminarian — why write a dissertation on something you think is wild *nonsense* — is it just to be stubborn?") and cry angrily, as she sometimes did, because he sat there mute and guilty, unable to defend or even to explain himself, and he would drag himself through the day, and at ten in the evening hurry to the telephone to call her to beg forgiveness: because he did love her and could not bear her scorn. (And what was more troubling to him was the fact that he was known as *Billy* among his friends, and *William* among his professors, but when he was on his own, among strangers, he fell into the habit of calling himself *William Japheth*, and tonight he realized he'd been thinking of himself simply as *Japheth* for some time, an endearingly foolish name, not really his at all: an inheritance from his great-grandfather, a minister in Edinburgh many years ago. As far as Audrey knew, as far as he wished her to know, the name *Japheth* was never used at all, reduced to an initial on his official papers.)

The arena was fairly crowded now. There were still empty seats at the very rear, and half the seats had been wisely roped off (for an evangelist of only moderate local notoriety could not hope to draw as many people as wrestling matches), but Japheth was surprised that so many people *had* bothered to come out on this dismal night. He tried to make an estimate. He'd never been good with figures — nor had simple arithmetic been one of his father's skills — but if there were approximately twenty-five rows of seats — or were there more? — or less? — he began counting again, badly distracted by the enthusiastic singing and handclapping all about him — if there were, say, thirty rows of seats and there were four separate sections of seats and in each section approximately   fifteen — twelve? — twenty? — seats — minus those that were unoccupied, of course, an average of two or three — might there be — he made a reckless stab — five hundred people here tonight? Or eight hundred? Or four hundred? But he had overlooked an entire section in the balcony, he realized. The balcony. Or *was* that a balcony? He turned clumsily in his seat, twisting his neck around, peering up. But he was sitting in such a position that he could not really see. . . . No, he thought irritably, it isn't a balcony: this isn't a theater but a sports arena: it's just part of the ceiling.

A cheerful ruddy-cheeked man in a dark brown suit with a handkerchief showing its corner in one pocket was at the microphone now, introducing Nathan Vickery. He was, Japheth gathered, a local minister: Baptist, maybe, or Church of God, or

Pentecostal. He seemed to be quite well-known. Pentecostal? But they were strong in this area, and throughout the state. (And in Japheth's own home town of Boston they were doing exceptionally well in recent years, strange and distressing as it seemed: imagine, Pentecostals in the year 1965 in America!) This smiling gentleman might have been a small-town druggist, or an automobile salesman, or a chiropractor, but he was by his own definition a man of God, and hundreds of people seemed willing to take him at his word.

A pause, and no clapping or vocal acclaim, though Japheth felt the arena fairly quiver with anticipation, and then Nathanael Vickery was on the platform, walking with a quick, stiff stride.

Japheth leaned far forward in his seat, staring. A pity he hadn't gotten to the arena earlier so he might be in the first row — back here in the ninth or tenth he could not see as well as he would have liked. *Which* of this strange creature's eyes was the real one, and which the glass? And were those gray hairs, or simply the way light happened to be reflecting . . . ? One thing was certain: Vickery's stage presence: his energy, his effortless confidence, the power of his raw, young, curiously aggrieved voice as it lifted to draw them all into prayer. He had no sociability, no platform ebullience or small talk, he hardly smiled, he did not seem to acknowledge his audience. He knew they were there and he spoke to them, brusquely and intimately, but he did not appear to *see* them in any ordinary sense. Listening to him, too surprised even to hear what he was saying, Japheth felt an unmistakable sensation of dismay, of dread.

This young evangelist did not look young. Japheth had been expecting to see a boy's attractive but inconsequential face, something like his own; but Nathanael Vickery was very peculiar-looking indeed. Though he was only twenty-five years old he had no air of youth, of youngness, about him. His face was lean and angular, his untidy dark hair swung harshly about it, the severe line of his jaw gave him an intense, hungry, almost greedy look. The prayer continued, melodic and yearning and eerily confident, and Japheth found it difficult still to fasten upon any of the words. He had begun to shiver. What was Vickery saying? — addressing God in that manner? — it had to do with the Holy Spirit, and the Seeking for Christ, and the Chosen of the Lord, and the intervention of Jesus Christ, and the Last Things: the Final Days of civilization, the completion of a cycle, the end of history. Japheth would have liked to take notes but he found himself leaning forward in his seat, stiffly, afraid even to glance away from Vickery for fear he would miss something. All about him people were shifting in their seats, leaning forward, straining to hear as though Vickery's words were indistinct, when in fact the amplifying system was more than adequate.

The prayer's intensity came to a kind of climax: with his head bowed and his bony hands pressed together in a classic attitude of supplication, Nathan Vickery called upon the Lord to intervene tonight, to send His power into the heart of each person present who truly wished to declare himself a Seeker for Christ. "There are those who know not what they do, or why they have been drawn here," Vickery said, his voice tremulous, "but I say unto You, Our Heavenly Father, that You see fit to show these people the miraculous light of Your love and forgiveness — that You awaken them to Your being, regardless of the ignorance in which they abide — !"

The prayer ended, much to Japheth's relief.

Now the preacher began to speak more humanly, though his manner was still peremptory; he spoke of his gratitude for the warm welcome the Seekers had received so far in Port Calmar, and for the generous introduction Reverend Weston of the Disciples of Christ Church had given him, and for the fact that so many people had come here tonight, some of them already declared for Christ, and others still awaiting baptism in the power of the Holy Spirit. Japheth tried to relax; he would have sat back in his seat, except someone directly behind him was pressing forward with his knees and breathing onto the back of Japheth's head. (The seats in the arena were uncomfortably small and jammed close together, as if, having been constructed some decades ago, they had in fact been designed for a smaller race of people.)

There was an interlude of gospel singing. The woman in the white dress stepped forward, beaming. Her face was shiny. Japheth had no interest in her or in the song, which he found no more annoying than the earlier songs, though he could not help becoming caught up in the rhythmic handclapping; he continued to watch Nathan Vickery. How very *odd* he was. His skin was pale and appeared to be luminous, as if lit, uncannily, from within. His eyes were half-closed. He stood perfectly erect in a nondescript costume — a cheap gunmetal-gray suit, a white shirt, a dark necktie — and Japheth had the idea that he was trembling, attuned not to the boisterous and aggressive song, but to a private, interior rhythm.

The song ended. The preaching began now in earnest. Japheth dropped his pen — his fingers appeared to have gone numb — and it rolled somewhere off to the right, past the feet of the young man beside him. There would be no reaching for it, no possibility of asking someone to pick it up. Even the children were staring ahead, enraptured. *I don't want this*, Japheth thought. *This is a mistake.* Nathanael Vickery was not a man but a voice, and the voice was otherworldly, serenely and maddeningly Biblical, the spirit of the Bible (or of certain books of the Bible: Japheth was alert enough to recognize Revelation, and Daniel, and Isaiah, and Ezekiel) come alarmingly to life.

Though his gospel was one of love, and though Japheth gathered that the Seekers, like most Pentecostal groups, would accept anyone who claimed to be baptized in the Holy Spirit and "washed in the Blood of the Lamb," much of what Vickery was saying was upsetting indeed. Nothing matters except God: nothing. Not war, not struggle, not poverty, not disappointments, not physical or mental anguish; not the deaths of oneself or one's family; not even happiness. Most of all it was happiness, Vickery exclaimed, that tempted man away from God. Ordinary worldly accomplishment, and love, and joy — these were more dangerous, perhaps, than suffering, and even more dangerous than sin itself, because they blind us to our predicament. Angrily he spoke of the Age of Nonbelief that was now upon us, the loathsome twentieth century, the completion of the sixth millennium since the creation of Adam and the possible — no, probable — end of history. The Last Things are upon us: it is all as the Bible predicted, and where shall we turn for aid if not to the Lord?

But the age was materialist, skeptical, blinded, atheistic; set upon its own destruction. The human race was committing suicide and would *not* be deterred, because it worshiped not Jesus Christ but the Devil himself, called by many names. He knew! Nathan Vickery knew! God spoke clearly and angrily to him every hour of every day, bidding him step forward to help those who craved help — to save those drowning in the pool of filth that was the contemporary world. *He that is not with me is against me:* you must choose either Christ or Satan.

And what of Satan?

Vickery spoke coldly and passionately, beginning now to pace about, to move his arms in wide, accusing gestures. He had not been smiling earlier, Japheth realized, shocked, because he was murderously angry. Satan was the secret god of America and it was given to only a few of God's Chosen to comprehend this fact. They were in danger of being broken by their knowledge and of falling into despair over the crisis to come, for they *knew* exactly how many years the human race had remaining, and consequently how little time they had to rescue souls. It was a bitter, bitter knowledge! Yet they lifted their voices in prayer to the Lord, Who will bring all history to a close, a continual prayer — *Come, O Lord, cloaked in Thy wrath and righteousness, come with Thy vengeance, come!*

Japheth felt a hot wave of disbelief. Was this madman praying for the end of the world?

Vickery went on to speak of Satan in the churches. And of Satan in the schools. In government. Pride, materialism, drunkenness, drugs, the sinful use of one another's bodies, the making of war upon defenseless people. From all the pulpits

come hollow faithless cries. American Christians! American hypocrites! Sinners! Devil-worshipers! Their fate will be that of their
secret, invisible god; they will not escape any more than *he* escaped, before the start of human history.

And in a voice of heart-stopping beauty, fairly trembling with
feeling, he spoke those verses from Isaiah that had captivated
Japheth for many years —

> How art thou fallen from heaven, O Lucifer, son of the
> morning! how art thou cut down to the ground, which
> didst weaken the nations!

> For thou hast said in thine heart, I will ascend into
> heaven, I will exalt my throne above the stars of God: I
> will sit also upon the mount of the congregation, in the
> sides of the north:

> I will ascend above the heights of the clouds; I will be
> like the most High.

> Yet thou shalt be brought down to hell. . . .

On all sides the arena rocked with emotion. There were scattered outcries. Japheth felt his jaws lock tight: his teeth had begun
to chatter: he was astonishingly weak and for a moment did not
know where he was. *Yet thou shalt be brought down to hell.* The
way Vickery had spoken those words, the exquisite way his voice
had dropped from the earlier pitch of feeling. . . . Japheth could
not stop himself from shivering. He sat hunched over in his seat,
his glasses halfway down his nose, damp with perspiration,
chilled to the bone.

Vickery continued to speak of Satan, and of the monstrousness
of the contemporary world, and of the continual defilement and
crucifixion of Our Saviour, and of the impending doom. Japheth
felt suddenly very lonely. His legs and arms were weak, his throat
ached as if he wished to cry but dared not make a sound. He was
so very much alone! So lonely! His grandfather was William Japheth Sproul of the Harvard Divinity School, a Biblical scholar

who had been one of the first men to work on the Dead Sea Scrolls; his father, dead at the age of forty-four, had held a chair in sacred literature at Union, and had been considered the most formidable commentator of his time on the New Testament. And they were both dead, and he too would die. And he would die without having known them. Without having known anyone. There would be no woman for him — in his misery he could not even recall the name of the woman he loved. He would not marry, he would not love anyone, he would not know anyone, he would live for a while longer and then die and then —

The notebook slipped through his knees. He stooped to pick it up and his forehead struck the back of the seat before him, and he whimpered with the pain and surprise of it; and when he straightened again his curious mood had passed. Nathanael Vickery was telling the crowd of tense, expectant people that they had only to ask God to make Himself real to them, and God would respond. "You must pray. I will lead you. You must empty your heart of willfulness, and pray to Our Lord that the Holy Spirit will descend into you this evening and baptize you with His power. Without the Holy Spirit you will not know God, you will not be able to welcome Christ into your heart, you will not become a Seeker for God, and in the Final Days you may become lost to all help and hurtled deep into the pits that wait for all who have rejected God's love. Do you hear? Do you understand? Oh, my brothers and sisters, if I could breathe in you, if I could see through your eyes, if I could *become* you for only a few minutes — if through God's miraculous love I could dwell in your heart and prepare the way for Christ — if I could see to your salvation, my brothers and sisters in Christ, then I would want nothing more on earth, nothing more on earth! — do you understand?"

His voice was incantatory, the gestures of his hands mesmerizing. Japheth shook himself away, apart. He was not going to listen any longer. He had heard enough. Not a madman, perhaps, but a criminal: a manipulator of others' souls. "I will lead you," Vickery was saying, his arms spread wide. "You must come forward. You must give yourselves to the Holy Spirit. You must pray. I will lead you. There is little time remaining. You must pray. You must surrender. I will lead you. I will lead you now and always."

The woman to Japheth's left was obviously distressed. She kept moving from side to side, hugging herself, moaning softly. Japheth did not wish to look at her; he did not care to see how she might be transformed. A few rows down, another woman had risen from her seat and was swaying from side to side, her hands pressed flat against her lips. As Nathan Vickery continued to speak, moving along the very edge of the platform, his arms opened for an embrace, his long, lean, pale face the only focus of attention in the entire arena, others half rose, or stumbled into the aisle, and began to speak or call out, abashed, whimpering, frightened, ecstatic: as if they were beginning to see something materialize before them and were not *yet* certain whether it was a thing of great beauty or of surpassing horror.

Japheth calmed himself by pressing the backs of his hands against his forehead. His face was hot, his hands had gone cold. He must escape. Around him people were becoming hysterical just as he had suspected they would, and as he had half-hoped they would so that he might witness, in person, the phenomenon of "conversion." A sudden shriek that ended in high clacking gibberish — a young man elsewhere who got to his feet and began shouting incoherently — a child beginning to cry, his voice climbing higher and higher in terror: it was as Japheth had supposed, yet it was terrible, terrible. He must escape. He did not want to observe anything more.

"Excuse me — let me pass — Please let me pass —"

He found himself stumbling over feet, desperate to get into the aisle. Already people were coming forward for Jesus. Two or three were descending the last of the steps, to be greeted by others — members of the Vickery church, presumably — "Seekers" who were positioned there to welcome the converts. And more were preparing to descend. Japheth hurried up the steps, hunched over, genuinely frightened, for what if someone mistook him for a convert and turned him about and forced him to go kneel at Nathan Vickery's feet?

An elderly man stumbled into Japheth's arms.

"Excuse me, sir — Please —"

The man's milky eyes rolled. A string of saliva hung from his lips. He pushed at Japheth and nearly knocked him down. "Fool! Sod! Stand aside! Don't you block my way! Don't you block my way this time like you done last time! *Stand aside!*"

Japheth ducked around him and ran up the last of the steps.

Now the organ music had begun again. The entire building shook with its relentless beating chords. In his mind's eye Japheth saw with perfect clarity the merciless accusing face of Nathanael Vickery, he saw Vickery's eyes fixed upon *his* fleeing back, he could hear, piercing even the organ's frantic noise, that terrible admonishment that was meant for *him: Yet thou shalt be brought down to hell. . . .*

ii

It had been his expectation that the stabbing would kill Your faith in him: would reveal at last his unworthiness as one of Your Chosen. But it was not to be. During the long months that followed, during the confused nights and days of his convalescence, it was gradually revealed to him that his action had no more significance in Your sight than that of a fly's buzzing in an attic room.

The dullish blade of the kitchen knife had been a kind of baptism. He had not known beforehand how You led him to such knowledge.

Afterward he woke gropingly to the realization that he was now above sin.

"So it's God Who chooses," he said slowly. He spoke to his grandmother, who helped nurse him. "God acts. Not us. If we submit to Him perfectly we are above sin."

"I don't understand," Mrs. Vickery said.

Her hands shook; her own vision had become clouded.

"I can do anything at all," Nathan said, "so long as it isn't my own will, but God's; it's impossible for me to sin."

"How do you feel? Are you stronger today?"

"This," he said, touching his cheekbone beneath the wounded eye, "was my sanctification."

Small liquid-light creatures brushed against him. Birds, butterflies, tiny fish. Your fluttering fingers: blessing after blessing. He woke to the warmth of such caresses, his good eye reluctant to open as if fearful of banishing You from the world. As the small creatures touched him, the envelope of his skin dissolved and they passed into him and through him. His flesh rippled with pleasure, his eyelids trembled.

Creature upon creature, delicate as vapor. His heart stilled in wonder as they approached — and as they touched him, and passed through him, he sighed aloud.

Seven months You bathed him in Your infinite warmth as he slept, gathering his strength. Seven months, he was told afterward, he lay in the convalescent home, near-oblivious of his surroundings. His grandmother was always near. He begged her forgiveness, he raved that she should leave him, he forgot her for days at a time. One of the pleasurous creatures was a hard, plump, glassy fish, a tiny sunfish. It swam against his face. It butted against his face. With a groan he surrendered and it burrowed into his empty socket, a queer tight hard stubborn substance.

The hand mirror, turned critically from side to side, revealed a deathly pale face coarsened by the beginning of a beard. Nathan ran his fingers across his chin, struck by the fleeting thought that he was, after all, a man. His grandfather had had a beard. Gone? Dead? They had burned him. Thrown him onto the small mountain of debris and wetted it all with gasoline and tossed a match onto it and that was that.

"Grandpa was trying to talk to me," Nathan said one morning. "I don't know what he wanted."

"What? What are you saying?" Mrs. Vickery whispered.

"He's alone. He's lonely. He doesn't know where he is. He kept asking me what had happened — where he went. I told him to pray to the Lord for guidance but he didn't seem to hear," Nathan said slowly. In order to wake each morning he had to fight the drugs. He pushed his way up through layers and layers of an element treacherous as water.

"What are you saying? *Who are you talking about?*"

"He isn't dead," Nathan said. "But he isn't alive either."

"Your grandfather? Thaddeus? You dreamed about him?"

The old woman was alarmed. Nathan squinted at her with his good eye, taken aback at her agitation. He wished only to make contact with the Holy Spirit in her, which was their usual way of communicating, but her excitement distracted him. She wanted to know where Thaddeus was, did he have a message for her, was he in distress, did he forgive her, did he love her, did he have a message . . . ?

"He was wandering somewhere that looked like . . . like a lane," Nathan said. He spoke slowly and reluctantly, disliking his grandmother's agitation. If she carried on so, one of the nurses might appear. ". . . a cow-lane between fields. The old farm, I think. It was almost dark, so I couldn't see well. But I saw *him*, I saw him before he saw me. He was waving his hands as if he was blind and asking where he was, as if he knew I was there though he couldn't quite see me; he asked where the family had gone, what had happened, who was living in his house, what would become of him? He wasn't himself: he's lost some weight. His cheeks are sunken in. His hair is all gray. I wanted to come close to him but the Lord held me back because if I felt pity for him, if I ran over to him, I would be insulting the Lord by coming between Him and one of His souls. *Pray to the Lord God for guid-*

ance, I said. *Pray without stopping. Never stop!* It's what I tried to tell him in life. . . . But he didn't seem to hear."

"Then he isn't dead!" Mrs. Vickery cried.

"Yes," said Nathan. "But he isn't alive either."

Not long after his new eye was fitted into the socket and, in the hand-held mirror, acquired a steely black-brown authoritative gleam, a woman said to be Nathanael Vickery's mother came to the hospital. She stood in the doorway out of sight and had to be coaxed inside.

"If you've come this far, Elsa — !" Mrs. Vickery said.

"But he doesn't know me, he doesn't want to see me —"

"He certainly wants to see you."

"Is he awake? He isn't? Oh, I'll go away and come back tomorrow!"

Nathan turned to her, squinting. The breathy girlish voice belonged to a full-bodied woman of about forty who stepped timidly into the room. She wore a polka-dot dress with long sleeves and carried a patent-leather purse. Her hair was brassy but rather attractive. "I'll go away and come back tomorrow," she said to Mrs. Vickery, blundering into the door frame.

His mother?

Had he believed it was so, he might have been speechless; but he did not believe it.

And so he had the strength to welcome the woman into his room, to invite her to sit down. She stayed for an hour and forty-five minutes on the first day. Mrs. Vickery talked most, asking her questions about her husband, her children, her home. There were presumably two half-brothers of Nathan's, and one half-sister. He smiled in response to such extraordinary news, though he did not quite accept it. His mother! His long-banished mother! Mrs. Vickery rarely spoke of Elsa except to allude to her in cryptic exasperated terms, but she was curious about the children, very curious about the husband. What sort of job did he have? What sort of salary? Had the children been baptized? Did she and her husband go to church at all?

"It's wonderful to see you," the woman said, making a clumsy gesture with both hands. She might have been offering to take Nathan's hand, but she stood too far away. "I was so, so. . . . So shocked. . . . Why, everybody was talking about it! I mean, you know, the accident. . . . What you did. . . . It was on all the radio news, I guess; it got carried on television two or three times in one day; I like to died, just hearing that name spoken like that! Never, never in my life . . . such a fright. . . . Wesley came home and there I was sitting in the kitchen in the dark with the two youngest running wild around the house and none of the lights on and . . . and it was just the most awful shock of my life. . . ."

"I'm sorry," Nathan said.

"But here you are looking well," she said, blushing. (For it was not true that he looked well; but the eye at least was in place. Suppose she had had to stare at an empty eye socket! Two drinks in a tavern just down the way had been necessary to get her to the hospital, and she would need another before she started back home.) "And they're saying what? — another week or two and you'll be discharged?"

"Is that what they're saying?" Nathan asked.

He had not known so much time had passed.

"Then we'll have to see each other real often, now that we're together again," the woman said. She began to cry. Now she did take Nathan's hand, both his hands, and Mrs. Vickery stood at the foot of the bed, crying also. Nathan gazed upon them both with love. His mother, his grandmother. Someone squeezed his fingers, and he squeezed her fingers in return. His mother? But what did that mean? He had no mother, strictly speaking; and certainly no father. He had been born of a woman, but the woman had been merely a vessel, a vehicle, wasn't that understood?

He was being lifted from bed. Swung about in the air.

A gigantic face drew near, he could feel its heartbeat, he began to tremble in expectation. His fingers flailed the air but could grasp nothing. How hungry he was, how terrifically hungry! His body was a tiny void that must be filled. A tiny universe that was empty and ravenous and must be filled.

Something metallic and cold touched his mouth, prying its way in.

That too was Your blessing.

"I wasn't a good mother to you," someone was saying. Her sobs were coarse and anguished. "I wasn't myself then! — I didn't *know!* I was too young, I was just a girl. Will you ever forgive me —"

The balloon face was wet with tears. It smelled of warmth, of blankets, of milk. A single eye was like the moon, fiercely glaring. Nathan could not determine whether all this had happened long ago or whether it was happening now; or would happen sometime in the future.

He swung his legs, slightly stiffened from lack of exercise, out of the bed. His grandmother helped him with the terry-cloth bathrobe (one of the many gifts he had received) and he stood beside his mother, barefoot, anxious to comfort her. "Will you ever forgive me," she wept.

"The Lord forgives everyone," Nathan said.

His voice too was stiffened from lack of use.

"If we could pray together," Nathan said, "it might be that Christ would come into your heart — it might be that you are really a Seeker for Christ — which is why you were led here today —"

The woman stared at him, uncomprehending. Except for faint lines about her eyes, she looked quite young, almost girlish. *Was* this person his mother? *His?* Her dark-pink pearlish lipstick was smeared and she was panting as if she'd just hurried up a flight of stairs.

"Pray?" she said. Her voice lifted wildly, almost shrilly.

"Pray to God. Now. Pray to Him. On our knees. Now. Here," Nathan said urgently.

She glanced at Mrs. Vickery but must have found no comfort or allegiance there.

"But I — I don't want to ruin my stockings," she said with an embarrassed, despairing laugh. "If I kneel I'll —"

"Do as your son tells you," Mrs. Vickery said.

"Here? Right here on the floor? With that door open and people out in the corridor gaping in — ?"

"The Lord forgives everyone, everything," Nathan said. He gripped his mother by the elbows as if to force her to lift her face upward, to listen. But he saw that she did not comprehend. She was frightened, even repelled by him. "You have only to ask forgiveness of Him," Nathan said less certainly, "and He will . . . will respond."

"Elsa, do as he says. This is Nathan Vickery talking to you," Mrs. Vickery said sharply. "*Nathan Vickery*. Why, he's come to change the world, he's been sent by God to. . . . And you worry about your stockings! Isn't that *just* like you, Elsa, after all these years!"

Mother and son knelt on the cold hospital floor. Nathan clasped his hands together and lowered his head and began to pray in a low, soft, groping voice. That God would forgive, that God would bring them together again, that Christ would enter their hearts and make them truly kin to one another, that the Holy Spirit would descend upon them, that time and history and sorrow and shame and anguish would be annihilated and forgotten, that they should know each other in Christ, in Christ, not mother and son but Christ in each speaking to Christ. . . .

From a distance he heard again the hoarse, irregular sobs, which, after a time, no longer disturbed him.

iii

When Nathanael Vickery came out of seclusion in the autumn of 1961 it was to discover that his act of penitence had worked to greatly increase his influence; so much so, in fact, that he shrank from identifying himself as *that* person, and half-wondered whether he should change his name and journey to some distant part of the country and begin his service for God anew. . . . The irony of the situation did not escape him, and allowed him to see Your design as it manifests itself in all things; nor did the irony of the situation escape Marian Miles Beloff, who had immediately and publicly dismissed Nathan from his staff.

(Reverend Beloff had been unable to avoid newspaper reporters, and even network television reporters, who sought him out within minutes of Nathan's act, and in the confusion and rage of the moment he had said certain things — that the young minister was insane, for instance, that he was willful and selfish and possibly even guided by the Devil, and needed psychiatric rather than medical care, and had, moreover, needed it for months — which he came to regret later. His personal anger came through with despairing clarity in the many articles and interviews, several of them in national magazines, and it was not only public opinion that swung violently against him but the sentiment of his own deacons and close associates, and the feeling of his own daughter, for where was his Christian love? — his charity? — his forgiveness? Local ministers were eager to preach from their pulpits in favor of the spirit of Nathanael Vickery's act, if not in favor of the *act* itself; not perhaps because they truly valued martyrdom or even penitence, but because the situation gave them the opportunity to attack Marian Miles Beloff. It turned out that he had no friends or supporters at all among the religious leaders of Port Oriskany. One by one they condemned him and stood apart from him. It was even said he had no fundamental grasp of Christ's message or of the meaning of his crucifixion; that he did not adequately comprehend the meaning of suffering; that he did not seriously believe in hell. He had had altogether too easy a time in his ministry, building that pretentious church, bragging of his followers' devotion and their constant generosity, preaching a superficial, sentimentalized kind of Christianity that was an insult to Christ Himself. And he had long been notorious for seducing well-to-do parishioners from other churches, even upon occasion from the Roman Catholic Church itself: and then boasting of their gratitude. Rumors surfaced concerning his relationships with certain women, his expensive cars, his having been seen at the race track, in cocktail lounges in distant cities, in suspicious company. . . . His television ratings fell off as a consequence of these rumors, or perhaps because Reverend Beloff seemed to have lost his old zest, his old amiable *certainty* about every word he uttered; attendance at the Bethany-Nazarene Church following the publicity rapidly declined, in a matter of weeks, when it became clear that Nathan Vickery would not return. For a while Reverend Beloff continued to preach and to be seen about the city in his handsome wide-brimmed black hat, carrying now an ivory-topped cane, and he gave the impression of being confident enough, defying some of the charges made against him by continuing to use his Rolls-Royce even for local trips; but it was understood, and he seemed in a way to accept it, that his day was over. He went into semi-retirement in the summer of 1960 and by the time Nathanael Vickery was beginning his ascent, in the years 1964–65, the old man was in complete retirement in Douay, Arizona, a senior citizens' community in which he had a considerable financial investment.)

"The Lord guides us in all things," Nathan realized. "The Lord provides."

It had seemed rather unfair to him that Reverend Beloff should be considered so unchristian when, in fact, it was through Beloff's agency that the hospital and doctor bills were paid — or by way of the shrewdly high insurance coverage he had on all matters concerning his church (since an extraordinary incident in the early fifties when an angry husband had attempted to sue him for alienation of his wife's affections after she became a fervent convert to his church); and it was through Beloff's son-in-law, Harry Dietz, that he and his grandmother acquired rent-free a hunting lodge on Wolf's Head Lake where they could live in seclusion as long as they wished, responsible only for keeping the place in good repair. Had he been willing to talk to reporters or other inquisitive parties, he would certainly have stressed this aspect of Beloff's behavior; but he shrank from all visitors, even the most devout, even Leonie herself, and by the time he was willing to allude to the situation, some years later, Marian Miles Beloff had left the Bethany-Nazarene Church for good.

In his convalescence and in his seclusion he dwelled for the most part with You, in Your constant regard. He strengthened; he gained back all the weight he had lost, and more; he walked for hours by himself along the edge of the lake, or through the pine woods, contemplating Your being and what possible use You might find for him in this world. He read the Bible, drawn to the Revelation of St. John the Divine most of all. It seemed to him that *here* was a message, a riddle perhaps, for his own scrutiny . . . for him to meditate upon and decipher. . . . He was given to know that it would not matter how long he took preparing his own gospel: whether it took months or even years: for You guided him in all things, according to Your design.

Idly I turn the dial of my compact little radio, encased in its red plastic; though it's past 2:00 A.M. the void is alive with sound — languorous dance music, jazz nearly lost in static, a man's angry voice, a woman's voice lifted in improbable melodic joy. . . . Like Nathan, who was led to listen for long, tense hours to a floor-model radio in the hunting lodge, and who began to scrutinize newspapers and magazines, searching for Your meaning in them, I am continually astonished by the *varied* nature of the world: of even the human world, which no one can chart.

Sometimes I can get a gospel program from as far away as Chicago, late at night. With the volume turned as high as it will go, with my head inclined meekly, I can listen for minutes at a time to a man named Brother Reed, whose message is mainly the good news of Christ's coming and the importance of the fact that Christians love one another and join in a great community able to withstand enemies arising on all sides, in Asia, in Europe, even in South America, even at home. Then the station suddenly fades and my ears are blasted by static. Or another station intrudes, drifting effortlessly across Brother Reed's eager voice: once it was rock music, another time an uncannily beautiful harpsichord concerto that made me start and stare helplessly at the floor, for here was a language I could not comprehend and could not imitate, though it had the power to touch my very soul, as if You Yourself had returned to me. But then that too was lost: furious waves of static dominated the night; and I turned off the radio in despair.

That too was a music. Jarring and discordant. Mocking. Blasphemous. The pitch and rhythm and message of the era as it was communicated to Nathanael Vickery by way of the radio, the newspapers and magazines, and certain people he befriended at the lake — older people, mainly, who lived at Wolf's Head all year, and who complained with a cranky zestful patience about their children and their in-laws and the Government and the summer people and their neighbors and their own pastors who never seemed to take a stand on anything, who didn't seem to *know* anywhere near as much as the young people claimed to know, or practically any news announcer on television, or any politician. . . .

They were angry. But why? The Holy Spirit in them had turned sour. Though they lived in peace in a remote and beautiful part of the mountains, though they were by no means as poor as people Nathan had known in the Marsena area, they were very angry. He was careful not to tell them anything that might identify him, and he never made any remarks about religion, and so they spoke to him with a bitter frankness and even a kind of energetic malice he had not experienced in people before. He reasoned that to their own pastors they spoke quite differently, if they spoke at all. And in church their expressions would be blank, or blankly benign. It was a small revelation to him that quite ordinary people, even the elderly, could be so passionately *angry*.

He had never felt anger in his life. Could not remember having felt it.

"But *why* so much feeling, one person against another?" he

asked his grandmother, groping for words. He felt in a way obscurely ashamed, as he'd been when arithmetic problems back in
his old school in Marsena had baffled him. A hot coarse blush
rose from his neck. "God is within everyone, so isn't it God
hating God? If you hurt another person, isn't it you hurting yourself? There seems no *point* to it," he said slowly.

"I don't know how to answer you," Mrs. Vickery said. It rather
unnerved her that her grandson who knew everything should
appear to be so attentive to *her* words. She wondered if he might
be testing her. "Isn't there hatred in the Bible, Nathan, and cruelty and war and. . . ."

"Yes," Nathan said.

There was a long pause. He would have liked to tell her that
the coming of Christ had changed everything; that His crucifixion had very much altered the world. And it had always been
difficult for him to take seriously the hatred of man for man in
the Bible, in the Old Testament especially, for many of the men
involved seemed merely childish . . . to have belonged to a
cruder, less evolved race. They were human; yet not human in
the way Christ and His disciples were human.

"It might be that you were shielded from things over the years,"
Mrs. Vickery said falteringly, "but I didn't see any point in em-
phasizing all that's wrong. . . . Nor did the Sisleys. There's only
so much time in the day, you know, and if you make room for
the evil, for even knowing about it, why then . . . why then you
are hurting your own self. Don't you think so?"

Nathan did not reply. It seemed to him quite reasonable, ab-
stractly, that human beings should make war upon one another,
for the nature of the world *was* fallen, and it was very likely that
history was easing into the Final Days of which St. John the
Divine spoke; none of this was surprising. The radio news was
always disturbing, as were the newspapers, but it was not quite
the same as hearing anger and hatred in the voices of people to
whom you are speaking on an ordinary sunlit day, and seeing in
their faces a certain mad gleefulness aroused by hate. He was

impatient with himself often, and presumably he had *hated* the evil in himself that had so distracted him from God back in Port Oriskany, but it would have seemed to him pointless to direct this hatred against another human being. As for striking another person, evoking pain in another person. . . . The very thought of it filled him with despair.

"The Jews crucified Our Redeemer, didn't they," Mrs. Vickery said. Her voice had become slow, wondering, hoarse. Since Nathan's "accident" the year before she had grown less certain of herself; she sometimes broke off her sentences without completing them. "There was *that* evil in the world from the start. . . ."

"Everyone shared in the crucifixion," Nathan said. "The whole world was present."

"The Jews. . . ."

"The whole world," Nathan said excitedly, "not just the Jews. But the world *was* Christ. It was His body."

Mrs. Vickery stared at him. She was now seventy-one, still big-bodied, heavy. The flesh had begun to hang from her in odd clumps at the tops of her arms and beneath her chin. She no longer had her hair set professionally, and so it had begun to turn yellowish, the color of faint tobacco stains. She was so close to her grandson that he rarely *saw* her; but there were times when she appeared to be anxiously scrutinizing *him*.

"Yes," she said, "but there were the Jews clamoring for His death, and the soldier who pierced His side. . . ."

"He willed it all! They were merely actors in His imagination!"

Again she stared at him, frowning. Another consequence of Nathan's accident was her intermittent deafness. Though she had been sitting as usual in a pew near the very front of the Bethany-Nazarene Church on that Good Friday, and though she had seen her grandson plainly enough, she had not heard most of his sermon, and she had heard none of his confession at the very end.

"Christ was a form of God and He was never not-God and so He willed everything that happened to Him, just as we will everything that happens to us," Nathan said hurriedly. "It would be blasphemous to think that Christ had *not* willed His own agony . . . or that we don't will ours, regardless of what we think."

"Yes," Mrs. Vickery said, looking away from the young man's pale, heated face.

He continued speaking. The present-day era bewildered him, he said; he could not comprehend it. Christ was immediate, Christ was ever-present, yet people seemed totally unaware of Him. Everything seemed to be disintegrating: hundreds of thousands of people divorced every year; innumerable children abandoned or injured by their own parents; alcoholism and drugtaking and crimes and acts of violence; and a war on the far side of the earth that seemed to be sucking the nation's vitality into it, like a whirlpool. What did it all *mean*? *Why* did it have this meaning? If God spoke through history, what was God's message? Nathan felt that he *must* know. . . .

Mrs. Vickery only half-attended to her grandson's words. The ring of his voice, the timbre of his voice . . . wasn't it familiar to her . . . didn't it inspire in her the sudden impulse to throw up her hands in mock despair . . . to contradict him bluntly and walk out of the room. . . .

Thaddeus?

"I will have to go back again," Nathan was saying, rubbing at his good eye. It was not possible to determine whether he spoke sadly, or proudly, or merely with resignation. "I can see that God is leading me somewhere. Has been leading me. Another six months or so . . . six months spent in preparation. . . . And then I'll return again to the world, and begin again as if I were no more than a child; as if I were newborn. You needn't come with me if you'd rather not. The strain might be too great. I have no idea what God expects of me but it won't be easy: it won't be anywhere near as easy as before. This time I won't have Marian Miles Beloff supporting me. I won't have any staff, or any money . . . at least at first. So if you'd rather not come with me, I understand."

Mrs. Vickery cupped her hand to her ear, as if she hadn't heard. She had been staring at his face intently. "Yes? What?"

"I said you needn't come with me if you don't want to," Nathan repeated. "You can stay here, or I could find a place in town . . . but I don't know yet *which* town . . . I don't know where God wants me to have my base. Maybe a large city. . . . I must wait for God to speak."

"What?" said Mrs. Vickery, her hand still cupped to her ear. "Did you say . . . *God* . . . ?"

iv

The windowpanes crack alarmingly with the cold. It is still January. A January of the spirit. I huddle beneath the covers and see my breath in shy vaporous spurts. While Nathanael Vickery chose freely to fast and (despite the admonition of Christ) thereby asserted his infinite will over his finite appetites, I lie in my rumpled bed numb with hunger because it is simply too cold to get up.

His fasting must have pleased God, in some ways. For God did reward him. In some ways.

His fasting brought him God's presence. Your presence.

But are You not *always* present . . . ?

In which case the fasting was superfluous. Is superfluous.

Nevertheless I too have visions fleeting beneath my eyelids. I too drift into sleep and am rewarded with astonishing, unspeakable sights. In fact, I have grown to fear sleep; at the very edge of sleep my entire body jerks, waking me. But the visions are not always nightmares. They can be sweet, soothing, hypnotic. I think they are the dreams of others, former occupants of this rented bed. Surely they are not my own.

Query: If You are unknown, how do we *know* You are un-known? For You are always and forever invisible, lacking even the substance of the wind, or my steaming breath.

Query: If You were with me once, before my plunge into mat-ter and consciousness, isn't it inevitable that You are with me now?

Query: If You are with me now, why am I so utterly alone . . . ?

▪ ▪ ▪

Imagining Nathanael Vickery is far more difficult a task than I had anticipated. Perhaps it is the cold: my fingers are numb most of the time, the nails a peculiar bluish-purple, until I warm them by closing them about a cup of hot coffee. But then they are warmed on the insides, the very tips of the fingers especially (where the flesh seems particularly sensitive), warmed and over-warmed, at times almost scalded.

I sit huddled now in an overcoat, at a kitchen table with a chipped enamel top. The little red radio is within reach but I will not turn it on this morning: so much squawking cheerful vitality depresses me. If I had Nathan's conviction that Your secret mes-sage was contained within that vitality — in its innumerable un-fathomable aspects — I should turn it on, certainly. For the jig-saw puzzle pieces of Your voice would fly at me and I would be in awe of Your majesty once again. But unfortunately I don't have that conviction.

Imagining Nathanael Vickery. . . .

It is easier to imagine William Japheth Sproul III. Whom I rather like. But he does not enter Nathan's orbit until 1965, and though he believed he was of crucial importance to Nathan's career, I suspect in fact he was not. (Just as poor Leonie Dietz went about giving interviews in the late sixties, fantasizing herself as Nathan Vickery's first and only love: blaming the failure of their love, in retrospect, on her father. But the hypothesis of a *married* Nathan Vickery, a *married* Saviour, was always ludicrous and no one took the woman seriously.)

(It sounds as if I am angry with Leonie. But that can't be — for *why* would I be angry with Leonie?)

Imagining Nathanael Vickery: addressing curious, half-smiling strangers in Heywood Park in the nondescript city of Derby, population 80,000. At the very periphery of a county fair, on a makeshift platform, in the autumn of 1962. That winter, in a store-front church in Yewville, the Tabernacle of Zion, speaking earnestly and ecstatically to a congregation of twenty-five people, three of them stone deaf.

Are you washed in the Blood of the Lamb . . . ?

He must have endured numerous hours of ordinary unecstatic life. He must have eaten, must have fed himself (or allowed himself to be fed: for he never lacked warm, concerned, maternal women who wished only to put some flesh on his bony frame, in the name of the Lord), must have showered or bathed occasionally (not often, I suspect), must have found accommodations for his many itinerant nights, must have slept, must have bought himself clothes when his old clothes wore out, must have gone to a barber to have his unruly hair trimmed. . . . He must have done these things, I know. Yet I can't imagine them. I can't remember them. Deeply absorbed in his experience of God he might come to, suddenly, and find himself in a warm, noisy diner, crowded in a booth with three or four well-wishers whom he had never set eyes on before (though in fact he was shrewd enough to always know that he *knew* whatever it was one might expect he should know), a fork halfway to his mouth. Left to itself, his body was hungry enough and his jaws gratefully devoured eggs and ham and hashed-brown potatoes and toast and even jelly, so there was no danger of his fading out of existence; but when he recovered consciousness he was often overwhelmed by the fact of other people, the reality of other people, living and breathing temples of the Holy Ghost, aspects of himself, brothers and sisters to him . . . and when he became aware of them in this way he quite naturally lost interest in eating, in his own bodily processes, and wished to address his fullest attention to *them*.

He must have met opposition from the very first. There were drunks on park benches, hecklers who waved their fists and shouted with voices as strident as his own, there were amused policemen, and intolerant policemen, and in the town of Rockland (ironically, for it was in Rockland many years before that he had preached as a child, with gratifying success) an agitated state trooper forced him into a patrol car and drove him out to the highway, saying he had best hitch a ride to the next town, no one wanted any trouble in Rockland, no one wanted any religious advice. "We got more'n enough preachers of our own," the man said in a not unfriendly voice. He must have been jeered at, interrupted, even threatened. He *must* have felt demoralized at times. But his later, rapid success seems to have obscured these early months and years, and in a way Nathan Vickery did not experience them, since by then You had allowed him to know that the trials of daily life were to be felt as *history*, as mere background to his ministry. For he never doubted his destiny. Not for an instant. He walked a high wire secure, and even at times rather brashly confident in the fact that You were the net beneath, and that should he fall — but he would not! — You would save him.

"The Lord guides us in all things," he taught everyone who would listen.

It was true that certain individuals invariably turned away from him, irritated or insulted or frankly discomforted ("Has Jesus come into your heart? Why do you keep Him waiting? How long are you going to keep Him waiting?"), and certain individuals responded with shouts and catcalls and even childish violence (throwing horse chestnuts at him in a downtown park one autumn, and once, when a local church had generously donated the use of its small building for the evening, silly young men rode motorbikes through the door and up the aisle); but no one was really indifferent, and always, always there were those who were profoundly moved. Of twenty-five people he was sure to capture four or five. Or more. It was as if he tossed something out to them, something invisible, that nevertheless caught in their unprotected flesh, in their very souls. And he knew, he sensed, that he had them. He was never wrong in estimating how many he *had*, for between these individuals and himself there was an immediate rapport, a kind of startled, frightened love that neither they nor he could deny.

Churchless and itinerant, without the support of local ministers, without the visible support of any believers or family, Nathan Vickery nevertheless made his way forward according to Your design. He accumulated believers; he took their money gratefully, shyly, but without false reluctance; if anyone guessed his identity he did not hesitate to acknowledge that he *was* the young preacher who had mutilated himself up in Port Oriskany a few years before, but he asked that this identity be kept secret because it was his belief that the Lord did not wish him to profit from that hurt . . . at least at this time. His natural modesty pleased everyone he encountered. He spoke of himself frankly as a seeker — a Seeker for Christ — and he wished only to bring others along with him on his quest. In the Mt. Shaheen Baptist Church one evening in 1963 he preached a sermon so effective that all but a half-dozen of the fifty people present came forward when he called for fellow seekers, including the pastor's son; and later that evening the pastor himself, Marcus Lund, made the extraordinary decision to become a Seeker and for the rest of his life to help Nathanael Vickery with his campaign for souls.

Reverend Lund was a stocky, stern man of middle age, with faint, fair wisps of hair combed damp across his head, and a rather thick, strong neck and a curious round face, like a child's, and again like a monkey's, appealing in its own way. It was said of him that he was tyrannical — he ordered his wife and his son and his associates around as he pleased, and he had once criticized his organist during church services, in front of the entire congregation. His son Mark was seventeen years old and extremely shy, with a slight stammer; his wife was a plain, sweet-faced woman in her early fifties, given to nervous smiling. Reverend Lund spoke in a high, rapid, inflectionless voice, as if it wearied him, this constant ordering of people about, yet what choice had he . . . ? When he met Nathanael Vickery he began to speak to him in this manner, asking him curtly just what he wanted, what he hoped to achieve in Mt. Shaheen, with whom had he worked in the past, why he hadn't a degree from a Bible college; then in mid-sentence he paused, and his shrewd, cold, monkeyish face seemed to freeze; and he could not remember what he was saying; and a kind of power seemed to pass over from Nathan to him, with his full assent.

(Later he whispered to Nathan when no one else was about, his cheeks reddened, his eyes gleaming with a childlike daring, *"I baptize with water: but there standeth one among you, whom ye know not; He it is, who coming after me is preferred before me, whose shoe's latchet I am not worthy to unloose. . . ."* Nathan, hearing this, turned upon the man a sharp, critical stare, and did not reply, did not even smile. For such words seemed to him blasphemous.)

Now gradually there was financial support. There were people who volunteered to share their homes, to lend automobiles and pickup trucks, to feed Nathan and the several members of his "staff" when they traveled about. In Indian Springs he was welcome to stay for as long as he wished with the sister of a woman who had found Jesus through him at a revival meeting in Hazelton, and in Yewville he and the Lunds and two other Seekers were given the use of an entire house for a week, through the beneficence of the publisher of the *Yewville Journal*, who had heard of Nathan's itinerant ministry and was very much interested in it. (Word had come to him by way of a relative in Kincardine, who claimed to have been cured spontaneously of sinus headaches during one of Nathan's meetings.) The campaign in Yewville was so successful that it had to be extended to five days, since on the third and presumably final day so many people had turned up at the rented hall — a Legionnaires' Hall that could accommodate only about two hundred people — that many were standing in the aisle and at the rear, and still others had to be turned away. The *Yewville Journal* covered the campaign in surprising detail: there were photographs of Nathanael Vickery with his arms outspread, welcoming converts; there were photographs of the newly saved, tears streaming down their faces — women, men, even children; and front-page interviews with people who claimed to have found Jesus through Nathan's intervention and whose lives were now completely changed, and with a half-dozen people who claimed they had been cured of ailments simply because Nathan Vickery had touched them in passing. ("I kept it a secret from everybody about these terrible pains I was having in my chest, and when he called for us to come forward for Jesus I could hardly stand, I didn't see how I could make my way through the people in the aisle to where he was, but I did, I did, and when I got there I was bawling like a baby because it was like a veil or a grimy windowpane had been taken away and I could *see*, I could *see* it wasn't just a man standing there but Christ Himself smiling at me and welcoming me, forgiving me for everything, and he came to touch me, just laid his hands on my head, a touch light as a bird's wing brushing against you. . . . And the pains lifted at once: just went away: and it's the Holy Spirit in my heart now instead of what was there before. And I know I have life everlasting, and that there is no need for fear, because God is with me always, and Nathan Vickery is with me always in his prayers. . . .")

In Woodside they rented the Air Force club hall for three days, and had a full crowd every evening; in St. Joachim they rented an enormous tent (used during the summer for bingo, at church picnics) and filled it every night; in Chautauqua Falls they were given the use of the Eden Pentecostal Church for several days, and were willing (though Reverend Lund had to bargain a bit) to share the collection with the pastor in an arrangement equitable to both. In the mill town of Aynsley, on the Alder River, they were warmly welcomed by the pastor of the Mount Zion Tabernacle of God in Christ, who was convinced that Nathanael Vickery was the challenge from their part of the world to all the rest of the world: that he would meet and overcome the fraudulent ministries of such hypocrites as Billy Graham and Oral Roberts and Farley Meikar, who were traitors to the Pentecostals, and who were always aspiring upward in society, greedily seeking con-

verts among the well-to-do and the famous. Even Baptists and
Methodists were too free-thinking and hypocritical, pretending
to be superior to the Pentecostals, when anyone who knew his
Bible could point to those passages in Mark that upheld the Pentecostal truth in defiance of all challengers. . . . And it was in
Aynsley that Nathan experienced his most prodigious success so
far: some twenty-five or thirty members of the Mount Zion Tabernacle of God in Christ, and a half-dozen people from outside,
claimed to be cured or healed of afflictions either because Nathan
laid hands on them, or prayed for them, or merely looked at
them. ("Nervous headaches," painful boils, toothache, earache,
rheumatic pain, cloudy vision, "lumps beneath the arm," dizziness, a sense in the head of things pressing tight, a sense of
unreality that had been plaguing the sufferer for weeks: Nathan
cured them all.) The *Yewville Journal* covered the Aynsley campaign in almost as much detail as it had covered the Yewville
campaign the year before, and other newspapers in the state
reprinted portions of the story, including photographs of converts
to the Seekers for Christ who claimed to have been miraculously
cured. The Sunday feature of the *Port Oriskany Gazette* did a
story on the Seekers that ran for four pages, and though Reverend Lund had been quite certain he had handled the reporter
shrewdly and had been absolutely obliging in every way, the story
that appeared was not *altogether* satisfactory: there were testimonials by the cured and the converted, and two very favorable
comments on Nathan's ministry by local pastors, but the article
ended with three paragraphs of harsh and even contemptuous
"assessment" by the pastor of the Paulin Memorial Presbyterian
Church, whose credentials were impressive indeed — he had a
number of degrees after his name and was the author of several
privately printed books on religious matters and was, evidently,
an expert in the spiritual life. He rejected the entire notion of
"faith healing" and dismissed the Seekers as yet another splinter
group among the Pentecostals, fighting for their life in 1965, an-
achronistic, reactionary, possibly even fraudulent. (Reverend
Lund was furious, and telephoned the man without consulting

Nathan, and called him a liar and a hypocrite — for he hadn't attended a single evening of Nathan's campaign, and had never heard the man preach! — and possibly even an agent of the Devil's. "We want a retraction!" Lund shouted. "We want a front-page apology and a retraction or we'll take you to court for libel!" But the Presbyterian minister merely hung up, and though Lund did consult an attorney, there was no lawsuit.)

Nathan read none of the news stories about himself, and after a while Lund stopped urging them upon him. He learned not to distract or trouble Nathan with trivial, worldly matters — the exact number of people who showed up at a service, the exact amount of money they contributed, rental charges for halls, insurance payments, traveling expenses. After the publicity in Yewville Nathan had been rather upset, for so far as he knew God had *not* called him to a healing ministry yet, and possibly He never would . . . and the news articles seemed to be centered on healing; why was that? "The principal thing is to awaken people to the presence of the Holy Spirit, and to get them to welcome Christ into their hearts," Nathan said earnestly. "Curing headaches or making warts disappear or easing arthritis, why, that's just secondary, that's just the consequence of the Holy Spirit, isn't it . . . ? It has nothing to do with me! God has never instructed me to go out and heal the sick and cast devils from people, God has *never* hinted a word. . . ."

"But you have the power," Reverend Lund said, puzzled. "It's obvious that you have the power and you're not exploiting it."

"The Lord guides me in all things," Nathan said. "I do only what He wishes."

"Maybe the call has come to you and you haven't understood. . . . If you have the power to cure sick people, why not exploit it? There isn't any better witness to the world than miracles! Christ Himself. . . ."

"I'm not Christ," Nathan said sharply.

Reverend Lund's expression shifted, like a child's; for a moment he looked as if he might cry. It had been with pride and excitement he'd shown Nathan the news clippings: so much excellent publicity! "I really don't understand," Lund said softly. "It seems to me. . . . If a fellow Christian is suffering. . . . It might be the case that God has given you this talent and He assumes you know what to make of it. Isn't that possible?"

"Someone once advised me to stay away from healing," Nathan said, frowning. He could not remember who. Had it been a man, or had it possibly been Christ? Years had passed since his last communication from God, and though he thought often, eagerly and wistfully, of those visitations, he did not allow himself to hope that another would come soon, or at all; and his obsessive contemplation of the experiences tended to confuse them. In some ways the earliest visions were the most vivid. And the one in which Christ had taken him to hell. But these were jumbled with the more frequent, almost daily, intuitive flashes he had of God's presence, and the remarkable dreams he had almost every night, empty of content or instruction but filled to bursting with the presence of the Divine. And he spent much of the day in solitude, studying the Bible, allowing his mind to drift to a pure, perfect emptiness, above the world of material shape and form, above even his own body and his "personality." At such times all earthly and human images were obliterated and forgotten; the vision in his good eye went dead; his senses, one by one, became extinguished; he was no longer Nathan Vickery, no longer finite. In this state God communicated with him silently, neither in words nor in sensations, and when he woke from his trance he was never able to remember *precisely* what God allowed him to know: yet he knew nevertheless. So it was difficult for him to judge not only what he knew but why he knew it, and whether it had come to him by way of a human or a Divine agency. (But he halfway thought that the Divine might occasionally use the human, and that possibly the two were one: which further complicated things.)

"Who was it? A fellow minister? He was *jealous*," Lund said flatly.

"I don't remember," Nathan said.

"If it was another minister he was just jealous and to hell with him," Lund said. "Look: you're twenty-six years old. You have the maturity of a much older man. The things people say about you, the absolute gratitude they feel. . . . It's amazing. In a few years you could be known throughout the country, maybe even the world. . . . Other ministers will try to hold you back, they're afraid and jealous because they *know* the power in you and where it may take you! I might have been that way myself. I saw you and heard you speak and a kind of devil leaped up in me, wanting to push you aside, wanting to ignore you, or even impede you — yes, really! But I conquered it. I think the Lord conquered it for me. So I understand that meanness, that jealousy, and I don't think we can ever let it stop us, Nathan. I don't think we can ever let *anything* stop us."

Nathan nodded slowly. He had not been following Lund's words with much concentration. (Lund talked constantly, as if he were thinking aloud; and this "thinking" was both a kind of dialogue with Nathan and an interior monologue of his own, centered about plans for the future. Even when he was with his son Mark, or his wife, or others among the Seekers staff, he talked in this rapid, groping way, sometimes using the word *we* as if he and Nathan were both speaking.)

"The call from God might come through another person," Lund said suddenly. "How can you know? There've been people who have told me about dreams of you, and seeing you in places where you *weren't*; and all sorts of . . . all sorts of things. Like seeing your hands and your face glow. Like seeing Christ where you're standing. I know you don't like to hear it, but. . . ."

"Seeing *Christ* where I stand?" Nathan asked quizzically.

"Yes. Just the other morning a woman came in, after services Wednesday night, and told me there was no mistaking it: she had seen Christ right where you were standing: and it upset her so, she went right home to bed but the next morning she accepted it and was all excited, so she thought she'd better tell me. She wanted to tell you in person but I said you were busy."

"She saw Christ where *I* was standing . . . ?"

"She certainly did. But you've been told this before, haven't you?"

Nathan rose. He ran both hands through his hair; he dug into his scalp with his fingernails. For a strange moment he felt he would laugh. There was the danger of laughing. But it passed, and he merely smiled at Lund and made a gesture that could not be interpreted. He wanted now to be left alone and to contemplate his situation, and it was a measure of the older man's rapport with him that he understood at once, and apologized for having taken up so much of Nathan's time, and went out, closing the door carefully behind him.

"If I am Christ, then who will save *me?*" Nathan murmured aloud.

V

Everywhere he went he discovered the Spirit of the Other already present, waiting for him.

In the quizzical expression of a shopkeeper, a stranger. Yes? What do you want? What are you doing *here?*

In the unsettling, vaguely mocking dogma of his most cherished professor, a Pole who had emigrated to America nearly forty years before: "All of mankind's convictions are merely temporary holding actions — plunges into diversion. They allow us to forget that we're *here* rather than where we feel we ought to be."

In the loose, casual gathering of acquaintances on the street, or on one of the sidewalks on campus: four or five or six young men who, when he hurriedly approached, would materialize into people already known to him, and no one of them the person he sought.

In the ringing of the telephone in his room, in the somnam-
bulist space of time during which he moved to answer it: sluggish,
his legs near-inert with the dread of encountering — of encountering whoever it was he wished not to encounter.

"There's a curse on me," he said cheerfully when, at lunch
with friends in a pub near the university, his fork slipped from his
fingers and clattered to the table and to the floor — and not for
the first time, either, in recent days. (Rising to go to the bathroom during the night, he had banged his forehead hard on a
door frame, having unaccountably turned in the wrong direction;
in his haste to get to a class on the third floor of an aged building,
he had slipped on the smooth-worn steps and had stumbled upstairs and fallen, practically on his face, his notebook and books
flying in all directions. Most perplexing and alarming of all, he
had had a freak accident while peeling an orange — he'd torn at
the rind so fiercely that one of his fingernails had ripped into the
flesh of his left hand, just below the ball of the thumb where
there was a vein close to the surface of the skin: the bleeding had
been remarkable for so shallow a cut.)

As long as he could articulate his condition and express it in
concise, witty language, he believed he was safe. So he took notes
on his own dilemma. Fancifully he imagined a film — it would
have to be a short, rather amateurish, but *artful* film — that dealt
with the comic predicament of an accident-prone individual
whose accidents become increasingly comic and increasingly
dangerous. It pleased him to think of himself in the third person,
especially as William Japheth, or as Japheth (with no last name),
who was an original invention. No one knew this Japheth: not his
mother, not his family, not his girl Audrey, none of his friends
and acquaintances, none of his professors. A secret, a stranger.
(Or was it the case that someone somewhere *did* know him, and
awaited him? But he shied away from thinking of that.)

Invited to afternoon tea at the home of one of his professors,
he heard himself, Billy Sproul, chattering knowledgeably and
wryly about Craveri's *Life of Jesus*, which he supposed to be a
classic of its type; he made several halfway intelligent remarks

about Schweitzer's *Quest for the Historical Jesus*, though he had, in fact, never finished reading the book. His bright, boyish face was set to advantage in the book-cluttered, dark-paneled room with its framed charcoal rubbings from a Buddhist temple in Ceylon and its unused pewter candlestick holders and its air of pleasurable weariness. His host had written, in his youth, a nine-hundred-page study of the influence of Greek ideas on Christianity; a study of Greek cosmogony; and innumerable essays and reviews. He was an altogether admirable scholar whose very habit of pausing between words Japheth had once discovered himself fondly imitating, but this afternoon everything seemed slightly amiss between them: the man talked, Japheth talked, words coiled about one another and sank beneath their own weight, but nothing was said.

The older man possessed an encyclopedic knowledge of many religions but he believed in none of them. Having such knowledge, how was it possible to have faith as well? While he talked Japheth grew more and more uneasy, sensing the presence of the Other. His heart beat; his face grew warm. He glanced surreptitiously into the corners of the room.

And when he was alone with Audrey, finally, it seemed to him he was not truly alone with her. Instead, a third party was close by, witnessing and judging. "Why are you so nervous?" she asked impatiently. "I can practically feel your mind racing." They wished to marry, but it struck them as preposterous: how *did* two individuals finally marry? How did they exclude all others from their lives? In her small tidy room in Quincy, lying on her bedquilt while the day thickened soberly to dusk, Japheth felt his consciousness drift inexorably back to that drafty sports arena . . . to the barred windows and the raised platform and the row upon row of earnest, staring people who wished *merely* to have their sins lifted from them and to be assured of life everlasting. He lay with his face pressed against a young woman's fragrant hair, and in his mind's eye there appeared an image of a pacing, improbable figure, his long lean face pale with passion, his eyes glittering.

"You've been distracted all day. You aren't *yourself*," Audrey said.

"But who else can I be?" he asked, startled.

"I don't know you at all. I don't know what we have to do with each other."

"Don't be silly," he whispered. "There's only. . . ."

"Yes?"

". . . only you."

But it was not true, and in the end there was nothing to be done: so he surrendered.

He joined the Seekers for Christ at a weekend convocation in Fort Gambrell, making his way forward with the other newly converted souls, unashamed, though tears streamed down his cheeks. Kneeling, he bowed his head before Nathanael Vickery, who paused long enough to lay both his hands on Japheth's slender shoulders and to give him a welcoming squeeze: a joyful childlike gesture of triumph.

He handed over seventy-five dollars and made a pledge of several hundred more. And volunteered his services. How could he help their mission? What sort of work might he do?

"It's utterly ridiculous," he said, laughing hoarsely. "I haven't any money left and I have nowhere to go and I don't for an instant truly believe in any of this. . . . Nevertheless I'm here, far from home. What do I do next?"

They saw that he was exhausted; they helped him to his feet.

"You can stay with us," they said warmly.

"What about *him?* — Nathanael? Will I see him?"

All the new converts wished to see Nathanael, but naturally this wasn't always possible. He was very busy; he rarely had time to talk.

"I'll wait," Japheth said. He wiped his eyes, not wanting them to see that he wept. "I have the rest of my life."

vi

Though there was scarcely an hour, scarcely even a minute, when Nathanael Vickery did not hold himself in trembling readiness for You, eight years were to pass between Your manifestation on the eve of Good Friday, 1959, and the fifth of Your manifestations in late September of 1967.

It was in Windigo Falls, at the headquarters of the Seekers for Christ, at that time housed in a twenty-five-room mansion built in the 1890s by one of the lumber mill owners (and in the 1940s and 50s allowed to tumble into disrepair): there, in the plain, ascetic, rather cell-like room Nathan had chosen for himself at the very top of the house, overlooking the river, You manifested Yourself to him in a vision that appeared to consume several days of his life, though in earthly time it was to be measured in terms of an hour and twenty minutes.

This was the Vision of the One.

(Of which I am terrified. From which I retreat. For how can I be equal to Your uncanny power, using mere words to represent You? There are times when I despair even of suggesting Nathan's response to You. I despair even of suggesting how *he* despaired when it became evident to him that he could not communicate the power and brilliance of his visions to anyone else — not even to his most adoring, uncritical followers, not even to the young man who was to become his closest and most devoted disciple. When he woke from his sweat-drenched trance, when he shook himself free of his speechlessness, he wanted only to bring to others Your message . . . he wanted only to impress upon others the incontestable fact of Your existence. But though they listened to him, and appeared to honor his words, it was transparently clear that they did *not* comprehend. For if they did . . . why

weren't their lives revolutionized, why wasn't the world transformed?)

The One: the Spirit of Absolute Illumination: the Many-in-
One: You.

■ ■ ■

He staggered into a room and someone arose immediately and
went to help him, gripping his arm tight, saying, "Where have
you been? What has happened to you?" in a voice of terror. (For
it seemed at first that Nathan had been physically attacked, or
had suffered a violent seizure of some kind.)

The voice was Japheth Sproul's, the warmth and the terror
were Japheth's. From the very first he would have preferred that
his Master be attacked by enemies than that he risk the closeness
of the living God: which was like the fury of a blast furnace.

When Nathan was able to speak he told him in a hoarse, faltering voice, "He — it — The One — The — "

And how weakly his voice dropped on that weakest of words
The — !

That was in Windigo Falls, where the first Seekers' Home was
founded: the first of the many hundreds of homes Nathan envi-
sioned as one day spreading across the continent so that his people could live in seclusion, in simplicity and celibacy and mutual
charity, with no need to defend their beliefs. Indeed, he envi-
sioned a network of Seekers' homes so that it would be possible
within a few years to traverse the entire United States without
being forced to spend a single night with strangers. It was necessary, he taught, for them to take care how they mingled with
others. All unbelievers were strangers: and most strangers were
unbelievers, the not-yet-baptized.

Curiously enough, many of the unbelievers were Christians,
so-called. In a way they were more troubled spiritually than those
who considered themselves agnostics or atheists. They *imagined*

that they were Christians when in fact they were nothing at all: empty shells out of which the Devil had sucked life. "They are not evil," Nathan taught, "but only ignorant. We must free them of their ignorance by showing them the love in our hearts, and we must be very careful not to seem impatient with them. For they are God's own children, like us. . . . At the same time we must be very careful not to be contaminated by them."

Ideally, Seekers' homes were to be in rural areas, removed from the active, striving, commercial world. If death-clouds swept upon the earth (as it appeared they might, possibly as early as 1974), they would hover and condense over the large industrial cities, and their poison would be drained into those cities and the inhabitants destroyed. No Seeker feared death — for death did not exist, as Nathan Vickery taught — but it was necessary for as many Seekers as possible to survive, since unbelievers would be horrified by the catastrophe and would then hunger for salvation; and it was to be part of Your design that they turn at the very end of history to the church founded by Nathan Vickery. So the Seekers must guard themselves carefully, not out of vanity or selfishness or fear of death, but out of charity for the not-yet-baptized world.

As early as 1967 the organization owned a fair amount of property: several farms, three or four houses in residential areas in small cities, fifty acres of undeveloped land in the Eden Valley. It was thought wisest and most pragmatic to maintain headquarters in the old Travis home in Windigo Falls because of the convenience of the location and the size of the house, despite the fact that Windigo Falls had grown to a population of over a hundred thousand and was a rather dirty, busy place — a pulp paper factory, a textile mill, and Greendale Chemacryl Plastics Inc. were all located on the river north of town. The house, however, was a windfall: a Greek Revival structure with four stately columns and a grandiose (though rotting) portico and an extraordinary number of high, narrow windows and many spacious rooms. The outside badly needed painting and repairs, the inside was rather shabby, but Seekers who had come to live in the house were eager to fix it up and, all in all, it was a considerable acquisition for the church — given to them outright by an enthusiastic convert in her late seventies who had inherited it, along with a great deal of money, upon the death of a senile woman named Alice Hull Travis, who had lived to be a hundred and three.

Nathan made his home here except when he was on the road; as did most of the permanent members of his staff — Reverend Lund, the choir director, several volunteer secretaries, Japheth Sproul and the printer Donald Beck, and Nathan's grandmother Mrs. Vickery, who had been given a suite of rooms on the second floor. What had been the living room was set up as a kind of chapel, with some fifty-odd folding chairs arranged in a semicircle, and a plain lectern at the front; other downstairs rooms were used for printing pamphlets and broadsides, and as mailing rooms. Reverend Lund had his own office and his own secretary (his wife, for a while; then his wife left the organization suddenly and went back to Mt. Shaheen, taking their son along; and so a volunteer worker took her place).

"I don't believe we'll stay here more than another year or two," Reverend Lund told Nathan. "Even if no one donates a larger, better place in a better location, we should be in a position to buy one, don't you think?"

"Yes," Nathan said. "It's possible."

"I'm thinking of Pittsburgh, maybe. A good central location, eh? Or maybe Cleveland. Or Chicago."

"Someday we'll have homes in all those cities," Nathan said.

Reverend Lund stared at him, smiling. "Yes? Will we? I do believe you're right," he said.

It was in the Travis house on a mild, ordinary morning in early autumn that You appeared to Nathan for the fifth time, without warning, sweeping down upon him as he was dressing to go out. He had no more than his usual hope, or apprehension, that You would declare Yourself to him; the evening before, he had participated in a quite successful (though tiring) service in a Disciples of God church a few miles away, and his mind had been dragged downward to some extent by a reluctant consideration of the number of Seekers who had joined in recent months, and the amount of money they had given thus far or pledged — details Reverend Lund never tired of talking about and bringing to the attention of others (for he believed passionately that the *number* of Seekers was very important: it was a witness to the world of the authenticity of God's blessing). Nathan was not truly surprised by the growing success of his church, nor was he very much concerned with the various problems Reverend Lund continually brought up, which were mainly financial and clerical; and he was not troubled, as Reverend Lund and Japheth Sproul and others of his staff were, by the hostile nature of recent news articles — which he read carelessly, with as much indifference as he read articles of praise. He had felt purely himself on that morning: dressing quickly, without regard for what he wore, without much awareness of the fact that he possessed a physical appearance, a physical being others might observe.

("Let me take you shopping, let me buy you some decent clothes," his friend Japheth begged. "You're worse than I am — everything hangs on you, there's no style or color — you look *forgotten*. The visual impression you make on an audience, Nathan, could be so much more powerful if you took my advice. Don't you care? Aren't you listening? *Why?*")

One moment he was in time, aware of the time: 7:45. The next moment time had stopped.

You descended.

A radiance swelling to such intensity that Nathan's eyeball was seared: scalding wires seemed to run up his nostrils, into his brain. The radiance grew, pulsating, until it began to burn, the very air turned to flames, invisible and silent flames, blackening. He tried to move but could not. The light turned suddenly dark, as if it had been forced inside-out.

"My Lord and my God . . ." he tried to whisper.

As a child Nathan had loved the Sunday-school cards with their pictures of Biblical scenes in soft reds and blues and yellows and browns. And he had stared for long minutes at a time at the illustrations in his grandmother's Bible, and afterward in the Bibles Reverend Sisley owned. The Adoration of the Shepherds . . . Abram's Covenant with Lot . . . Joseph Meeting his Brethren . . . the Finding of Moses in the Bulrushes (one of the loveliest pictures of all, sky and water blended to a fine ethereal mist, and Pharaoh's daughter and her maidens dusky-skinned and exotic and girlishly surprised) . . . Moses and the Burning Bush . . . the Tabernacle in the Wilderness . . . Elijah Calling Down Fire on Mt. Carmel . . . Daniel in the Lions' Den . . . Jesus Healing the Leper . . . Jesus Healing Peter's Wife's Mother . . . Jesus and the Barren Fig Tree . . . Jesus Stilling the Storm . . . the Crucifixion . . . the Resurrection . . . the Ascension. . . . He knew each of the pictures as intimately as if he had created it himself, out of his own awe, and even in recent years he found himself sometimes glancing at these or similar pictures, comforted by their simplicity, their air of placid finality: for even the Crucifixion, which should have been disturbing, was in fact pastoral as a watercolor.

Now he saw the pictures though he was blind; they were being flicked toward him in the dark. From where did they come, to where did they go, where was he himself now standing . . . ? He had known in the first instant to surrender at once to Your power. He would never have resisted, despite his body's panic; his soul had absolute dominion over his lower self and acted swiftly, without hesitation. *My Lord and my God*, his lips would have shaped, had it been possible. . . . The pictures were being flicked toward him through the bright-dark air: Jesus's soft blue robe, the bizarre but very pretty feather headdress worn by Pharaoh's daughter, the yellow-orange flames of the burning bush. The darkness swelled and pulsated. Was it Your breath, Your very being, inside which he stood, immobile? A sea of glass and fire, fiery glass, throbbing and beating until it seemed his brain would be destroyed by the pressure: and then suddenly the pictures burst into flame and there came to his ears a terrific howl, soundless, sheer sensation that was the howl of the damned of hell he had heard many years ago and had never forgotten.

About him pages of the Bible were blown, catching against his legs. The heat was nearly unbearable. The surface of the earth had cracked and blasts of fetid, fiery air came forth, catching up the pictures, the pages, and whirling them about. A ghost-image of his hand and arm materialized, instinctively reaching for one of the pages; but the fingers closed upon nothing, upon air, and were themselves no more substantial than air. One by one the pages exploded into flame. There were hundreds of them, there were thousands: scattered across the earth's surface, blown by demonic winds, fanned into flame. The howl of their destruction was terrible; Nathan felt it in his very soul; he would have joined the soundless, agonized weeping had he not been too frightened by Your wrath to turn aside from You for even a moment.

The Bible: the thin, delicate pages: the childlike pictures: a chaos of flame.

And You asserted Yourself then in Your infinite, writhing, coiling majesty, Your radiance once again so heightened that it turned pitch black, and the black then beat itself, frenzied, into light, and the light again black, by which Nathan came to know the power of Your breath, which is the breath of the living earth. Something brushed near against his face, like wings. Feathery-light, exquisite, faintly stinging. . . . He was frightened. No, he was not frightened at all: there was no part of him not utterly absorbed in You, not utterly surrendered to You.

My Lord and my. . . .

The enormity of You, a colossus! A vast membrane swelled to the breaking point with its own great breathing, its own wild life-heat. *My Lord*, Nathan wished to pray, while about him the flames leaped and the cries of the damned quivered in the darkly-bright air, communicated to him as vibrations are communicated through matter, language as sheer sensation. *My Lord. My God. Have mercy.* Underfoot were images of Moses, and Paul, and Mary with the Christ child in her arms; and Christ Himself, pale and gaunt on His cross; Christ Himself resplendent in His white robes, risen from the dead. The fiery-hot winds blew them about mercilessly, savagely, until they burst into flames and shriveled in a matter of seconds and were gone.

Whereupon Nathan Vickery learned that You will tolerate no other gods before you, no other forms of godliness.

A sleeping giant, You were. And in Your sleep Nathan stumbled, utterly alone. One of his eyes had been sacrificed to You and the other was now blind, blinded by the terrible radiance of Your love. No other gods before you! No images of Your being! You are the Many-in-One, the One-in-One, the One. Nothing before or after. Nothing except the One. Your breathing caught him up and threw him about, heedless of his panic. He did not resist. He knew enough never to resist. Christ appeared some distance before him, whitely-flaming, and by his side was a ladder, and up and down this ladder enormous angels moved, their hair streaming fire, their eyes burning white with agony. In Christ's face Nathan saw his own face: in those hotly-dark, moist eyes his own, what had once been his own, the face of his youth. And in an instant Christ and His attendant angels disappeared: were sucked into crevices in the very air. As Nathan stared, the crevices deepened, darkened, and then flared open again, and the figure of Christ reappeared, and His angels, as if they had not been sucked into oblivion; and in another instant they disappeared again, annihilated; and in yet another instant reappeared. . . . And so it was given to Nathan to know that You give birth to Your creations and suck them back into Your oblivion as You wish, time and again, for all eternity. The creations are fluttering images, fiery light, godly enough, and even human, but they are visible only in Your regard, and should You choose to make them invisible they will disappear in an instant. When they reappear it is out of Your immense heartbeat, not out of their own will. Your breath! Your muscular protoplasmic breathing! In the distance Nathan saw individuals straying too close to Your pulsating radiance, and one by one they were drawn to it, pulled into it, and destroyed in a soundless explosion of fire. He must wave them back! Must warn them! The energy of their beings that they saw

as their own was in fact Yours, and they had no awareness of You
at all, wandering careless as children on an ice bank. . . . Their
heads were filled with babble, shrieks and cries and howls, their
eyes were clouded with the thoughts of demons, evil spirits that
had insinuated themselves into their souls and urged them reck-
lessly onward to their destruction. Suddenly Nathan saw the
faces of people he knew: the faces of many of the Seekers: Reverend Lund and Japheth among them. He must warn them, must
wave them back. Must exorcise the evil spirits from their souls.
He must run forward into that immense heartbeat secure in the
knowledge that it would not destroy him so long as he subordi-
nated himself to it with every particle of his being.

vii

After his recovery it happened gradually that the young man
Japheth Sproul became his chief comfort.

He no longer wished to upset Mrs. Vickery. She had been
ailing for some time, and the mere suspicion that her grandson
was not altogether well excited her dangerously. So Nathan and
the others took care that she should know nothing alarming.
How was Nathan today? In excellent health. How did last night's
service go? Excellently. Was anything wrong, was there any bad
news? Never.

He loved his grandmother and he loved his followers. But he
could not talk to them, not even to Reverend Lund, who grew
uneasy in his presence after more than a few minutes and drifted
onto subjects that did not interest Nathan. It worried him that he
should love these people so deeply, so purely, and yet have very
little to say to them. Always, they looked to *him* for wisdom.
They looked to *him* and fell silent themselves.

But Japheth was rarely silent. He loved to talk, and talked very
well, with a stammering, stumbling fluidity, a cheerfulness that

enlivened his small, rather boyish face. He had come to the Seekers out of nowhere — descending with a number of other converts at a Sunday-evening service in Fort Gambrell some time ago. Nathan had sensed from the first that Japheth was different from the others; vastly different; he had been clumsy, and deeply embarrassed, his intelligent features shrunk with a kind of bemused chagrin.

"But what did you think would happen?" Nathan had asked, astonished.

"I thought — I had the idea — I was afraid that if you laid hands on me," Japheth said, blushing, "I would fall over *dead*."

He had noticed Japheth for a while, and forgot him for a while, since he had been traveling a great deal at that time and new members were joining the church every day; and many of them, like Japheth, were eager to give all their money and their material possessions to the organization in return for the privilege of living close to Nathan, and of sharing in his work. Reverend Lund had been suspicious of Japheth during the first weeks: he had believed the young man to be a spy of some sort, possibly a newspaper reporter, possibly an associate of a rival church. And then Japheth had worked so frantically on one of the campaigns — canvassing half a city on foot, patiently ringing doorbells in the cold, distributing handbills, helping to set up Nathan's platform and address system, and even volunteering to help clean the hall when it appeared that the owners had not fulfilled part of their agreement — that even Reverend Lund had been impressed. Tireless, of a sunny temperament, in the habit of making small and sometimes not quite intelligible jokes, Japheth Sproul was generally well-liked and it was not surprising that Nathan himself began to spend more and more time with him.

After he staggered from his room that morning, and woke sometime later in Japheth's presence, it seemed to Nathan that he might be able to explain what had happened to him to Japheth, and that he might speak as frankly and as freely as he wished, not taking care to measure his words and the effect of his words, as he did in public. That he had been frightened and for a while even repelled by God, that, as far as he could judge, God did not value any of His manifestations over any others — Christ being revealed as no more significant, apparently, than Nathan himself: if only he could share this extraordinary revelation with Japheth, what a relief it would be! To say finally that You are indeed a God of wrath, and the vials of Your wrath will be poured out upon the earth as it was foretold; to say finally that the race of men and the race of devils were intermingled, and must be forced apart, in order that Your kingdom be restored on earth. . . . But the vision had so exhausted him that for hours he had been unable to speak coherently, and for the rest of that day, and part of the next, he had had to sit in his room with the blinds pulled, alone, only his lips moving in a constant, near-silent prayer of supplication, waiting for the new, fragmented, confusing bits of wisdom to coalesce. He knew himself — Nathanael Vickery — to be a frail vessel composed of particles of light, atoms of energy, that could at any moment be sucked into utter oblivion, except that You had chosen him for Your specific purposes as You had once chosen Jesus of Nazareth. As Christ Himself had been an idea of Yours, given flesh and blood and a fate He must have felt to be unique, so Nathan realized that he too had been given life in order to fulfill Your wishes: *but what might those wishes be* — *!* He would have liked to confess to someone, to anyone — anyone who might take pity on his bewilderment and not mistake it for humility — that he had witnessed the extinction of Christ, His form blasted into its elements and then reassembled, sucked in and out of existence, and his kinship with Christ was therefore a terrible one: they were linked not in their power but in their powerlessness.

Someone knocked softly at his door but he did not answer.

And again someone knocked, later. Nathan heard his raw, surprised voice lifted in irritation: "Go away! Leave me alone! Why are you tormenting me!"

It had been Japheth, he guessed afterward. But the incident was never mentioned between them.

Once he began to recover from the shock of the vision, however, he allowed Japheth to visit him whenever he wished. Instead of having his meals alone, as he commonly did, Nathan asked Japheth to join him, and afterward they walked out along the river bank; or worked together on the land that was to be used to grow vegetables — for it was Nathan's ambition that each of the Seeker homes would someday be self-sufficient: each "family" would grow its own vegetables, bake its own bread, raise its own cows and chickens. At such times Japheth did most of the talking. He seemed eager to speak, of even the most private things, and while Nathan was sometimes surprised at the personal, and therefore inconsequential, nature of his remarks, he found himself strangely intrigued. Japheth spoke of his childhood in Boston, which he characterized as lonely; he spoke of his father and his father's scholarly work, which sounded to Nathan like sheer vanity: a life's work poking and prying at the edges of God's Word; he spoke of his tormented adolescence, which he *hoped* he had finally outgrown; he spoke of the guilt he felt over the breakup of his engagement to a young woman whom he had loved, or believed he had loved, very much; he spoke of his queer, inchoate, and to Nathan's mind rather mild, religious experiences, which seemed to have died out before his sixteenth year. "For a long time I waited for them — for it — to return, and then I gave up. And then I met *you*," he said breathlessly. All this was offered to Nathan in a quick, light, undramatic voice, as if Japheth Sproul wanted him to understand he did not take himself altogether seriously. Frequently he concluded his remarks by gesturing wryly and saying, "Well — that's how it is." At other times he shrugged his shoulders, murmuring almost inaudibly, "But why should *you* care about all this. . . ."

Nathan responded by saying that he did care, of course.

And it was true: he cared, with one part of his mind. He found himself caring very much. It moved him to hear another person speak of his childhood, confessing that it hadn't seemed right, somehow, not *the* childhood everyone else seems to have had. Nathan would have liked to speak of his own childhood, but he didn't know quite what to say. Had he been lonely? No. At any rate, he didn't think so. (But what was loneliness? Was it possible to be lonely when one was with God?) He began to tell Japheth about his mother, and his grandmother, and his grandfather who had died so suddenly, but the words struck him as hopelessly inadequate, and something in the young man's keen, assessing gaze made him falter. Japheth Sproul did not want to hear that Nathan Vickery was similar to him; he surely did not want to hear that Nathan had had a childhood that hadn't been altogether. . . . But Nathan would not have known what to call it. Happy? Unhappy? The words seemed to him misleading and trivial. What did happiness matter, really? His soul turned away in revulsion from the tawdry happiness of ordinary life. The God of his visions was not a God concerned with anything as banal as happiness; there was only His will to be lived.

Friendship puzzled him. Erotic love puzzled him. (There were young women who approached him even now, staring at him as if they saw, in him, a creature of their own invention; but since his experience with Leonie Beloff and the terrible penitence God had exacted from him, he appeared at last to be invulnerable.) He understood that men are commanded to love one another, but not how: and not why. The love he had felt for his Grandfather Vickery had not helped his grandfather, nor had it helped him. Love for one another. . . . Brothers and sisters in. . . . If God was in all, what difference did it make whether the parts loved one another or were even aware of one another? As Japheth spoke of some humorous, complicated incident that had taken place a few years ago, Nathan listened intently to his words without hearing them, and gazed at the young man as if he were watching him from a great distance. He *loved* Japheth because Japheth was a fellow Seeker for Christ, but he did not know whether he *liked* Japheth: for what did that mean, *liking*? Every earthly attraction was in conflict with one's absorption in God. . . .

"Ah, I'm boring you! I can tell!" Japheth laughed harshly.

Nathan blushed. He tried to protest.

"No, no, I understand! I shouldn't be telling you these ridiculous things. Your time is far too important. There are hundreds of people who'd like to tell you their life stories, and most of them would be far more meaningful than mine. . . ."

"I was thinking," Nathan said, "of loving and liking. Of friendship. . . . I was thinking that I didn't really understand what they mean."

"Understand what they mean?" Japheth repeated blankly. "Why, they mean . . . they mean. . . . People are attracted to one another, that's all. It can't be explained."

Nathan nodded slowly. "And sometimes they fall in love."

"Well, yes. Sometimes. But it doesn't last," Japheth said, frowning. "It always *appears* as if it will last, but it doesn't."

"Nothing abides but God," Nathan said faintly.

"Nothing abides but God."

Nathan looked at Japheth, wishing to see whether the cloudy spirit did indeed dwell in his soul: but he was distracted by the young man's quizzical expression.

"Why are you staring at me?" Japheth asked. "Did I say something that offended you?"

"I'm sorry," Nathan said.

"You have a certain. . . . It's uncanny. . . . Oh well," he said, grinning, "I'll never understand, so why should I try? Sometimes I think I want to establish a human contact with you, Nathan, even if it's only to make you draw away from me in disdain; at other times I know I don't want that. I joined the Seekers, I'll confess to you, not because of the Holy Spirit or God or Christ or whatever, but because I couldn't shake you from my mind: because I dreamed about you night after night. I was convinced that you are the . . . you are the center of. . . . My life turns about you; why should I pretend it doesn't? I tried to tell myself for a while that I joined your church in order to get close enough to you to determine whether you were a conscious fraud or simply a madman. I tried to rationalize my behavior. But it's hopeless, it's degrading. I dreamed of you as an avatar of Christ and I think . . . I really think, you know," he muttered, "that you *are*."

"An avatar of Christ," Nathan said softly.

They walked for a while in silence. Neither was conscious of the sky above, or the earth below. Neither was conscious of the mist that lay lightly upon the river. After some time Japheth began to speak of a childhood fantasy, an imaginary playmate he had created out of his loneliness, being the only child of older parents; his friend's name was Billy-o, and he had had red hair and a reckless, rather naughty manner, unafraid to speak up for whatever he wanted . . . most of the time a companion to Japheth, but occasionally an enemy. It was as if, Japheth said, some power of his own had flowed into Billy-o and might then be turned against *him*.

"In the end he frightened me. He threatened to make me say things and do things that weren't what I wanted at all. And he grew so big . . . a head taller than I was. My own age, and so big! He tried to force me to knock things over, or spit in my father's face, or shout in church. The little bastard."

"What happened to him?" Nathan asked.

"I don't know: he died, maybe. I think he died."

"How did he die?"

"Why, I suppose I must have killed him," Japheth laughed. "When I was older . . . ten or eleven. . . . Billy-o was teasing me one day and I ran across a busy street and almost got hit by a car, and he *did* get hit, and that was that. I felt the *crunch* in my own body, and that was that."

"And he never came back again?"

"Oh no. Absolutely not. . . . Look, did I embarrass you before? That business about Christ?"

Nathan shook his head wordlessly. He had no idea what to say. The image of Christ had burst into flames and burned to ashes, inconsequential as any ashes. But he could not tell Japheth that; he could not tell anyone. That "Christ" was a mere image? He dare not tell anyone that truth.

"My mind veers off into two wholly distinct directions," Japheth said. "The earthly, the mundane, the practical; and the ethereal, the spiritual, the . . . utterly outrageous. I can't bring the two directions together. For a while I tried, I tried very hard, I had intended to get a PH.D along the way while forcing the two together, but it simply didn't work. So I've given up. The earthly must go its own way while I cast my lot with the other. I *did* dream of you as Christ, and in my imagination I call you *Master*. I'm a year or two older than you but I call you *Master*. Am I ashamed? A little. Not much. A few years ago it would have been preposterous, but not now. I accept a certain truth about you that possibly you can't experience yourself. But it doesn't matter. I don't even care if I embarrass you. An avatar of Christ! What nonsense! What an absurdity! . . . Yet I *believe*. I *know*. The doubts I have concerning the Seekers are of no more substance to me than mosquitoes whining about my head, or a fly buzzing in an empty room: they are merely thought-clusters, the inevitable doubts the mind casts up simply to keep itself going. Do you understand? Yes? We doubt just to assert our existence. *I doubt, hence I am*. But it can't be taken seriously. None of it. The earthly, the mundane, the practical . . . the *sane*. . . . Can't be taken seriously once one has tasted the other world. *Though our outward man perish, yet the inward man is renewed day by day. . . . for the things which are seen are temporal; but the things which are not seen are eternal*."

Nathan stared at him. Was it true? He had seen that very page of Scripture burst into flames and shrivel into ashes, he had seen the ashes scattered wildly across the earth. . . . But perhaps You had spoken to Japheth with a message for *him*? Perhaps he had misinterpreted You? But it was hardly possible, Nathan thought, for him, for Nathan, to have misinterpreted. . . .

While Japheth chattered on, he walked in silence, unaware of his surroundings. The earth that received his footsteps, the caressing air through which he moved, even the sunshine that caused his one good eye to squint: they were of no consequence beside the beam of power that was Nathan's own soul, stirred to a frenzy by a stranger's words, a brother's words. Surely it was God speaking through this person. Surely it could not fail to be God. *Master*, Nathan was called: in mockery, and yet not altogether in mockery. Japheth laughed at himself, touching Nathan's arm as if to draw attention to the willingness with which he laughed at himself, for had he not become a fool in glorying, wasn't he defiantly proud of himself for speaking as a fool — for declaring his love? "The first time I heard you speak I wanted to stand up and shout that you had no right to terrify us with those specters out of Revelation — and did you understand the Book of Revelation yourself — *did* you have any idea in your passionate zeal that the book can only be interpreted in the light of its historical context — that it was written during the reign of the Emperor Domitian, who wished to persecute Christians all the way to Asia, and so John — whoever John was — saw the world divided into good and evil, into Christians and their persecutors? Did you have any idea that the Beast you referred to was simply Nero, *the beast that was, and is not, and is to come* — that Nero had killed himself and there was a legend that he would be returning from the underworld, and John obviously took this legend seriously — just as he took everything seriously and inflated a political situation into a vision of the end of history — Armageddon? I wanted to shout you into silence, I wanted to drag you off that platform and take your place myself and tell the frightened audience that — that — But you kept speaking, and I just sat there, and I realized that it didn't matter what you said — just as it didn't matter what John said, or what he imagined he said — It didn't matter that the Beast was or wasn't Nero, that St. John the Divine was or wasn't a paranoid schizophrenic, that the entire Bible is or isn't a direct revelation from God — Do you see? Do you understand?" he said, in his excitement gripping Nathan by the forearm. "*Can* you? It took me almost thirty years to come into the presence of the Divine, but that presence is unmistakable, and I'm not ashamed to call you Master, or to follow you wherever you go — to sacrifice my life for you, in fact! The way of my father — my fathers — is not the right way, it doesn't lead to salvation or even to earthly happiness — for what does it profit anyone, to know all there is to know but to *feel* nothing? — to know the causes of all human motivations, and the backgrounds of every collective event, but to share in nothing, to experience nothing? When I joined the Seekers I gave you all the money I had and about half of it was money I'd gotten from selling my books — some of them rare books — my father's, my grandfather's — and it isn't that I reject that knowledge, and I certainly don't reject the scholarly world, but — but — But I had to do it, do you see? Otherwise I would have drowned! Suffocated! The weight of so much knowledge, so many books, the entire life's-work of innumerable men, and — and the prospect of — I was to be one of them, do you see? I was fated to be one of them! William Japheth Sproul the Third! And so I — I — I saw you, and heard you, and ran away in disgust: and for weeks afterward I struggled with you: but as you know I was no match. I had to return. I have never experienced God as you have, Nathan, and so I don't know whether God exists — I hardly know whether *anything* exists, in fact — especially when I am so rattled — but there is one thing I know without question, to the very depths of my being: and that is the fact that your divinity acts in me. I see in you — I recognize — You have come into the world to save us, Nathan: to heal us. Some of us are very, very sick, and require your healing. There *are* devils. Wicked, capricious spirits. Are they demons, are they neuroses, are they the species' wishes for death — what are they — *how* are they able to exist, and to thrive — why do human beings tolerate their presence — open their lives to them? I don't know. Can't begin to know. And what God intends — whether we are coming to the end — whether you're right or are merely echoing the words of the chiliasts who have been with us from the start — I don't know. I don't know whether God exists, Nathan — but I know that *you* exist."

It was sometime afterward that Nathan approached his friend and said simply: "God exists."

And Japheth's bright, expectant gaze was lowered in sudden meekness, in absolute submission. For he knew it to be true; and all that was required was that his Master touch his shoulder — lightly, in passing, in a gesture of unconscious benediction — for him to know he would carry this truth with him to the grave.

viii

Master, he was called.

Sometimes he acknowledged it, sometimes not.

It was held against the Seekers for Christ that they had no need to *seek* their Christ: for he dwelled among them and his name was Nathan Vickery. So spoke critics of the church, worked to a frenzy at the spectacle of so many converts in so brief a time. And the infantile simplicity of the prayer Nathan sometimes led them in, repeating over and over, chanting, droning, a prayer that was (so he explained frankly enough) meant only for unbelievers who despaired of being healed — *Jesus loves me, Jesus loves me, Jesus loves me, Jesus loves me*. One was instructed to take a full breath and to expel it slowly while repeating the prayer, slowly, slowly enough so that one's entire being was filled with the rich vibrant sounds of the words. Only when all thoughts were obliterated through the power of the prayer, and when the meaning of the prayer's individual words was obliterated, could the Holy Spirit descend. And even then, Nathan cautioned, it was possible that nothing would happen. For You do not act in everyone according to how You are bid, but according only to Your desire.

The Seekers was not a church for everyone, it was explained carefully in official publications. No matter that during services Nathan Vickery and his associates sometimes spoke of rival churches as being "of the Devil without knowing it" — in pamphlets and booklets printed by the organization with such titles as *Are You Curious About God's Most Democratic Church?* and *Are You A Seeker For Christ Without Knowing It?* it was set forth in clear, simple prose that each Christian was drawn to the church most suited for *his* spiritual needs, and that no church was really superior to another; for Japheth Sproul, who put together most of the publications, knew it would have been a mistake to bring upon the Seekers the jealous wrath of other denominations. (He compiled and edited various sermons of Nathan's, arranging them in brief paragraphs with spaces between them for easy reading, and the creation of these essays gave him a curious sense of pleasure and satisfaction. In the old days he had written lengthy research papers on obscure Biblical and theological subjects, and though two or three of them eventually made their way into print, he had known all along that no one, with the possible exception of the professor who was grading him, would ever read the papers in their entirety or with any degree of attentiveness. But the twenty-five-page booklet *Are You A Seeker For Christ Without Knowing It?* went into innumerable printings, and eventually sold — first at a price of $1 and then at $1.50 — over four million copies. And perhaps it is selling still, or at least being read.)

So the church advertised itself as both democratic and exclusive: open to anyone, yet clearly not suitable for everyone. There was only one test of faith and that was the baptism of the Holy Spirit, which manifested itself in ecstatic states of mind, usually accompanied by speaking in tongues, or fainting, or the spontaneous healing of disorders. And afterward converts frequently chose to call Nathan *Master*, for how could they resist? — seeing that he had saved not only their souls but their lives as well?

After the Vision of the One, Nathan instructed Reverend Lund to cancel his engagements for six weeks, knowing he would need time to absorb Your message; and when he returned to public life in the late autumn, with a three-day crusade for souls in a small industrial city on the Alder River, he told no one, not even Japheth, of the decision he had made. And so his staff and his followers were taken by surprise, though many were to claim afterward that they had had premonitions that something extraordinary would happen.

Greedy for his Master's preaching, Japheth sat at the very front of the church. He was to help when converts came forward and he was, despite his weak, flat voice, part of the Seekers' choir. But he was as exhilarated as any newcomer, and it seemed to him very nearly unbearable, the ten minutes or so of singing and music before Nathan appeared. (He sang the gospel songs without hearing them, loudly and mechanically clapping his hands, his mouth stretched into a smile: the words did not matter, all that mattered was the emphatic, joyful rhythm, the sense of magic, as if the crowd in its enthusiasm were drawing Nathan Vickery closer and closer.) And then Nathan did appear, and Japheth saw that he was at the top of his form. He had totally recovered: his voice had regained its strange melodic authority, he did not look so pale and drained and thin, he strode to the center of the raised platform with his arms outspread as if he would embrace the entire room.

He began softly, even conversationally. Welcoming them — expressing his gratitude — asking them to join him in a prayer to bless the evening. Then he went on to speak of Christ's love and sacrifice, and the necessity of humbling oneself, opening oneself fully, to God; and then, his voice growing stronger, he began to speak of the possibility that the Final Days were approaching — given the evidence of war, and riots in the cities, and assassinations, and crime, and divorce, and alcoholism and drug-taking, and immorality of all sorts; and Japheth sat listening as if he were hearing all this for the first time. There were beasts abroad, and angels of death. And devils. Demons. The signs were unmistakable. There were false prophets in the established churches, and unbelievers — mockers of Christ — in positions of power. Government, business, education were contaminated. Good was mistaken as evil, and evil as good. Many feared that the Kingdom of God was at hand and yet they did nothing — knew not what to do, even to save themselves. What a horror it would be, what a chaos! The bravest men and women had become cowards, eager to placate Satan and his manifestations, turned aside from the Lord though they knew very well the wrath that lay in store. They knew, they knew very well! Yet they pretended not to know. And it was his duty, Nathan Vickery's duty, to call them back to their senses, to shout into their faces the truth of God's love. *Be not afraid of them that kill the body, and after that have no more that they can do. But I will forewarn you whom you shall fear: Fear him, which after he hath killed hath power to cast into hell; yea, I say unto you, Fear him.*

And then, suddenly, Nathan fell silent.

He stared out at them, as if alarmed. Japheth was shocked. Was something wrong? Had something gone wrong? Around him people were murmuring. A few seats down, Reverend Lund glanced toward Japheth suspiciously; he must have believed Japheth knew what was happening.

Nathan stepped forward, peering into the crowd. He brushed his hair out of his eyes in a simple, disarming gesture, like a man who has become suddenly self-conscious. "I don't think I can continue this evening," he said. "I feel the force of the demonic so strongly, coming from certain individuals here in this church. I *feel* it. I can't go on — I can't speak of Christ and love and forgiveness and Heaven and the Holy Spirit awakening in you unless these evil spirits are driven out — unless you surrender them to me and allow me to drive them out. . . . Do you understand?"

Japheth felt waves of alarm and panic run through the church. He felt, in that first instant, a sensation of sheer guilt: as if Nathan had looked into his very soul and had discovered evil there, where he himself had not known it dwelt.

"Do you hear? Do you understand?" Nathan was saying in a singsong voice, as if he were speaking to stubborn children. "I *feel* the evil in certain individuals here. I can see you — I can see into you. You've come here tonight because the Holy Spirit has led you to me, because it is ordained that tonight you are going to be made well and brought into my church. You didn't know: maybe you came out of curiosity, but the Holy Spirit was guiding you. And now you are here. And now I know you. And I am telling you that some of you can be saved and some of you can't be saved, because it is God's will. If you are sick at heart, if you are ailing, physically or mentally or spiritually ailing, you *must* surrender yourself to me — and if it's God's will I can exorcise the principle of the demonic from you and make you whole again, as you were as a child. I can do it with God's help. God can do it with my help. I had intended to preach as usual tonight and to call for the saved to come forward and be welcomed into my church, but I can't continue — I can't go on. *You* can't go on. There's no point in my addressing you as if the majority of you were healthy and free of evil influences — God has allowed me to know I can't continue as I had planned. Some of you are seriously sick — deathly sick! And you know who you are! And *I* know! And God has given me the power for only tonight to drive the sickness from your souls and make you well — He has called me to a healing ministry right here before you — He has instructed me in all that I must do — in the works that I must work during my time on earth —"

For the first several minutes there was confusion, since no one had been prepared for Nathan's pronouncement. Japheth himself sat stunned, hardly attending to the whispering and murmuring among the Seekers. Was Nathan speaking to *him?* Had Nathan discerned a certain lack, a certain unhealthiness, in *his* soul? Somewhere toward the rear of the church a woman began to sob, and at once others joined her, and Nathan's organist began to play — lurchingly at first, so that it was several bars before "Thus Christ Approaches" was recognizable.

And then everything fell into place: the aisles were jammed with people pushing their way forward: a few of the Seekers, quick-witted enough to know they must help, got to their feet and stood ready.

"Is God present? Is the Holy Ghost present? Tonight? Now? Here? In us?" Nathan cried. "I think so. I *feel* that it's so. Don't hold back, come forward, come to me, I can help you, come to me — yes, like that! Is God present? Is the Holy Ghost present in us? I feel so many wonders in me! So many marvels! My head is filled to bursting with them! Such power! Such love! Yes, like that, yes, come forward — we'll help you — come forward, come forward — you will be baptized in the Blood of the Lamb

— your sins will be washed from you and your soul will be clean
as a newborn child's — you will belong to the Lord forever and
He will never neglect you — you will belong to us forever —
we will love you and take care of you and never, never neglect
you —"

Japheth would have liked to help but the situation terrified
him. Many of the men and women were perfectly ordinary
churchgoers — Pentecostals, probably — with their grim, hopeful, seedy faces and their cheap dress-up clothes; but here and
there Japheth could see people who were genuinely not well —
some were crippled, some were very weak, some had the shrink-
ing glittering look of madness. All were pressing forward. The
organ's massive wheezing chords and the near-hysterical singing
and clapping and, above all, the call, the cry, of Nathan's voice
drew them irresistibly forward. "Is God present? Is God in me?
Am I God? Tonight? Now? Here? I feel His power in me! To
the very tips of my fingers! I am filled with strength, with marvels —"

And yet, when he considered the situation afterward, Japheth
had to admit that Nathan had been in complete control all the
while. There was the appearance of ecstatic chaos, of near-
danger, and certainly there were a number of hysterical people,
men and women both, but Nathan controlled them wonderfully
with his voice and his gestures: drawing them forward, greeting
them one by one, laying hands on them and gazing into their
eyes with a peculiar intensity, as if he were seeking someone,
looking for someone he knew. It was evident that Nathan could
tell in an instant whom he might help, and who was beyond his
help. He knelt before an aged, badly crippled woman who had
been led forward by her daughter and, taking both her hands in
his, he pressed them against his forehead and prayed in a loud,
plaintive voice that she would forgive him, for he could not help
her, he had not the power to help her. And as he leaned forward
to greet a young blond man Japheth saw his expression shift, his
good eye narrow: and this man too was beyond his help. (The
man was in his twenties, very thin, with a skimpy beard and a

trembling head and a keen, gaunt look that frightened Japheth
for no reason he could have said: Was the young man insane?
Was he dying?) Nathan gripped him close in an embrace and
then stepped back and begged to be forgiven, and in his confusion the young man stood there for a moment, blinking, trembling, until someone else pushed up close behind him, and one
of the Seekers — Reverend Lund himself, it was, perspiring
freely — gripped the young man by his arm and pulled him aside.
It was necessary to keep the aisles clear, to keep traffic moving.

But those he could help Nathan spent some minutes with, his
hands on their shoulders, his face brought close to theirs. He
spoke to them cajolingly, murmuring that the Holy Spirit had led
them forward and was now descending into them, flowing from
him and into them, bringing them strength and purpose and
well-being and love. Did they feel it? Did they feel it? At times he
cupped a believer's face in both his hands and the look that
passed between them was one of urgent, almost terrified love: of
recognition and love. He prayed for them in a whining, pleading
voice, his own face hotly pale, damp with sweat, his eyes glittering. What devils could withstand his power, the power of the
Holy Spirit! What cloudy devilish thoughts could withstand *his*
power! After a brief while the believer began to sway from side to
side as if losing consciousness, and his head rolled on his shoulders, and still Nathan gripped him tight and stared into his eyes,
and it happened in several instances that the person shrieked and
began to fall and was caught in Nathan's arms. As the service
continued and the air became more and more highly charged,
Nathan had to do no more than merely approach a believer, or
touch him — a woman collapsed with a groan, a red-faced man
of middle age fell heavily sideways and would have struck his
head against a pew if Japheth himself hadn't caught him, a girl of
about fifteen began weeping uncontrollably and slipped to her
knees at Nathan's feet.

A number of the newly converted did faint, but came around
again almost immediately, helped by members of Nathan's staff.
They babbled in delight, clutching at strangers' hands, declaring

the Holy Spirit was in them and they were well, perfectly well, Nathan had cured them, Nathan had brought them God. Japheth crouched over a woman in her mid-thirties who was lying on a pew, breathing rapidly, on the verge of hyperventilation; she gripped both his hands so tightly he had to steel himself against crying out in pain. "My God! My God!" the woman wailed. She was amazingly strong for her size, and with her eyes shut tight and her cheeks wet with tears she put him in mind of a woman in childbirth: the ecstatic abandon, the strength of her hands, the almost inhuman expression on her face: giving birth to — birth to what? Japheth's teeth chattered with excitement, or perhaps it was with fear. He tried to calm the woman. It was his responsibility to get her name and address and to find out from her whether she was a regular churchgoer, who was her pastor, was this the first time she had heard Nathan Vickery speak, did she intend to become a Seeker for Christ, did she wish to become a full-time member of the church or a part-time member, and how large was her family . . . ? But it was nearly twenty minutes before she could reply coherently to his questions.

The service lasted for hours. At the end Japheth was staggering with exhaustion. He squatted in the aisle beside a man in his late forties with a closely shaved head and an odd pattern of purplish-red birthmarks on his left cheek and for some minutes Japheth could not tell which of them was sobbing, which of them was babbling wildly about the Holy Spirit and Christ and Brother Nathan and some bad, some very bad, bad thing, that had happened back in 1939. Was there forgiveness, the man wept, would Brother Nathan forgive him if he knew . . . ? "I did it with full knowledge of how sinful it was! It wasn't the Devil, it was me! It was me alone! I did it and knew it was wrong and never, never told anybody and now it's too late!" he cried. And Japheth managed to comfort him. Of course he was forgiven: hadn't the Holy Spirit descended into him, wasn't he like a newborn child, washed and cleansed and pure?

The man turned his contorted, weeping face to Japheth and would have hugged him had Japheth not kept his distance. De-

spite his exhaustion Japheth had the clear, penetrating, triumphant thought that in his Master's name he had done good: had
performed a kind of miracle: for the man would believe anything
he was told in that mental state, and so he was indeed absolved
of his sins. How could there be any doubt of that? Hadn't Nathan
Vickery touched him tonight, bringing him the baptism of the
Holy Spirit?

On the second night of the Crusade nearly everyone who had
attended the first night returned, bringing others with them; the
crowds were such that a number of people had to be turned away.
But Reverend Lund made the promise that another, larger
church would be rented, which could accommodate everyone.
And so on the third night hundreds of people showed up, many
of them converts from the first two nights; and so it was with the
fourth night, and the fifth. . . . (The Crusade was so successful
that it was extended for a full week.)

There were newspaper reporters and photographers, and even
television cameramen and their equipment, and the Seekers were
violently divided about them: should they be allowed inside the
church to witness the services, though most of them were unbelievers and some were probably outright enemies . . . ? Or should
they be turned away? Since Nathan Vickery kept to himself for
the entire week, speaking to no one at all — not even to Japheth,
who was surprised and hurt — they could only speculate about
his wishes. Many of the Seekers wanted the reporters banned,
but Reverend Lund pointed out that it was only through publicity
that the church could attract members — and, strangely enough,
it didn't seem to matter whether the publicity was good or bad.
An article so hostile as to have been nearly libelous had appeared
the summer before in an upstate newspaper, yet attendance at
Nathan's subsequent meetings had been higher than ever, and
membership in the church itself continued to climb.

So a number of reporters and photographers were admitted,
and on the fourth night of the Crusade photographs were taken
of an extraordinary incident: as people were making their way

forward to be greeted by Nathan Vickery and given his blessing, a disturbed young man in a canvas jacket appeared suddenly at Nathan's side and, accusing him of something in a loud, braying voice, made a swipe at him with a hunting knife. Japheth, who happened to be standing only a few yards away, saw to his astonishment that Nathan appeared not at all alarmed: without hesitating, he reached for the knife as if to simply take it out of the man's hand. His fingers closed ineffectually about the blade, however, and the young man drew the knife back violently, and Japheth saw that Nathan's fingers were slashed. Yet in the next instant Nathan managed to disarm the man, this time by seizing his wrist. There was a great deal of excitement — the scuffling of Nathan and his attacker, and the screams of witnesses, and the flash of cameras.

"Call a doctor! Someone call a doctor!" Japheth cried.

But Nathan turned to him in surprise. He didn't want a doctor, he didn't even want the police; everything was under control.

"But your hand —" Japheth said.

"There's nothing wrong with my hand," Nathan said irritably.

He held out both hands for Japheth and the others to see — and indeed there was no blood on either hand, no marks at all.

"But he cut you — The knife blade cut you —"

"No," Nathan said. "I'm not hurt."

"But I saw —"

"You're mistaken," Nathan said, turning away.

And so the service continued, and Japheth stood staring, unable to comprehend what had happened. He had seen, clearly enough, Nathan's fingers close about the blade of the knife — he was positive he had seen the blade slash Nathan's palm — he *had* seen blood. Yet there was no blood, there was no wound. Nothing at all. The young man had been led out of the church and his knife was pocketed by one of the reporters (so Japheth believed, and this turned out to be accurate) and Nathan simply continued with the ceremony.

Much later, when they were leaving the church, Japheth asked nervously if he might see Nathan's hand again.

"My hand? Why? What do you mean?" Nathan asked. His voice was hoarse and his skin had gone clammy from exhaustion. He walked like a man in a dream; like a sleepwalker. It was evident that he did not remember the incident, and when Japheth reminded him of it his expression remained blank. "What knife? What man? Nothing happened; everything went as it was ordained. What do you mean?"

"You took hold of his knife by the blade and he jerked it back and — and your fingers were cut —"

"I tell you, nothing happened," Nathan said.

There were others listening, other members of his staff. They watched him rather timidly, knowing he did not care to be bothered at such times. (Only if he needed help walking out to the car, or seemed about to keel over, would anyone dare to approach him; even Reverend Lund had learned to keep a respectful distance.)

"What are you all looking at?" Nathan said. His voice rose hoarsely and cracked. "I tell you, nothing happened, I'm not hurt, I can't be hurt. Did you think it would be that easy?" He looked at them, forcing a queer, strained smile. Again he showed them his hands, the palms exposed, and they were unharmed — untouched. "Why are you so fearful? Why so anxious? You should have more faith in me after all these years. Don't you know at last *who I am. . . ?*"

ix

Were You present when Nathan Vickery healed the sick, did You indeed pulse along his veins, breathing in unison with him . . . ? Did You whisper to him who might be saved and who was beyond his ability to save, did You coil about him like a lover, did You strain his heart to the bursting point?

Do You abide with him still?

My prayer continues, but now it is without hope. I continue, but without hope.

There are small tasteless meals to be prepared and eaten; there are interminable nights to be endured; there are thoughts tormenting me that I cannot escape. I live now without hope.

It must be evident to You that I know very little, that I am as ignorant as certain of Nathan's disciples, who wanted only to kneel before him in brainless adulation, begging that he allow them to call him Master. (For it was a word that exasperated him.) My efforts to give substance to a wraith cost me a great deal of pain and yet are inadequate, and *yet* I must continue for I am powerless to bring my prayer to an end . . . to a premature end.

I am discovering, O Lord, that my prayer is my life: my self.

To break it off would be to break off my own being.

The skein of words connects me to You (or to the memory of You), and I myself am the word made flesh, stubbornly living though my reason for living has fled.

The composition of this long, torturous prayer is exhausting, and yet I cannot give up. I want to *know*. Were You indeed present in the form of the Holy Spirit when Nathan performed his many cures? — his "miraculous" cures? Did You instruct him in everything? Was it Your power that healed his slashed hand, and allowed him to rise from a hospital bed (in the winter of 1969 he was badly ill with pleurisy) in order to continue his Crusade? Did You pulse and flow into him, and breathe with his eager lungs, and fill him like warm honey to his very fingertips? Was it Your passion that made his voice tremble, Your uncanny beauty that made so many of his followers fall in love with him . . . ? If so, You had no mercy: no pity.

Japheth saw, Japheth was a witness.

■ ■ ■

"God exists," Japheth went about muttering, in a state of almost continual excitement. "God exists. *Exists*." He found it

difficult to sit still long enough to eat; there was always something
to do, a telephone call to make, mail orders to send out, a con-
sultation with the printer or with one of the secretaries. Though
his reaction immediately following one of Nathan's services was
never as extreme as that of Nathan himself — for it wasn't uncommon that Nathan would lose seven or eight pounds in a few
hours and collapse into a deep coma afterward and not wake for
a full day — he was nevertheless profoundly affected: his skin
broke out in angry red rashes, his bowels writhed, his teeth chattered with the exhilaration of plans for the next service.

Now there were church groups and even secular organizations
eager to bring Nathan Vickery to them, now there were fifteen
and twenty-five and forty and seventy Seekers' communities
springing to life, some of them no more than a few friends who
happened to have been converted together, some of them genuine communities with houses and land and dizzyingly ambitious
plans. (Under Nathan Vickery's general direction, and Reverend
Lund's meticulous guidance, the Seekers' communities were established in order to provide a place of sanctuary for believers: no
one could move into one of the houses without surrendering all
the debris of his past life, including savings, property, personal
attachments, habits involving sexual behavior, or alcohol, or
drugs; and of course all emotional, assertive, non-Christian behavior had to be given up.) Now there were accountants and
attorneys and tax specialists; and a staff hired to deal with the
press and with public relations in general. (For a while Japheth
headed this staff, and throughout his relationship with the Seekers he met regularly with press reporters and photographers, who
seemed to appreciate his quick-witted eloquence and his disdain
of solemnity, and were inclined to be merciful to him. With one
part of his mind he despised publicity, but with another he appre-
ciated the soundness of Reverend Lund's strategy. "You can't
control the bastards by turning your back," Lund said, "but you
can *halfway* control them by meeting them face to face." Japheth
became professional enough to see the interviews as games from
which he sometimes emerged victorious and sometimes emerged

looking like a fool. And since Nathan never condescended to speak with interviewers or, as time went by, with people from the "outside" at all, it was necessary that someone intelligent take charge. *Let not then your good be evil spoken of:* thus did Japheth mutter at Nathan's chaste back.)

Now there were dismaying entanglements: a lawsuit initiated by the family of a cancer patient who allegedly broke off her cobalt treatments after having been "cured" by Nathan, and who subsequently died within a few months; and though it was protested that Nathan had not pronounced the woman cured, and that the Seekers hadn't even a record of her conversion, the case went to court nonetheless. (I believe it is unsettled still, awaiting appeal on one level or another.) And astonishing windfalls: a tax-free inheritance of half a million dollars from the estate of an eccentric philanthropist who, as far as anyone knew, had never even heard Nathan preach. . . . There were gifts of jewelry and insurance policies, houses, automobiles and trucks and vans, even offers of partnerships in businesses; and as always there were gifts of cash, made outright, without requests for receipts.

For by grace are ye saved through faith; and that not of yourselves: it is the gift of God.

So taught Japheth's Master; and in the early seventies it seemed as if everyone was hungry for this teaching. Salvation had nothing to do with social responsibility or action of any kind; it had nothing to do with human relationships; the believer's allegiance was to God, and God was all in all, absorbing everything into Him so that nothing remained.

It astonished Japheth that more and more young people of the middle class were attending Seekers' meetings, even when they were held in churches and auditoriums and sports arenas many miles from suburban communities or university campuses. Haggard smiling boys with their hair tied back in pony tails, girls with their long straight hair falling to their waists, in scruffy khaki windbreakers or ankle-length capes or hand-woven Indian shirts, wearing sandals or costly leather boots: Japheth picked them out at once, the very first night they appeared, their eyes already glassy with a certain hard, willful desire before they even heard Nathan Vickery speak. Japheth was somewhat disturbed. He could not really comprehend what it might mean. These were *his* people, in a sense; younger than he, but sharing certain economic and social and political concerns; and of course they were well-educated. At least they had been educated at considerable expense.

"Do you realize who these people are?" Japheth asked his associates. "These young people? That group that came in the van all the way from New York City?"

Of Nathan Vickery's closest associates, only the printer Donald Beck, who had attended college for two years, had a background comparable to Japheth's. His father was said to be an executive with an insurance company in Indiana, and Japheth gathered that Donald had attended an Eastern preparatory school. But when, in the presence of Reverend Lund, or another staff member, Japheth allowed himself to make certain clever remarks (for he was sometimes maddeningly frustrated by the obtuseness of his associates), Donald merely smiled and blinked at him, seemingly without comprehension. He was a strong-bodied, shy man in his late thirties, who wore his thinning blond hair combed back away from his forehead so that the strong ascetic bones of his head were prominent. He spoke infrequently, and always in a subdued voice. Japheth had had little success in becoming acquainted with him, for Donald evaded his questions, and it wasn't possible to know whether Donald had been married or not — it wasn't possible to know, even, whether he might still be married. He was very religious: when he wasn't working he stayed apart from the others, reading the Bible and praying; it was said that he kept the same general hours Nathan Vickery did, and tried to fast as he did, though extreme bouts of fasting were more or less forbidden in the Seekers' communities. (After a great deal of worry and discussion they had had to adopt this "law" — a nineteen-year-old girl had collapsed from malnutrition a year before, and there were bizarre episodes of hallucinations and

paranoid terror in a number of the homes.) Donald Beck, like
many of the other church members, had appeared one day out
of nowhere, eager to hand over to the Seekers all his money and
material goods and to volunteer his skills in exchange for the
privilege of living in the community. He had been drawn to the
Seekers in a fairly typical way — struck by a poster announcing
Nathan Vickery's imminent Crusade for Souls (in the small city
of Dunes, near Port Oriskany), fascinated by the sharp bony
planes of Nathan's face, his stern half-smile, the frosty *certainty*
of his eyes; and troubled as well by the small headlines beneath
the photograph, *What Does It Truly Mean To Be Washed In The
Blood Of The Lamb?* and *Are You A Seeker For Christ Without
Knowing It?* It had never occurred to him that there might be a
truth about himself that had not been revealed to him; he had
always found it difficult to believe that the world's — and his
family's — assessment of him was just. And so he had gone to
Nathan's service, and within half an hour something extraordinary had taken place in his soul, and he found himself weeping
as though his heart were broken, on his knees, his head bowed
before Nathan Vickery's warm, low, richly vibrant voice. When
Nathan touched him, pressing down firmly on both his shoulders, he experienced a violent, almost convulsive shock: he
nearly lost consciousness: and afterward he realized that at Nathan's touch something had rushed out of him, a queer sub-
stanceless yet writhing, stinging *thing*, in shape rather like an eel;
he had known, even before one of the Seekers explained, that
the thing had been a demon.

The torment of his former life, the relative aimlessness and
insecurity, the frequent half-wishes for death, had been caused
all along by this poisonous spirit, which he had sheltered without
knowing it; which, perhaps, he had even defended in his stubborn
pride in his own self-reliance. Now all that was changed. All that
was past. He lived no longer in and for himself, but only for
Christ, and for Nathan Vickery, and for his fellow Seekers. (He
even wore, tight about his left arm a few inches above the wrist,
a braid of dark hair, which was usually kept hidden by his sleeve:

which Japheth assumed to his dismay to be Nathan Vickery's hair. But how the man had obtained it without Nathan's knowledge he could not imagine. . . . For Nathan would *certainly* forbid such behavior if he knew.)

When Japheth brought up the subject of the young people, Donald Beck was strangely offended. He stared at his hands, he began to crack his knuckles unconsciously, he would not meet Japheth's eye. "There's something in the air, something new and not yet formed," Japheth said eagerly, "a kind of miracle. . . . An entirely new type of Christian."

Donald merely made a guttural sound, vaguely affirmative. But he continued to frown and would not look up.

"When Reverend Lund gets back from Cleveland we must talk to him. We must make him understand how important this is. Instead of booking Nathan in the small towns and the usual places, he should be arranging for him to visit cities, particularly cities with universities. A new plan of attack is called for, don't you think?" Japheth asked. His anxiety about even the simplest conversations had become rather amusing: he could see how absurd it was for him to be trembling and perspiring, as if he were imploring Nathan Vickery himself to take him seriously, and not merely Donald Beck. But tremble he did, and it took an effort for him to keep his teeth from chattering. "It's so important that Reverend Lund *understand*. He's an excellent businessman, I acknowledge that, but he's narrow-minded, and obtuse, and he has never seemed to trust me — not even to accept me. Brothers in Christ, we are! *Brothers!* But he pretends to ignore my suggestions, and then a few weeks later he implements them without giving me credit, and Nathan would naturally think that *he* — Reverend Lund — thought them up. And I hardly want to degrade myself by telling Nathan what the situation really is. . . . What do you think, Donald?"

After a pause the older man glanced uneasily at Japheth and said, so softly that Japheth could hardly hear, something about the commandment of Our Lord: *That ye love one another.*

"What? Oh yes. Yes," Japheth said. "But at the same time — I think it's sometimes necessary to — You see, Donald, we may be on the brink of a new era. Not just the Seekers: but the nation itself. The young people who were at the service last night — I was talking to them for quite a while afterward — they're profoundly disillusioned with the secular life, not just with their parents — they rejected *them* years ago — but with the secular world altogether, with politics and social action and *getting things done*. One of them was a law student at Columbia, and he told me he'd been on the edge for months, on the edge of a nervous breakdown, or worse, and he'd heard of the Seekers from someone else and thought we might possibly be the answer. He dropped out of law school and is living on a farm in upstate New York and — Well, I don't want to get carried away," Japheth said, laughing, troubled by Donald Beck's impassive face, "I just want to explain — You see, these are wonderful young people, intelligent and well-educated and sensitive — they've had all they ever required in terms of material possessions, and their parents have loved them — for the most part, I mean — they've done everything for them, anyway. And so — And so it would be a marvelous thing if we brought the faith to them, if we made a real effort to win their souls — Don't you think?"

"I think," Donald said slowly, gripping his hands together tightly, and managing a timid glance at Japheth's face, "that it doesn't matter to Christ or to Our Lord or to Nathan who people are. There is neither rich nor poor, nor. . . ."

"Yes, yes," Japheth said, hardly listening in his excitement. "But for the first time Nathan seems to be drawing people from the middle class, the educated class — For the first time since I've been working with him there seems to be the possibility of — of something wonderful, something marvelous — a revolution of consciousness! And we might be — Nathan might be — at the very center of it: don't you understand how urgent it is?"

Donald shook his head, frowning. "All things unfold as they must," he said.

"But at last he seems to be reaching out to the kind of people who scorned him in the past."

"*He*," Donald whispered. "Who do you mean by *he*? You shouldn't talk about Nathan Vickery like that: not *he*."

Japheth stared at him. Donald was deeply tanned from working in the sun, and the whites of his eyes appeared to be unusually white. Where Japheth was quivering with passion, Donald was rigid, as if he did not dare allow himself to move; even his restless hands were stilled.

"You have no right," Donald whispered, "to speak of Nathan Vickery like that. To degrade him like that. As if he wasn't here with us, as if his spirit wasn't here." He glanced about the room, as if to seek out Nathan. "You have no right to make plans for the future in his name. Not even to think of them. For all things are done in Nathan's name in their own time, as we've been told. And the Kingdom of God is close at hand: you know that. The church can take only so many souls with it to heaven, there isn't room for everyone, the Chosen of the Lord number no more than a hundred and forty-four thousand, you *know* that . . ."

Japheth swallowed uneasily.

". . . and the adulation of the world is vanity," Donald continued in his slow, groping voice. "*Woe unto you, when all men shall speak well of you! for so did their fathers to the false prophets.*"

After a long moment Japheth began again, though without as much confidence, to explain that the United States might be on the brink of an entirely new consciousness: a revolution in Christ's name. And after the United States . . . ? Possibly the entire world.

Donald Beck stared, as if not recognizing him.

"It's my personal theory that — that the younger generation is turning aside from material things," Japheth said, "and — and from certain of the old cultural ideals — they were originally Greek ideals, I believe — the desirability of combat, of strife and competition and endless contests — the worship of masculine *virtue* — virility — I think we've come to the point in the evolution of our species where we're ready to — to make a leap to another — The cruelty of the Hellenistic ideal has had its day, after so many centuries: at last we can be brothers and sisters in Christ! At last —"

Without speaking, Donald Beck rose and left the room. And Japheth remained where he was, staring after him.

Some days later Beck took him aside and informed him that he, Donald, had been praying for him almost constantly, that his troubled soul be at peace. "There is something poisonous in you," the man said frankly, "something restless and grasping and evil. You don't realize it because it's so close to you. You've lived with it all your life. But even after Nathan Vickery has accepted you and taken you in, you're not whole, you're not one of the Chosen. . . . So I've prayed for you. And I've asked others to pray for you too."

Japheth managed to stammer something. "What? Why . . . ?" But the man did not hear, or did not choose to hear; he simply walked away.

"You *bastard*," Japheth muttered.

And his bowels ached with hatred, and his eyes filled quickly with tears.

X

If any man come to me, and hate not his father, and mother, and wife, and children, and brethren, and sisters, yea, and his own life also, he cannot be my disciple . . . !

So he cried out to the multitude, his arms held wide. White-gowned, impatient, he called to them in a half-wailing, seductive voice, his hair swinging savagely about his face. *If any man come to me, and hate not . . . he cannot be my disciple.* All were silent, listening. The electric organ was stilled, the choir was stilled, as if in terror of his passion; everyone sat hushed before him, each alone with him and his voice. Was he angry, his eyes flashing, his hands closed into fists? Or did he tremble with desire for them, in a strange half-fainting trance?

Come forward, he pleaded. *Come forward.*

The white robe was dazzling. The voice lifted higher and higher, and dropped suddenly, richly commanding. *Come forward, come forward and make your commitment to Jesus.*

As he spoke they began to stir, and then to rise, some of them doubtfully, fearfully, making their way to the aisles. Staring at him, mesmerized by his face and his ceaselessly moving arms, there were those who stumbled on the stadium steps, and had to catch themselves by taking hold of the railing. *Awake. Now. Come forward. Tonight. Now. Jesus is waiting. I am waiting. Now.*

A lone airplane flew overhead, quite high. Nathan's voice pierced its familiar companionable drone, amplified many times. *The sick-at-heart. The weary. The lonely. You who hear my voice and would resist, groveling in your skin. You too must awake: must come forward. Jesus is waiting. Jesus is impatient. He has been waiting so many, many centuries, waiting for you to cast off the bonds of sin, to step forward into his embrace . . . ! Those who have suffered for the sake of righteousness, and those who have suffered for the sake of sin: awake now and come forward before the Lord God turns His wrath upon you. Do you hear? Do you understand? I am the Lord God beseeching you through the person of Nathanael Vickery . . . I am the Lord God crying out to you to come home, to come home.*

Now the organ began again, softly. Now the choir began to sing.

He paced about the platform restlessly, calling them to him. They listened, and shuddered, and could not resist. Already the first of the converts were making their way down the steps to the ground, their movements tentative, their expressions dreamlike. The Lord God called them out of their seats and they could not resist, they did not dare resist. *The sick. The ailing. The weary. The frightened. The lonely. The sufferers in silence. The bewildered ones, who cry aloud each day: Why was I born? Those who are burdened with their own sins, their own offenses against the Lord. Those who fear death, knowing they will be cast down to hell. . . . For it is impossible but that offenses will come: but woe unto him through whom they come! It were better for him that a millstone were hanged about his neck, and he cast into the sea. . . .*

One by one they came, and in small faltering groups, their eyes wet with tears and their lips murmuring prayers. Slowly they made their way forward out of the tiers of seats, slowly the streams became one large, formless stream, pressing forward. Nathan called them to him and they could not resist. The Lord God called them and they could not resist.

You are all Seekers for Christ, are you not? From the day of your birth until tonight, the hour of your awakening? You are all my children, are you not? Shaking yourself free of the terrible weight of sin. . . .

So they came to him, several hundred altogether. And he greeted them individually, hungry to seize their hands, to welcome them in the name of the Lord. They shuffled forward, their faces transfigured. Not a one was ugly! Not a one was haggard, or exhausted, or drawn with age! One by one they made their commitment to the Lord Jesus Christ, one by one they gave their names to him, and he repeated their names, his voice beginning to crack but his face still ecstatic. *My brothers and sisters in Christ! My dear ones! Now you are come home at last, now you are come home . . . !*

Middle-aged men in sports clothes and pregnant young women in billowing dresses and boys in white shirts, their eyes damp with fear; men leading their elderly, crippled mothers down the steps and across the grass, slowly, slowly, making their way to Jesus; the young, the old, the dreamily smiling, the quick, brisk, exuberant ones whose hearts were already with Jesus: so they came to him for they could not resist. He seized their cold perspiring hands in his, and rubbed them together in triumph, a smile of sheer joy transfiguring his face. And sometimes he grasped their heads as if he meant to embrace them violently, welcoming them in the name of Jesus. There were those who stumbled to him, and pushed themselves in his arms; there were those who collapsed in tears before him. Some shrank from his touch involuntarily, and staggered as if they would fall, and then came to their senses; and were welcomed in the name of Jesus. And God was all in all: and there was nothing that was not God.

(Except there came before him a panting, full-bodied woman, her face rounded and shining, her hair fixed in a plump, glossy chignon from which stray tendrils escaped; and her expression was both desperate and cunning. So close to hysteria was she that others stood aside to let her pass, and one of the staff members helped her forward, staggering in her high-heeled shoes, so that she could stand before Nathan Vickery and make her commitment to Christ and accept His blessing. But she merely stared at him, and raised her hands to him. *Nathan? Nathan?* He gazed upon her with the radiance of Christ's love, but did not offer to take her extended hands. *Nathan? Don't you know me?* He smiled at her, his single good eye shone with love for her, and recognition of a kind; but it was clear that the woman was hysterical and must be led away, for she was no one Nathan Vickery knew.

Nathan? Don't you know me? Don't you forgive me?

Close about him stood his highest associates and, in plain clothes, several security policemen, and when the woman sought to press herself forward into Nathan's arms, she was immediately held back. Sobbing, sobbing helplessly and angrily, she tried to sink to her knees before him, and made a gesture as if to clutch him about the legs — but this too was prevented, and she was hauled to her feet and led to the side. *Nathan! Please! I only want* — But he knew her not, he knew nothing of her, and in the next instant he was welcoming in the name of Christ a young man of about nineteen who was so agitated he could barely stammer, and who, when Nathan Vickery laid his hands upon him, began at once to weep like a child.

And so the woman was led away, gasping and muttering, around and behind the raised platform and toward a rear exit, where several others had been led, gently but swiftly. *He does know me! He loves me! Let me go, let me go to him —*

They let her say what she wished, but walked her to the exit nonetheless.)

Be ye in the world and not of it.

Tough and fibrous the root forced itself up out of the earth, and grew strong and powerful and majestic as a tree, pushing defiantly upward, straining upward into the sky. It was gigantic: no longer a tree but a tower. A day and a night Nathan gazed upon it, in helpless rapture. He could not move. He could not think. His mind was broken and gone, his very being sucked out of himself. *Be ye in the world and not of it,* You cautioned him.

The sun blazed and the winds blew hotly across the curve of the earth, yet the tower remained firm.

He saw the immense desert spaces of the earth stretching out before him; he saw strange desert birds flying close to the cracked ground, ungainly creatures, solitary and triumphant. In his ordinary life he had gazed upon birds and animals and his fellow human beings, yet it had not been granted to him to *see;* nor had he felt the profundity of their separateness, their stubborn and inexplicable reality. Now You allowed him to realize the *otherness* of these creatures, and of all creatures, and You gave to him dominion over them, over all manner of life that crept about the face of the earth. There were the great sunless darkly heaving oceans of the earth, beneath their surfaces choked with life, and over this life, which swam and coiled about itself and devoured and excreted itself constantly, You gave absolute dominion to Nathanael Vickery: for he was the root, the tree, the living tower that held together earth and heaven. The birds of the air, the creatures of the deep, and all life that sprang out of the earth, including man, You placed under his dominion. For he was the seed, the stem, the blossom; the gigantic tower that heaved with life, and that no earthly power could overcome.

He was allowed to see, then, at the base of the tower that was himself, the Tribulation that was to be the fate of ordinary men and women. Seven years it would rage, seven chaotic years, and there would be great suffering, and weeping and gnashing of teeth, and he must steel himself against pity: for pity for mankind would melt his bones and he would be lost, as Jesus of Nazareth was lost. *Be ye in the world and not of it, as Jesus was of it; his worldliness cost Him His life. In you I am come again. In you I will not fail.*

After the seven years' horror there would be visited upon the earth the warm bliss of Your love, and the new Saviour would descend, and for one thousand years would reign; and the Chosen of the Lord would rejoice, and the dead would be resurrected, and all would be well. The Saviour would walk upon the earth *as if* he belonged to the earth. But he was Your son: Your being: the heavenly tower itself. And this heavenly tower was Nathan, who gazed upon it in rapture, his soul drawn out of his body in a swoon of bliss. *In you I will not fail*, the voice declared.

Nathan whispered: *O Lord I am not worthy — !*

But You brushed away his doubts. You stooped to him and whispered in his ear *I am thy salvation, I and no other*, and he stirred, he threw himself about, he groaned to wake and embrace You: for he wished suddenly, greedily, that he could press You against his body and make his claim upon You, as You made Yours upon him. But he was the radiance that forced its way out of the earth, he was the tree, the great tower, the fortification that reached to heaven itself, and he had no human body, only the semblance of a body . . . his very soul that had gone hard with rapture, linking earth and heaven, the earth of mankind and the heaven of the Lord. And so no human wishes were granted him. No human desires, or gratifications. *Be ye in the world*, the voice cried, *and not of it*.

Jesus of Nazareth had failed, but Nathan would not fail: so You allowed him to know.

Many were the false prophets and lying Messiahs, and the bitter, broken Christs out of Galilee. Many were their unsubstantial images, blown about the face of the earth, reduced to ash.

Fraudulent signs and wonders, spurious miracles, idols and creatures of straw: none of which pleased You. But Nathan would please You. In Nathan You descend again to the earth, in Nathan Your Kingdom touches the earth once again, and brings the heartbeat of history to a stop.

Knowing this, he groaned and thrashed about, hardly able to bear such joy, such pleasure. His backbone seemed to come alive of itself: exploding with radiant light: he could not bear it, could not bear it! That he gazed upon the wondrous tower and yet was the tower, was himself the tower — he could not bear it! Yet You whispered to him, and comforted him, allowing him to know what no other man had ever known. *You and I are one. You and I have always been one.*

A day and a night the vision endured, yet when he woke no time at all had passed. A rivulet of perspiration ran down his side, and the back of his neck was damp, and the skin of his face was feverish; but no time had passed. Between one heartbeat and the next You had spoken and Nathan had been snatched out of himself and flung far, far distant, and yet his body had remained in its seat, and his voice had continued, and no one could guess that You had shown Your face at last.

About the long candlelit table Your creatures sat, gazing upon Nathan, seeing Your radiance in him, and in honor of him they chattered as always, in the harmless melodic sounds of human creatures, looking to him for his judgment. Who were these people? Had he known them in another lifetime? He, who had been shown the secret axis of the earth, he who was the very axis himself, was expected to take them seriously and to reply to their childlike questions . . . ! He laughed aloud with the absurdity of it. He *laughed*, that these people should imagine he shared a common language with them, or dwelt in his body as they in theirs, a stranger to You.

Echoing voices. The sound of silverware, china. A half-familiar voice that was — whose? — commenting upon the strong, warm, exhilarating atmosphere of the college. (For it seemed that earlier that day, a thousand years ago, Nathan Vickery had

held a prayer meeting in a gymnasium, and hundreds of young
people had crowded in, curious about him, some of them skeptical, some of them eager. So long ago! He had braved their bold,
frank, inquisitive eyes, he had spoken slowly and quietly of the
Lord Jesus Christ, and of their own apartness, and gradually his
voice had risen to passion, and gradually, very gradually, the
atmosphere in the overheated room had quickened: and he knew
he had them: not all of them, but the great majority. He knew;
and so it came to pass. He led them in a prayer that was childlike
in its simplicity, and he told them that this prayer, and this prayer
alone, was suitable to people like themselves, who lived at the
very tops of their heads, overly conscious, overly wakeful, in utter
isolation from one another and from the Holy Spirit. And so they
must make themselves as little children again, they must break
and humble themselves, saying again and again *Jesus loves me,
Jesus loves me, Jesus loves me, Jesus loves me.* . . . Their voices
rose, the gymnasium vibrated and echoed with the prayer *Jesus
loves me*, half mournful, half hopeful, a droning chant that
forced a considerable number out of the building — and these
Nathan followed with his stern, knowing gaze, and he sensed
their dislike of him, their outraged contempt, that he should have
hypnotized so many young people with *Jesus loves me*, reducing
them to piteous infants in the name of the Lord. He knew, he
sensed his enemies' accusations; and yet he forgave them, even
as they made their way noisily out of the gymnasium. *You are
beyond my reach now*, he called to them, *but there will come a
time when you will grovel at my feet.* . . .)

The root of all life, the stem, the tree, the tower: the magnificent tower reaching from earth to heaven, from heaven to earth.
He felt its power throbbing in his veins, beating in his head so
emphatically that his right eye began to ache. . . . What was Japheth Sproul talking of, punctuating his remarks with nervous
bursts of laughter? He was seated beside a diminutive, soft-spoken
gentleman in his sixties, a professor of philosophy whose name
Nathan could not recall, for it seemed he had been introduced to
these people, these warm generous kindly inquisitive people,

many years ago. The university chaplain was trying to make conversation with him, with Nathan, and a thin, intense young
woman with fashionably angular glasses was turned to him as
companionably as if they were old friends, smiling at him, addressing questions to him, while about the table others chatted in
the rhythms and nuances of human speech — quite as if the
human world were not nearing its completion, its final disaster.
The university chaplain's first name was Rick; he had been a
professional football player for a brief while; though he was about
Nathan's age — thirty-two — he looked considerably younger,
with his thick red-blond beard and his engaging smile. Nathan
returned that smile as he returned all human smiles, out of cour-
tesy, for the Lord God Himself would not be discourteous, not
even to self-deceived fools. Rick was saying that the afternoon
session had been a wonderful, wonderful experience, that a
dozen or more young people had crowded into his office afterward, talking excitedly of Nathan, and of the decisions they had
made for Christ, and of how they firmly believed their lives would
be transformed. "One of them is a boy I've been very worried
about," he said, shaking his head in simple awe. "Brilliant kid, a
physics major in his senior year with a Woodrow Wilson fellowship for graduate school, a fellowship he'd been thinking of turning down, actually . . . can you imagine? Wonderful, brilliant
kid! But so troubled. His parents are both Methodists and I gather
fairly old-fashioned and of course he . . . and he's in love with a
girl . . . and. . . . Well, this afternoon has turned his life around,
he says. His face was glowing, it was an astonishing sight, I almost
wish we'd had room to invite him to dinner tonight so that he
could talk with you a little further, but my wife drew the line at
. . . and you might want to relax a little, Mr. Vickery . . . Nathan. . . . Isn't that so? You must be exhausted after meeting
with that group this morning, and then the afternoon session
lasted almost three hours. . . ."

The vision had lasted a day and a night, and it was true that he
felt rather drained. Yet no time at all had passed: at the end of
his fork was a morsel of food that had been raised to his mouth

and lowered to his plate and slowly raised again: less than a minute had passed.

"Yes," said Nathan, clearing his throat, "but there's no need to flatter me."

The chaplain and the young woman with the glasses looked surprised.

"Flatter . . . ?" the chaplain said in a hurt voice. "I only meant. . . ."

"The Lord God acts in our hearts, we don't act of our own volition," Nathan said. His throat ached; his voice sounded raw, a little too loud for this intimate setting. He made a conscious effort to speak more softly, as people speak to one another in such circumstances. (What was this place? Why was he here? A college in eastern Pennsylvania, a liberal arts college, and there was some connection between Japheth and one of the professors, or perhaps the chaplain. . . . Nathan looked down to the far end of the table where his friend was deep in conversation with the professor of philosophy and a rotund, merry person of indeterminate sex, and he perceived that Japheth was behaving out of vanity, that beneath his artless boyish talk of the renewal of faith and the "warm, generous, exhilarating" atmosphere at the college there was the ugliness of egotism: and an unclean inclination to boast of Nathan's success as if this success were somehow his own. He perceived as well that Japheth, in his awareness of him, of his physical presence, was deluded into imagining that this presence *was* himself; it might even be the case that Japheth was in love with. . . . But of that he did not care to think.)

". . . only meant that you've helped certain of these young people very much . . . you should hear them rave about you! Isn't that true, Sandra?"

"Yes, you should hear them, it would be . . . I think it would be very gratifying. . . . Of course we don't mean to embarrass you, Mr. Vickery."

"But it has nothing to do with me," Nathan said, forcing himself to speak in a normal voice. "The Holy Spirit speaks to them, and wakes them, and they come forward and make their commitment for Jesus, and I have nothing to do with it: I'm transparent as this glass. See? Transparent as this glass."

He raised the water goblet to eye level and rather playfully stared at them through it with his glass eye; he touched the eye to the goblet and there was a tiny clicking sound; but the noise about the table was such that the chaplain and the young woman probably did not hear.

A third party, a smiling middle-aged man in a vested suit, with mutton-chop whiskers, leaned into their conversation by laying a hand on the young woman's arm. "Ah, but you must not undervalue yourself," he said heartily. His accent was guttural; he might have been German. "Modesty is a virtue that is certainly rare these days, but at times it is rather misleading, Mr. Vickery! For if you had not come to Oakville and had not met with so many of our students, if, for instance, the gymnasium had been merely empty today, and no one at all had stood where you stood, there would have been no — no instances of conversion, eh? Or whatever you may wish to call the phenomena some of us observed. Without you, Mr. Vickery, none of it would have come about, and so you must acknowledge your role . . . your responsibility."

"Why *must* I acknowledge anything?" Nathan asked. "Who are you to speak to me like that?" He laid his fork down carefully on his plate. Your wrath flared up in him for an instant, rising from the base of his spine. It was white-hot: he halfway imagined it might be visible. "You look at me and see a certain form, and this form is nothing more than an idea in your head. *I* am not contained in that form, and still less in your idea. And the Holy Spirit who speaks through me is invisible even to me. And is not contained in me. So you have no right, a stranger to the Lord like yourself, and with that little mocking smile of yours that the Lord is well aware of, and perceived early this morning, in fact — you have no right to speak to me about these issues, or about anything at all."

The man stared at him. His smile faded at once, his expression went blank. Nathan looked frankly upon him and perceived, as though he could read the man's thoughts, that never in his life had the creature been so profoundly insulted. His geniality masked a ferocious egotism; like many of the chaplain's guests at this dinner, he was not truly a Christian, he merely played at being condescending and tolerant of Christians. Ah, Nathan knew him, Nathan knew him well! For it was by Your grace that he had the ability, at times, to peer into the souls of others; to swim through the tangled, cloudy thought-clusters that were consciousness and to penetrate the soul that lay hidden far inside.

"I really don't understand," the man said, flushing. He too set down his fork on his plate. "You seem to be saying . . . taking the position. . . . You *seem* to be saying that I can have no true idea of you at all, no idea of your existence at all?"

"No idea at all," Nathan said softly.

"But that's ridiculous!" the man laughed. "It might be that I know you better than you know yourself: know your type, that is, and something of the background of your church. When we were introduced I saw that my name meant nothing to you, and no doubt that's as it should be, for I hardly imagine myself famous! . . . but I am, in fact, the author of a study on the sociology of religion in America, with an emphasis on the fundamentalist and apocalyptic sects . . . the Jehovah's Witnesses, for instance, the Millerites. . . . And someday, perhaps, I will do an assessment of the Seekers for Christ: if the movement lasts beyond a few more years."

"You know your own idea, you write about your own idea," Nathan said calmly. "Your consciousness turns round and round, going nowhere, while your soul stands apart, contemptuous and bitter. Your soul *despises* you, which is why you carry about with you that mocking little smile, the smile of the Devil, that devalues other people without seeking to love them. You look for the living God among the dead, the dead ideas of your own consciousness. And you will suffer for it: you will receive the due reward of your deeds."

The man laughed in amazement, looking around at the other guests. Japheth's expression was one of utter dismay.

"I don't think you ought . . . don't think we ought to be too *hard* on Frank, after all he's . . . he's not really of the Devil's party," the chaplain said in a high, jovial voice. "He may cause us a bit of trouble in the college senate, but. . . ."

"Of the fourteen people at this table," Nathan said, clearing his throat, "surely *one* of you is a devil . . . ?" And he smiled broadly, to show that he was joking.

The young woman stammered a question. She wished to draw the conversation into another area, she wished to have them talk of the history of devil-belief: the worship of devils, and the exorcism of devils. But the man with the mutton-chop whiskers interrupted, saying in a flat, jeering voice, "Mr. Vickery is an expert on devils because he drives them out of the afflicted, don't you? Heals the sick! Cures the incurable! Unfortunately, we hadn't anyone sick for you to work your miracles on this afternoon, wasn't that a pity? The press photographers felt a little cheated."

Nathan gazed upon the man and saw him disintegrate into the elements that composed his heavy body and his flushed, beefy face. Last of all remained the pinpoint of consciousness that was the soul: wild and bitter and terrified; and this soul, Nathan perceived, wished to call out to him. But it was too remote, it was locked too far behind that coarse mocking face.

"Well, Mr. Vickery *has*, you know, he *has* performed certain . . . has had a remarkable effect on certain people," the chaplain said, smiling nervously. "It's incontestable, Frank. I know what your position is on such matters, but . . . but, well . . . there *are* miracles of a sort. . . ."

"Those are ridiculous claims," the man said rudely. He seemed as angry at his host now as he was at Nathan. "Self-diagnosed illnesses that were never illnesses at all, miraculously cured! Cancer, heart trouble, tumors, deafness, blindness — all of them hysterical symptoms, the symptoms of hypochondriasis — nothing but nerves and imagination. And so the tent preacher comes along and gets the "sick" to cough up their demons, and they're well again. Perfectly well again! And willing to go about the countryside raving about the preacher and Christ coming into their hearts, or the Holy Ghost, or whatever gibberish they've been told — and unshakable in their beliefs. Even if the symptoms return, even if they eventually *die* of whatever it was Christ cured, they're unshakable; fixed for life. But I don't think the rest of us have to be impressed on that account."

"Well, we all have different interpretations of such phenomena," the young woman said slowly, "and I think. . . . It's only fair that. . . ."

"Very little is understood, yes," the chaplain said. "After all, it's recorded in the Gospels that Christ *did* work miracles . . . even raised the dead . . . or the comatose, at least. . . . I've personally taken a very, very careful position on these matters, Frank, because after all there's more in heaven and earth than . . ."

"But you do believe in devils, Mr. Vickery? Eh?" Frank asked.

"*Devil* is a word, a human word; a sound merely," Nathan said.

"A what?"

"One of your words. One of your human thought-clusters."

Frank cupped his ear as if he could not hear, though Nathan spoke clearly enough.

"A what? — Thought-cluster? *What?*"

You rose majestically in Nathan, lifting Your strength up his spine. Slowly, slowly, with regard for Nathan's comparative weakness, slowly You rose to the base of his neck, and then into his skull. A warm, powerful, yet somehow *muscular* radiance: which began to show in his face, which had been sallow from exhaustion.

"One of your ridiculous human words," Nathan said, smiling.

For a brief while there was silence around the table. Then Japheth murmured something about the lateness of the hour, and the fact that Nathan and he had to be up quite early; at six o'clock. The professor of philosophy was staring fixedly at Nathan. Small-featured, rather comely, a death's-head of a skull, with stiff white hairs in his ears and his eyebrows; Nathan gazed upon him and saw a sudden manifestation of the man as a form of God, and read in his thoughts a profound, almost frightened sympathy with Nathan that the circumstances of the evening would not allow him to express. *The Lord God blesses you just the same*, Nathan told him in a smile.

But Frank would not allow the subject to die. He shifted his weight violently in his chair and raised a forefinger and said, "But you *do* believe in devils! In demonic possession! And in godly possession! You *are* responsible for what you tell people! — The horror of it today, hearing you tell our students those primitive, barbaric, *sick* things, things they no doubt wish to hear, in their crudest and most infantile souls: *If any man come to me, and hate not his father, and mother, and wife . . . and his own life also, he cannot be my disciple.* A gospel of hate! Of regressive disdain for human relationships! You tell them it's perfectly all right, it's even necessary, for them to kick themselves free of their families, and of the past — you tell them they *must* kill all human, natural feeling in themselves in order to enter the 'kingdom of heaven.' But what *is* the kingdom of heaven? Where *is* it? Surely not the womb, not after twenty centuries of consciousness! — not after our struggle to preserve civilization in our own century! These things cannot be countenanced. They simply cannot be. Many of us on the faculty intended to be sympathetic with you, and even supportive of you, because we wanted to learn — because we are genuinely interested in the new religions and what they have to tell us about contemporary life, and about ourselves as well — our failures, I suppose, as teachers and adults — we were even quite enthusiastic about bringing you here — we were *not* being hypocritical or cynical, as you seem to think. But your attitude is astonishing — to me, at least, it's astonishing! You disclaim all responsibility for what you say, and consequently for the results of your preaching: you sit there quite calmly and tell me I can have no idea of you at all, and that the words you use are without meaning, and —"

Nathan interrupted and said in a serene, measured voice: "*I am come a light into the world, that whosoever believeth on me should not abide in darkness.*"

"Now, what is that supposed to mean!" the man laughed

angrily. "Tell us — what *is* that supposed to mean! Light, darkness — your Biblical intonations — your air of insupportable hauteur — If you would break down and admit to us that the Seekers for Christ is a money-making organization, that you and your associates are in business, and doing very nicely, I understand — investments in real estate and in the stock market — imagine, Christ investing in the market! — if you would share with us your trade secrets, or at least the spirit behind them — why, we might admire you in a way: we would admire your honesty at least. But under the present circumstances what can we do but reject you as —"

"Frank," the chaplain said sharply. "I really don't think —"

"Please don't interrupt me. Please. I know no one intended this dinner to be an occasion for the uttering of truth, of certain truths, but if the time has come — if I am the only person willing to speak —" He looked around the table, his shoulders hunched forward. "If I am the only one among us honest enough, unintimidated by this charlatan and his quackery and —"

Everyone began to speak at once.

The ungainly, solitary birds flew across the polar cap, while Nathan gazed in helpless rapture. To be one of them! Alone, in utter isolation, in a cold so bitter it could not be gauged, where even Christ could not have hoped to follow! Their white feathers were waxen, and icy, their long crooked necks and hooked beaks had the look of sculpture, unliving, perfect in exquisite ugliness. What had love to do with them? The God that was Love had not yet come into existence, and what need was there for Him? Nathan gazed upon the sweep of the ice cap, the lonely dazzling curve of the earth, and saw from the great tower that was himself how all creatures shrank to pinpoints of consciousness, and came close to extinction, yet were not allowed the release of extinction — for it was not Your wish that they escape Your dominion.

"Come," Nathan said, rising, and extending a hand to the man who mocked him, "come, my brother, and let us touch and forgive each other, before we both regret what has come to pass."

Something had fallen to the floor — a white napkin. Nathan

stepped away from the table and stood with both hands extended, and as the others stared, as even Japheth stared, he smiled a broad, uncanny smile.

"I don't — I don't think I want — I — What is there to forgive!" the man shouted. "You are outrageous, really! A clown, a fool! And like all clowns, cruel and antagonistic and inhuman! You won't respond to my charges against you — you won't behave as we must, in civilization — You skip away from the most serious of charges as if they meant nothing at all, as if we were only passing the time with one another here tonight! And now you expect —"

"Come, are we not brothers in Christ?" Nathan said, lightly mocking.

"I am not a brother to you in any sense of the word!"

"But we share the same anatomy. The same language. If we are deluded, we share some of the same delusions. We've broken bread together tonight, haven't we! We've shared a certain space of time that will never come again. Come now," Nathan said cajolingly, as one might speak to a child, "come before it's too late and you regret bitterly how you kept yourself apart from the Holy Spirit. Devils are mere words, and yet it's a devil that has hold of you! Yes, at this very moment! A devil that keeps you away from me, holding you paralyzed in his grip! Break the hold of your devil, my brother, and come and receive my blessing, and allow the Holy Spirit to touch you, and to flow into you, before it's too late."

The man remained seated, staring at Nathan. His forehead was damp; his eyes bulged slightly. "You are outrageous," he whispered.

"*You* are not outrageous," Nathan said, "but merely pitiful. Locked in the grip of a cloudy, waspish, sluggish devil — not even a very attractive devil — certainly not a very formidable devil, compared to those I have driven out of others. Believe me, my friend, your soul stands apart from you and despises you, and works against you, seeking your own destruction. I hardly know you and yet it's perfectly clear to me, as it must be clear to everyone close to you, that you care very little for life: imagining your-self a failure as a scholar and as a man, imagining your life is bound up in the accomplishments of the ego, and of the body, and so condemning yourself to death! Your health is poor: your heart is pounding at this very moment. How red your face is, beet-red! It looks as if the skin is about to burst! Your blood is pressing against it, and against your organs, a terrible pressure, a merciless pressure, for it's life itself you despise, having turned aside from the Lord God many years ago. How can you keep yourself from me? — from the power of the living God?"

"He's mad," the man said.

In Nathan alone was the link between earth and heaven, and in Nathan alone the power of life and death, but he held himself apart from the brandishing of this power; he felt a sudden pity for the very person who mocked him, and did not wish him harm.

"The Holy Spirit has the power to heal as well as to destroy," he said softly. "Won't you come to me and allow the Spirit to pass into you? Don't be afraid. Don't hold back. If you feel a terrific pressure, if you feel you're about to faint, it may simply be the passage of the devil out of you — rushing out of you and leaving you exhausted — but it will be only temporary, and when you recover you'll give praise to the Lord —"

"Make him stop," the man begged. He did get to his feet; his chair nearly fell over. "Rick — make him stop. Otherwise I — I must leave — This is hideous," he said, swallowing so that his words were nearly inaudible. "I'm leaving."

"But without shaking hands?" Nathan said.

Japheth rose and hurried to Nathan's side. He was very excited; he grinned broadly. "We should leave," he said. "It's late and we should leave. The day has been exhausting, everything has been exhausting, I think it would be better if —"

Nathan approached the man, his hands held out to him. He was smiling his wide radiant smile. The streaks of silvery-gray in his hair were picked up by the candlelight and gave to his appear-ance a ghostly, altogether bizarre air. It could not have been determined which of his eyes was his own, and which a hard nugget of glass, so frostily did both gleam. "Come, my brother, let me touch you in love —"

The man backed away, as if frightened. He stumbled against someone who had arisen at his side — one of the wives, in a long flowered dress — his own wife perhaps? — but seemed unaware of her. "*Don't* come near me," he whispered. "You're insane."

"Insane just to want to shake hands?" Nathan laughed. "Ah, my friend, it's the devil that keeps you from me, it's nothing but the devil who wishes to keep you in *his* grip! He wants you to remain a self-despising failure, a hollow rotting husk of a man, he wants you to worry yourself into a premature death — a heart attack in a year or two, and possibly sooner! He *wants* your destruction; but I am here to thwart him and to bring to you the power of the Holy Spirit. Why else was I brought here tonight? Money, do you think? Money, did you say? But I have no money! I know nothing of money! The Holy Spirit neither knows nor cares about worldly things, nor do I know or care about worldly things, except insofar as the husks of men walk about on the earth, in their pitiful physical forms, and cry out to me for salvation. What does it matter if my touch will burn, if your heart will beat so rapidly you'll fall into a faint? — it will only last a few minutes, no more than an hour! A slight convulsion as the devil rushes out of you and releases his stranglehold on you, and you'll black out, and in a short while you'll rise again giving thanks to the Lord — surely you aren't afraid of that? Of *that*, when your very life is in danger if you resist? My friend —"

"Keep him from me, he's insane," the man whimpered, still backing away.

The others watched in amazement, and Nathan could not help but smile upon them. How serious they were, how alarmed, as if a solemn rite were being performed — when in fact it was nothing more than Your playful expression of Yourself, like a colt galloping in a puddle-rich pasture in spring; like a bird soaring and dipping in graceful abandon in the sky.

Japheth tried to step between Nathan and the man, saying in a high, cheerful voice that Nathan was only joking; it was all a joke. But because of the late hour perhaps they should —

"No? No handshake? No banishing of the devil? Nothing? You'll walk away and leave this opportunity, turn your back on the living God Himself?" Nathan said.

Flushing, deeply embarrassed, the man muttered something to the others, made a gesture of farewell in the chaplain's direction, and turned to leave.

"But where are you going?" Nathan called after him. He would have followed, but Japheth blocked his way. "My friend, my brother, where are you going? Do you think you can escape the living God? Do you think your devil can carry you away from the living God? Why, you may fall down dead on the sidewalk in front of this house — your poor overtaxed heart might suddenly burst — and should you like me to raise you from that state, perhaps the Holy Spirit won't accommodate me, and then what? Then what? The Holy Spirit chooses the time and place of my power to heal, and not I," he shouted after the man, "for it's exactly as Scripture tells us: *The wind bloweth where it listeth, and thou hearest the sound thereof, but canst not tell whence it cometh, and whither it goeth. . . .*"

"Nathan," Japheth said, trembling, "please don't. Please. It's late and we should leave. They don't understand you," he said in a low voice. "You've frightened them, Nathan. Please."

"I've frightened them but not you, eh?" Nathan laughed. He passed a hand over his face, which felt surprisingly warm, almost feverish. When he drew it away time seemed to have passed, and it was much later, and yet his host and the others were staring at him as before. He felt Your strength begin to ebb in him, dropping slowly from the base of his skull and into his spine, and down his spine by inches . . . and it was with an effort that he resisted a sudden convulsive shivering that would have shaken his entire frame.

"Yes," he murmured carelessly, "it's playfulness . . . it's fool-

ishness, as he so shrewdly noted. . . . Like Paul, I am a fool for
the Lord and can't help myself. So I hope you will forgive me."

The chaplain hurried to him and offered to shake hands, smiling in his exuberant red-blond beard, his eyes creased and wary.
And Nathan did shake hands with him, and apologized again, in
a slurred, careless manner, as if he were suddenly very tired. The
others rose and milled about, eager to show that nothing was
amiss, that they were *not* frightened, not at all. (Yet Nathan
noted to his amusement that they obviously wanted to run after
Frank, or at least to check the sidewalk in front of the house, to
see if perhaps he had collapsed — when there was no likelihood
of it at all, since Nathan had been merely joking, and the Lord
God merely joking.)

"There's nothing to forgive! Nothing to forgive!" the chaplain
said with slightly hysterical laughter. He stared at Nathan with
teary, doglike eyes. "It's been our honor to have you here tonight,
and we hope you'll come back soon, and —"

"*That* I can't promise," Nathan said rather sharply.

And so the evening ended, and Japheth led him away, and he
felt an extraordinary lassitude drawing him down, as if his feet
were lost in shadow and the candlelit room and the faces of the
others had never existed, had never come into being, except as
Your phantasmal dream.

xi

Where You have once been, and have departed, there is mere
devastation: the tangle of uprooted things after a violent storm,
the brute shapes of things once living.

Muddy abysses no more than a few inches deep into which one
may sink, nevertheless, forever!

I wake before morning, before dawn, when there is neither sun nor moon to guide me. My mouth is bitter and toad-spiteful. Should I dare touch my face, I would be alarmed indeed, for a gargoyle crouches atop my shoulders and twists my soul out of shape. *God of radiance, God of dark*, I pray, but my mouth twists in mid-prayer, and surely You will never hear me.

When the floodwaters recede there is a jumble of things: broken parts, fragments, coils and loops and shreds. Shall I seek myself among them? Shall I seek You among them? God-intoxicated am I, or only stubborn? Or defiant? Calling to the one least like me, to the One Who has swallowed me up and forgotten me. Who gave birth to me, and devoured me, and excreted me into the drifting, clamoring world. God-mad, God-infatuated am I, calling to the one least like me, to the One who will never reply, who has turned away from me forever. . . .

Nathan atop his tower, which was himself, yet more than himself: Nathan in his God-trance: spying upon the world, which did not very much interest him. Nathan ascendant, and I prostrate on the ground. Nathan who was nourished by Your grace those many years; and I who languish for love of You. You coursed along his veins and arteries, it was Your voice that throbbed so passionately in his own, Your spirit that fed his spirit constantly. (So that he easily comprehended the nature of addiction, and was warmly and in a sense *insatiably* sympathetic with those followers of his, young men and women, occasionally no more than teen-aged boys and girls, who were addicted to drugs, and who credited Jesus Christ and Nathan Vickery and the grace of the Holy Spirit with their ability to free themselves of their habits: all of which brought highly favorable publicity to Nathan's church in the early seventies.) Nathan richly and ceaselessly nourished by Your presence; and I skeletal with hunger. Nathan moving through a universe that was melodic, beating with a blood-heavy rhythm, opaque and yet transparent, its outlines lovingly blurred, softened, Nathan in love, Nathan the living vein that linked earth and heaven; and I alone in my rented room in a city whose name I have forgotten, if I ever knew. Nathan in constant communication with You (and shifting reluctantly to the other, drably real world: where he might find himself sitting at a gleaming conference table with people said to be vitally linked with him and his church, his closest associates among the Seekers, and certain outsiders who were attorneys, tax specialists, accountants, bookkeepers, and stenographers: wanting from him responses he could not proffer, though he gave every appearance of listening, of listening critically and even suspiciously, and when he signed his name to the documents they presented him it was always with a gesture of reluctant finality, as if he knew very well that these terms could be better, but — ! He would accommodate himself to the world to please the world, and not himself.) And I in communication with no one.

A quarrel in another flat, downstairs; in the basement; a man's voice raised, a woman's shriek; the shock of utter silence. I stand barefooted by my door, whimpering with the cold (it is January, an infinite merciless seamless January) or with apprehension, or with shame at my own cowardice. (For I have heard these people quarreling in the past, usually late on Friday evenings, and I have done nothing to interfere, not a thing; not even shout down at them as certain of the other tenants do. The police arrived one night and so someone must have telephoned them but it was not I, I have no telephone, and anyway no courage, no wish to inter-fere.) Where Nathan Vickery was so courageous as to alarm his disciples, I know myself a coward, and take no pleasure in the knowledge; where Nathan Vickery possessed — somehow, no one knows how — a remarkable physical strength, I know myself a feeble, diminished, broken creature, prone to headaches and humiliating bouts of the flu, one of my molars decaying, my left leg stiff in damp weather (which is near-constant in this climate). Where Nathan Vickery was, in his prime, strikingly attractive — not handsome, perhaps, but striking indeed, with his bony, hawk-ish profile and his intent stare and his dark hair, shot weirdly with gray, silver, and bone-white, falling to his slender shoulders; his movements that were, without logical transition, graceful and jumpy and somnambulistic and threatening, like those of a giant cat; his musical, raw, whining, cajoling, lulling voice (or voices) — where he was a remarkable creature to gaze upon, I know myself utterly ordinary, even ugly, and if it happens that people do glance at me when I venture out, to buy a few groceries, or to wander listlessly about the streets with the aim of exercising my aging muscles and perhaps overhearing conversations (for I forget, if I keep to myself, how people in the world *do* talk to one another; it's substantially different from the conversations one hears on the radio), then they glance at me merely with curiosity, or pity; it cannot be said that they *gaze* upon me, for certainly I am not that intriguing.

A door is slammed downstairs. Someone runs out noisily. A woman screams after him. She is drunk, she is evidently swearing, but the words are slurred, indistinct. The door is slammed again.

I stand here shivering. Blows and screams like that indicate passion; indicate love. Is it so? Must it be so?

Blows. Screams. Rage. The desire to murder. Then again caresses, love-whispers, love. The desire to complete oneself in the body of the beloved. A riddle: a riddle in which I am drowning.

Nathan too was the object of passion. He felt it keenly, he could not escape it: the realization that another person wished to complete himself in *his* body.

He recoiled in disgust. In disbelief at first, until You allowed him to know that it was indeed true; and that he must purge the world of such uncleanness. It was lust, it was filth, there was nothing sacred about it. *Leave me*, he would say, mouthing the words in private, *leave me and make no attempt to return*. But for a long while he held back, out of disgust. For it was a terrible insult to him, and to Your spirit that dwelt in him, that another person should desire him in the flesh.

You allowed him to comprehend that Jesus of Nazareth was a form of Yourself crucified by the world upon the cross of the world, the fleshly axis of the world. A soul crucified upon its own body. A spirit crucified upon its own animal desires. It was Nathan's belief, and soon became one of his principal teachings, that suffering of all kinds was to be experienced with resignation, even with joy, for it was a means of subduing the flesh, and of testing the soul's strength. (It happened that this aspect of Nathan's teaching was misinterpreted by certain enthusiastic but impetuous disciples, and there were instances of fasting to the point of near death, and self-torture, and even beatings of one church member by others: in Seekers' communities in the Southwest, and in Southern California, and in northern Minnesota, and even close to church headquarters in Windigo Falls, where it might have been thought his teachings were better understood.) The euphoria a Seeker experienced when the Holy Spirit came into his heart was an endless source of strength, and could be drawn upon at any time, even when unexpected blows or pain or grief descended. So Nathan taught, and so he believed.

Be ye in the world and not of it. So the body dwelt in the world, and took its crude nourishment from the world, but the spirit dwelt elsewhere, taking its nourishment from God. So the body's experiences were not truly authentic, not truly *real*. (It happened that one of Nathan's more articulate converts, a researcher in neuropsychiatric studies at one of the California universities, went about giving lectures on this aspect of Seekers' belief — for he was convinced Nathan had an intuitive grasp of a mind-body relationship that eventually would be substantiated by science.) The soul interpreted the body, in a more or less constant, helpless process, but if the soul chose to delimit itself, and to interpret only those aspects of the body it considered significant, then it would triumph over the flesh and its distracting, degrading temptations, and align itself more securely with God. Fasting, celibacy, manual labor in the Seekers' communities, abstinence from nearly all rich foods, and from all alcohol and drugs and stimulants — these were the conscious means by which a believer delimited his body's control over his spirit. It should not have surprised Nathan's observers and critics that young people who had been sexually promiscuous since their early teens, or had been drug addicts, or alcoholics, or had been wandering aimlessly about the country for years were attracted to the Seekers, for it was precisely this disciplining of the flesh and its appetites that such young people craved, though they could not have articulated their craving, and had not sufficient consciousness to understand the gravity of their predicament until Nathan Vickery explained it to them. *Be ye in the world and not of it.*

At the foot of the tower there was suffering, seen dimly. It was experienced merely by the body and by the outermost and least significant part of the soul, and so in a sense it was not quite authentic. The repetition of the sacred words *Jesus loves me* was all one needed to protect oneself against the exterior, ungovernable world: words that might be whispered with every breath, throughout one's life. So Nathan Vickery taught, and so it was.

(Rumors arose that many of the Seekers, adults as well as young people, substituted *Nathan loves me* for the words Nathan himself prescribed. And many of them referred to him as *Master*. And credited him with various miracles — the curing of incurable illness, the raising of the dead, the calling forth of the Holy Spirit. Before as many as six thousand witnesses an unearthly radiance sometimes played about his face and hands, yet left him untouched.)

In a state of euphoria he witnessed his own mock-death. For You allowed him to see, a full twenty-four hours ahead of time, how out of the corner of his eye the Angel of Destruction would dart, shrieking gibberish at him, bringing down something on his head — and while he flinched in his imagination, he was not to flinch when the incident took place.

In July of 1973, visiting a Seekers' community in White Springs, he was shown several acres of cultivated land — tomatoes growing beautifully, lettuce, carrots, corn — and he withdrew himself from his companions to walk in solitude through the rows of corn, which were nearly shoulder height; and by his act he put himself into Your trust altogether. For he knew his doom was upon him, or nearly so. He knew someone wished to kill him.

Why?

He did not ask. He would not question Your wisdom.

The violence that was gathering must be allowed to break free; it must be allowed to express itself. Otherwise it would fester, and grow ever more poisonous. Nathan knew this, You allowed him to know it. He accepted it. He would not rebel. At the very foot of the tower there must be suffering, and this suffering would inevitably turn into hatred and violence. And sorrow. And grief. One act of violence would cause another and still another, and yet it was Your wisdom that Nathan play his role, not rebelling, not running away in terror. (For with one part of his mind he wanted very much to run away. To break into a desperate, shameless dash through the cornfield back to the safety of the house. To cry out for help. To cry, "Save me! Don't let him hurt me! Save me! I don't want to die!")

But what was sorrow, what was fear. . . ? His own emotions were of no more substance than anyone else's and all emotions were wisps, vapors, chimeras. Delusions. No emotion could make itself heard at the top of the tower, which reached unto heaven; it referred only downward, downward, to the doomed land. Your wisdom was imprescriptible and Your faith in Nathan Vickery justified: for he did not run.

Why must he be killed, or nearly killed . . . ? Why must he suffer violence in his own body?

On this warm sunny day, and in this sun-warmed paradise!

He did not ask because, in a way, he already knew. And knew he would not lift a finger to defend himself.

Some months before, he had had to banish one of his disciples.

"You must leave the Seekers. You must leave me. And make no attempt to contact any of us again," he had said.

But why, why?

The man had pleaded with him to explain.

Why?

The man had fallen to his knees before Nathan and begged him to explain. Sobbing, his hands clasped together, his soul writhing in distress and incredulity. *Why?*

Nathan had not replied.

He had been forced to banish the man because You had allowed him to learn, in a dream, that the man harbored a certain
lustful secret perhaps not adequately known by the man himself.
To utter it would be to defile him, to destroy him. And so it was
best for him simply to be banished from the Seekers in order that
his craving — his sickly, frenzied lust — might be thwarted and,
in time, overcome.

Love? Desire? Physical love and physical desire?

Homosexual desire?

Nathan contemplated the phenomenon as one might contemplate an insect of hideous and yet exotic markings. He held it at
arm's length, unmoved by pity or even disgust; for what *was* one
to make of such a thing? To Nathan, homosexual desire was as
pointless and futile as heterosexual desire, and less plausible.

The thing to do with the insect was to flick it away — to see
that it landed somewhere in safety — to get rid of it as quickly
and as chastely as possible.

All this You allowed Nathan to know, and guided his every
word. And everything came to pass as it was ordained. Nathan's
peremptory words *You must leave the Seekers, you must leave me*
— the young man's stunned but guilty expression — the way he
fell to his knees, weeping and begging for an explanation — begging to be allowed to remain in the church, at least — clutching
at Nathan's hands, which Nathan suffered him to grasp though
the very touch of him was repulsive. Such scenes, such emotions,
were of no consequence whatsoever; they were of no more meaning to You and Your design than a fly's buzzing in an empty
room.

But I don't believe it, Japheth whispered. I don't believe you
can mean what you're saying . . . .

On his knees he grasped Nathan's cold, unresisting hands. And
his eyes swam with tears of terror, of reproach, but also (so Nathan saw, to his disgust) of love. For it was so, it was obviously
so, that the dream You sent to Nathan of Japheth in the flesh
embracing Nathan in the flesh, with no shadow of Your presence

between them, was Japheth's own dream, which perhaps he had
never experienced, and would never acknowledge.

Love. Desire. Physical love and. . . .

Leonie had knelt before him too. Pleading with him, grasping
at him. But you love me! You once loved me! And I loved you:
you know I loved you! Oh Nathan will you forgive me — She
had knelt before him, and he had banished her. *Christ* he
would honor in her, of course, but *Leonie* he would not recognize, he felt only contempt for her and the weakness she em-
bodied; he had plucked her from out of his heart long ago, in
another lifetime.

And now Japheth. Pleading for a forgiveness it was not Nathan's to allow him, since only Your will exists. Pleading and
begging and weeping like a child, utterly broken, without pride.
Without shame. *Nathan, you can't send me away, I have no life
apart from you.* . . .

But it did not matter. Such emotion did not matter. It does not
reach to the top of the tower and so it is of no consequence.
Even Nathan's trembling on that terrible morning was of no
consequence, forgotten in a moment. You flowed into Nathan
and in a brief while all was calm and serene and rippleless, and
You told him once again that he was sanctified here on earth,
that he might do or say anything and it was blessed from all time;
for such was Your plan. Was he capable of committing a sin? Not
really. No longer. For as You dwelt in every pore of his flesh, in
every atom of his being, it was not possible for him to sin. What
might be sinful in others was sanctified in him, for he did nothing
that was not ordained by You. Like Abraham, he might sacrifice
his son or he might *not* sacrifice his son and neither action was
sinful: the only sin for him, as for Abraham, would have been
refusing to play his role.

And so it came to pass that on that morning in July Nathan
chose to walk apart from his disciples, brooding over Your design
and waiting for it to unfold. Alone in the cornfield he saw a door
open at the rear of his mind, and saw a figure suddenly appear,
and knew that the figure was that of his murderer — his banished

disciple Japheth Sproul: and knew, even as the distraught man appeared beside him, stepping into view, that You would protect him against all harm.

Nathan! There you are! Japheth cried.

His heart had begun to beat quickly. He would have been afraid, but at once his own teaching calmed him: *Be ye in the world and not of it.* The body dwelt in the world, the soul dwelt elsewhere. Had You not instructed him in this simple wisdom many years ago, and were You not close by him now, protecting him against Japheth's murderous rage. . . ?

It was as the dream had warned him. The Angel of Destruction crept up softly behind him and then began to scream at him. *Nathan! Nathan!* Something was raised high into the air — a hoe, Nathan thought at first, though in fact it was a crowbar Japheth had taken from one of the barns — and brought down on his shoulder. He staggered but did not fall. He maintained his distance from his attacker, his gaze turned away as if out of shame for what was being done to him. While Japheth screamed incoherently — accusing him of beastly, abominable things — he stood with his feet apart, swaying, waiting for the next blow, for it was ordained that You would protect him, and that this violence must be allowed to run its course.

Panting, Japheth came up close behind him and struck him this time on the back of the neck — and You consoled him yet again with Your ageless wisdom, *Be not afraid of them that kill the body, and after that have no more that they can do. . . .* By this time Nathan's companions were running to him, shouting. Japheth grunted and reared back to swing the crowbar a third time, and still Nathan did not look at him, and still he waited, half stooping, his heart now pounding in his chest as if it were a wild thing desperate to escape. *Nathan,* Japheth cried, *Nathan, why did you — Why are you —* Before the blow fell, Nathan extended his hand toward Japheth without turning, and it was a gesture acknowledging guilt and forgiveness — a benediction: yet the gesture did not appease Japheth but seemed to madden him all the more. For the third and final blow was the most brutal of all, striking Nathan on the forehead, just above his good eye. The violence of the blow was such that the skull was crushed, and blood exploded outward, and Nathan's spirit fled from his body, and time came to a stop.

xii

And began again, of course.
  And again, again.
  And again.

For Nathan Vickery, the Chosen One, was immortal: unkill-able.

For it came about as it was ordained, that the three savage blows should fall, and that Nathan should resist none of them, and that his life would be protected by Your love.

  And indeed it was a miracle. A miracle before witnesses, and before the murderous disciple himself, who later testified to police that he had struck a killing blow to Nathan Vickery and had indeed *killed* him but in the next half-minute life had been restored, and he knew it was hopeless, and had thrown the bloody crowbar away before he was seized.

"I am guilty of murder," Japheth Sproul insisted, laughing and pushing his glasses up his nose. "I did what I set out to do. I killed him. Ask him — he knows! His skull crumpled, the brain was pierced, he died; just ask him and he'll admit it, he won't dare deny it, he can't tell a falsehood because he's the Son of God! He's God Himself! He is, that's why I tried to kill him — tried to rid us of him. And I did kill him. But he came back. But I *am* guilty. . . . You know, he *is* the Son of God. He has replaced

Christ. It's true, ask him, he'll admit it! He admitted it to me once or twice. It was I, Japheth Sproul, who cautioned him against releasing such news to the world, for fear he would be misunderstood. But it's true, it's true! Ask him! Go ahead and ask him — he can't lie! He is God Himself come to us because the time of wrath is near. Everyone knows this but won't acknowledge it! Everyone knows! The end is come upon the four corners of the earth and no one will be spared except those Nathan has lifted up — ask him, he'll tell you! Ask him! The rod has blossomed, violence is risen up, you will seek peace and there will be none. *There will be none.* I tried to avert all this. I tried to stop him. I did it alone, without any help, all alone I tried to save the human world from him, and he halfway wanted me to succeed, I *know*, I know him so well; and though I failed in the end I *did* kill him, I did accomplish what I set out to do, for at least a minute! — I, Japheth Sproul, *did* kill Nathan Vickery. But he came back to life again because he isn't a human being, the Spirit of the Lord is in him, protecting him, lifting him up. He isn't human, he can't be killed, not really killed. Just ask him, go and ask him, he'll tell you himself, he'll admit it, he can't lie!"

And they went to Nathan Vickery and did ask if he was the Son of God, or God Himself: but Nathan withdrew and would not reply. He had stopped speaking directly to "outsiders" some time ago. He answered certain summonses because it was ordained that he obey the law of the land until such time as the law was overthrown or annihilated, but he would not reply to such questions and to a number of others. Why did his former friend and disciple want to kill him? Why had he not protected himself? Why had he not pressed charges, why had he not even wanted medical attention? And how was it possible that the attack had injured him so slightly? (He had only a few bruises and scratches, and a swelling the size of a robin's egg on his forehead.)

Lawrence R. Pearce, of New York City, the Seekers' new chief counsel, instructed Nathan in what he might say and what he need not; and Nathan in his wisdom prudently obeyed.

xiii

Late February.

A universe of snow.

As for Nathan Vickery time stopped and then began again, so for me also it has stopped. Some weeks ago it stopped when I found that I could not continue. But now, today, time begins again as it must. For despite my inertia it is still day and I must work, for the night will come when no man can work.

You who read this — you cannot guess at my dread, or my self-contempt because of that dread. I am sick with apprehension, I am a gargoyle crouched atop human shoulders, boar's head, dog's head, swollen beastly lips wet with saliva. The phenomenon of language draws us together as sisters and brothers, sisters and brothers not in Christ but in the Word; yet the phenomenon of language falsifies my experience as it is transmitted to you, for you cannot know, you cannot guess, at the meaning of the spaces between words, the blank white emptiness of silence. . . . Into which I might plunge myself yet, for perhaps only so desperate an act would return the Lord to me.

The skull was crushed, the spirit fled from the body, time came to a stop. With the ease of a sail suddenly filled by the wind and borne away by the wind did Nathan's soul detach itself from his body and fly some distance away, weightless, invisible, quick as a spark of electricity, unharmed. From a great height Nathan's soul appeared to watch the clumsy activity surrounding Nathan's fallen body. It observed with a curious detachment, and yet with absolute clarity, Nathan's ashen face his partly closed eyes, the blood that ran so freely and horribly from his wounded forehead. . . .

Not for the first time did Nathan shake himself free from his flesh. Not for the first time did he squirm out of the compact, rather wonderful prison of his skeleton. But it was the first time he dissolved the union of his own accord, as an act of his own will: in the past You had snatched him away, bidding him fly to You. Perhaps for that reason he felt nothing more than a queer clinical dissociation. He watched the men grappling with Japheth Sproul, he watched Japheth Sproul struggling hopelessly and stupidly, he watched even his own life's-blood draining away. A spark of light, a scrap of dandelion fluff, a mere pinpoint of consciousness: so his soul vibrated above the human spectacle, untouched, unmoved. You drew near, the radiance of old, yet invisible. *Is it time to die*, Nathan asked without hope. *Is it time for me to come to You* . . .

There was no need for You to reply. For You and Nathan were always one, and he understood Your wishes as if they were his own.

The spirit fled from the body, darting clear of its distress. Time came to a stop. And then — suddenly — suddenly the spirit woke again in the body: and all began again.

One moment he had been a great distance away, contemplating without emotion his own dying self, putting his question to You. *Is it time . . . ? Is it time for me to come to You . . . ?* One moment he had been free; the next he was back in his body again, trapped in the skull of a stranger said to be himself: Nathan Vickery.

He had not died. Yet he had not exactly continued to live.

There was a break, a bubble, a missed pulse beat: and suddenly he woke again in his body and all was as it had been. For, as we know, there is no death without Your blessing, there is no peace without Your will.

Nathan stirred and came into consciousness, amazing all who were witnesses. Only his murderer Japheth was not surprised — not really surprised. "He can't be killed," Japheth said wildly, grinning. "Some of you try it! Go on and try it! There he is, now's your opportunity, save us from him, just *try!* It can't be done."

Time began again and continues still.

Yet Nathan's doom was upon him, as Japheth understood.

Still, he continued to bring many more thousands of souls into his church. With a strange, renewed, feverish vigor he traveled across the North American continent and met with unparalleled success in every church and arena and auditorium and hall and stadium the Seekers for Christ procured for him. By September of 1973 he was sufficiently recovered from the attempt on his life to begin a massive crusade that kept him and his staff on the road for nearly twelve months, covering some twenty-five thousand miles and eighty cities, and bringing him into contact with several million people. In all that he did and said he was carried out of himself, a vessel for Your wisdom, and many were the miracles performed in Your name, and in the hundreds of thousands were the joyous converts to Your church on earth. Cleveland, Cincinnati, Nashville, Chattanooga, Tampa, Miami, New Orleans, Houston. . . . And on and on, across the continent, north and south across the nation, and into Mexico and Canada, a tireless crusade-for-souls that wore out all but one or two members of Nathan's staff, so that they had to be replaced by others whom he knew less well but whom he trusted implicitly, for You guided him in all things. September, October, November, December . . . and the new year, the ceaseless progression of months, weeks, days, nights, hours . . . Nathan in a state of euphoria before thousands of believers crammed into a baseball stadium, Nathan crying out to the multitudes that the Holy Spirit had guided them to him, and him to them, and would very shortly make itself known in their hearts. Because of the power and the possible danger when the Spirit flowed into Nathan Vickery, it was the case that no one should share a platform with him: services began with an introduction by a local minister, or a fellow Seeker, and involved the testimonials of five or six or more people, some of them fairly well-known in their part of the world, and then everyone left the platform, and there was a moment's pause and a terrific hush before Nathan himself appeared in his white robe, his arms always held aloft, opened as if in a great embrace. And how the multitudes thrilled, seeing him — knowing they were to share a certain space of time with him, who had been proclaimed as the incarnation of God Himself!

At the state fairgrounds in Patagonia Springs in one of the western states, You sent to Nathan the seventh and most violent of Your visions, and it was here, on the eighth of August, 1974, before an estimated crowd of over a hundred thousand people, that the ministry of Nathan Vickery came to an end.

He had known, and yet he had not known. So rarely was he lowered into his finite self, so vaguely did he attend to the details of his personal life, that perhaps he had not known at all — until the very moment of Your attack. Since he came to life only when completely surrendered to You, and when preaching Your word, the spaces between convocations became increasingly blurred. Eating, drinking, bathing, dressing and undressing, going to bed — these activities were performed for him by the fleshly creature he inhabited, done mechanically, effortlessly, while his spirit brooded over Your design and had only the most slender attachment to the exterior world.

Thus he knew, and did not know. He knew there was dissension among his staff, that certain accusations had been made — either by Reverend Lund, or about Reverend Lund — but he did not know the details, he could not tolerate a knowledge of the details, and so he thrust the matter from him and left it with his attorneys; who (it was revealed afterward) quarreled bitterly among themselves. He knew, and did not know, that he and his church had become famous: that unauthorized articles about him appeared regularly in the public press, that fraudulent confessions by former associates were published and read eagerly by millions of people. There were cover stories about his ministry, there were bizarre photographs showing his radiant, contorted features, his wild, graying hair, his broad entranced smile; pho-

tographs of those he had converted, some of them lying on the
ground senseless, or staring glassily at the camera, their faces wet
with tears. He knew, and did not know, that hundreds of spurious
relatives emerged to make their claim upon him in the public
press, and that his convocations were often picketed, and his life
threatened; and that he was protected at all times by a guard in
plain clothes whose salary was — or so the rumor went — well
above fifty thousand dollars a year.

Still he continued his work on earth, fasting for days, kneeling
for hours in Your presence, rising only when You bade him rise.
It was Your wish that he arrange for more meetings than his staff
had originally planned, for it was a pity that remote corners of
the country might be slighted; and there was great urgency in the
land, which the multitudes felt. It was Your wish that he avoid all
strangers, all outsiders, for fear that his presence might confuse
them, and something pass from him to them that might be harmful. It was Your wish that he make no comment on any of the
worldly problems that arose: the picketing of his San Diego convocation by a disorderly group of young people claiming to be
Maoists, and their subsequent injuries at the hands of the police;
the claim made by an insurance company that one of the Seekers'
houses had been deliberately burned to the ground in Seattle and
that no insurance payment would be made; the ugly news that
surfaced again and again that his former disciple, Japheth Sproul,
had killed himself in a private mental hospital in Massachusetts.
Because he needed all of his energies for the times when he
preached Your word, he could not attend to these matters, and
indeed they seemed insignificant to him, and even ludicrous. For
they belonged to the world and were lodged deep in time, and
both the world and time itself were coming to an end, according
to Your will.

To have assimilated everything completely in himself, to have
obliterated the false barriers between one form and another! —
to have experienced Your grace as the cessation of all duality, all
struggle! — thus he knew himself one with You, thus he gazed
out upon the multitudes and proclaimed Your wisdom, that none

who heard should fall by the wayside and be lost. Around him, about him, beneath his straining triumphant voice, hundreds of believers sang hymns that were like the murmuring of Your own voice, exquisitely beautiful. "The Old Rugged Cross." "Faith of Our Fathers." "Are You Washed in the Blood of the Lamb?" The sun reeled in the sky, Nathan himself set his foot upon it, and was one with it, and shone out upon the thousands upon thousands of adoring faces, that they should never suffer, and should never die, but have life everlasting. In their gratitude they cried out to him: *Nathan! Brother Nathan!* And they cried out to him: *Master!* And knelt before him, in utter submission to him. For days and nights on end they traveled to the great fairgrounds at Patagonia Springs, for many miracles were expected to take place here, in this enchanted land in clear view of the Rocky Mountains, beneath an extraordinarily rich and endlessly blue sky. *Brother Nathan!* went the cry. And *Master! Master!* And he held out his arms to them as if he would embrace them all, and the sound of their gratitude swelled to heaven itself.

And —

And yet he knew, he knew, that his doom was upon him: the time of his ministry was at an end.

It happened that, in Patagonia Springs, crouched before a microphone, gazing out into the vast crowd of expectant, greedy believers, rocked by their thunderous voices, half mesmerized by their ecstatic love for him, Nathan Vickery saw, for the first time, for what he realized was the first time, Your face — he saw You.

He was in the midst of crying out that we are indeed living in the Final Days, that the earth's population is convulsed with sin, that there is corruption and futility and death — and even death by suicide — ah, how many deaths by suicide in the United States alone, committed by young people, by children, at younger and younger ages — we are in the midst of the Devil's Kingdom, and only Christ's Kingdom could do battle with it! — he was in the midst of an impassioned plea, as raw and direct as any he had ever given, when You allowed him to know that Your love for him was at an end. Quite suddenly, after so many years — it was over.

He knew. In the space of a pulsebeat he knew. Yet, though his voice faltered, he tried to continue: he skipped to the final part of the sermon and spoke of the need for sin to be expelled, the need for sinners to come forward, to come forward immediately —

Yet You had retreated from him, and it was over. His ministry and his life were over.

How suddenly, how vividly the world declared itself! Even as he was faltering through the end of his speech he became aware of the odd ineffable *reality* of what was outside him. The choir, in handsome velvet robes, was singing "Are You Washed in the Blood of the Lamb," the sky was hard and blue and depthless, he was standing, alone, perspiring, in some sort of robe himself, before a microphone, before thousands upon thousands.

He saw. He lost the pattern of his own words. He stood there, bent, swaying, staring out into the seething mass of life before him, life that knew him not, even as he knew it not, the life that is You, a chaos of molecules dancing wildly and drunkenly in the sun.

The sermon had ended abruptly. Individuals were standing in the aisles, blocking the aisles, halfway to him, their faces streaming with tears. But suddenly his words stopped. His voice died. The mass of quivering life stared at him, there was a sudden silence as the choir came to the end of its song, a greater silence as You dropped away from Nathan and declared Yourself in Your primary form, mocking him, a stranger to him. From the raised platform Nathan Vickery stared, his parched lips trembling, his hands, suddenly useless, ungainly, raised before his stricken face as if to ward off a blow.

"My Lord and my God," he tried to say, "please save me from — Don't let —"

But he saw only You: shapeless, twisting and undulating and coiling and writhing and leaping.

A great hole. A great mouth.

Ah, he stood at the very brink, at the very edge! — in his frail, rather foolish being, in his utterly insubstantial *human* form. In that instant, as Nathan gazed into God, he knew that this was the vision Christ had seen: certainly He too had seen it: they were not rival sons but brothers, as all men are brothers. Standing on the edge of You. On the edge of Your ravenous being. . . . He knew, and yet the logic of his wisdom, the very words themselves, were snatched from him, blown away; and now he went completely speechless.

"I — I —"

But no sound came. He stood there, crouched, cringing, his skin dead white, and he saw that the hole before him *was* a mouth, and that the writhing dancing molecules of flesh were being sucked into it, and ground to nothing, and at the same time retained their illusory being. What he knew to be You before him imagined itself quite otherwise — imagined itself broken and separated into parts, into individuals, into people, "men" and "women" and "children." It was madness, their madness, Your madness, and he was paralyzed before it.

"My Lord and my —"

But he could not speak.

The mouth remained, the molecules remained, in their ceaseless dance, even while the outlines of certain people returned, and their small frantic gleaming faces became clear again. And then in an instant they faded, dissolved into You. And *then* in another instant they appeared again as You allowed them their delusion. . . . Nathan stared in horror. For it was evidently the case that these creatures, mere bubbles in Your mind, were staring at *him* as if they expected something from him. They were hungry for something, ravenous, worried, intense, pleading with outstretched arms.

"What do you want — Who are You — What do you want from me —"

He was about to collapse. The terrible danger was that he would topple forward from the platform, he would fall and sink and be swallowed in You. But instead he sank to one knee. Grabbing at the microphone, his entire body shivering. His good eye went clear for an instant and then darkened.

On his hands and knees he tried to crawl away. His head swung from side to side, his long coarse hair swung, the nugget of flesh that was his eye throbbed with pain. For some minutes now the singing had stopped. Everything had stopped. There were isolated cries, even screams, and someone was bending over him, he half-saw legs, feet, incongruously shiny shoes, but really he heard nothing and saw nothing, for You had swallowed the entire world. He knew his ministry was over, his life was over, that everything had come to pass as it was ordained, but he knew also — for even then You allowed him the realization of certain truths — that his terror had just begun.

EPILOGUE

the sepulcher

i

Thus Nathan Vickery was extinguished, and sank into oblivion. And lies there still in his death-trance. And passes from my consideration, belonging to You and not to me, who despaired of him from the first and wished with all my heart that Japheth Sproul had indeed killed him. So it was, and ever shall be.

So it was: I am capable of no more pity than You are.

∎ ∎ ∎

Now it is late winter; by the calendar, early spring.

My downstairs neighbors have moved away. I helped them move: loaded cardboard boxes and pieces of battered furniture into the back of a pickup truck, astonished that the husband and wife should turn out to be, close up, so very *ordinary*; not violent at all; rather subdued, abashed. (After the police came for the second or third time, our landlord asked them to leave.) The woman flame-haired, with a white, unhealthy complexion and a small plump body; the man surprisingly slight, half a head shorter than I, with a small dark mustache and a furtive, shy manner.

In the kitchen of their vacated apartment they offered me a drink. The three of us finished a bottle of red wine, drinking it down ceremoniously. They did not know me, yet did not wonder why I had come downstairs to give them a hand. Neither asked my name. When I asked where they were going, they looked sullen and vague. "That depends on somebody's brother — is he going to take us in or not," the man said, laughing. The woman grinned but did not laugh. She poured the last of the wine into my glass, shaking the drops out.

In this cold reluctant spring everything is scaled down and precise. I count the bills in my wallet, I count change, pushing quarters and dimes and nickels and pennies into little piles.

I listen to the radio, my head inclined toward it, bowed in expectation.

Since You have not come to me, what choice have I, my Lord, but to seek You in the world, limping from one consecrated building to another. The Gethsemane Lutheran Church. St. Barnabas' Anglican Church. Church of the Nazarene. St. Andrew's Presbyterian Church. St. Vincent De Paul Church. Church of Jesus Christ of the Latter-Day Saints. First Church of God. Christian Reformed Evangelical Church. Emmanuel Baptist Church. Our Lady of Perpetual Help Church. Church of the Resurrection With Signs Following. St. Michael and All Angels Anglican Church.

(What is a *church*: God's dwelling place, four walls meant to contain the invisible; ceiling above and floor below and pews set neatly in place, the infinite scaled down by stone and glass and wood. And human flesh: for in all churches abides a person set apart as Your spokesman, and in his face there is the old uneasy claim of proprietorship, and the dread that You will someday expel him.)

In St. Vincent De Paul's I sat for hours staring at a stained-glass window. Human figures were represented in the window but I could not identify them. A man and a woman in brilliant robes, and an infant in white. Halos circled their heads. The sky behind them was a rich glaring blue. I stared and saw the figures slip into their separate parts, their separate colors. Blues, yellows, reds, greens. Flat. Blunt. The sun glowed behind the window and the colors lifted into life and were almost too brilliant to contemplate. *My Lord and my God . . . !*

But as I stared, the sunlight faded abruptly and the colored glass became merely colored glass again, fitted cleverly together. It was meant to represent — what? A man and a woman in absurdly bright robes, an infant in swaddling clothes with a halo about its head, human figures, highly stylized, flattened human figures, meant to represent — ?

After some time people began to come into the church. Mainly older women. A priest and an altar boy appeared. I remained in my pew, I knelt, I made every effort to pray, leafing through the prayer book, wishing to be drawn to You through the priest's chanting, and through the congregation's response. There were not many of us. Our voices were alternatingly feeble and overloud. Did You hear? Were You touched by our effort?

You withdrew and contemplated us from afar. You were not coaxed down into the priest's magical instruments — You did not enliven the wine, or slip into the stamped-out bits of bread. The priest's face was flushed with a kind of busyness and self-importance: for though You did not appear in his church he had to pretend You did, in order that his communicants not be dismayed. He was an actor performing for an audience and there were certain conventions that must be observed; otherwise the performance would come rudely and comically to an end. You did not indicate Your displeasure with the charade, and so it continued, harmless as before; but neither did You indicate Your blessing.

During a Sunday-morning service at St. Andrew's Presbyterian I saw in the third row from the front, near the center aisle, the man who had been Nathan Vickery's disciple — Japheth Sproul himself. I saw only the back of his head and a sliver of his face.

He was wearing glasses. As the minister spoke to his congregation of Christ's mission on earth, and the progress of the building fund, and the importance of voting in the upcoming municipal elections, I stared at Japheth Sproul and felt a great chill rise in me and could not move; it was as if I were paralyzed, I could not move, until something happened — the minister concluded his talk, another part of the service began — and I was released.

Strangers glanced at me as I hurried out, surprised and curious and pitying.

In St. Barnabas's drafty tomblike space I sat alone one weekday at noon, listening to an organ. There were no services, the church was empty and unheated. Far above and behind me someone was playing a complicated piece, rather difficult to follow, ferocious and elegant. I sat listening. I sat in a kind of daze, listening. The invisible organist stopped suddenly and repeated several bars, stopped again, and then played again, practicing a complex run.

Alone and invisible I sat in the darkened church. My hands rose suddenly to my face, I found myself weeping, but there was no need for self-consciousness, there was no one to see.

ii

He was extinguished, he died and slipped into oblivion, and after many months stirred to life again, and was cast upon the shore again — for You did not intend that his earthly existence should end, only that he be destroyed.

It was rumored that a furious glaring † had appeared on his forehead at the time of his collapse: the flesh raw and bleeding as if slashed by a knife. Dozens of people claimed to see it, a woman fell into a dead faint at the sight of it, and could talk about nothing else for weeks. It was rumored that enemies of the Seekers for Christ had poisoned him; a rival church, Devil-worshipers in the guise of mainstream Christians, had infiltrated Seekers' headquarters and had been trying for months to kill Nathan. It was rumored that the United States Government itself, frightened of the growing membership in Nathan's church, had ordered his death; for the Seekers wished nothing less than a revolution — a revolution of the spirit that would bring about, almost immediately, a revolution of the state. (The deceased, traitorous disciple Japheth Sproul was in some cases an agent of the Government, in other cases a member of a rival church, in still other cases a manifestation of the Devil himself.)

What was clear was the fact that Nathan Vickery had been struck down. Thousands upon thousands of people had witnessed his collapse. And afterward it was believed he had died; despite news of his hospitalization it was believed he had died; for hundreds of people claimed to see his soul fly out of his mouth, something vaporous and writhing, near-transparent. It flew out of his mouth as he sank to his knees — so they claimed. Hundreds of people, perhaps a thousand, made their claim. The Master was dead — had been struck dead! Like Jesus Christ before him, he had been cut off at the height of his powers! . . . It was rumored that his body had mysteriously disappeared before burial, and that the authorities were suppressing the facts.

He was hospitalized as any human being would be hospitalized, at first in a Denver hospital, and then in a clinic nearer Windigo Falls; he was given treatment, and after several weeks he was discharged: not well, perhaps, but no longer sick. Overwork, exhaustion, near-malnutrition, a slight heart murmur. His voice was gone. He could make only a hoarse, rasping, painful noise and his throat burned almost constantly. His voice was gone, he sounded hardly human, rather more like a broken, wounded creature of some kind, utterly baffled by his fate.

Very late one night Japheth appeared in the clinic. His thin boyish face was ashen, his glasses were slightly crooked as always, his fingers trembled as he reached out to touch Nathan's hand.

He was still very angry. Murderously angry. His fingers closed
upon Nathan's, hard. He began to squeeze. Like a woman enduring the agony of childbirth he squeezed, squeezed, his face glowing now with sweat, with rage. *Why did you betray me!* he whispered. *Why did you deny me! I loved you and you cast me down,
you cast me aside like rubbish!*

Eventually, as the weeks passed, Nathan was able to speak, in
a low, hesitant, rasping voice. But it did not much matter, because he spoke rarely. What was there to say? A great cooling
silence had bloomed in him, Your flower of a mouth, darkening
his brain. What was there to say, even to Japheth? Nathan sank
into the bliss of oblivion where there were no words, where there
was no language, where You never visited. What was there to
say?

Six months, ten months, fifteen months in seclusion. Eighteen
months. It was said that with Nathan Vickery's collapse and his
resignation as head of the Church of the Seekers for Christ, a
kind of empire was coming to light, and even as it came to light
it was disintegrating: there were bitter accusations, hysterical re-
plies and counteraccusations, there were lawsuits on behalf of
individuals, and on behalf of municipal governments, and the
Internal Revenue Service was investigating the church's income
and holdings; there were charges of mail fraud, and even embezzlement, and rumors of attempted suicides. And at the head of
the church was a broken, utterly bewildered man, weighing only
one hundred and eight pounds, subject to bouts of delirium and
forgetfulness; *non compos mentis.*

You observed but made no comment.

You observed, surely — ? But kept Your distance.

O Lord, he prayed in his broken, scraping voice, his face hidden in his hands, *why do You forsake me? Why do You deny me?*

And again, baffled by Your silence, Your absence, yet not despairing: *Lord, there is none like You! None! Let all the nations*

*hear, let all of mankind praise! . . . But why do You keep Yourself
from us?*

It was an oddity, it was not *quite* to be grasped: Your absence.

And so he slipped away from the city and for months wandered
about the countryside. He sought You there, in solitude. In the
inhuman vastness of the landscape: the hills and mountains of
his youth. One morning, after an hour of agonizing prayer, he
rather boldly renamed himself *William Vickery:* rebaptized himself in a mocking little ceremony on the bank of the Eden River,
near his birthplace in Marsena. *Nathanael* that was, was no
more; *William* that had never been, was now come into existence; *Vickery* was a dead man's name but all he had. "William
the offspring of Nathanael," he whispered, flicking water onto his
forehead. He was utterly alone. No one watched, no one listened. No one: and Your absence was palpable, incredible. But
he was utterly alone and might have baptized himself any way he
wished, or might have thrown himself into the river to his death;
no one observed.

A lifetime's habit of addressing You could not be broken so
easily, and so he continued to speak to You as if You were indeed
near.

What was there to say, and to whom might he speak . . . ? He
wandered about the countryside seeking bits of himself, odd stray
memories that might be stirred, overturned, like broken crockery
or bricks in a garden exposed accidentally as the soil is being
tilled. In Mt. Lambeth there was only a boarded-up frame building where he remembered the church of Brother Micah. How
long ago it had been, in another lifetime — the Mt. Lambeth
Tabernacle of Jesus Christ Risen. He walked about the building,
which was only four walls and a sway-backed roof and five windows, all of them broken behind the Xs of boards. Mt. Lambeth
itself seemed not to exist: two other frame dwellings in the area
were abandoned, a one-room schoolhouse nearby had been al-

lowed to rot and collapse. He stood for a while with his cheek pressed against the wall of the church, his eyes closed, his mind brought to a halt. He wanted to remember what had happened here, for he knew something profound had happened here. There had been heat lightning, and his grandmother's feverish excitement, and singing and hand-clapping and Brother Micah's passionate raised voice, and the Spirit of the Lord had manifested itself, and. . . . Something scuttled overhead. He started, and looked up to see a gray squirrel hurrying across the roof, unaware of him.

He remained there for a while, until early evening.

And there was Mt. Ayr in the distance, unchanged; and the countryside unchanged; the dense, lush, overgrown vegetation silent as always, in his mind's eye trembling with meaning but in itself merely dense and lush, silent. For You had departed from the countryside, just as You had departed from the city. And Your absence was palpable and terrible as any presence.

Won't You show yourself . . . ? So went William Vickery's frightened prayer.

In Marsena he saw the old places, which were changed a great deal, and he saw that You had departed from them as well. The Baptist church where Reverend Sisley had been pastor: small and inconsequential and rather dreary, with asbestos siding that had already begun to stain. The red brick building his great-uncle had owned: the general store now closed, empty, the barbershop gone, the post office expanded, with a smart-looking plate-glass window. He could not remember his great-uncle's name. Carlson? He could not remember. The man had died long ago, had been tilled back into the soil long ago, what did it matter what his name had been? A girl of about seventeen in a short dress with a halter top came out of the post office, dragging a small child with her. From across the street he stared at her, his heart suddenly beating, for perhaps it was someone he knew — someone from his school — one of the girls he had noticed on the periphery of his life, while You claimed all his attention in the center. She had long brown hair, her manner was abrupt and irritable, she was pretty, or not pretty; he stared at her and it seemed her features were familiar, and then he realized, with a startled gasp, that she was hardly more than a child and he was a man in his mid-thirties.

He turned aside, laughing silently.

How You led him on, how You played with him . . . ! But he recognized the joke, the jesting spirit, behind all Your cruelty.

And there was the old Vickery house. And of course he had to see it, had to force himself to walk to it, prepared for a shock. It had been allowed to deteriorate like the other buildings. A rain-streaked gray, many of the shingles missing, one of the upstairs windows mended with plywood, a scrubby front lawn, only one of the blue spruce remaining along the drive. Dr. Vickery's little brass sign was gone, as was the iron pole itself. The brick walk was a mass of weeds. He stood and stared and waited for You to speak to him, waited for You to instruct him in what he should feel. He had loved Dr. Vickery. He had loved him very much. And he had killed him: had looked him full in the face as You struck him down. . . . And there was a woman who sang to him, hugging him close. *O Galilee, sweet Galilee where Jesus loved so much to be*. He had killed her too. No, he had not killed her: she was still living. Her hair a shock of white, her face deeply wrinkled, a crazed wide-eyed stare and a haughty, whining voice that spoke of her son who had been the Son of God, and who had been crucified, and who dwelt now with his Father, but would return to earth in a very short while to reclaim his Kingdom. In a nursing home in Windigo Falls an elderly, petulant woman awaited the restoration of the Kingdom of God, and spoke only of her son who was the Son of God, and when her grandson visited her, infrequently as he did, she did not recognize him at all. (Who was this stooping, haggard, gray-haired stranger with the trembling hands? *Her* son had been magnificent: the Messiah Himself, wrathful and gentle and lamblike and merciless all at once. And very tall, and strong, and handsome. And possessing a marvelous voice.)

The old Vickery house had fallen into the hands of a family with many children and was no longer the house he remembered. And the village itself seemed sadly impoverished. As he walked away, a skinny mongrel trotted along behind him, sniffing at his heels. Another dog joined it, a mongrel as well but larger, with curly black hair and long floppy ears. One of the dogs growled deep in his throat. William Vickery looked around at them nervously, but saw they were keeping their distance. The skinny dog was obviously quite old and appeared to be blind in one eye; at any rate the eye had turned a queer milky white.

Next to the old Vickery place was a farm he half-remembered. It had belonged to a family named Bell. It seemed in better condition than the Vickery house but he had no interest in examining it closer. William, he was. William Vickery. A stranger. The Vickerys were gone, the Bells were probably gone. No one knew him. No one observed. Something had happened to him one summer day behind the Bells' house, back by the outbuildings. He had crawled through a barbed-wire fence to get to it. *Pride*, someone had whispered. *You are guilty of pride*. But he could not remember. *You must be defiled*, someone had said.

The mongrel with the black fur was barking at him now, its ears laid back. But it kept a certain distance and was obviously afraid of him.

"Go away," he whispered, gesturing vaguely. The dogs were not very real to him, nor was the old Bell place. The barn, the chicken coop, the white and red chickens that picked in the dirt even now, after so many years: none of these things was very real to him, or very significant. He awaited Your instructions but You were silent. What should he feel, what was the proper human response, what, precisely, should he remember? Shreds of himself were everywhere in this village, in this landscape, but he could not assemble them, could not bring them together. Was it possible he had been born in that falling-down house a hundred yards away? And his mother had nursed him there for a while, and then had turned from him, had wept and run from him, and had never come back. Her brother Ashton Vickery too had been driven from home. He had fled, had returned briefly and disappeared again, lost, a wreck of a man, smelling of cheap whiskey; it was not possible to believe he had once been young. *They weren't really my children*, Mrs. Vickery had said. *Only you. God sent me only you.*

In that ruined house Mrs. Vickery had loved him. And his grandfather too had loved him. And had died. You dwelt with them for a while and then passed on and now You were nowhere near. What did it mean? What should he feel? He remembered how You had filled him at all times, how You had whispered in secret to him, telling him things no one else could know. One summer day You brought him to a small barn behind this house, You forced him to crawl beneath a barbed-wire fence, You were pitiless, terrible in Your wisdom, and something had happened, something had transpired, he had been broken in utter humility and degradation and You had claimed him then as Your own: but he could not remember clearly and had no real conviction that it had happened to *him*.

My child, You had whispered, gloating.

But perhaps that had not been William Vickery, who stood now in this place. And perhaps it had not really been You.

iii

The pavement, the cobblestones, are splattered with sudden angry pellets of rain. An impatient look to the river: white-tipped tongues rising and heaving and slapping. My shoes are wet. My cheeks are streaming. I am not angry, that is the river's mood; I stand here broken and acquiescent and waiting.

As I have been waiting for years.

Nathanael that was, and is no more: William that was not, and is; has one given birth to the other, or are we brothers . . . ? The birth cord that linked us was stretched thin, thinner and thinner until, like a thread, it snapped, and now there is oblivion on both sides, as if You in Your invisibility, in Your secret wisdom, closed above our heads Your great darkling wings and all was erased. Or nearly so.

It has been many years.

If necessary I lie to them about You. And Nathanael. I tell them in their own neutral tones that You were a delusion and Nathanael mad: and, disappointed, halfway suspicious, they are, forced to accept my judgment. . . . But tell us, others say, slyly, greedily; tell us about God. About Jesus, the Son of God. And the person you were: you *were*, weren't you, one of the Chosen . . . ? A delusion, a dream, I tell them gently, with the tractable smile that performs such feats, such small tidy wonders, here in the world.

Time, that was to be no more, endures. Continues. Nor am I out of it.

Though in Your time not a day — not a moment! — has passed. (For I vividly remember that birth, the flashes of light assaulting my teary eyes, the salt taste of blood, the water that, lapping wildly against the white porcelain of the basin, took on the hue, subtly, delicately, of a somewhat turgid blue sky that was — or am I mistaken? — glimpsed in a mirror, obliquely through a mirror; I remember the birth as if it were only this morning. Such is Your gift, which I retain still though You have departed.)

Man's hunger for God, I might tell them, the curious greedy disbelieving ones, cannot be satisfied by earthly food. Don't speak to me of "human" love. Don't speak to me of "making a place for oneself" here. It is quite pointless. It is not even cruel: only pointless.

I would ask them only — Am I a brother to anyone in this agony? In this terrible loneliness? For it is a question I cannot ask You. It is a question You — even if You would speak — cannot answer. *Behold me O Lord*, I mouth to the petulant waves, *for I* am one of those who has been cast down; who has been broken and obliterated. And in whose obliteration even You have been extinguished.

So I stand here at the railing. Waiting. My lips moving with an old prayer. There is a low dull droning from the edge of the earth, where many winds converge. I am shameless. Look at my cheeks streaming tears. I am in exile, I am proud and broken and absurd, and so shabby it is quite natural that people stare and children jeer — whom else can they mock, if not me? They know that my task is to become one of them, and that I have failed — more, I have failed even to mourn my loss. It is only You I mourn. It is only You I know. *They* do not exist, any more than Nathanael Vickery exists.

So I wait. I am quite patient. The river's violence is not my own. I expect nothing. I hope for nothing. I will stir no one to expectation or hope, still less to hysteria; my voice is still hoarse, the back of my mouth scrapes raw if I lift my voice above a whisper. So it is, and evidently must be. In Your justice. In your infinite mercy.

And Your playfulness —

For I came upon, just last week, a tabloid newspaper of the kind that is sold in drugstores and grocery stores, and often left on park benches or, partly crumpled, in trash baskets, and my attention was drawn to a three-inch headline UNDERGROUND RELIGION FLOURISHES and a somewhat blurred photograph of a man in an ankle-length gown standing on a platform with his arms raised and his head thrown back, his expression rapturous. For a terrible moment I thought the man was myself. Then I saw that it must be another preacher, a much younger man with wild shoulder-length hair, who stood with his legs parted and his knees slightly bent and his long, thin fingers stretched wide, so wide that one would think he must be experiencing great pain. A spotlight behind the preacher created an aureole about his head — a fortuitous effect! — that gave him an uncanny look while it blurred and softened his features. I held the newspaper close to my face. It trembled slightly; I held it firmer. And after a long moment I saw that the preacher *was* myself. Or Brother Nathan.

Yet we looked in no way alike. It was not even possible that we were brothers. Yet there was, there is, no *we*: there is only an *I*. My vision cannot be double, I have not the anodyne of madness. . . . The young man in the gown, Brother Nathan who is no more. Yet evidently exists: in fact, flourishes. I skimmed the smudgy dancing print to learn that the Church of the Seekers for Christ is rumored to be active on the West Coast, despite official pronouncements that it had been disbanded and its property and assets seized after innumerable legal entanglements and a declaration of bankruptcy by its board of directors some years ago. (There had been, according to the disjointed article, a number of embezzlement charges brought against high-ranking Seekers, and more than a hundred lawsuits, most of which were settled out of court.)

But the most extraordinary news was the fact that Nathan Vickery still heads his church.

According to a Seeker identified only as Brother Donald, Vickery maintains absolute authority over the Seekers and, though necessarily in exile, conducts services regularly for a "small, select group of disciples who have proven themselves worthy." These services are clandestine, of course, kept secret from all non-believers, since the Church of the Seekers for Christ has many enemies who wish to destroy it. "Our Master is in exile, not in hiding," Brother Donald said, "because of the many vicious threats against his life. But he has not turned away from us. He is still our Master here on earth, and our pathway to the Lord." But where is the commune, reporters inquired, is it somewhere in California — ? But Brother Donald declined to answer. He was described as a tall, exuberant, friendly man with a firm, powerful handshake, eager to talk — to talk for hours, it seems — about Brother Nathan and the Church of the Seekers for Christ, though without revealing any secrets. He is himself head of a small Seekers' house in Los Angeles, an "independent" community formed after the breakup of the original organization some years ago. Is there any possibility, reporters asked, that Brother Nathan would come out of exile? And speak once again to the entire nation? "We have only a few more years," Brother Donald said, "before the end. It's coming: it's on the way. And about six or eight months before that time the Master plans to reappear and lead his people out of bondage. I mean bondage to illusion, to the material world, to sin. If he appears that close to Armageddon the police state will not have time enough to apprehend him. And if they try to arrest him, and persecute him, as they did last time, we have more sophisticated means now of dealing with them. *I bring not peace but a sword*, Christ told us. The police state has been in the hands of the Devil for the past seventy-five or eighty years. . . . All this will come to pass around 1982, or 1985. Only the Master knows for certain."

The vision in my eye faltered as I read. On an inside page I discovered still another photograph of myself, on another raised platform, and as the photograph was taken I had evidently whirled about violently so that droplets of perspiration flew off me and were caught strangely in the glare of the spotlight. The caption beneath this photograph claimed it had been taken only a few days before by a photographer who had infiltrated one of the clandestine Seekers' ceremonies, despite rumors that non-believers were dealt with harshly.

The man in the photograph *was* Brother Nathan. But the photograph must have been taken years ago. . . .

In the end I stuffed the newspaper back into the trash basket and walked away. And tried to put Your playfulness out of my mind.

Still, I am faithful. I am Yours.

Will You not whisper unto my soul, as You once did, *I am thy salvation* . . . ? For Your cruelty has not broken me, nor has your inscrutable mercy; and even Your irony — which I could not have anticipated, in that place long ago where light did not hurt and the taste of blood did not sting — has not discouraged me. Death has no appeal; nor has suicide; for if I be washed in the Blood of the Lamb but it is my own blood, it will not be cleansing, it will not be according to Your design.

So I wait for You, and will wait the rest of my life.

61774